Praise fo

Book III in the Roma Nova series

"If there is a world where fiction becomes more believable than reality, then Alison Morton's ingenious thrillers must be the portal through which to travel. Following in Caesar's footsteps, she came with *INCEPTIO*, saw with *PERFIDITAS* – and has well and truly conquered with *SUCCESSIO*!"
– **Helen Hollick**, author and Managing Editor Historical Novel Society Indie Reviews

"Alison Morton has done it again. *SUCCESSIO* is the latest in her series of powerful tales of family betrayals and shifting allegiances in Roma Nova. Once again, I was gripped from start to finish."
– **Sue Cook**, writer and broadcaster

Praise for *Inceptio*

Book I in the Roma Nova series

"Terrific. Brilliantly plotted original story, grippingly told and cleverly combining the historical with the futuristic. It's a real edge-of-the seat read, genuinely hard to put down."
– **Sue Cook**, writer and broadcaster

"I loved it! Intriguing, unusual and thought-provoking. Karen develops from a girl anyone of us could know into one of the toughest heroines I've read for a while. Roma Nova was a world I really wanted to visit – and not just to meet Conrad – vivid and compelling. A pacey, suspenseful thriller with a truly dreadful villain, I can't recommend *INCEPTIO* enough."
– **Kate Johnson**, author of *The UnTied Kingdom*

"Tense, fast-paced and deliciously inventive, Alison Morton's *INCEPTIO* soon had me turning the pages. Very Dashiell Hammett."
– **Victoria Lamb**, author of *The Queen's Secret*

"Gripping. Alison Morton creates a fully realised world of what could have been. Breathtaking action, suspense, political intrigue… *INCEPTIO* is a tour de force!"
– **Russell Whitfield**, author of *Gladiatrix* and *Roma Victrix*

Praise for *Perfiditas*

Book II in the Roma Nova series

"Alison Morton has built a fascinating, exotic world! Carina's a bright, sassy detective with a winning dry sense of humour. I warmed to her quickly and wanted to find out how she dealt with the problems thrown in her path. The plot is pretty snappy too and gets off to a quick start which made it easy to keep turning the pages. There are a fair number of alternative historical fictions where Rome never disappeared, but for my money this is one of the better ones."
– **Simon Scarrow**, author of the Eagle (Macro and Cato) series

"I can't resist an alternative history and Alison Morton writes one of the best. Powerful storytelling, vivid characters and a page-turning plot makes Alison Morton's *PERFIDITAS* a must read."
– **Jean Fullerton**, author of the historical East London novels

"Pure enjoyment! A clever, complex plot set in the beguilingly convincing fictional country of Roma Nova. Scenes and characters are sometimes so vividly described that I felt I was watching a movie. This compelling tale rendered me inseparable from my copy right up to the last turn of the page."
– **Sue Cook**, writer and broadcaster

Alison Morton grew up in West Kent. She completed a BA in French, German and Economics and thirty years later a MA in History. She now lives in France with her husband.

A 'Roman nut' since age 11, she has visited sites throughout Europe including the *alma mater*, Rome. But it was walking on the mosaics at Ampurias (Spain) that triggered her wondering what a modern Roman society would be like if run by women...

Find out more about Alison's writing life, Romans and alternate history at her blog www.alison-morton.com, or on Facebook at www.facebook.com/AlisonMortonAuthor and follow her on Twitter @alison_morton.

·SUCCESSIO·

ALISON MORTON

SilverWood

Published in 2014 by the author
using SilverWood Books Empowered Publishing ®

SilverWood Books
30 Queen Charlotte Street, Bristol, BS1 4HJ
www.silverwoodbooks.co.uk

Copyright © Alison Morton 2014

The right of Alison Morton to be identified as the author of this work
has been asserted by her in accordance with the Copyright,
Designs and Patents Act 1988.

All rights reserved. No part of this publication may be reproduced,
stored in a retrieval system, or transmitted in any form or by any means,
electronic, mechanical, photocopying, recording or otherwise,
without prior permission of the copyright holder.

This novel is a work of fiction. Names and characters are the product
of the author's imagination and any resemblance to actual persons,
living or dead, is entirely coincidental.

ISBN 978-1-78132-218-5 (paperback)
ISBN 978-1-78132-219-2 (ebook)

British Library Cataloguing in Publication Data
A CIP catalogue record for this book is available from the British Library

Set in Bembo by SilverWood Books
Printed on responsibly sourced paper

HISTORICAL NOTE

What if King Harold had won the Battle of Hastings in 1066? Or if Julius Caesar had taken notice of the warning that assassins wanted to murder him on the Ides of March? Suppose Christianity had remained a Middle Eastern minor cult? Intriguing questions, indeed. Alternate (or alternative) history stories allow us to explore them.

Whether infused with every last detail of their world as in S M Stirling's *The Peshawar Lancers*, or lighter where the alternative world is used as a setting for an adventure such as Kate Johnson's *The UnTied Kingdom*, or a great and grim secret as in Robert Harris' *Fatherland*, alternate history stories are underpinned by three things: the point of divergence when the alternate timeline split from our timeline; how that world looks and works; and how things changed after the split.

SUCCESSIO focuses on one main character, Carina Mitela, and her struggle to defeat a nemesis threatening to destroy her family and her country. As the title suggests, this story is 'what happened next' after *INCEPTIO* and *PERFIDITAS*, the first two in the series. But *SUCCESSIO* in Latin also suggests 'the next generation'. Times move on and new history is made.

I have dropped background history about Roma Nova into the novel only where it impacts on the story. Nobody likes a straight history lesson in the middle of a thriller! But if you are interested in a little more information about the mysterious Roma Nova, read on…

What happened in our timeline

Of course, our timeline may turn out to be somebody else's alternative one as shown in Philip K Dick's *The Grasshopper Lies Heavy*, the story within the story in *The Man in the High Castle*. Nothing is fixed. But for the sake of convenience I will take ours as the default.

The Western Roman Empire didn't 'fall' in a cataclysmic event as often portrayed in film and television; it localised and eventually dissolved like chain mail fragmenting into separate links, giving way to rump states, local city states and petty kingdoms. The

Eastern Roman Empire survived albeit as the much diminished city state of Byzantium until the Fall of Constantinople in 1453 to the Muslim Ottoman Empire.

Some scholars think that Christianity fatally weakened the traditional Roman way of life and was a significant factor in the collapse. Emperor Constantine's personal conversion to Christianity in AD 313 was a turning point for the new religion. By AD 394, his several times successor, Theodosius, banned all traditional Roman religious practice, closed and destroyed temples and dismissed all priests. The sacred flame that had burned for over a thousand years in the College of Vestals was extinguished and the Vestal Virgins expelled. The Altar of Victory, said to guard the fortune of Rome, was hauled away from the Senate building and disappeared from history. The Roman senatorial families pleaded for religious tolerance, but Theodosius made any pagan practice, even dropping a pinch of incense on a family altar in a private home, into a capital offence. And his 'religious police' driven by the austere and ambitious bishop Ambrosius of Milan, became increasingly active in pursuing pagans...

The alternate Roma Nova timeline

In AD 395, three months after Theodosius's final decree banning all pagan religious activity, over four hundred Romans loyal to the old gods, and so in danger of execution, trekked north out of Italy to a semi-mountainous area similar to modern Slovenia. Led by Senator Apulius at the head of twelve prominent families, they established a colony based initially on land owned by Apulius' Celtic father-in-law. By purchase, alliance and conquest, this grew into Roma Nova.

Norman Davies in *Vanished Kingdoms: The History of Half-Forgotten Europe* reminds us that:

> ...in order to survive, newborn states need to possess a set of viable internal organs, including a functioning executive, a defence force, a revenue system and a diplomatic force. If they possess none of these things, they lack the means to sustain an autonomous existence and they perish before they can breathe and flourish.

I would add history, willpower and adaptability as essential factors. Roma Nova survived by changing its social structure; as men constantly fought to defend the new colony, women took over the social, political and economic roles, weaving new power and influence networks based on family structures. Eventually, daughters as well as sons had to put on armour and carry weapons to defend their homeland and their way of life. Service to the state was valued higher than personal advantage, echoing Roman Republican virtues, and the women heading the families guarded and enhanced these values to provide a core philosophy throughout the centuries.

Roma Nova's continued existence has been favoured by three factors: the discovery and exploitation of high-grade silver in their mountains, their efficient technology, and their robust response to any threat. Remembering their Byzantine cousins' defeat in the Fall of Constantinople, Roma Novan troops assisted the western nations at the Battle of Vienna in 1683 to halt the Ottoman advance into Europe. Nearly two hundred years later, they used their diplomatic skills to help forge an alliance to push Napoleon IV back across the Rhine as he attempted to expand his grandfather's empire.

Prioritising survival, Roma Nova remained neutral in the Great War of the 20th century which lasted from 1925 to 1935. The Greater German Empire, stretching from Jutland in the north, Alsace in the west, Tyrol in the south and Bulgaria in the east, was broken up afterwards into its former small kingdoms, duchies and counties. Some became republics. There was no sign of an Austrian-born corporal with a short, square moustache.

Forty years before the action of *SUCCESSIO* in the early 21st century, Roma Nova was nearly destroyed by a coup, a brutal male-dominated consulship and civil war. A weak leader, sclerotic and outmoded systems that had not developed since the last great reform in the 1700s and a neglected economy let in a clever and ruthless tyrant. But with characteristic resilience, the families' structures fought back and reconstructed their society, re-learning the basic principles of Republican virtue, while subtly changing it to a more representational model for modern times. Today, the tiny country has become one of the highest per capita income states in the world.

Dramatis Personae

Family

Carina Mitela	Major, Praetorian Guard Special Forces (PGSF), commanding Operations, nicknamed 'Bruna'
Conradus Mitelus	Senior Legate, PGSF and regular Praetorian Guard, 'Conrad'
Aurelia Mitela	Carina's grandmother, head of the Mitela family
Allegra Mitela	Carina's and Conrad's eldest daughter
Antonia and Gillius	Twins, (Tonia and Gil) Carina's and Conrad's younger children
Helena Mitela	Carina's cousin
Dalina Mitela	Family recorder
Lucilla Mitela	Lieutenant, PGSF

Household

Junia	Comptroller/steward of Domus Mitelarum
Galienus	Under-steward/housekeeper
Marcella	Aurelia's assistant

Tellus family

Quintus Tellus	Head of Tellus family
Caius Tellus	(Deceased), Quintus's brother, unsavoury rebel

Military

Daniel Stern	Colonel, deputy legate, PGSF
Fausta	Captain, PGSF, Digital Security
Sepunia	Major, PGSF, Intelligence Directorate
Carina's Active Response Team	Paula Servla, Flavius, Trebatia, Livius, Atria
Rusonia	Legate's executive officer
Sergius	Captain, PGSF, Training and Personnel

Palace

Silvia Apulia	Imperatrix
Stella Apulia	Silvia's eldest child
Hallienia Apulia	Silvia's third child 'Hallie'
Favonius Cotta	head of protocol, ex-Washington legation

Outside Roma Nova

Michael Browning	Captain, British special forces
Wilson	Lieutenant, British special forces
Nicola Sandbrook	Sergeant, British special forces
Johnson	RSM, British special forces
Andrew Brudgland	'Commissioner', British security services
Christopher Newton	Ex-British special forces
Janice Hargreve	A teacher

Other

Lurio	Department of Justice Commander, Urban Cohorts (*Custodes*)
Pelonia	Department of Justice *Custodes* special investigator
Octavia Quirinia	Head of Quirinia Family
Maia Quirinia	Her daughter, a typical teenager
Philippus	Bar owner, ex-associate from the Pulcheria Foundation
Dania	Upmarket restaurant owner
Lucius Punellus	Retired adjutant, PGSF, Conrad's ex-comrade-in-arms
Paulina Carca	Life partner of Lucius Punellus
Sertorius	Pompous, but effective, Mitela family lawyer
Faenia	Professor of Medicine, Central University, PGSF consultant

'What do you mean? Who was she?'

Part I

Generations

I

It was far too quiet. Only an occasional owl call, the odd flutter of feathers and pitter-patter of a small night creature. Sure, the training area was literally kilometres from anywhere, somewhere called Norfolk, but a hundred people couldn't stay that quiet, not even — arguably — the best special forces in the world. Beside me, the two centurions, Livius and Paula Servla, were motionless; I couldn't even hear them breathe. I peered through the face veil hanging from my helmet. My eyesight was still good at thirty-nine, but I didn't see a thing in the dawn light. I relaxed; we had a full five minutes before we needed to move.

I'd been crazy to agree to take part in this exercise; I'd sat at a desk for too long. Commanding Operations did *not* mean taking part in every exercise. It'd been my vanity that made me put myself down for the ultimate — training with the British special forces. No, *against* them. Even more insane. I was no slouch and worked hard to keep my fitness up, but I really should have left it to the super-fit like Paula and Livius and, of course, Flavius. But a small country like ours didn't refuse such invitations twice and the competition to be picked for this exercise had been near lethal.

Each year we invited a small number of allied countries' special troops to Roma Nova to take part in our annual fitness-for-purpose exercise; thanks to our legate's connections, there'd always been some British. Very effective and highly competent, they were reserved at first, like they'd swallowed some kind of 'how to behave abroad' manual, but by the end of the week, they'd usually relaxed. But this was a first for us to have an exclusive exercise with them, and on their ground.

The first night we'd arrived, we'd had all the 'swords and sandals' cracks in the bar from those who'd never met us. Sandwiched between New Austria and Italy, people thought Roma Nova was a cross between the *Sound of Music* and *Gladiator* with a dash of Ruritania thrown in. But when their commander welcomed us formally the next morning, he told the assembled host troops about our sixteen-hundred-year traditions and that the Praetorian Guard Special Forces were just as fearsome as they'd heard. And that Roma Nova had survived, clawing its way through the centuries, was in no small part down to the Praetorians. The British grunts tried not to appear impressed, but I saw a little more respect in their eyes after that.

Livius lifted his index finger a few millimetres from his rifle and glanced over at me. I gave a hint of a nod. Ahead of Paula and me by a body length, he started crawling forward. Using our elbows, we pulled ourselves behind and a little to each side of him across the forest floor covered in pine-needles. Three others, Allia, Gorlius and Pelo, followed in the same arrow formation. Reaching the crest of the washed-out shallow valley, we spread out behind it and froze. After five minutes watching and listening, I nodded and Livius took Allia and Pelo into the trees behind us and set off for the other side of the depression. Raising my hand a couple of centimetres from the sandy ground, I signalled Paula to maintain position here. I grabbed my assault rifle and in a crouching run made my way to the dip twenty metres away at the entrance. I glanced up to see Gorlius scrambling up into one of the trees behind Paula to act as lookout. As he drew one of the new individual cam nets over himself, he disappeared. I pointed my pocket scope up at him. Even his heat signature was pretty near neutral. Expensive but impressive. Now we waited out ten minutes to let the wildlife settle back down.

'Contact.' That one word hissed in my earpiece told me Gorlius had spotted them. We'd tabbed to this location by forced march – an old Roman tradition – so we could surprise them. And there they were, walking single file, sweeping their route with their eyes and weapons, watchful, but not wary. Too professional to make any unnecessary noise, they were nevertheless a little over-relaxed.

Their commander sent two ahead to check. Now they concentrated, their weapons raised and arms and legs tensed. Just before they reached the edge of the depression, one turned back to the commander and shook his head.

Livius dropped the two of them in rapid succession. Allia and Pelo launched at the main group from the far point and downed another three between them. Paula slammed the radio operator to earth, pinioning his flailing arms and legs. Gorlius fell on two others. I tripped the last one as he tried to escape and jammed my weapon in his throat as he attempted to struggle up. I didn't need to look at my watch to know we'd done it in under two minutes. Hm, slowing up.

We secured and tagged them. While Livius and Pelo swept the back area for a possible second patrol, Paula scanned their radio with an electronic logger.

'Can't see any transmission within the past ten,' she said, looking up. 'But I think they check in every thirty.' She spoke in fast street Latin in case any of these clever boys turned out to be linguists.

I turned to their officer, Lieutenant Wilson, from his jacket tab. 'Now, Lieutenant, I hope we're not going to go formal here. I just need you to confirm the time of your next radio check.'

'Not a chance in hell.' His eyes half closed and he snorted.

I sighed and signalled Allia forward. From her sleeve pocket she extracted a slim tin containing two syringes and an ampoule, knelt down by the officer, prepared a needle and waited for my confirmation.

Wilson drew back. 'What the fuck is that?'

'A fast acting relaxant that'll have you chirruping like a mongoose on holiday. No permanent effect, you may be a little disorientated for ten to fifteen minutes afterward. We need to move on now, so I can't wait for you to have a mothers' meeting about whether to tell me.' I nodded and Allia pulled his sleeve up, jabbed the skin and depressed the tiny plunger.

I counted to twenty before I stood over him and asked again, 'Time of next radio check?'

'Get—no, not—' Sweat broke out on his face with the effort of defying the chemical. 'Twenty, no—, twenty-two. No—'. He dropped his head as if humiliated, but it wasn't his fault.

We now had a generous margin before any alarm was given. Paula threw the opposition's radio batteries into the woods. Allia checked out the other captives, but they only had hurt pride and a few bruises. We looped a line through their cable-tied hands, securing it to a tree and left with mildly obscene curses and promises of revenge behind us.

Setting off north at a fast march, we circled around after five minutes to parallel the trail for the exercise headquarters. We'd finished our tasks half a day early. Now we'd eliminated our closest rivals, I figured we'd be the first team back. After three days out in the field, we were looking forward to hot food and a chance to clean up properly.

Allia jogged beside me and I could see a question ready to burst out. She was very young, around twenty, and this was her first time on overseas exercise. I checked the proximity sensor; no biosignatures apart from ours for at least three kilometres.

'What is it, Allia?' I whispered. 'It's okay, just keep your voice down, though.'

'Why are they all men, ma'am? I mean, I saw some women at the start, but only a very few and we haven't come across any out in the field.'

'Western forces don't generally have women in front line combat units, and only a few in their special forces. You'll probably see more in the American military, if you ever go there.'

I saw the disbelief on her face. I smiled at her, but said nothing. I wanted to conserve my strength and wind.

Fifteen minutes later, Livius stopped, held his hand up. We dropped to the ground as one. Between the trees, I could see the edge of the clearing housing the exercise headquarters. After a long five minutes, Livius sent Gorlius and Pelo forward to check out the approach. It was such a classic trick to stake out the base camp approach. So near our goal, no way did we want the embarrassment of falling for a classic. I watched the two of them walk in, circling back to back, across the innocent-seeming twenty metres. The remaining four of us took shallow breaths and readied ourselves for reaction.

'Clear,' came Gorlius' disembodied voice. I signed Livius to cross next with Allia; Paula and I brought up the rear.

The exercise gate passed, we checked in at the admin desk with the sergeant, one of the few women Allia had seen. Her dark blonde hair was plaited and piled up on top of her head, almost like a Roman. Something familiar yet repelling about her distracted me. Nothing in her face was wrong; she smiled pleasantly enough, her light eyes shone with interest. She noted everything down efficiently; her checklist was marked up neatly, spare pens in perfect parallel to each other. I rolled my shoulders to disperse my unease; I had so much else to do. But still...

Behind her stood an older man, around fifty, built like a block of muscle. He reminded me of our former *primipilus*, the senior centurion. He wore a leather band on his wrist with a crested metal badge, so a traditionalist, but the standard uniform button tab showed he was a warrant officer, like a top sergeant. I glanced at his name tab as he nodded to me.

'Morning, Major.'

'Mr Johnson.'

'Enjoyed yourself?'

'Oh, I think so.' I grinned and he smiled back, one per cent off a smirk. Yeah, just like the *primipilus*.

'You'll find fresh food for your team in the mess tent.'

They'd reached the tent first while I'd been doing the nicely-nicely with Johnson. Livius beckoned me over to the table they were clustered around and he thrust a plate of some kind of brown meat stew, potatoes and vegetables toward me. I poked at it.

'It's all right, Bruna, it's dead,' Paula Servla said. 'Quite tasty, in fact,' and followed her words by loading a spoonful into her mouth. The others laughed at my expression, even Allia and Pelo who were very junior. My friend and comrade for nearly fifteen years, Paula had used my *nom de guerre* – Bruna – with ease as she teased me. But she was right, the stew was good.

Afterwards, I told them to go grab a few hours' rest. I settled down to write my report. I was finishing the first draft when a shadow fell across the table.

'Major Mitela.'

Crap.

'Lieutenant Wilson.' I looked up at him. He winced.

Damn. I'd used the American pronunciation. The Brits hated that.

'Have you recovered?' No harm being polite.

He snorted. 'That was an illegal procedure and I intend to report it to my and your senior command.'

I shrugged. 'Fine by me. Do it.' I bent my head back down to my report. He had no choice but to go. I watched through my eyelashes as he stomped off to the command tent. Gods, some of them took it so badly. Tough. We trained like every exercise was a live operation, usually without any blood, and used all the techniques, equipment and training at our disposal. When it came to it, a live operation unfolded like an exercise, but sometimes included casualties. A hard way, but successful. Sometimes a little too robust for outsiders.

More of our teams drifted in through the afternoon and I went and spoke to them as they settled down to their food. Two had been brought in as captives, so commiserations to them. Overall, though, we'd acquitted ourselves well.

A joint senior staff mop-up meeting was held before the evening meal where I had the impression we'd won a few friends, one unfriend and a decent amount of respect. Nobody said a word about our unorthodox methodology.

Making my way over to the wash tent later, a tingle ran across the back of my neck. I whirled around but nobody stood behind me, nor anywhere in the clearing. I stood completely still and listened. But I knew somebody was watching, and purposefully. I pulled the outside flap aside slowly. Nobody. No sound of water falling. I checked all the canvas-sided cubicles. Only the smell of soap, and the sheen of wastewater with a few surviving bubbles in corners of the trays. But I still felt uneasy. After a few moments, I decided that I was being ridiculous. Maybe it was tiredness. I shrugged and chose one of the cubicles to the right.

As I dressed afterward, I glanced up at the sign 'Female showers'. How had showers acquired gender? You didn't get that ambiguity in Latin, even in the 21st century.

Early next morning, I went for a run with Flavius. Now a senior centurion, he and I had met fourteen years ago on an undercover operation. He was smart, aware and physically tough. He wasn't a pretty boy like Livius; his light brown hair and mid-brown eyes together with the other standard features you got in a face made a pleasant, but not outstanding combination. This was a great asset for a spook as nobody remembered the average. But when he smiled his soul shone out from his eyes. He gave me balance, sometimes quite starkly, other times humorously. He was my comrade-in-arms, but above all a friend.

'How do you think it's going?' I asked.

He grinned at me. 'I heard you pulled one of your little tricks.' He ducked my flying hand.

'All perfectly routine,' I said.

'Yeah, but this lot play by the rules, generally. Rules of engagement, they call it.'

'I bet they don't when they're in the middle of some covert op in the African mountains,' I snorted.

'Well, I gather we're making a good impression, at least in

comparison to the Americans and the Prussians.'

I showered and went for breakfast, getting waylaid in the mess tent by one of their captains, called Browning. His long sculptured face was lightened up by a charming smile. I had a penchant for blond hair, which in his case topped blue eyes and, curiously, a scattering of freckles over his nose.

'*Salve* Carina Mitela,' he began and went on, in slow but correct classic Latin. 'Your forces fight well, with much courage and cunning.'

'Thank you, tribune,' I replied, trying my best to match his formality of voice. 'I accept your praise on behalf of my troops. Your Latin is excellent, very cultured. May I enquire where you learnt to speak so well?'

'Universitas Sancti Andreae.' He smiled at my puzzled look and reverted to English. 'It's a university in Scotland. I tried it out on some of your people, but I quickly realised it hadn't moved on since Augustus.' He smiled ruefully and led me towards an empty table.

'Hey, no problem,' I said. 'I'm happy to speak English – good to pick up on my native language.'

His turn to look confused.

'I was raised in the Eastern States, you know, America. I lived there until I was twenty-four. My mother was Roma Novan so when I emigrated there, I re-joined her family. I became a member of the PGSF a little later.'

'Fascinating! Do you go back much?'

'Only twice in the past fourteen years, the last time a year ago. I found it quite weird – a lot had changed.'

Yeah, and apart from the cleanliness, not for the better. Or maybe it was me. Time to switch subjects.

'Are you going to try out the Roman games later? I'd be happy to take you through some of them.'

'I think I'll watch first.'

I grinned, finished the mug of strong tea the Brits drank, piled my dirty plate on the service table and made my way back to our admin tent.

Flavius was designating teams for the games this afternoon. We were giving our hosts a demonstration just for fun, but he wanted it to be perfect and was choosing carefully.

'Ah, Major,' he caught my approach, cast his eye down at his el-pad and asked, 'can I put you down for the link fight?' His half-smile was a little too knowing.

The guards fidgeting in a cluster around him, eager to find out their assignments, stopped. The chatter dried up instantly and two dozen pairs of eyes focused on me.

He knew I was the most experienced link-fighter. He also knew I loved it. I'd been practising it with Daniel, now Colonel Daniel Stern and deputy legate, for years before it became legal. It had been an illicit pleasure we'd both relished but contests had been banned for years because of the lethally high casualty rate. I was knocking on the door of forty, for Juno's sake, but if I said no, Flavius would needle me about it for months. Worse, I'd be letting the detachment down in front of foreigners. If I said yes, I'd have to win or lose face. Asking me in front of the troops meant I couldn't refuse.

Crafty bastard.

'Of course, Senior Centurion, I'd be devastated with delight. Now do tell me, who have you volunteered as my partner?'

He had the grace to look away, but after a second found a beaming smile to throw at me. 'Your choice, ma'am. Centurion Livius is a possibility, or perhaps Pelo.'

Livius! The fittest soldier in the unit. He was raving. And Pelo was a younger version of him.

'And yourself, Flavius?' I smiled as sweetly as I could without causing a stampede for sick bags.

'Oh, I think I'll be needed to supervise everything. I must regretfully decline your invitation.'

I sighed. 'Tell Livius to report to me and we'll practise a few moves.' I looked at my watch; we had four hours before lunch. I might get lucky and break my leg before the games started.

'C'mon, Bruna, wake up!'

We'd been practising for fifteen minutes now and I wanted a break. My breath was rasping through my lungs in shorter and shorter gasps. Blood thrummed around my system as my superfit opponent exerted every gram of his formidable strength against me. I was more skilled and agile than him which was, thank the gods, more important.

'Screw you, Livius.' I jumped over the chain right into his field of contact and slashed at his arm. He nearly drew away in time. I left a short, red gash on his forearm which leaked slow droplets.

I brought my short sword around before he could recover, feinted right in his face, jerked the chain, thrusting my foot out at the same time and tripped him up. As he hit the ground, he found the tip of my sword pressed against his larynx. He dropped his weapon and opened his arms, laying them on the ground, the palms of his hands upwards in a signal of surrender. He grinned up at me as he lay there, his blond curls dishevelled but his pale eyes laughing. Even defeated, his good humour didn't fail. No wonder women fell for him.

I sheathed my sword and held my right hand out to him. I saw the measuring look in his eye.

'Don't even think about it,' I said. He sat up, studied the ground for a few seconds and chuckled to himself. He sprang to his feet, giving me my hand back, all in one graceful movement. His tall frame hadn't filled out a millimetre since we'd met on that first training exercise fourteen years ago. He still towered over me and I knew how crazy I'd been to accept him as my opponent. Small wonder I was still trying to catch my breath.

Lined up after a light lunch and the gods knew how much water, we occupied two sides of a cleared area, ready to start our skills demonstration. I noticed a couple of empty chairs between the exercise commander and the Latin speaker, Browning. Were they expecting guests? I sighed. Sometimes I felt we were like a circus, parading our Roman-ness, satisfying some half-baked nostalgia based on epic movies. Some clown had even wanted us to stage a mock battle against one of the Roman re-enactment groups. They forgot that while we were proud of our history, we were a forward-looking 21st century country.

Flavius got it all underway, with pairs demonstrating sword skills. Not practised these days outside the professional games arena except by the military, training with a sharp, double-edged fifty centimetre carbon steel blade tended to concentrate the mind as well as honing reaction skills. Not mandatory – we used state of the art weaponry as normal – but all members of the unit were encouraged to become proficient with a *gladius*, if only to get used to close physical combat with an opponent. If you got cut, you got cut, then chewed out for being careless. Contrary to popular belief, the Roman short sword was more than fine for cutting and chopping motions as well as for thrusting. Not much had changed in shape since the Pompeii pattern used in the fourth century which had been spectacularly successful.

After a while, Flavius invited the Brits to come forward to try it out. His opposite number, Johnson, and around a dozen of them did well despite their unfamiliarity with the weapon. After watching for a few minutes, I nodded to Paula and we left them to it.

In my tent, I got kitted up with Paula's help. I stripped off my fatigues jacket, leaving my black t-shirt and donned the thin leather undershirt, lined with Kevlar fabric. I changed into my studded leather arena boots, bound my plaited red-gold hair up on top of my head. Paula clipped a leather-and-mail protective band around my neck.

'You okay, Bruna? You seem a bit quiet.'

'Sorry, just thinking about a strange feeling I got this morning. I was outside the showers and I got a distinct feeling of being watched.'

'Some perv wanting an eyeful?' she smirked. Her brown eyes reflected cynical humour.

'No,' I smiled back, lifting my arms for the chain mail *lorica* she was slipping over my undershirt. 'More than that. I got a definite tingle of danger.'

'Not that young officer Allia stuck her needle into? He was pretty pissed about it.'

'I don't think so. No, something bigger.' I shook my head to get rid of the thought as I buckled the wide leather belt she'd handed me. She fastened the leather Kevlar-lined lower arm guards and I was ready.

As we got back to the edge of the clearing, they'd just finished demonstrating the *cuneum formate*, a shock tactic in the form of a wedge. Like a treble-sized sabre-toothed tiger coming at you; incredibly scary if you were on the receiving end of it.

The next thing I saw was that the two empty chairs were now occupied; a slim junior officer, sitting upright and formal, and next to her, the legate.

What in Hades was he doing here? And why had he brought the ghastly Stella?

II

A sharp tug jolted my arm again. Livius was pulsing them to break my concentration. I doubled my guard as we circled again. The gravel crunched under the soles of my boots as I kept my feet dancing. At the other end of the two-metre chain, Livius caught me in a fixed stare, trying to unnerve me. I glared back. I feinted forward, letting the chain go slack, then yanked and slashed down with my blade. A thin ripple of blood appeared on his upper arm in the gap between arm guard and sleeve of his chain-mail *lorica*. It matched the one I'd given him this morning. He swore. Not a trace of good humour in his face now. I laughed at him. I was going to win. He looked as mad as Hades.

The leather cuff at the end of the chain binding my left wrist to Livius's started to chafe. The sweatband underneath was saturated. The links clashed and groaned with the intensity of our pulling and straining. Sometimes I imagined a ripple of fierce, lethal energy running up and down the chain. All you wanted to do was destroy your opponent.

I heard cheering, shouting of bets placed, heckling, but filtered most of it out. I had to concentrate on Livius's weapon slicing the air and jabbing at me. and his attempts to defeat me. I was used to the merciless force as the opponent pulled, but he was wearing me down. Sweat ran down my back and between my breasts with the effort of thrusting and dodging.

I must have been crazy to do this. I felt a rush of fear mixed with adrenalin as I leapt over the chain to avoid a vicious stab. Gods, he was furious now, his eyes as hard as stones. As I dodged faster and faster, I missed my step, he tripped me and I was on the ground. As I went down I grabbed the chain link near his wrist and pulled him to earth with me. As he fell, I used the momentum to throw him over my head while I rolled away. We both scrambled up, panting, measuring each other up.

The violence in his eyes, now tearing with the dust we'd raised, made me determined to finish this quickly. As we sprang up,

I feinted to the right, distracting him, leapt into his now opened guard area. Using my whole body, I felled him and landed hard on his chest. Within nanoseconds I had jerked my elbow up to the grey sky, my arm and wrist folded in one downwards line, hand poised ready to thrust downwards. The tip of my sword grazed his throat.

For a few seconds I thought he was going to try something stupid like bringing his sword up from behind and slashing my unguarded flesh. His linked hand was trapped under his body, but his right hand was still free holding the lethal blade.

'Drop it.' I pushed the sword tip harder against the stretched tan skin of his throat, just nicking the surface. A tiny spot of red seeped out.

His eyes narrowed, making them darker. His mouth was still a single hard line. The shouting and heckling from the audience had died. Intense stares lapped at us, but nobody moved.

'C'mon, Livius,' I whispered. 'Give it up. I'm dying for a drink.'

The rigid body under me seemed to harden. Suddenly, it relaxed and I was sitting on softening flesh. The fire in his eyes subsided and a ghost of a grin flitted across his lips. He uncurled his hand and released his blade.

I stood up and brandished mine in the air with a shout of 'Victis'. Flavius came forward and, mildly pompous like any referee, declared it finished. I ignored the applause and exuberant shouting around us.

Unlacing my leather cuff, I glanced at Livius, doing the same. 'Friends?'

'Of course, Bruna.' He smiled and shrugged. 'But I can see why they banned it for so long. I wanted to destroy you.'

'I know. That's why I had to end it.'

We weren't offering our hosts the chance to participate in this particular exercise.

We grasped forearms in the traditional way. His gaze was steady now.

'You know what we have to do now, don't you, Bruna?' He raised an eyebrow as if expecting me to protest. 'As the old man's here,' he looked me direct in the eyes.

'I suppose so. Let's get on with it, then.'

'Don't be so grouchy.'

'Huh.'

We marched across the ten metres or so, he impeccably, me

adequately, but in step. We stopped two metres away from the front rows of our hosts. Some were sitting in canvas field chairs, others on the ground. Swords still in our right hands, we raised them, swinging them around to the front in a wide arc to rest, blades vertical, flat side facing, our hands close to our faces, paused for three seconds, then slashed them down to the right. And waited.

The legate stood and assessed us with his hazel eyes, his face showing no sign of emotion, no reaction. Even the scar from his recent accident that ran along the hairline by his temple looked calm. He saluted back and we stood easy, but not relaxed.

'A good demonstration,' he said in English. 'I commend you, Centurion Livius, for going up against the most experienced link-fighter of this generation.'

Was that a compliment?

'Well done, Major.' He smiled at me, his eyes crinkling, betraying a trace of mischief. Good thing his back was to our hosts. 'I think you've frightened everybody sufficiently for one day.'

He dismissed us. We saluted again, turned smartly to the right and marched off. After a few steps, we relaxed into a normal walk and joined the others, milling around with some of the Brits. I looked back, searching for the legate, but he and other senior officers had vanished into the staff tent.

'Excuse me, ma'am,' came a voice behind me. That tingle ran across my shoulders again. The blonde sergeant I'd last seen at the check-in table was standing in my blind spot. I hadn't heard her approach in the noise of the talking, joshing and laughter around me.

'Yes?'

'The Colonel's compliments and would you and the senior members of your detachment care to join him in twenty minutes' time for a pre-supper drink?' Her face was neutral, but despite her pleasant tone, I was strangely reassured to be holding my fifty centimetres of carbon steel.

'Er, yes, of course, we'd be delighted.'

Showered, changed and relaxed, I made my way over to the staff tent. I enjoyed the social stuff that went with military life. It was far less hypocritical than civilian parties; you had straight talking and the chance for genuine friendships based on common experience.

I exchanged smiles with the dozen women and men loitering outside holding plastic cups containing different coloured drinks.

The entrance flaps on the tent had been pegged back for air circulation; it was a warm evening. I ducked through and found the rest of our officers and non-coms talking to their hosts.

'Major. Here, take this.' Captain Browning materialised beside me and handed me a cup of what turned out to be warm white wine.

'Thanks, Captain. Hey, what's your first name?'

'Michael,' he said grinning. 'And it's not shortened.'

'Okay, Michael,' I smiled back. 'Carina.' We shook hands. He really did have the nicest smile.

'That was an impressive display earlier,' he said, standing near to hear my answer. The alcohol and testosterone in a confined space made it pretty noisy. 'Do you teach it?'

'Only to the most agile and those who can handle the emotional side, otherwise the casualty rate is too high.'

'I suppose it's the chain that induces the desperate need to fight so savagely,' he mused.

'Yeah, it's pretty much do or die. Well, it was in the old days.' Criminals awaiting a death sentence had been offered the option of link fighting. If they won, they got off. But the state had usually put a champion gladiator on the other end which weighed the odds steeply against the likelihood. These days, because of the danger of emotions racing out of control, only the military or licensed gladiator schools sanctioned it, and under restricted circumstances. 'It was illegal until a few years ago. I was, er, instrumental in re-introducing it.'

'Yes, after a spell in the cells for illegal fighting, if I remember correctly,' a cool voice added. I shut my eyes, suppressing both irritation and pleasure at the sound.

'Sir,' said Michael, finding our legate in front of him. He took in the other man's tall, athletic frame, dark blond hair slicked back behind his ears and hazel eyes which glinted more green than brown at this precise moment.

'Captain Michael Browning, Legate Conradus Mitelus.' I vaguely waved my hand from one to the other.

Michael, being a Latinist, got it immediately. 'Ah, I see. If you'll excuse me...' He nodded and left us in our group of two.

'Well, that worked,' I said, rolling my eyes at the legate.

'He was getting a little too friendly, I thought.'

'For Juno's sake, Conrad, he was being collegiate.'

'Does staring down your front count as collegiate?'

'He was not!'

He snorted. Although a bone-and-blood Roma Novan, despite his foreign name, my husband of fifteen years was still prone to jealousy attacks. I smiled to myself but I wasn't going to let him off too easily.

'What in Hades are you doing here, anyway?' I said. 'I thought you were in London with the children, and Stella.' I found his daughter, Stella, from his previous relationship awkward and difficult. I didn't like it one little bit that she'd joined the PGSF as a cadet officer and had accompanied her father today. But I knew how to be civilised.

'That's not a very friendly welcome – I thought you'd be pleased to see me. I came to see how you were all getting along.'

'Right, like we're a load of kids, needing our babysitter?'

'You seem a bit tense, love. Are you all right?' He stroked my cheek with the back of his fingers. A wave of warmth rolled through me. How could he have the power to do that after all this time? We were an old married couple.

'I'm fine, really. Maybe a bit tired. But there's something else. Probably nothing to worry about, but—'

'Ah, Legate,' interrupted a muscular man of medium height, with a self-important air. He was a Brit, around mid-fifties, his neck chafing on the collar of his new-out-the-stores fatigues jacket which carried red tabs. So some kind of general. His eyes flicked over me casually. 'I'm sure your officer will excuse you. I'd like you to meet some people.' Our host, the local commander, Colonel Stimpson, hovered behind him with a totally neutral expression on his face which to me signified he thought the other guy was a pain in the fundament.

Conrad's expression contracted and his mouth retreated to a straight line. 'Just before we circulate, I don't believe you've been introduced to my wife, Major Carina Mitela, who is leading the training detachment.' He turned to me with a big smile. 'Carina, this is Brigadier Furnell from the Department of Defense. Oh, excuse me, the *Ministry* of Defence.'

'Oh, pleased to meet you, I'm sure.' He looked as if he was eating grit. 'Well, you'd better tag along, Major.'

He turned away and set off through the crowd. Conrad looked furious. I laid my hand on his forearm. 'It doesn't matter. Really.

They're like that here, especially the top brass, as Michael calls them.'

'Hades, I don't know how you put up with it. I can't remember it being like that when I trained here.'

'Well, love, you're a man. And you were very young. You wouldn't have noticed.'

Eventually I broke free and went outside for a few minutes' fresh air.

'Aunt Carina?'

I turned to see a brown-haired girl, slim to the point of skinny, in tailored fatigues. Her fingers on one hand twisted and twined around those on the other.

'Hello, Stella. Are you all right?'

She glanced away, then back to me, with none of the assurance of a normal twenty-one-year-old.

'What can I do for you?'

'Dad said we'd be staying here tonight, but I don't know where I'm supposed to go.'

At that moment, I felt sorry for her; she was alone amongst strangers and not very skilled at reaching out.

'Let's find Centurion Servla – she'll know, or if she doesn't, she'll sort it out.'

Back inside the staff tent, I cornered Paula. It was unfair, I knew.

'Centurion, do you have space in your tent for an extra one? Cadet Apulia needs a bunk for the night.'

Not one scrap of reaction showed on Paula's face. 'Of course, ma'am. I'd be delighted. I'll go and sort it out right away.' As she turned to make her way back to the accommodation area, her shoulders set, I knew I was going to pay for it later.

'I thought I'd be in with you,' said Stella. 'Why can't I?'

'Really, Stella. That was rude. Centurion Servla may have heard you. You're very junior. Just do as you're told.'

Gods, she looked truculent. She stuck her chin out and her dark brown eyes boiled. That was the problem with rich kids – they didn't have a clue. Officer Cadet Stella Apulia had enjoyed a privileged upbringing – she was the eldest daughter of Imperatrix Silvia – but despite her mother's best efforts, she hadn't grasped that she needed to take on responsibilities in exchange. 'Serve to lead' was no empty slogan.

'Centurion Paula Servla is a very senior soldier and I'm grateful to her for looking after you. You will treat her with maximum courtesy and fit in with her. She's not there to run around after you. Nor is anybody else in the unit.'

Stella looked mutinous.

'If you want to stay, you have to knuckle down, work hard and accept discipline. You wanted to join. Of course, you always have the choice.'

'Why are you so horrible to me?'

'Oh, please! I'm trying to show you how to behave. Gods, Stella, you're twenty-one, not twelve.'

We stood there, glaring at each other. The trouble was, nobody wanted to cross her. I was one of the few who would. Not only did I have the social rank, but her mother, Silvia, was my cousin and friend.

'Look, Stella, you're not in the palace now. You're a small, but promising, cog at the lower level of a very efficient machine. Once you've grasped the knack of working *with* others, and respecting them for what they do, you'll find it very rewarding and you'll make real friends.'

'It's alright for you, everybody likes you,' she said, her face sullen.

'Well, news for you – it didn't happen overnight. I had to earn it.'

I wasn't about to tell her the full story of the difficulties I'd had; it was done and gone. But the twin burdens of being married to the boss and being joint head of one of the most powerful and wealthiest families in Roma Nova hadn't made my initial path as a junior officer in the special forces very smooth. Navigating between the toadies and the spiteful in order to find true friends and comrades sure had honed my people skills. But the difference between me and Stella? I loved the life, the excitement, the sense of fulfilment, the buzz, from the work I did. She didn't know what she liked or wanted.

Later as we lay together on sleeping mats in my tent, Conrad told me about the small act of vengeance he'd enacted against the pompous Brigadier. After the post-supper port at the senior staff table, the Brigadier had invited Conrad to stay at the local hotel where he and his Defence Ministry people were putting up. Conrad said he'd prefer to sleep with his wife, and begged to be excused.

'I thought Furnell was going to have a stroke. Stimpson, who was standing a little behind him, gave a little smirk – not at me, love,' he added, seeing my reaction, 'but at the shiny-arse from the ministry.'

I laughed, bent over and kissed him lightly on the lips. 'Thank you. You really are the nicest man.'

He didn't say anything, but the warmth grew in his eyes. Even in the dim light, I could see them darken. He leaned over and kissed my eyelids, my jawline, making his way up gently but determinedly to my mouth. Oh, the warm pleasure of it. The graceful line of his throat stretched above me. His masculine scent overwhelmed me. His body always excited me. Although military bedrolls were not the most comfortable or sensual surroundings for passionate love-making, we managed to frighten the local wildlife.

Beginning the day with a fresh egg and bacon roll – hot, salty bacon coupled with the firm liquid of a fried egg bursting in your mouth – in the quiet of a pine forest with the sun starting to shed its early light on you took some beating. The cook grinned at me, sensing an appreciative customer.

'Like another one, ma'am?'

I swallowed the last piece and grinned back. 'No. No, thanks. Nothing could better that.'

'Coffee and tea are inside, but come back if you want another,' and he winked.

I pulled the heavy canvas flap of the mess tent aside and found a few other early souls. Passing on the muddy-looking coffee I filled a mug from the tea urn.

'Sleep well?'

Cute question.

'Hi, Michael. Yes, thanks. I've always loved camping out and it's so quiet here.'

'We're either not trying hard enough to make it sufficiently uncomfortable or you lot are tougher than we think.'

'Yeah,' I smirked at him. 'Get over it.'

He chuckled and raised his mug of tea, toasting me.

The rest of that day, we packed up the camp into cargo trucks. Even Stella helped, acting as Conrad's runner. That strange young woman, the admin sergeant, seemed to be everywhere, but as I stood up, pausing for a moment after securing the straps on my own pack, I caught her staring at Stella and Conrad. He turned away to sign Flavius's el-pad, and Stella watched the two men, oblivious to the interest from the sergeant. What jolted me was the violence in the British girl's scrutiny. Her mouth twisted in anger and her eyes shone hard and pitiless. Then in a nanosecond, it had all vanished and her serene expression was back. I blinked. What in Hades was that about?

I watched her covertly for a little longer, but she disappeared after a few minutes. After personal farewells to our hosts and final parade, we drove back to the main barracks allocated for our use, until recently an RAF base given over to the EUSAF. I'd decided to grant the whole detachment three days' local leave before going home to Roma Nova and Flavius was briefing them about observing local sensitivities. He organised them into groups of three or four, with the youngest guards paired with more experienced ones.

'The gods help us when this lot hits London,' he muttered under his breath to me while Conrad was giving them a lecture about English dos and don'ts.

'No problem, Flav. I'm more concerned about the stuff they'll absorb from the locals.'

'What do you mean?'

'You haven't forgotten Operation Goldlights, surely?'

Flavius and I had met when I'd been undercover fighting the wholesale introduction of illicit drugs into Roma Nova. We'd stopped it then, but it was one of the biggest worries faced by our law and security forces.

'Of course not!' He rolled his eyes. 'They've all been warned specifically – no tabs, no powder, no sprays or they're out. They're meeting up with some of the English we've been training with, so I hope that'll help.'

'You're kidding! You know how they drink.'

'C'mon, Bruna, they're not kids.'

I shrugged. I just prayed there was one particular English sergeant they were not meeting. If Fortuna was smiling on me, she'd sent that girl back to the Brits' permanent base in the west and we'd never see her again.

III

On the second day in London, we arrived back at the hotel suite late afternoon after an activity-packed day; the Tower, the Battersea theme park, a burger stop, Skateboard Central and a browse through the City children's farm. I thanked fate yet again for my cousin Helena. When she'd given up teaching and taken on supervising my kids, it had been one of the luckiest days of my life. She'd turned out three happy, inquisitive, healthy but immaculately mannered beings.

Well, mostly.

Allegra had started teenage grunting recently, which Helena assured me was perfectly normal. I wasn't too sure. She was the child of my heart and until a few weeks ago, I had been almost smug about how much pleasure we gave each other. Most fourteen-year-olds, when I'd been one in the States, were beyond embarrassed to admit they actually had mothers. I hadn't been so lucky; mine had driven herself off a cliff when I was three.

But Allegra and I had been friends always. We'd sit together, she curled in my lap when little and close by my side when older, as we read books, talked, played on the games console together. I'd sit by her when I could, helping her with homework assignments, giving her confidence to try new things and consoling her when she failed or fell. She poured her heart out to me, sometimes teaching me things, and listening seriously to what I said. She'd send me a soft smile, followed by a chuckle then a full throated laugh. Then a few weeks before we came here she'd transformed, like she had a split personality; flirting with her father, still giving Helena respect and polite to everybody else, she saved all her grumping for me. Fabulous.

The twins, Tonia and Gil, at ten were über-boisterous after an exciting day out in London but that didn't entitle Allegra to drag along all day saying how bored she was. She knew better. And that made me angry. She knew it would be her turn tomorrow and we'd leave the small ones and Helena behind.

'I don't know what you're worrying about, love,' said Conrad. 'It's just a phase.'

'Right. A phase. Sure. You're getting all the Daddy's girl treatment and I'm Cruella de Vil.'

'Forget about it tonight. We've got dinner with Andrew Brudgland later, so you can relax and leave it to Helena.'

'You don't think that's the problem? I mean, Helena and not me?'

'Carina, look at me.' Mm, always a pleasure. Although he was gaining one or two more lines around those mesmerising eyes and tiny grey wings at his temples, his smile was so warm and sexy, I forgot everything else.

'Hey!'

'Yes?' I said.

'You are a great mother. You love our children unreservedly, you nurture them, help them, defend them. You have responsibilities, sure, but they know that and none of them feels any less loved because of it. So stop it.'

'But why—'

He laid the tip of his finger on my lip. 'It's not you. She's just trying to work out who she is. She's an adolescent.' He shrugged.

'Helena says I have to persist, keep talking, support her, talk to her as an adult. But all I get back are grunts.'

'It'll pass. Honestly.'

'And what makes you the great expert?' He had no sisters and only distant female cousins. Then I remembered. Stella. He saw I'd got it.

'Quite. Remember her at fifteen? I know she can still be awkward, but she's a great deal improved. I think living at the palace has kept her a bit immature. Hopefully, that'll go when she gets to the officer training school.'

Personally, I had my doubts.

Rules Restaurant belonged to another world. Welcomed by a smile from the top-hatted commissionaire, tall with the assured, disciplined air of a former soldier, we passed into the care of wonderfully polite, hyper-efficient servers sporting tab-fronted aprons and tailcoats. Light bounced between the gold-framed mirrors, reflected off the fabulous coloured glass ceiling and fell on our party dining in a discreet corner. The spaciousness, soft leather benches and thick carpet recalled a more comfortable and relaxed age.

Andrew Brudgland had that confident British air of looking as if he was sitting up straight when slouching. He ate his food with smooth, precise movements, nothing dropped or spilled and no crumbs or drips left. Fascinated by such fastidiousness, I studied his unremarkable face closely. Half-closed lids couldn't disguise the directness of his gaze as he talked with Conrad about some shared past adventure. They'd met and trained together when Conrad had spent time on detachment in England as a young soldier. Andrew worked now in one of the British government's security services. From his fit appearance he didn't sit at a desk so much.

'I'm sorry I missed you both last time you came to London, Carina. How are you enjoying it?'

He watched carefully for my response to his formulaic question. I had the impression he never wasted a word.

'Good to have a few days to recover after the exercise – something I guess you know all about,' I said, and looked up at him through my eyelashes. I saw a half-smile of appreciation and heard a chuckle from Conrad.

'Sorry,' Andrew said, and smiled. 'That was rather trite. Seriously, let me know if there's anywhere particular you'd like to visit and I'll do my best.'

'Well, thank you. That's a great offer.' But I doubted he'd get us into Buckingham Palace, something that would have been pretty intriguing.

When we'd finished eating, I excused myself, making my way through the frosted glass door and up the narrow red and gold papered stairway to the restrooms. Back down again in the tiny lobby, I stretched my hand out to open the door back into the restaurant when I heard Conrad's voice, clipped and tense. But strangest of all, his usual faultless English was spoiled by traces of a Latin accent. Only when he was exhausted or stressed out did his accent slip.

'... not a clue. It was hand delivered. As soon as I read it, I stuffed it back in the envelope. Gods, I can't believe it! The signature just said "Nicola". Who the hell is she?'

That got my attention. I froze where I was.

'Let me have the letter, Conrad, and I'll get somebody at the lab to process it. If there's anything, even a partial, we'll find her. Don't worry, I'll be careful. Not a word to Carina.'

'Jupiter, no. She's as sharp as all hell and can pick up a conspiracy in a breath of air.'

'So I've heard,' came the dry reply.

What in Hades was that about?

I shucked off my shoes and crept back up the stairs. At the top I slipped them back on and came down the stairway making light shoe noise on each uncovered tread. I swung through the door, a smile on my face. The two men smiled back equally blandly and we made nice conversation for the rest of the evening.

Next morning, I woke at the touch of Conrad's lips on my forehead. Totally relaxed, I enjoyed the soft tingle as it spread through my skin. I smiled before I opened my eyes. But when I did, I was disappointed to see him dressed, and in sweats and sneakers.

'Just going for a run in the park.' He pulled his glance away a little too quickly, turned and shut the bedroom door behind him before I could say anything.

That was weird. We ran together whenever we could. He'd recovered so well from his accident earlier this year that he'd now resumed full-on training. The first proper run, he'd scarcely managed a kilometre before collapsing, heaving breath like a suffocation victim. Luckily, we'd kept to the parkland behind Domus Mitelarum but it hadn't lessened his humiliation and anger at himself. He hadn't said a word as we walked back, him limping badly. But for Juno's sake, his leg had been smashed in several places by that truck running him down. I'd reassured him, but his confidence had suffered. Although he seemed fit now, months later, even he had to admit he'd lost his edge.

If I hadn't overheard his conversation last night with Andrew Brudgland I would have shrugged it off as quirky, or thought he was letting me rest some more. But not this time.

I leapt out of bed and frantically pulled on my own jogging sweats and sneakers. Yanking the door to the landing open, I startled the guard and tore down the service stairs. Would Conrad have taken the elevator? At the foot of the narrow stairwell, I hurried past a surprised maid and headed for the staff door leading to the lobby. No sign of him through the shaded window panel. Damn! I edged into the main lobby, sidled along to the elevator doors then stepped out briskly across the marble lobby. Outside I glanced up and down Park Lane. It was only half seven in the morning, but already busy. I peered between the traffic and spotted Conrad's figure across the road as he ran along the park railing at a gentle pace.

Shadowing him on my side of the road, I jogged in parallel, but staying a few steps behind. After he disappeared through the park gate, I counted to five, saw a space in the traffic and sprinted to the middle. A taxi screamed past me. Crap, I forgot they drove on the wrong side of the road. Once safely across, I made for the gate Conrad had taken.

Concealed behind a tree, I watched as he trotted in the direction of the Serpentine lake. I set off down the Broadwalk, keeping him in my line of sight at all times. It was too open for me to follow him directly. A little further south, the added cover of shrubs and trees let me cross westward past the bandstand towards the lake. I closed up on him, but keeping a healthy distance between us. Was he simply out jogging? Where did he get the energy after last night?

I followed him across the bridge, hiding in a small group of other runners. If he looked around, I didn't want him spotting me. He started back along the south bank, switching on to Rotten Row and diverting through the formal gardens and stopping eventually on the east side of some Greek warrior statue. He affected some stretching exercises, but by now I had caught him up and was hiding only a few metres away behind a tall shrub.

He tracked an imaginary line running from the middle post around the statue and a tall chestnut tree at the park railing. He turned to look at the statue itself, but all the while glancing around him checking that nobody else was in view. His hand came up and he rubbed his fingers along the hairline above his right eye. Gotcha! Now I knew he was up to something. Love him as I did, I thought his tradecraft was sloppy. He strolled over to the tree, sat at the base of the trunk and made a call on his cellphone.

A vibrating buzz from my pocket answered. It sounded as loud as a jackhammer drill. I leapt up, sprinted away to a safe distance out of earshot, careful to remain just out of his line of sight. I found a shrub to crouch down by.

'Oh, hi,' I answered.

'You sound out of breath. Are you all right?'

'No, I'm fine. You surprised me. I was in the bathroom when you called. I just swallowed some water.'

He laughed. 'Well, take it easy. I'll be back in about ten.'

I signed off and crept forward a few centimetres. Conrad pocketed his cell, then too casually laid his hand on the tree root. His fingers contracted, darted under the root and picked something up. He stood up, put it in his pocket and jogged off.

I made it back only seconds ahead of him, threw my sweats under the bed and ran into the shower where he found me. Thank Juno, he didn't hear my heart thumping with the exertion of getting back first. Leaving him to finish, I skipped out of the bathroom and found his discarded sweats on the floor. I hesitated. Surely I could trust him. I pulled the towel from my hair and started rubbing it dry. I stared at the sweats again. It was too tempting. In Conrad's pocket I found two pieces of paper stapled together; a handwritten letter in precise blue ballpoint ink and Andrew Brudgland's report.

We left from Heathrow later that day, arriving at Portus Airport in Roma Nova in the early evening. As we clattered down the steps we were engulfed by hot, humid air. By the time we reached home, my head was starting to throb. Juno knew what it would have been like without air conditioning. Helena and I settled the three wilting children and I looked in on my grandmother, Aurelia. It was late when Conrad and I sat down to supper.

'I'll wait till morning to check up on work,' Conrad said, reaching for his glass of beer. 'I don't want to disturb Daniel now, especially as he's tied up getting ready for his anti-terrorism exercise. I had the last contact report this morning, so I can't think anything drastic has happened since.'

'That's good, as I want to discuss something with you in private.'

'Oh?'

'Why didn't you tell me about Nicola?'

He looked down and stabbed the breadcrumbed pork with his knife, swishing the meat around his plate, giving the beans a hard time. He didn't speak for a full two minutes. I watched his jaw working as he ate, his face impassive. I found the silence oppressive, but I knew I had to wait.

'Did you read it all?' His voice was subdued and his eyes remained focused on his plate.

'Yes. Conrad, I—'

'What the hell were you doing rifling through my stuff?'

'Excuse me? Why were you hiding such a letter from me? And asking a foreign security service to investigate it for you?'

He waved his hand and looked irritated.

'How did you find out?'

'I heard you in Rules.'

'Gods, do you always eavesdrop on private conversations?'

'That's in my job description, remember?'

He was as mad with me as Livius had been during the link fight.

'I'm not your target,' he said. 'Or have you decided to make me one?' I winced at the sarcasm. His eyes narrowed and slanted upwards and the skin covering his cheeks tightened. When he closed his face down like that, he closed down mentally as well.

'Why didn't you tell me?' I smiled a smile I didn't feel. 'Surely this is some con woman on the make? We can deal with it together, like we always do.'

I touched his forearm.

He shook my hand off. 'For Jupiter's sake, don't give me any platitudes.'

'Okay,' I said and swallowed. 'We'll do it straight.'

He glanced at me, then went back to looking at his plate.

I waited, but he kept silent.

'This is how I see it,' I continued. 'As family head, I have to know about anything that threatens us. So give me the full story.'

He took a large swallow of his beer, stared at the bookshelves behind me.

'I'll deal with it. It's nothing to do with you or your family.'

'What do you mean, *my* family? It's *our* family.'

He'd belonged to it for nearly fifteen years. In Roma Nova, men married into their wives' families, taking their *nomen*, the family name, and leaving their birth name behind. Although my grandmother headed our family, I was taking on more of her responsibilities, trying to keep the hundreds of cousins in order, running the businesses, deputising in the Senate as well as my day job. It was pretty tiring, if I was being honest. I could do without any further complications.

'It's a Tella family matter.'

A door slammed in my face. He'd ceased to be a Tella the moment he signed the family register on our wedding day. His eyes refused to meet mine and a pink flush appeared on his face. The cords in his neck stood out. I'd have bet my last *solidus* he was deeply embarrassed as well as angry.

'Okay, I realise this is difficult for you, but let's try and look at it logically...'

'Don't you ever turn off the logic and reason button?' He snorted and I thought I saw contempt, but also uncertainty.

'Look,' I said, and laid my hand on his, 'I'm trying to understand how upset you must be, but you'll have to help me out. Of course, anything affecting you affects me and I'm not talking family politics here.'

He said nothing. He pulled the letter and report out of his pocket and laid them on the table, drawing his hand back as if to disown them.

I picked them up and read the letter again.

Hello, Dad.

I expect you're surprised at being called that by a complete stranger, but then I'm not a stranger.

You met my mother, Janice, when you were here twenty-five years ago. Her diary is full of the good times you had together. I expect you thought it was a few weeks' fun with an easy English girl, but my auntie told me you broke Mum's heart.

She brought me up by herself, on benefits, too proud to contact you for help. Auntie said you probably didn't know I was on the way, but you didn't bother to check, did you?

I looked into you and your family. Not very good you having a human rights abusing traitor as your stepfather, was it? Or a slippery politician like the uncle who brought you up.

That posh wife of yours won't like me popping up, so I think we need to come to some arrangement. You wouldn't want me turning up at your ex-girlfriend's palace, or telling my story to your daily rag, would you?

You owe me and I'm going to collect.

Nicola.

I found it as crude and tasteless as when I first read it in London. Andrew Brudgland's report identified her as likely to be Nicola Hargreve, born twenty-four years ago in Darlington Memorial Hospital. Finger print data were not as strong as Andrew would have liked, but he was eighty-five per cent confident. Why had she been finger-printed? I thought they were pretty tough on destroying them after a specified time in the UK. So why were hers still on record?

With dark blond hair, shifting copper-brown and green eyes and strong, sculpted lines to his face, Conrad was an attractive man. When he smiled, he was devastating. I'd met him when he was thirty-two, in his prime. It wasn't merely his face, his athletic body or his fascinating cat-like walk. It was his plentiful charm. At twenty-one, in an English army town full of young soldiers, he would have been the hottest thing in pants.

'She says she's my daughter, mine and Janice's.' His shoulders slumped and he brought his hands up to support his head. 'Mars help me if I've abandoned a child of mine.'

After a few moments, he stood up, catching the end of his knife and fork which clattered on to the table; the sound echoed through the room.

'I'll talk to Uncle Quintus. Perhaps he'll have some ideas how to deal with this. And he's the head of *my* family.'

Quintus Tellus, who'd retired as Imperial Chancellor a few years ago, would no doubt have all kinds of clever advice, but I was unnerved to see Conrad at such a loss. Not a trace of his famous detached decisiveness; his mind was like a bowl of *puls* porridge. And this reverting to his previous family. My instinct would be to pay this Nicola a little visit and scare the crap out of her. Unfortunately, the letter had bitten straight into Conrad's Achilles' heel.

What made him such a good father was his determination that none of his children would want for love or care. It was an obsession that reached back into his own ruined childhood.

'Of course, we'll consult Uncle Quintus,' I said, 'but we'll handle this together. Between us, we can see off this little blackmailer. She's probably only bluffing.' I smiled at him and reached out my hand.

But he kept his own back and looked down at his dirty plate.

'I know that after we met, I was a coward not to tell you about my children with Silvia,' he said, his voice only just above a whisper. 'Or about Silvia herself, but I was shit-scared of losing you.'

It had been a bitter time when I'd discovered the truth in the most humiliating way possible. We'd parted for nearly a year, each nursing a deep hurt. It was only after hunting down the killer who was after me that we'd been reconciled. It was simple – we'd found we couldn't live apart. A cliché, sure, but that's what clichés were – common occurrences. But it hadn't been a smooth run in anybody's language.

'But this, this…' He failed to find the words.

'Little accident?'

'Don't be facetious' He looked as angry as all Hades.

'Sorry. That was insensitive.' I waved my hand at him and stifled my irritation.

'I swear I didn't know about this.'

IV

The gods knew what Conrad discussed with his uncle the next day, but he didn't, or wouldn't, tell me anything when we met in his office in the afternoon. I decided to pay a call on Quintus Tellus myself.

Domus Tellarum was even older than ours, some parts dating back over a thousand years. Not so tall and less pristine than Domus Mitelarum, it exuded a shabby charm. Today's strong sunlight emphasised the flaking portico columns, and the red brickwork exposed here and there, but the world wouldn't end if they weren't re-faced. I left my side arm in the vestibule safebox and made my way through to the atrium.

'Carina. I *am* honoured. Both of you within a day. Dear me.'

'Don't give me that bullshit, Uncle Quintus.' I grinned at him, leaned over and kissed his cheek. 'You know why I'm here.'

A little over eighty, Quintus still thought and spoke like the clever politician he'd been. Not only that, he had the sharpest sense of survival I'd ever seen and everything was subordinate to it. I loved him dearly.

He gestured me to a seat by the window overlooking the garden. Only the night irrigation was keeping anything green in this summer's heat. But this evening a breeze was just starting to relieve the heaviness of today's exceptional temperature. I was sure we'd have storm rain tonight. A servant brought us wine, then we were completely alone.

'Is this an official visit?'

I wore my PGSF summer uniform; I'd come straight from work.

'Believe me, Quintus, if this was an official Mitela family visit, I'd have half the family council here to support me.'

The Mitelae were the senior of the original Twelve Families who'd founded Roma Nova. Endowed with privilege, the Twelve had been the ruler's supporters and servants for over sixteen hundred years. But to balance it, they had greater responsibilities. They served the imperatrix while protecting their own families and the Roma Novan society they'd helped found. The Families' Code regulated and balanced affairs between these powerful families in a fair but disciplined way. Undemocratic, but it kept order. It worked.

Technically, Conrad had violated the code by not disclosing voluntarily about Nicola, but how stupid would it have been for me to discipline him for that?

'You underestimate yourself, Carina. You're sufficiently terrifying by yourself.'

I smiled at him. He smiled back.

'I thought we'd have a little chat, just between ourselves,' I said. 'Not only do I not want to make it official, I want your advice.'

'Oh?'

'C'mon, Uncle Quintus, don't be difficult. I really do need your help.'

His eyes scrutinised my face for some moments. He waved his hand, inviting me to speak. I knew he'd manoeuvre me to be first up to bat.

'I don't know what Conradus has discussed with you and I don't suppose you'll tell me.' I glanced at him. The expression on his face was impassive. He waited for me to continue. 'I'm concerned he didn't confide in me when we were in London,' I said. 'I only found out by accident.'

He grimaced. 'Conradus put it in rather stronger terms. "Sneaky" and "underhand" were somewhere in the conversation.'

'Whatever. What did he expect from another spook?'

We sat in silence for a few moments. I heard faint sounds of crockery being set on surfaces from his dining room. Of course, like many older people he ate early.

'Quintus, I only want to help. I'm worried he'll internalise it and get depressed like after the accident.'

A little over six months ago, Conrad and I had been out on a rare shopping expedition in the old quarter of the city. Fed up and impatient to get home, we'd headed for a short cut through a narrow alley behind the shops. Just before it opened on to the Via Nova, we'd heard shouting and crying. In front of a recessed timber-framed building we found a stocky, middle-aged man smacking a kid of around six or seven. The kid cowered in the old beam-framed doorway, pinioned by the man's hand against the timber door. The man's other hand travelled back and forth across the boy's face and side of his head, palm and back of hand hitting the child with increasing ferocity. It wasn't a casual slap or two, it was systemised beating.

With an almost feral cry of 'Nooo!' Conrad hurled himself on the man and smashed him to the ground. Then he knelt down by the kid to comfort him, but the boy pulled away, terrified. I caught and held the kid, murmured reassurance and wiped his dirty, bloody face already starting to bloom with bruising. Conrad called the *custodes* and the medics but kept his eyes fixed on the boy. Neither of us was watching the guy Conrad had felled. Sloppy in retrospect, I guessed. Next minute, the man was on his feet and punched Conrad hard in the small of his back and ran toward the Via Nova. Conrad grunted, caught his breath and sprinted after him.

Next thing I heard was a screech of brakes followed by the dull thump of something bouncing off a vehicle to the ground, then metal crunching metal. The beater was dead under the vehicle's wheels. Conrad was blue-lighted to the Central Valetudinarium. Apart from the broken leg and multiple bruising, the most serious injury was to the side of his head. The MRI and CT scans cleared him of permanent damage, but he became frustrated and depressed at how slowly he'd recovered. He seemed cheered when I told him the kid had been fostered with a decent family in the city.

Conrad was cleared physically fit, although not for active operations as his reflexes had been dulled. He'd never be able to go out in the field again, something I still wasn't sure he'd accepted. The Senate had reconfirmed him in his command post, but I still worried about the overall effect on him. I'd stopped mentioning it as he hated being reminded that he could no longer be the super-perfect special forces officer.

'I wouldn't worry about it,' Quintus's voice brought me back to the present. 'He'll sort it out.' He gave me one of his politician's smiles. 'Now, what are you doing for your birthday? Anything special?'

I was stunned by Quintus's lack of cooperation. No, it was a thin slice off wilful obstruction. What the hell was going on? Had he lost it?

No, it was their damned bond. Quintus had rescued Conrad from a disastrous early childhood; Conrad's step-father, Caius Tellus, had launched a coup and imposed a repressive regime afterwards that lasted barely twelve months. In the aftermath, with the family ruined politically and their property confiscated by the state, Quintus was lucky to have survived, exiled to the east as a lowly country magistrate. He'd fought his way back, gaining a compassionate patron, some say lover, who'd brought him into the circles of power.

He'd sent his tough little nephew into the legions, where Conrad had thrived, enduring the strenuous training and the contempt for his name. Invited to join the PGSF as a young officer, he'd worked tirelessly to reach the top. It probably hadn't hurt him any that his wily uncle had risen to be the imperatrix's Chancellor for the last fifteen years. Quintus was retired now and although he still had personal influence, the power didn't flow from him in the same way.

But he still acted like a politician. I couldn't coax a further word out of him. As I left Domus Tellarum, I almost forgot to smile at the steward as she murmured a farewell.

I drove into the town centre and called Lucius, more properly Lucius Punellus. He'd been the PGSF Adjutant for many years and knew everything about everybody. More importantly, he'd been Conrad's best friend and comrade-in-arms since they were recruits.

Would I get the same stonewalling from him? Had Conrad gotten to him first?

Lucius had retired last year and lived with his long-time companion, Paulina Carca in a tasteful, but fairly modest, apartment block halfway along the Via Nova. His spiteful ex-wife had divorced him without a *solidus* over the minimum legal settlement. Paulina only had a teacher's pension plus a run-down little farm her aunt had left her. But they were refurbishing it little by little and looked happy together.

'Lucius? Carina. Can I drop by for a few minutes?' Pause. 'Outside your street door.' I'd parked up in the courtyard already. I looked up and saw his figure standing at the window, but he was too far away for me to distinguish anything else. I heard the entry lock buzz and slipped in.

'Always pleased to see you, Carina,' He bent down to kiss my cheek as he ushered me across their threshold. 'What trouble are you in this time?'

Paulina Carca coming into the hallway saved me from giving an impolite reply. She shook hands, smiling nervously. She'd accepted me as one of Lucius's colleagues, but he told me she'd never forgotten that night nearly seven years ago when I'd burst into her apartment with a bunch of heavies. A desperate time when we were fighting off an attempted coup. I was deep undercover and wasn't particularly happy about it, but we'd had to get to Lucius quickly. We hadn't trashed the place in any way, but she was still resentful. One of those I'd never win over, I guessed.

He gave her a reassuring smile and gently steered her back into their sitting room. Lucius took me into his tiny study, firmly shutting the door.

'Okay, what's this about?'

Lucius had run the admin side of the PGSF with ruthless efficiency and could snake his way though any bureaucratic maze. He settled behind his desk, his eyes staring unblinking at my face, his tall upper body leaning forward. He was concentrating every gram of his mental energy on me. I'd forgotten how formidable he could be. I took a deep breath and started.

'Totally off the record, okay?'

He said nothing, but I saw his shoulders tense. Was I too late?

'Has Conradus been in touch about a little problem that's come his way?'

'What sort of problem?'

'Um, a family problem.'

'Isn't that your domain?'

'Yes, it should be. I'm perfectly happy to deal with it, officially, if I have to. But he's closed me out.'

'Really?'

'Yes, really. Don't look so smug, Lucius. That's my job, to protect my family.'

I told him about the contents of the letter and Andrew Brudgland's initial findings.

'I don't know, Carina. Perhaps he wants to do this one himself.'

'Why?'

'Don't quote me, but he's a proud man and perhaps underneath he's terrified of hurting you again. He thought he'd lost you all those years ago when he didn't tell you about his previous children.' He got up and closed the drapes. He picked up a paper clip from his desk and teased it out straight before looking me direct in the eye. 'He doesn't want a repeat.'

'But by hiding this business with this girl, he's doing it again.'

He snorted. 'Whoever said he'd be logical?'

'C'mon, Lucius, he's one of the coolest, most decisive people I know.'

'Yes, but remember his upbringing.'

'Meaning?'

'I'm no head doctor, but when people feel a threat to something they hold dear, that's vital to them, they often lose it and act very strangely. They're in survival mode. Sometimes, they even strike out at the people nearest to them.'

'Has he been in contact with you?'

'No, he hasn't.' He grinned. 'He probably knew I'd tell him not to be such an arse and let your family council sort it out for him.'

I chuckled. 'You're such a sensitive soul, Lucius.'

'I'm not going to tell you your job. I expect you've got some wild plan to sort it out. But you know I'll help, don't you?'

'Yes.' I laid my hand on the back of his and smiled up at him. 'Thanks.'

'Perhaps I'll call him anyway to see if he wants to go to the gym or for a drink.'

I struggled not to shout at him for such an elementary blunder. Conrad would know immediately I'd been at Lucius. It was different from talking to Uncle Quintus; Conrad would expect that. But Lucius and Paulina were so often at their farm that it would be reasonable to assume I hadn't been able to see him.

'Would you mind leaving it, Lucius? Just for a while.'

'Why? Oh, of course. It would be too much of a coincidence, wouldn't it? Mars, I'm starting to get old.'

'Go back to playing at farmers, Lucius. I'll try not to disturb you.'

'Cheeky little tart – we don't play, we're serious. We want to move out there permanently, so it's got to work.'

I couldn't see Lucius digging around amongst rows of salad or doing unspeakable things with cows, but he seemed to want it.

The next afternoon, Flavius and I waited. And waited. Where the Hades was Branca? Flavius started tapping on his el-pad, unusual for him to show impatience. But I didn't think he had much time for the head of training. Nor, I admitted, did I. Lieutenant Colonel Tertia Branca was a pain in the fundament. One of the last of the old guard to come through, she still thought her rank entitled her to behave as she thought fit. After years of being contained in logistics, she'd been promoted to take the wonderful Julia Sella's place in training when Sella retired. Bad move. Luckily her staff managed to keep the department functioning at some level, but it was becoming more difficult as each week passed.

'If she doesn't turn up in the next five minutes, I'm off. Sorry, Bruna, but I've got better things to do than hang around for some slacker to get over her hangover.'

'Not very respectful, Senior Centurion,' I mock-admonished him.

'Sorry, ma'am, I'm sure.'

But Flavius was right.

I tried her personal commset again. It was switched off.

'Okay, let's carry on and send her the report afterwards.' Not that it would do much, but I'd blind copy it to her executive officer and something might get done. Gods, it was hard sometimes, dealing with idiots. I turned to my screen to begin, when a loud knock on the door interrupted me. The door burst open.

'I'm very sorry, ma'am, I only just found out this meeting was scheduled. I hope I'm not too late.' Lieutenant Lucilla Mitela, clutching her folder, chest heaving, gulped down some air; she must have run all the way.

'Come in, Lucy, sit down and get your breath back.'

Lucy smiled nervously at Flavius; he returned a grave, but not angry look. 'Where's Colonel Branca?' he said.

'She's... she's indisposed, Senior Centurion, so I thought I'd better come and take notes in her place.'

Flav rolled his eyes and muttered, 'For fuck's sake!' not quite under his breath.

'Well, let's get on with it,' I said. 'You'll have to convey our decisions back to her, Lucy. We don't have time to waste on another meeting. If she doesn't like what we agreed, tell her to take it up with the legate.'

Somehow, Conrad and I seemed to miss each other at home. Was it just a case of split work shifts or deliberate evasion? Either way, I didn't have the opportunity to raise the question of Nicola again with him. I had a Senate committee meeting this afternoon and spent lunchtime going through the paperwork. I hated being on the bureaucratic end of the security oversight group. I sometimes had to grill my own colleagues – a near impossible situation. I knew how tough their job was without having to justify every *solidus* of their budget or every tiny action. But I had no choice;

that was my job. One of my other jobs, I should say.

Giving up on reading the papers, I went through the main part of the house up to my grandmother's rooms as I did at least once a day. Marcella, her assistant, now grey herself, led me through to the bedroom. Nobody had used the D word yet, but Aurelia Mitela, my grandmother, my beloved Nonna, was dying.

She was propped up in bed, eyes half-closed. I looked down at her face, frail skin sagging over the shrunken flesh beneath. My hands balled automatically. I felt angry and powerless at the way the cancer was destroying her. She was only in her eighties; according to the records, our family usually reached the century. Gods, how unfair it was for such a clever and affectionate woman to be taken like this.

'Hello, darling,' she said. Her voice was surprisingly strong as was the sparkle in her eyes. 'You look so tired, Carina. You should try to rest, you know.'

What in Hades was I supposed to say to that? Nothing adequate presented itself, so I said nothing. I just held her skeleton's hand.

'I'm fine, Nonna, really,' I lied after a few minutes. 'I have to go to the security committee session this afternoon and the documents were giving me a headache.'

'Really? That's it?' I felt her eyes delving under my facade. 'I don't think that's everything, is it?'

'No,' I admitted, 'but I have something I need to sort out in the family and I haven't worked out what or how to do it. But I don't want to bother you with it.'

She snorted. More like a wheeze, but effective enough. 'I'm not on my bier yet, Carina. So tell me, please.' She never sounded more clipped as then. She was back in her role as head of a rich and powerful family with connections and influence all the way up to the top. She had more steel in her poor wasted hand than most had between their head and tail.

When I'd finished, she gave me a steady look.

'I know you felt you didn't have much choice, but I don't think you handled it very well, darling.'

'What do you mean?'

'It was a mistake to confront him as soon as you got back. I would have carried on my investigation behind the scenes for a little longer.'

I was hurt by her analysis; I was considered a strategic specialist.

Maybe I'd lost my edge during the past two years I'd commanded Operations. Or let my deep concern for Conrad interfere with logic. But no way was I going to start a major argument with her. I didn't go for the old and dying.

'Somebody cut your tongue out?' Her eyes glittered almost maliciously. 'Too scared to fight me?'

'You're impossible! Of course I can't fight you, you're—'

'Yes?'

'You are so unfair, Nonna.'

'Yes, I know, but you're so vulnerable, Carina, it's irresistible.'

'Well, behave yourself, Nonna, and try to help me out here.'

'Only if you stop being sentimental and pretending I'm not dying. You're wasting both our time.'

I choked on my next breath and felt my eyes tearing. She sent me an incinerating look. I drew myself up, swallowed and looked straight at her.

'Better,' she observed. 'Now, try and rescue some brains cells from the sloppy mush in your head and listen to me. Conrad has reached some kind of crisis, perhaps something from his past and the letter from this girl has triggered it. Your grandfather, Euralbius, went through a similar phase, so I know what I'm talking about. They do get over it, so long as you keep your head.'

I stroked her hand, blessing myself again for her wisdom and hard-headedness.

'Try very hard not to oppose him directly. It's like dealing with an adolescent, but a lot more serious. I'm not telling you to submit in any way. Be patient, but clever.' She gave me a measured look. 'You're crafty enough to be able to work this out, Carina. I suppose you've gone soft worrying about me. Well, you can stop that, right now. You're going to have to concentrate.'

How did she do this? I know she was a bone-and-blood Roman, but such toughness and selflessness was beyond anything. If I could behave one tenth as well, I should be very proud.

The next moment, she wilted, sinking into the cream lace-edged pillows. It was a small vanity of hers to have wide swathes of hand-made lace to frame her sleep. I would have bought her an ocean of it if it would have taken this evil disease away.

V

Checking my mails next morning, one sprang out at me – Conrad's executive officer, Rusonia, asking me to call by his office 'as soon as convenient'. Which meant now. I glanced at my watch. It was barely seven thirty. What was so urgent? He'd come home late last night, I'd been drifting off to sleep when I'd felt him slide into our bed, but he didn't say a word. Nor did he touch me. When I woke around six, he'd gone, not even appearing at breakfast. Was Nonna right? Maybe I should have left it.

I hurried along the cream corridors, el-pad in hand, my sandals scarcely sounding on the polished wood floor. I smiled at Rusonia as I entered the anteroom.

'Go straight in, ma'am, he's expecting you.'

Nevertheless, I knocked on the door and waited, my nerves jangling. For Juno's sake, I wasn't some lowly recruit in disgrace. I heard nothing; I knocked again and went in.

The legate's office was a large room, located in the corner of the building, with floor to ceiling bulletproof windows on two sides. The regulation cream was broken up with a lot of bookshelves, some prints and maps and a display cupboard. The little gold eagle I'd bought him at Christie's on our previous trip to London glistened behind the glass doors as it reflected the early morning light. Unlike other people's offices, the large meeting table was paper-free.

He was sitting behind his desk, head down signing some document. He finished, closed the folder, put the top back on his pen, laid it on the desk and looked up. I was shocked by the dark shadows under his eyes and taut lines around his mouth. What in Hades was happening to him?

I half-extended my hand, instinctively, but quickly drew it back. We were in our work environment; he the unit head, me a senior officer, but under his command. Not easy, but we'd made it work over the years.

'Sit down, Carina,' he said, waving me to the chair opposite him. 'Two things. Firstly, I've had a complaint from Colonel

Branca. She's aggrieved that she wasn't at the recent liaison meeting and you saw fit to carry on without her. She felt slighted to have been "relayed instructions via a junior officer." Any comment?'

Gods, he was all business this morning.

'It was a periodic meeting, with a month's notice. We were to address training needs in light of the recent overseas exercise.' Since I had nothing to lose, I let him have it. 'Training has been both inadequate and poorly organised this past year and operational arms are suffering as a result. If I may speak so freely, Colonel Branca has little interest or motivation for her job, to the extent of negligence where people may get killed or injured as a result.'

'A serious charge.' His voice was grim. 'Can you substantiate it?'

'How much evidence do you want?'

'Then why haven't you raised it before?'

I gasped. Anger swept up through me. 'May I bring the Legate's attention to my report last month and the report after the winter warmer exercise?'

Both had highlighted serious training defaults. Hadn't he read them?

'I raised them with Colonel Branca, but she considered you were exaggerating.'

'She what?' I took a deep breath. 'You didn't think to discuss it with me?'

'No.'

'Why ever not?'

'Not your domain.'

'That's it?'

He leaned back in his chair and sighed. 'I forget how argumentative you are. Yes, that's it. I'm perfectly aware she hasn't been the most effective training officer we've had. Her departmental staff has managed well, though.'

I was bursting with my own opinion, but kept it to myself, remembering Nonna's advice.

'This brings me neatly to the second thing. Effective tonight at 18.00 you're relieved of your command of Operations.'

No!

I stared at him. I couldn't move. I ran his words through my head again. Why? Gods, it was unfair. Just because I'd criticised a useless but well-connected old lush. Was Conrad getting personal here? Was he resentful of how I'd reacted to Nicola's letter? No, that was so out of character for him. I had no option but to accept it, but throwing me out of the job he knew I loved was unbelievably severe.

Then I spotted tiny creases around the edge of his mouth that had nothing to do with his tiredness.

'You're taking over Training and Personnel on promotion, with the rank of Lieutenant Colonel. Congratulations.' And he smiled at me with the warmth and sparkle of normal times.

'You—'

'Yes?'

I swallowed. Hard.

'You... you surprised me, that's all.'

He burst out laughing. 'You are such a liar.'

'Yeah, well. That wasn't nice.'

'But fun.' He smiled.

I didn't think so, but he had a more robust sense of humour than I. I think most men did.

He went over to his coffee machine and brought me back a cupful to which he promptly added a slug of brandy.

'For the shock, of course,' he said and winked.

Branca was 'retired' on medical grounds. She had to get dried out as a condition of drawing a full pension, which I thought was fair. Although I was functionally in charge of such things now, I lost interest once I'd seen the mess she'd left the department in. Branca's executive officer, Captain Petrus Sergius, had held it together as much as he could. His human resources background before joining the PGSF had been invaluable. No, it had pretty much saved it all from going under. I was mentally exhausted, but in a way grimly satisfied, after our long hours hammering out the new framework.

'Thank you, Sergius, good session. Let me have the budgets as soon as you can. Last thing, can you open up a feedback mailbox on the department intranet?'

'Do you mean like a suggestions box, ma'am?'

'Exactly so. I want input from everybody.'

His grey eyes looked wary.

'What?'

'Colonel Branca expressly forbade such a thing and made it a disciplinary.'

I couldn't believe it. She really had made the rules up as she went along.

'Well, Sergius, news for you. I want to know. You might find a revisit to the legate's standing orders about transparency and teamwork of, what, nearly eight years ago, worthwhile.'

His face closed down; he tightened his mouth, his eyes lost a little light.

Oops.

'Don't take it badly, Captain. You did a great job. Now you're going to help me do a better one. Besides,' I grinned at him, 'apart from knowing what they're bitching about, we may learn something ourselves.'

'Very well, Colonel, I'll get it set up.'

Colonel! I'd have to get used to being called that.

He ran his fingers along the side of his el-pad and hesitated.

'Something else?'

'It's something Colonel Branca dealt with. It's done, but—'

'Try me.'

'It's fairly routine, just a follow-up after the recent exercise.'

'Okay, Sergius, let's get a few things straight if we're going to work together. I don't play games with colleagues – I don't have time. If you have something to say, say it. I really don't mind if it's as trivial as somebody sniffing in a different way, or a major attack. If it has any significance, or it's bothering you, you tell me. Use your judgment, sure, but err on the telling side. Okay?'

He nodded, looking a little defensive. He'd get used to me, I hoped.

'It's a mail we had from the English liaison officer, Browning, enquiring about a familiarisation visit.' He paused, looking awkward. 'Although it was addressed to you, it got routed to us as it had a training code in the reference. I suggested forwarding it to you, but the colonel insisted we deal with it and replied that we were too busy to entertain such informal trips.' He threw a speculative look at me and decided to stop talking.

Good move. He learned fast.

'Okay, Sergius. Thanks for telling me.' I couldn't take it out on him. 'Forward it, and Branca's reply, to me ASAP. I'll sort it out with Captain Browning.'

He looked relieved.

'Oh, and don't call them English. They get seriously miffed if you get their complex nationality thing wrong. Their naval and air forces are "royal" and their army "British". And for Jupiter's sake don't ever call any Scottish people English. They have this love-hate thing. You'll know how annoyed they are by how hard they hit you.' I grinned. 'It's a bit like Castra Lucillans and Brancadori.'

After Sergius left, I called Colonel Stimpson's executive assistant at their base in the west of England and she patched me through to Michael.

'I don't know how to apologise for my predecessor's rudeness, Michael. She somehow didn't pass your message to me. Of course, we'll be delighted if you can find time for a liaison visit. How long can you stay?'

'I was thinking of a week to ten days, if you'll have me. I might add on some leave I've got due.'

'Great, I'll get a programme drawn up for the official visit. Is there anything you particularly want to see or anyone you want to meet in your free time?'

'I'd very much like to have a look inside your university, if that can be arranged.'

'Sure, easiest thing in the world.'

'I've also got a little bit of news for you, but we'll talk about that when I get there.'

'Don't be such a tease, Michael. What is it?'

'I'd rather not say over the phone.'

We had one of the most secure military comms systems in the world; even Fort Meade in the EUS had a problem listening in, and I doubted he was using a public payphone either. So what was the problem?

Nine days later I met Michael off his flight. I threw my weight around and took our wheelbase out airside and had him disembarked first. My driver loaded his bags, we processed him through the military side of Portus Airport and were soon on our way back to the PGSF building. He couldn't resist gaping like a tourist at everything. I recalled how entranced I'd been by it all when I'd arrived fifteen years ago, so I gave him the running commentary as we drove along. Cream stone with terracotta roof tiles mixed in with tall, much grander blocks and modern buildings standing alongside older ones; somehow it all fit together.

In the centre, we drove past one side of a huge open square, surrounded on the other three sides by a forest of stone columns and grand buildings – the forum – containing various public offices, including the Senate. The smaller ones were mostly temples. When I'd first caught sight of it, I'd thought it looked like a sword-and-sandals movie set with extras going up and down the steps, but in normal twenty-first century clothes.

Twenty minutes after we left the airport, we were skirting a hill rising steeply to an old castle ruin perched at the top of a cliff commanding the whole river valley. Halfway up was a beautiful stone house, the Golden Palace. With long single storey wings running out from each side, it looked like a bird poised for take-off.

I wasn't sure how much English my driver understood, so describing the scenery kept us to general topics until we were safe inside my office in the PGSF.

At the guard post, I'd retrieved a slim metal wristband with a tiny screen and clipped it on Michael's wrist.

'It's an ID and commset combined. Don't forget to wear it at all times, otherwise you'll have sudden company in the form of a security detail. If the guard watch office sees a biosignature in the building without an ID attached on their screens, they automatically respond. Pretty robustly.' I grinned at him.

'Consider me warned,' he smiled back.

'C'mon, I'll take you on the short tour before lunch.'

One military unit headquarters is pretty much like any another, but our sports area included a sand-floored arena and the armoury for bladed weapons. Michael was drawn to the small museum and talked in his stilted Latin to the curator. Marcellus Vitus had been the *primipilus*, the most senior enlisted man, before his retirement three years ago. He just knew everything, so I listened carefully too.

'I'd like to have another chat with Vitus, if that can be arranged,' Michael said as we made our way to the mess area.

'Sure, I'll—'

'Carina! Where've you been? I get back and you'd vanished. Oh, congratulations, by the way.'

Daniel. Now unit deputy, he'd been my buddy since we were junior officers together. Well, apart from a really frosty period seven years ago after the final Pulcheria operation. That had lasted a whole uncomfortable year. Eventually, he'd thawed and we'd mostly regained our friendship, but with a tentative note still hanging there.

The teasing expression in his dark eyes now was matched by his infectious grin.

'Good morning, sir,' I said formally, locking down my answering grin and switching to English. 'May I present Captain Michael Browning, of the British Army special forces? Michael, this is Colonel Daniel Stern, the deputy legate.'

'Oh. Morning, Captain. Good to meet you. You're with us for a couple of weeks, I believe?'

'Yes, I am, sir. We're scheduled to meet tomorrow, at 11.00 hours.'

The two men assessed each other. Daniel broke first, smiling, took the Brit's arm and pulled him along. 'Let's grab a beer then, before lunch, and get to know each other.' He turned his head over his shoulder towards me and winked. 'You can run along now, *Lieutenant*-Colonel,' he said. I said nothing, but smiled to myself as I walked back to my office, pleased the two men had gelled so quickly. I glanced at my watch. Half an hour before lunch. I'd quickly check my desk and join them in the bar.

'Colonel,' a sombre-faced Sergius greeted me. He had a naturally solemn expression, but now his features looked pinched in. 'Something unfortunate has occurred.'

Not my grandmother. Please Juno, no.

'What? Is it the Countess?'

He shook his head, but looked as if he was eating stale field rations. He shuffled his feet and looked away. Sergius's carefulness was starting to annoy me. Didn't he ever take a risk?

'Then what?'

'The DJ *Custodes* XI Station rang through. They've arrested a female juvenile. Drunk in a public place.'

'And?'

I didn't particularly care about some stupid kid pissed out of her head. Strictly one for the *custodes*. Then fear stabbed me in the gut. Please gods, not Stella. Silvia would be mortified. Good thing they'd rung me, not the palace, if it was her.

Sergius looked down at the el-pad in his hand as if to find some help there. He looked up at me and said in a totally expressionless voice, 'The name on the arrest sheet is Mitela, Allegra.'

VI

'Here, Bruna, drink this.'

A strong, masculine hand bearing a chipped mug came into view, interrupting my study of the skirting in this dismal room. I was crouching over with shame and tension.

Lurio had greeted me at the station house entrance, dragged me into the nearest interview room, thrust me down on a hard plastic chair and told me to stay there. When he came back, I took the mug automatically, sipped and nearly lost my ability to breathe at the fiery spirit he'd poured into the tea.

'Juno, Lurio, how much have you put in this?'

'Enough to wake you up out of drama queen mode.'

'Well, screw you.'

'Much better,' he replied and grinned at me. Cornelius Lurio, currently Department of Justice *Custodes* Senior Urban Cohorts Commander, had been my boss on my first ever undercover operation fourteen years ago. I'd been Senior Justiciar Bruna then, with a minus intention of going anywhere near the PGSF. The false name had stuck, although only used now as my nickname. We'd briefly been lovers during that year Conrad and I had parted. Lurio was one of my oldest and most acerbic friends.

'Look, Bruna, it's not a big deal. Kids are always doing stupid things. Be grateful it's nothing worse.'

'But she's so young. Allegra's different, she doesn't—'

'Don't be so bloody naive! Your fluffy little bunny is like anybody else. We're always scraping them off some pavement somewhere. Especially the gold-plated ones.'

I glared at him. He never failed to throw my family's wealth in my face.

'Yes, yes, you can look all Hades at me, but you know I'm right.'

'Give me the details, please.'

He looked at the arrest sheet. 'The local squad was called by the bar owner who'd chucked Allegra and an older girl out. The two girls had got rowdy and were starting to annoy the other customers.

The two of them started running across the Via Nova playing dodgems with the traffic.'

I swallowed hard to prevent a scream escaping. The Via Nova was not only incredibly busy; it was the site of Conrad's accident. How in Hades had she got so drunk? That bar owner should be flogged. I would make it my personal mission to have her licence revoked and her business ruined.

'Go on.'

'When the patrol got there, they found Allegra slumped by the side of the road, weeping, but truculent. No sign of the older girl. They arrested Allegra, put her in a general holding cell with the town tarts and petty thieves. Apparently, Allegra had used some offensive language when she was arrested. The custody sergeant thought it would teach her a lesson.' Even Lurio looked grim.

'Her name?'

'Don't go there, Bruna. I can understand why the sergeant did it. The shock often works. But she didn't realise they were dealing with such a protected little flower.'

I hated him at that moment.

'She refused to give her name. She didn't bleat, but as her clothes and accent showed she came from a well-off family, they got permission from the magistrate to scan her.' He snorted. 'Imagine the panic that caused when they read her identity on the display! With such a live coal landed in their laps, they called me.'

Screw the *custodes* having a bad day, Allegra would have been frightened beyond reason. Not just the *custodes*, nor the restraints, the arrest vehicle, the humiliation, but the rough element in the holding cell.

'Thank you for contacting me, Lurio,' I said stiffly. 'May I see my daughter now?'

'Are you sure you're ready? I won't have a screaming session or cat-fight in one of my stations.'

Juno, he was all heart. 'You may be reassured, Senior Commander, that we know how to conduct ourselves, even under trying circumstances.'

'Trying to put me in my place?' He smirked.

'Just get on with it.'

I tried to ignore the blue-uniformed *custodes* as we walked through to the cells. They were both wary and polite with us in the PGSF and I knew they'd be watching now. Many of my colleagues sneered at the *custodes* and used the public's name for them – scarab, or dung beetle. I'd been a DJ *custos* once; I kept it formal with them. Well, apart from Lurio.

Getting one over the PGSF would give them satisfaction. Having the junior heir to the most powerful of the Twelve Families in custody would have been the event of the year. But right now, I was only a mother with a wayward daughter. Through the observation panel of the cell door I saw her hunched over, perched on the edge of the bench, and sobbing. The bitter smell of vomit floated through. My heart ached for her. At Lurio's nod, the guard opened the door and I went in alone.

She looked up, eyes red, face streaked with traces of mascara. Any angry words I had for her died in my breath. I held her tight, gently rocking her in my arms on that hard plastic bench until she was all cried out. She glanced up at my face, turned nearly crimson and burrowed her head back between my chest and my arm.

'Hey, it's okay.' I stroked her hair, trying to comfort her. I never loved her more than at that moment.

Lurio countersigned the temporary release, muttering that he'd skin me alive if I failed to produce Allegra in court the next afternoon. I knew he'd been generous; normally they'd have held her overnight in the cells. As we rode home, Allegra didn't say a word, just gripped my hand with a desperately strong hold. My arm around her waist, I supported her along into her room, peeled off her soiled clothes and bathed her as if she were five years old. I fixed her a warm drink and put her to bed.

'Mama,' she whispered.

'I know, darling. You rest and we'll talk in the morning.'

Tears leaked out of the corners of her shut eyes. I kissed her forehead. She sighed and fell asleep within minutes.

I found Helena in the nursery dayroom, helping Tonia and Gil with their assignments. I kissed them both, giving Gil an encouraging rub on the back as he frowned over some math problem. Like Allegra, they'd elected to go out to school, rather than be home tutored and were finding it competitive. As they were absorbed, I looked at Helena and nodded for her to follow me into the nursery kitchen. I closed the door and turned to her, trying to keep my cool.

'Okay, Helena, when were you going to tell me?'

'Sorry?'

'Oh, come on. Allegra. You know, my daughter. The one you're supposed to be supervising.'

'What do you mean?'

'I think you'll find she's missing.'

'No, she's over at Maia's, Maia Quirinia's.'

'Really?'

'Now wait a minute, Carina, what's going on? Why are you looking at me like that? I'm not one of your suspects.'

'Not formally, no. Not yet.'

'What!'

'Suppose you tell me exactly what happened this morning.'

'Suppose you calm down,' she retorted.

I gestured her to sit and looked straight at her, waiting.

'Allegra went to school as usual. Quirinia's chauffeur collected her first thing. It was their turn to do the run. Maia invited her over afterwards and Allegra's sleeping over. I'm not expecting her back until tomorrow afternoon.'

My face must have reflected my anger.

'Whatever's happened, Carina? Where is she?'

'Safe in her bed, sleeping, thank the gods. As for tomorrow afternoon, she'll be appearing before the magistrate for public drunkenness, reckless behaviour on the public highway and insulting a law officer.'

'You're not serious.'

But I was already calling Domus Quiriniarum.

'Okay, Maia, suppose you tell me what happened after you picked Allegra up this morning?'

I stood there, in my uniform, side arm on my belt, arms crossed, legs braced, staring down at her. Helena stood a little behind me, to the side and attempted to smile reassuringly at a nervous Octavia Quirinia. I'd pushed through as soon as the steward opened the entrance door and marched straight into Octavia's dining room. She didn't get an angry special forces officer or acting head of the most powerful of the Twelve Families but a much more dangerous animal – an irate parent. I gave the impression Allegra was still missing.

'Well?'

Maia was completely frozen, her hands jammed into her arm pits.

Helena touched my arm. I turned and she mouthed 'Let me.'

I shrugged and plunked myself down in an armchair, still wound up, ready to spring again.

'Maia, look at me,' Helena started. But the child found it hard to drag her terrified eyes away from me. When she did, she managed a nervous half-smile at Helena who took the girl's hand in her own and gave it a little shake. 'Just start from this morning. Describe what you were wearing, what you had in your bag and what you were looking forward to. Try very hard not to hide anything. This is really not the time to keep secrets, even between BFFs. It's far too serious.'

Maia glanced at me and her mother, then retreated back to Helena.

'We'd asked to go to school early. I had my new trainers, the ones I'd bought with Allegra at the weekend. I hadn't worn them yet.' She dropped her enthusiastic tone and went into pseudo pious mode. 'We wanted to check our homework and get ready for the day.'

'Oh, really?' Helena said, her eyebrows raised.

Maia studied the floor.

'C'mon, Maia, the truth.'

'We were meeting Zenia,' she muttered to the carpet.

'Uh, huh. And who is Zenia?'

'She's our friend,' Maia said, emphasising the last word. 'She's cool and treats us like grown-ups. She wears all the latest stuff and make-up, and tells us little tricks—' Maia clamped her hand over her mouth. Her eyes bulged.

'Tricks?' Helena gave Maia's hand a little shake.

'To get stuff.' Maia glanced over at her mother. '*She's* always saying no.' Octavia looked shocked at her daughter's rudeness. I rolled my eyes; Octavia Quirinia was the most indulgent parent I knew.

'So, Zenia,' Helen continued, ignoring us. 'What did she ask you to do?'

'How do you know she did?'

'Well, friends usually do things for each other.'

Neat, Helena. Gods, she was good.

'Oh,' said Maia. 'She only asked for little things, tokens, mini-tribute. She'd given us cigarettes, so we were happy to do something for her.'

I thought Octavia was going to have cardiac arrest when her precious daughter said 'cigarettes'. I grabbed Octavia's hand and shook my head at her to stay silent.

'I pinched some sweets for her. I nearly got caught.' She gave a little sob. 'Allegra's dare was to drink alcohol in public. That was a laugh. The idea of Miss Upright getting pissed.'

Only the surprisingly strong pressure of Octavia's hand grasping mine stopped me from leaping up and tearing her child apart. Helena said nothing, just waited. Maia glanced at her mother who gave a sad little shake of her head. When Maia met my eyes, she shrank back in her chair. Her eyes darted around the room like a frightened rabbit searching for sanctuary. She looked at Helena, almost pleading.

'I didn't meant it, I didn't mean it like that. It was only a joke,' she stuttered and burst out crying.

'Okay, Maia,' Helen spoke at last. 'You've done well telling me all this, but you know you've let yourself down badly, don't you?' Helena was back in teacher mode. She'd say 'disappointed' any moment now. 'What I want you to do now is to apologise to your mother for your rudeness, then you can go upstairs, wash your face and get on with your homework.'

Maia sniffed, stood in front of her mother and made her apology. Octavia pulled her daughter down on to the couch, hugged her close and kissed the top of her head. Each to her own. I stood up and approached Maia. Helena gave me a stern look, but I'd prodded my temper back into its cage. I crouched down near where Maia was sitting on the edge of the couch.

'I'm sorry I frightened you, Maia. I'm very anxious about Allegra. Being cross and anxious makes some people want to hit out at everybody else. I guess I'm one of those.'

I stood and turned to her mother. 'I apologise for my discourtesy in barging in, Octavia. Please believe it only arises from my anxiety about Allegra.'

'I understand. You've certainly opened my eyes.' She gave her daughter a measured look.

'Oh, one last thing, Maia,' I said. 'How do you contact this Zenia?'

'We don't. She's just there, waiting for us. Not every day, but usually.'

I steeled myself and made the most difficult call of the year but Conrad didn't answer. He'd been away in the north overnight, but he should have been back by now. I was transferred to his exec.

'Where's the legate, Rusonia?'

She paused for a second. 'He's taking private time. He'll be back in a couple of hours, ma'am.'

That would make it after nine.

'Are you sure? I mean, isn't he coming straight home after that?'

'Not according to his schedule.'

'Okay, Rusonia. Here's the thing. We have a family emergency on a scale of ten out of ten. I need to speak to him. Is he contactable?'

Jupiter knew where he was. And Rusonia.

'Let me get back to you, ma'am, if you don't mind.'

'Sure.'

I was nursing a glass of Aquae Caesaris red and pretending to look through some mails when Conrad called.

'What is it?'

'I'm not discussing it on the phone, but it's about one of the children.'

'Not hurt?' He shot back.

'Not in the obvious way, but yes.'

'Jupiter, Carina, what's happened?'

'Just get back here.'

'Who the Hades is this bitch? I'll break every bone in her body.' He didn't pace. He didn't throw his arms around. He simply stood there humming like an unexploded bomb. He'd looked in on Allegra, but she was lost in deep sleep. He contented himself with a tender kiss on her forehead. He'd squeezed his eyes as he bent over and I'd seen a tear drop on to the sheet. We'd crept out of her room and he covered his face with both hands, leaning against the corridor wall. I'd led him back to our sitting room and given him a generous whisky and gently pushed him down on the couch.

'The public feed is the obvious starting point and I'll get a watch on the school for a week, if you're okay with the budget.'

He snorted. 'Screw the budget. Call it a training exercise, but do it.'

We lay together that night quietly, trying to heal each other from the hurt and anger at our daughter's first brutal encounter with the real world.

I called on my personal Active Response Team for the surveillance. ARTs were a strange leftover from the ancient days when each officer, mostly centurions, retained their own century whatever their function in the army. These days, it was a group of around six to eight. Mine had trained together, fought together and drunk together for years. I trusted them and relied on them unreservedly. We each knew exactly how the others thought. If the tactical situation went to Hades, and you didn't have time to think through what to do, the team adapted as if connected by telepathy.

I called Flavius from my study and told him to get them together for a video meeting in half an hour's time. I logged off, stood up and pulled the drapes apart. Outside, the city lights were switching off as the sun took over. I glanced at my watch; it was just after six thirty. I'd insisted Conrad went and checked in as normal, but I knew he'd be back shortly after seven so that he didn't miss Allegra before the lawyer arrived.

Right on cue, Conrad's voice came out of my commset.

'I've checked the joint watch report. Allegra's on there, but there's no sign of this little tart Zenia.' His voice sounded strained. 'I couldn't see anything obvious on the public feed recordings. But your team will be going through them in detail.'

'Come back to the house, Conrad. You can't do any more.'

A little before seven, I sat in my study in front of my blank screen staring at it equally blankly. Allegra was still asleep as of five minutes ago. A strange lethargy had occupied me, but leavened with spikes of intense anger. I hadn't worked through what I was going to do once we'd busted this Zenia; I was concentrating on catching her first. But why did such women want to attract these adolescents? Was it a substitute for their lack of friendships with their natural peers? Simple exploitation? The buzz? The money and gifts?

We dealt more with conspiracies and ideological attacks in the PGSF, but not exclusively. The grimmer possibilities – prostitution and trafficking – I didn't want to go near.

A beep woke me out of my trance and Flavius's face appeared.

'Bruna.'

'Flav. Everybody there?'

'All present.' The camera panned to show them in turn: Paula, Treb, Maelia, Nov, Livius and Atria. A sense of reassurance descended on me.

'Okay. First and most urgent, has anybody got a child around twelve to fifteen?' A question so out of order that it almost took my own breath away. But any embarrassment melted away quickly. Atria and Livius' kids must have been too young, they'd only been partnered for six years, but Paula raised her hand and looked at me with concern in her brown eyes.

'What is it, Bruna? Why do you need to know?' Then, quick as ever, she got it. 'Allegra. Of course, her name was on the joint watch report. What's happened?'

Their faces reflected the shock I'd felt when Sergius told me. I gave them the details and Maia's description.

'I can't order you, Paula, but I would deem it an enormous personal favour if you could loiter outside Allegra's school gate this morning and see if this Zenia turns up. If your daughter is with you, it'll look less obvious.'

'Bruna,' came Treb's voice. 'I could pass for a senior, if you want.' How blessed I was with this group. Treb was small, slim and could talk for Roma Nova. With her brown curls pulled back, no make-up and a change of posture, she'd be perfect.

'Thank you,' I whispered. 'Thank you both.' They'd gone before I could take the next breath.

'Leave it with me, Bruna,' said Flavius. 'I'll organise the shifts. How long?'

'A week, to start with. And we need to pull the public feed apart.'

'Already on the task list.'

'Put it on the training budget, Flavius.' Conrad's voice came from behind me. I turned and gave him a quick smile. His hand rested lightly on my shoulder. I placed mine over it and looked up at him. He managed to smile back, but it struggled with everything else on his face.

'Sir.'

'Flav, the *custodes* will be doing their investigation, but it'll probably be routine.' I said. 'Try to keep under their wire, please.'

'Don't worry, we won't upset the scarabs.'

Back upstairs, Conrad changed into civvies. We ate our breakfast in silence. As I was finishing my second cup of coffee, Helena put her head around the door.

'Allegra's awake.'

Unsurprisingly, she looked washed out. Her pale cheeks

emphasised the weary, unhappy expression in the eyes that darted everywhere.

'Allegra,' I said and swallowed. 'How's it going?' I smiled to reassure her.

She looked everywhere but at our faces, then settled on studying her hands. I sat on the bed and took one of them into mine. Her fingers lay cold and passive. Conrad pulled up one of her apricot velvet chairs on the other side. He stretched his hand out and slid the back of his fingers down her cheek.

'I feel so stupid,' she mumbled, 'really stupid. I thought I was being...you know, grown-up.' She wiped her eye socket with the palm of her other hand. 'I'm sorry,' she whispered.

'Hey, these things happen.' I smoothed her fine hair away from her forehead. 'I'm not going to yell at you. You know what you've done and you feel pretty bad about it, don't you?'

She nodded. Her chin dropped on to her chest and she gave one heart-rending sob. Conrad leaned over and grabbed her to him. She grasped one of his arms with both hands and settled into him, but she didn't cry any more.

After a few minutes she released herself, sat up, blinked hard and shook her head.

'What happens now?' she asked.

'Okay, now we need to get through this,' I said. 'Sertorius is coming to talk to all of us later this morning to set out the legal position. After lunch we go to the juvenile court where the magistrate gives you, and probably us, a hard time.'

To my delight, she actually giggled. Well, more a gurgle.

'Dad and I will sit just behind you, but you have to stand in front by yourself and take it like a Mitela.'

'Carina—'

'No point wrapping it up. They'll be watching her like a hawk.'

'I accept that, but she's not fifteen, a child.'

'Only a few weeks away.'

At fifteen I'd been learning the hard lesson of surviving, excluded from my foster family's love and Conrad was struggling with rural poverty and ostracism.

'Dad, I can do this, really. Mama's right. I have to.' She laid her hand over her father's as if to comfort him.

★

She listened carefully to everything Sertorius told her both before and in the courthouse ante-room. He was a boring, self-important fool, with a personality by-pass, but sharp as Hades and a fluent orator in court.

Dressed in a dark navy suit, Allegra approached the bar, listened without fidgeting while the charges were read out, then sat calmly on the defendants' bench through it all. To my surprise, Lurio presented the police report to the magistrate, adding the DJ would be content with administering a caution, as this was a first offence.

'No doubt, Senior Commander,' the magistrate replied, 'but I'm inclined to make an example. The defendant has had every advantage, and should know better. I hope her parents will bear this in mind in their future supervision of her.'

Ouch.

I gripped Conrad's hand, partly to restrain him, partly to channel my anger at this pompous little jerk.

'One month's community service, level four, subject to school hours. And tagged.'

I thought Conrad was going to leap off the bench and kill him. Level four meant the worst jobs and only potential runaways got tagged. What an asshole. After formally accepting the verdict – what choice did we have? – we filed out. My arm around Allegra's waist, and our heads raised, we were both prepared to die before we showed any emotion or reaction to the flashbulbs or dumb questions from the newsies sniping from behind the caged barrier.

Lurio met us in the back lobby where convicted defendants were processed. Windowless and painted in grey, it contained hard benches and bored *custodes*. Lurio waved away the two waiting to take Allegra for tagging.

'I'm so sorry, Bruna, I couldn't do anything. Usually they'll take the DJ's recommendation.'

'I know. Thanks for trying.'

Conrad, never comfortable around Lurio, was incandescent. 'Jupiter's balls! What right has that little prick got to dish out that kind of punishment to a child?'

'Conrad, you're frightening her,' I warned him.

Allegra's composure had melted away, she looked fearful, her eyes running from one to the other of us. 'What... what do you mean?'

'Well, young lady,' said Lurio, 'you have to come with me and get fitted with a new kind of bracelet. Your mother and father can come with us, if they want, as they're law officers.' He looked at us like we were idiots. I fumbled with my gold eagle badge and clipped it on to get through the security barriers. Conrad laid his arm protectively across Allegra's shoulders and nodded abruptly to Lurio to proceed.

Down in the cell block under the court, Allegra stood silently as the tag was locked on to her left wrist. Lurio stopped them fitting it to her ankle as was usual.

'Pointless really,' he snorted, 'since she's implanted with a tracker anyway. He just wanted to humiliate you through her. Stupid bastard.' He turned to me. 'If he so much as goes through a red light or overstays his parking meter, I'll throw the whole bloody *Lex Custodum* at him.'

VII

The evening of Allegra's court appearance, I checked in briefly with Flavius.

'No show, Bruna. Sorry. We'll see if we get anything tomorrow. I had a word with the DJ case officer. They're not going to do much more. Court conviction, so case over as far as they're concerned. No objection to us nosing around a bit more so I've sent Atria over to interview Maia Quirinia to put together an e-fit picture of this Zenia.' He hesitated. 'Would you let Atria talk to Allegra as well?'

'Gods, of course, Flav. She starts her work detail tomorrow at half five and finishes around half eight.' I sighed. She'd be so tired. 'Atria could come over at, say, four thirty.'

'She'll be there.'

Helena took Allegra to school herself the next morning and let the principal know the situation.

'Juno, Carina, I felt as if I was under lock-down. I got that "gravely disappointed" talk.' She rolled her eyes. As a teacher, she must have given that talk herself many times. I sympathised; I was finding it equally uncomfortable being on the consumer end of the justice system.

'How's Conradus doing?'

'Not taking it well. He thought the magistrate was over-harsh. He went into work ready to kill elephants.'

'You're not going to like this, but maybe it'll give her some first-hand experience of life at the other end.' She held her hand up. 'Don't look at me like that, Carina. You both had a difficult upbringing, so you're naturally over-protective, especially since that business with Superbus and his brutal goons all those years ago. Going out to school has been excellent for Allegra and toughened her up.'

'Finished?' I got up, pushing my chair back under the breakfast table.

'Take that poker out of your backside and think about what I've said.'

'I'm going to work now, Helena. Julia Atria will be here at four thirty. Please ensure Allegra is ready for her.'

'Carina—'

I was gone.

Still smarting at Helena's words and reluctant to admit there might be some truth in them, I grumped my way to my office. Sergius came in, protecting himself with a cup of coffee for me.

'Your Captain Browning's scheduled to go out with you to the training ground lunchtime to watch tactics exercises. Do you want me to re-assign it to somebody else, ma'am?'

'No, he's my guest, I'll take him. Besides, I'd like to get out in the fresh air.'

I smiled at him. He was being incredibly tactful.

'Okay, Sergius, what else is on the menu today?'

We finalised budgets and I signed them off which released the funds to get the new framework up and running. I'd have a whole branch meeting in a week's time to review how it was shaking down.

A knock on my doorframe let me lift my head from the bunch of files Sergius had left me.

'Colonel? Not interrupting, I hope?'

Michael. His attractive smile was like an instant tonic.

'Hi. Come in. I'll just be a minute. Grab a coffee.' I waved my hand towards the machine.

Around ten kilometres away from the city, the training ground consisted mainly of mixed woodland and ground scrub, with a couple of open field areas and an urban mock-up for house-to-house training. We stopped off at the admin building where Lieutenant Lucilla Mitela greeted us.

'Hello, Lucy. How's it all going?'

She drew herself up and saluted with a grave look on her face.

'Very well, ma'am. Only one broken arm and a few bruises.'

I smiled to myself at the deadpan way she described painful training accidents. I presented Michael and we made our way in for sandwiches in the staff cell where Lucy went through today's programme. Her English was excellent, but with a funny international accent. Maybe she could do a training period with Michael's people. Hopefully not with similar repercussions as Conrad's time in England. I batted that unpleasant thought away. At least we'd know in nine months and not twenty-five years later.

Michael was fascinated by the way we drew on over two thousand years of warfighting and bombarded Lucy with questions. She took him out to the mock-up street where they were practising hostage recovery. Halfway along, she got called in to adjudicate some point, so I seized my opportunity.

'Okay, Michael, we've got a few minutes in a nice noisy place where we can't be overheard. What's this news of yours you couldn't tell me on the most secure comms system in the world?' I didn't mean to sound sarcastic, but I couldn't understand his reticence.

'You remember meeting Andrew Brudgland in London after our joint exercise? I understand you're aware the contents of his report to the legate about Nicola Hargreve.'

I nodded. It was all I could do.

'Well, he asked me to delve deeper. He likes to be fully informed about his opposite numbers, and I think he genuinely wanted to help your husband.'

'Why you? I mean I'm not dissing you, Michael, but he has a team of specialist investigators to follow this up.'

'He knows I know you and your culture and I speak a little of the language. Also, I'm not on his budget.' He grinned. 'As it turned out, I was the perfect person for the job.'

'How was that?'

Before he could answer, a ball of fire erupted out of the window of the nearby building. We clapped hands over our ears and ran.

'Bugger me, that was loud.' He shouted. 'What the hell do you use?'

'Trade secret.' I grinned at him, as we reached a rise ten metres away. I shook my head to try to get rid of the blast effect.

'Anyway, your Nicola—' he continued.

'Not my Nicola. In any sense. Ever.' I heard the ice in my own voice; it mirrored the ice in my gut.

'Very well. Nicola Hargreve turns out to be a deceitful young woman. She was born in an Army town and like a lot of youngsters there, went into the armed forces herself. She applied herself and was promoted sergeant and because of her excellent record was accepted into the special forces. She had a talent for single-mindedness and was tough enough to stand the endurance training. Her OC commended her for her tradecraft and outstanding performance in two operations where she worked with the security services. The only problem was that she called herself Sandbrook and had been very clever in establishing that identity. It was only after she left and I started investigating that this all came to light.'

Gods. This was getting better all the time.

'In fact, you met her.'

I stared at him. 'No, how could that be?'

'She was acting as admin staff for your exercise.'

Click.

'Not the one with the plaited blonde hair on the check-in table at the end of the exercise?'

Lucy came back at that moment and we toured the rest of the training area. Michael took the opportunity to ask questions wherever he could, and try a few things. In a borrowed helmet, carrying a standard service weapon, he melded with the rest of them. Every step he took was purposeful and controlled; the slightly hesitant academic had completely vanished. Impressive. And dangerously deceptive.

As soon as my mind was freed up from concentrating on observing him and the others running through a rescue drill, Nicola resurfaced. Ignoring my instincts never did me any favours and they'd been right off the scale when I'd come across her in England.

What exactly did Michael's information mean? For one, she'd become a much more serious threat. She was trained in deception, had patience and endurance and fighting skills. And probably that damned Tella pride. Fabulous.

I absolutely had to know more so I tackled Michael on the way back.

'So, Michael, has your buddy told my buddy?'

'No, he thought I might run it past you first.'

'And why was that?'

'He thought you might be more objective,' he said, glancing at me. 'I'm not so sure now.'

'No, I don't think I can be objective. Like it or not, I'd like to beat the crap out of her.'

'Hm. Perhaps I was wrong, then.'

'Whatever,' I shrugged. 'I suggest you go and see the legate yourself and tell him your news. I'll arrange to collect your body after you come out of his office.'

'I see.'

We rode back in silence after that.

★

By the time I parked my car in the courtyard at home, it was a little after ten. I found Conrad in his study. I had to talk with him about the Nicola threat. Somehow we hadn't coincided during duty hours, not even at mealtimes. I was starting to think it was intentional. Or maybe he was just distracted.

'Hi.' He looked up as soon as I walked into the room. He half sat, half lay on the dark green leather couch, his ankles crossed on the second cushion with his feet hanging over the edge. He discarded his book on to a side table and looked at me intently.

I scanned his face for any signs of stress; I could see only a gleam in his eyes. A slow smile built on his lips and I felt twenty-five again. How simple it had been then, despite the danger. Warmth spread through me; I just wanted him. All my questions faded away, irrelevant. I bent down and kissed his cheek, a little up from that mouth. I laid my hand on his shoulder, knelt on his thigh and kissed his lips. Oh, the pleasure of it. His mouth was warm, soft, tender. I was intoxicated as his tongue sought mine. His arms pulled me to him and I fell in.

Later that evening in our bed, he was equally passionate, taking care to ensure my pleasure reached the maximum. As we climaxed, I was overwhelmed. My every nerve was singing. The rhythm of waves eventually slowed and I landed in a pool of exhaustion, warmth and deep content.

The early morning light was peeking through the drapes as we lay face to face, smiling, touching, hands teasing and tickling, but in a languid, contented going-nowhere way. I stroked the side of his face, paused at the tiny dip at his temple, then continued down over the curved edge of his cheekbone. His eyes closed at my touch and he almost purred. I leaned over and kissed the tiny line at the side of his mouth, his hand came up behind my waist and he pulled me on top. His eyes were wide open and glinting now.

Then his commset beeped.

'Mitelus. What?'

His mouth was an irritated straight line. As I watched, his frown became tighter. Whoever was on the other end had better have her asbestos suit on. He listened intently, his eyes wandering at first, then coming back to concentrate on the back of his hand. He grunted, then listened some more.

'Very well. I'll be there at seven. Out.'

He rolled his eyes, his mouth still peevish, but he started to move. He nudged me off gently, then sat on the edge of the bed, stretched over and ran the back of his hand down my cheek.

'Sorry, love. I wanted to have breakfast with you, but I have to go in.'

I was far too relaxed to do anything but smile back at him.

'Catch you later. Lunchtime?'

'Yes, I'll have sorted this out by then.'

I was on late shift so I went back to sleep.

It was only in the shower that I realised we hadn't discussed the Nicola thing at all. How could I have forgotten? Hades, I was slowing up. No, I'd gotten completely sidetracked. Mmm, but what a way to go. A mean thought wormed its way into my head. Surely, he hadn't used last night to divert me? He was perfectly capable of it, but he hadn't, had he? I didn't know whether to be furious at him or guilty at myself for thinking such a thing. I gave myself a mental shake. Juno, I'd start suspecting my toenails next. But still...

I'd hardly knocked on his office door at 12.30, when he came out, beckoned me in and told Rusonia he was taking personal time: no calls, no interruptions until 14.00. Her eyebrows shot up at least a millimetre.

'Look, sorry I had to go so quickly this morning. An emergency concerning the palace guard.'

The regular Praetorian Guard which he was also now responsible for acted as day-to-day security for the imperatrix and her palace, or wherever she was. One summer, while he was still junior legate heading the PGSF only, Silvia and all three children had come to stay with us for a few days at our farm near Castra Lucilla. Despite its remoteness, the guards turned it into Fort Knox. The children weren't even allowed to go for a swim in the lake without an armed escort. Until Conrad put his foot down. He banned the guards from the villa and garden and told them to stick to the perimeter. The commander looked as black as Hades at him, but couldn't argue. Conrad outranked him by several steps and was after all the children's registered father. No official report of the clash ended up on anybody's desk, but relations cooled considerably between the two branches. Conrad's appointment to commanding both branches as senior legate had meant dealing with some uncooperative egos.

I rolled my eyes in sympathy. 'So, obviously, a major incident?'

'Not really, just some tactless handling by a tired detail. A couple of grunts were a bit robust with some tourists who kept trying to get inside the palace perimeter last night. The guards moved them along. One tourist apologised, so they sent her on her way, but the other one wouldn't let it go, so they chucked her in a cell in the guardroom for the night. Unfortunately, she turned out to be a foreign investigative journalist and was screaming police brutality. They tried to explain they weren't *custodes*, but according to the guard commander that wound her up more and she started on about military dictatorships.' He shrugged. 'In the end, I rousted Silvia's protocol chief out to smooth it over.' He sighed. 'You'll never guess who the new one is.'

I shook my head. I'd dropped so far behind on reading routine appointments circulars.

'You remember Favonius Cotta?'

'You're kidding me?'

'He was as deeply thrilled to see me as I him, but he can do the job, I have to admit. He used just the right balance of serious attention and condescension. Very slick.'

And just as oily, would be my guess. Conrad looked like he had a bad smell under his nose. Favonius Cotta had been the senior diplomat we'd had a run-in with fifteen years ago when I'd sought asylum in the legation in Washington.

'Well, never mind that. I have to talk to you about something much more important. Nicola.'

I jumped at the name, and at his raising the subject. He'd told me so firmly to butt out before.

'I've been in two minds about her.' He set his elbows on his desk and tapped the fingertips of each hand against their opposite numbers. 'I can ignore her and hope she'll go away. Rarely a good option. These kinds of problems always come back, usually well-fermented. The other option is to see if we can't negotiate some kind of arrangement with her.'

He was discussing her like a theoretical case or an exercise scenario. His voice was dispassionate, disinterested even. Had he gotten over the emotional crisis Nonna referred to? He'd been so much happier yesterday, like he'd come to some conclusion. Obviously, her letter had caused a huge upset, but now he'd be able to resolve it, thank the gods.

I nodded and was about to suggest making an appointment with Sertorius to draw up an opening offer. Sertorius was so tough and slippery he could negotiate the palm off Victory, and she was a gold statue. We'd be rid of Nicola within a few weeks.'

Conrad said nothing. After a few moments, he smiled to himself. 'She seems to have done well in the military, though. Something to be said for the genes.'

Oh, Juno, he actually admired her. He bubbled with pride in his children and this visceral emotion was stretching to include Nicola. Not good. Not at all good.

He glanced toward me from across his desk. 'I know this may come as a bit of a shock, but I'm going to invite her over here.'

Speechless didn't describe my state even halfway. I stared at him as if I hadn't heard correctly. I swallowed hard as if it could stop my mind seeing images of collapsing buildings.

'Why do that? Can't the lawyers handle it?' I managed. 'I mean, by letter or mail?'

'It was Michael Browning's news that brought it home to me. She must have been so miserable to have gone to such lengths.'

No, Conrad, she's a conniving little madam.

'I feel I have to do this,' he ploughed on. 'She can stay with Uncle Quintus. He's sharp enough to contain her. Perhaps she'll come to see she doesn't need to fight against everything so desperately.'

I bit into one of the sandwiches that Rusonia had ordered, but it tasted like dry cardboard and rubber.

He picked up an el-pad stylus and played with it, but didn't touch the food.

'Um, not wishing to put a damper on it,' I tried, 'but do you have proof she *is* your daughter?'

'Always the careful one, aren't you?'

'C'mon, Conrad, you wouldn't be the first one to get caught.'

'You're assuming she's not.'

I said nothing and the air around us became heavy. No longer having an appetite for food or argument, I said, 'Get a DNA test. Take some precautions at least.'

Ironic he hadn't taken any twenty-five years before.

Michael was on the last day of his official tour tomorrow, scheduled to go out with Paula to watch for Zenia. The surveillance operation had been pretty fruitless, no show since the day of Allegra's arrest.

'Hasn't helped that the school's put a heavy on the front gate,' Flav grumbled. 'I did ask them not to, as they had us there, but the principal did that lemon-sucking face trick and insisted.'

'Don't worry, Flav, we'll finish it tomorrow. She's obviously gone after other prey.' Annoying that we hadn't found her, but we'd got rid of her at least. And Allegra wouldn't get caught twice. She was growing up a little too fast, my daughter.

I met them all in the mess bar and stood them a drink. Scant thanks, but Paula told me not to worry.

'Don't get worked up, Bruna. We've enjoyed working together again,' she said, 'although, being honest, it was a bit boring. Treb said it had been fun acting as a senior for all of three days, but got fed up with the hair and boyfriends obsession of her classmates.' She grinned. 'Still, any excuse to catch up. Did you know Atria's eldest has started school?'

I studied Paula Servla's face as she chattered on. She'd been my first friend in the PGSF, before even, when I'd still been in the DJ and come to train with them. A few fine lines had started to appear around her eyes, but not one white hair had dared show itself in amongst the tight brown curls. And her daughter Valeria was twelve now. Juno!

I opened my mouth to say something anodyne about us all getting a little older but that the up-and-comers weren't anywhere near as good as we'd been, when I sensed someone behind me.

Julia Atria, famous or maybe infamous for her persuading and influencing skills, was standing motionless, scarcely seeming to breathe. A wisp of a smile between her lips, she waited a full minute for me to give in and speak first. She was a natural, plus had been trained by one of the best psych teachers in the country. Charming fish out of the water to walk on dry land was a warm-up exercise before breakfast for her. I knew all about her little tricks, but in a fix I was glad to have such a manipulator on my side.

I did the really cheesy thing from the movies and raised one eyebrow, forcing her to begin.

She smiled in acknowledgement.

'I didn't get very good results from the girls' interviews. Quirinia was too nervous and a little hysterical. She couldn't make her mind up about anything. I got the impression she said what she thought I wanted to hear rather than admit she hadn't seen anything. She's very self-obsessed and doesn't notice much about the rest of the world around her unless it impacts on her.' She shrugged. 'Typical adolescent.'

'And Allegra?'

'Better. But her emotional upset about the whole thing was too strong and it clouded her recall. She remembered more of Zenia's mannerisms and her clothes rather than her face.'

'Hmm. Sorry you didn't get more.' Somehow I felt responsible.

'Hades, Bruna, not your problem. I did get that she was tall, blonde and monosyllabic.'

'So we have a third of Europe in the frame? Fabulous.'

Thankful it was Friday, I was finishing up my file reviews. I'd scheduled the whole branch meeting for next week and I wanted to be over-prepared. I unclasped my hands from the back of my neck and brought my shoulder blades together. Gods, I hated all this paperwork, even though the majority of it was digital. A knock on my doorframe woke me up; Flavius and Michael. I always left my door open, but Flavius took the handle and shut it as soon as he and Michael entered. Their expressions were as solemn as hired funeral mourners.

'What? You both look as if the Fates had descended on us.'

'In a manner of speaking, they have, Colonel,' said Flavius.

I waved them to chairs in front of my desk. 'Explain.'

They exchanged a glance.

Oh no, not one of those.

Flavius nodded to Michael.

'As you know, Colonel, I went out with Senior Centurion Flavius this morning as an observer on the surveillance exercise. We were sweeping the road near the school as our cover when a young woman who'd been lounging by the gate stopped and talked to a group of girls around Allegra's age.'

I held my breath. A surge of excitement ran through me. Had we got her then?

'We only had a back view, but she was tall and blonde. We held our cover, but advanced in her direction, as if we were going to empty our sweepings into the cart. About five metres from her, we were ready to snatch her. She half-turned and cocked her head to one side. In the time I turned to tell Flavius, she'd disappeared.' He looked embarrassed, but angry as well. 'God knows where she went, but when I recognised her, I stopped being surprised she'd done a vanishing trick like that.'

'What do you mean? Who was she?'

But I knew. I shut my eyes as I heard him confirm it.

'Nicola Sandbrook'.

VIII

Hades. Times ten. Not that it was Nicola. That was bad enough. But breaking it to Conrad. At least it would put his plans to invite her over on hold. I tapped into the system to put an immediate APB out on her at the airport and railroad stations plus alerted the DJ watch office. Now we knew who we were looking for, we had a good chance of finding her. Michael was less optimistic, but I was sure she'd stand out here. Besides, I posted a thousand *solidi* reward on her.

Conrad would be so disappointed and hurt, too, that she'd targeted Allegra. But at least he'd see Nicola for what she was.

We got a slot twenty minutes later and the three of us trudged along to Conrad's office. Rusonia took one look at our long faces and even opened the door and announced us. He was putting some book back on a shelf when we entered. He turned to us with a smile.

'Great gods, a delegation,' he said in a semi-ironic tone. I cringed inside; we were really going to ruin his day.

He perched on the corner of his desk and motioned us to sit.

'If you don't mind, Legate, I think we'll stand,' I said.

His smiled faded. 'Very well. What is it you want to say?'

'This morning was the last day of the surveillance operation at Allegra's school,' I began.

'Yes?'

'Senor Centurion Flavius and Captain Browning were observing. There was a development.' I couldn't bear to say it.

'What kind of development?'

'A sighting of the woman known as Zenia.'

'And?' He waved his hand impatiently. 'Are we going to get there sometime within the next hour, Colonel, or do I have to play twenty questions?'

I swallowed hard. 'She's been identified.'

'Excellent. Presumably you've put the usual alerts out, so we should have her soon.' He looked at us as if we were deficient. 'So what's the problem?'

'There's more.'

He raised one eyebrow, 'I can hardly wait.'

'Captain Browning ID'd her as former Sergeant Sandbrook of the British Armed Forces.'

The muscles on his face froze. He didn't even blink.

'I see.' The words fell out of his mouth as if by accident.

None of us moved. Conrad was as still as a block of Aquae Caesaris granite.

'Please tell me exactly what you were doing, Flavius, and then, Captain Browning, you can explain why you have come to this conclusion.' His voice sounded as cold and incisive as an ice dagger.

Flavius gave a precise report, detailing the minutiae of the whole watch. Conrad nodded curtly when he'd finished and looked toward Michael.

'Well?'

'Sir, I've worked with Sergeant Sandbrook. She was a member of a specialist unit trained to carry out close target reconnaissance, surveillance and 'eyes-on' intelligence operations. She knows exactly how to design and run a range of targeted operations in different environments.'

His voice was steady, but I heard the note of bitterness.

Crap. A talented professional. This was getting worse by the minute.

'When did you last see her?'

'At the exercise to which Colonel Mitela's detachment was invited. I have to admit I was surprised to see her. I know a circular went round asking for volunteers to participate and for staff support. Her role was specialist not general, but she seemed happy to serve as admin for the exercise. Perhaps she was conducting her own personal reconnaissance—'

'Enough!' Conrad's voice sliced through. 'I don't need junior officers' subjective comments. Dismissed. You, too, Senior Centurion.' He waved both men out and went to sit behind his desk as they made their escape.

'Go on, say it.' He glared at me. 'You can hardly wait, can you?'

I couldn't find any fancy words.

'I'm so, so sorry. You must be very disappointed.'

'Disappointed! Don't use your fucking weasel words with me, woman!'

I said nothing. He lifted his hand and rubbed the hairline over his temple near the accident scar. Placing both elbows on the desk, he dropped his head into his hands and I heard a deep guttural sound as the spasm racked him. I turned and slipped out, easing the door closed behind me.

The rest of the afternoon passed in a haze of nothingness. In the end, I gave up. I picked up my case and el-pad, slung my black uniform fleece over one shoulder and wandered through the outer office, giving Sergius a perfunctory smile. I was due to collect Michael from his last session in the signals office and take him home to stay with us for a few days.

Given the antagonism between Conrad and Michael, this was going to be a fun week. Conrad and I had worked hard to keep our work and private lives separate but Nicola's attack on our family threatened to throw that fine balance off. If we caught her, it could cause a huge personal rift. I couldn't figure out what to do next – it seemed too nebulous. Immersed in these unhappy thoughts, I hardly noticed where I was going.

'Hey, look out.'

Daniel. I'd almost walked into him. Difficult to miss his sturdy figure, though. I didn't realise I'd come as far as his office. His hand rested on the brass door handle.

'What's the matter?' He always switched to English when we were alone. 'You look terrible.'

I shook my head. His arm came up around my shoulders and he gently guided me into his office and pushed me down on one of the leather easy chairs.

'Tell me,' he ordered. A frown had replaced his normally cheery smile.

He knew some of it, of course, but he'd been wrapped up with the new anti-terrorist initiative and had hardly been at the house over the last few weeks. Daniel lived at Domus Mitelarum, in his own apartment in the south wing. Fifteen years ago he'd arrived in Roma Nova on a three-month training detachment from his home country, but had never gone back. Sponsored by Conrad, he'd been adopted into our family and become my buddy, my brother-in-arms. We'd worked hard together, and played hard, getting ourselves into and out of a load of trouble, especially when younger.

Once he'd dared me to a climbing race up the lower wall of the old fortress building, strictly forbidden, but I couldn't resist the challenging sparkle in his eye. Of course, we got an audience, of course, they made book on us, but the catcalls and shouts of encouragement spurred us both on. We'd almost got to the top, neck and neck, and muscles trembling and breath heaving, and I was about to swing myself up over the remains of the crumbling parapet, when the shouting died at a stroke.

A voice like a shotgun had rung out, ordering us down that instant. Major Mitelus, as he was then, was incandescent; his eyes blazed, he could hardly speak. Apart from our disobedience to standing orders, reckless behaviour and a poor example by junior officers to enlisted personnel, he castigated us for the waste of our expensive training if we'd broken our stupid necks. Daniel and I caught seven days in the cooler, but it cemented our friendship.

'Shit, Carina! How did it get to this?'

'The gods alone know. I've tried to be tactful with him, but I'm starting to get pissed with the whole thing. I know she's a destroyer. Look how she attacked Allegra.'

'Sounds a right little cow.'

I half-smiled at his Britishism.

'Maybe now that Conrad's realised what a threat she is, he'll drop the whole daughter thing and leave it to the lawyers,' I said. 'But somehow, I don't think she'll let it go that easily.'

'You're the strategist – what do we do?'

'What I'd like to do isn't legal.'

'So?'

'C'mon, Daniel, we can't go there.'

'Pity.'

He picked up a green marble paperweight from his desk and tossed it lightly from one hand to another as he walked backed and forth. He could never stay still. He frowned.

'Look, Carina, unless there's some sort of definite threat, we can't officially commit any further resources. It's a family matter.' He smiled up at me. 'But you know I'll give you a hundred per cent personally.'

'I have a few ideas chasing around in my head, but first we have to get hold of her.'

Daniel put Michael up in his apartment, which headed off most of the possible awkwardness with Conrad. Despite their different backgrounds, the two men got on well and were bantering when they came down together to the main dining room for breakfast next morning.

'Daniel's been telling me something about this house. I gather some of it's over eight hundred years old.'

'You know, the person you want to talk to is Galienus, Junia's deputy. He'll give you the tour. You'll only need five weeks.'

Michael laughed back at me. 'Daniel's taking me gliding this morning, so perhaps later.'

'Sure. I'll let him know to expect you.'

I left them talking about thermals and streamlining and went upstairs to sit with my grandmother. Her room had been transformed into a mini-hospital ward, complete with the antiseptic smell. The young nurse was tweaking a drip line fed from a transparent bag hooked on a stand as I walked in. He finished, nodded at me and withdrew. Nonna's eyes were closed, but I could see her shoulders moving slightly as she breathed.

'Carina?' she whispered.

'Here, Nonna.' I sat on the chair by her bed and folded her hand into mine. 'How did you know it was me?'

'Your footstep and your scent.' She paused, took several breaths. 'Yours are wired into my head.' Her eyes flickered open and a tiny smile appeared. 'I'm so glad to see you before I go into the shades.'

'Nonna... don't. Don't speak like that.'

She just smiled, then grimaced.

'What is it? Do you want more medication?'

'If I have any more, I'll be unconscious.' She grasped my hand, her poor weak fingers finding strength for a few moments. 'Listen, Carina. Listen properly, please.'

Tears swam in my eyes, but I nodded. I tried to gulp them back for her.

'You have to remember this. Make your decisions for the family.' She took short laboured breaths. 'It'll be hard, but you must be loyal to them. Whatever the heartache. Promise me.'

'You know I will.'

She scanned my face with eyes that could hardly see.

'Yes, I know. You're a good girl. Sorry to leave you. I love you so much.'

'Nonna.' Brown, sunken skin as thin as wrapping tissue and criss-crossed with lines surrounded her eyes. The brightness in them dimmed like the electric current had been stepped down to minimum. She closed them and sighed. I leaned over and kissed her forehead. 'I love you, too. I always will.'

I crept away next door into her private sitting room and found Marcella talking to the doctor.

'How long?' I asked, baldly.

'A week at most. I'm very sorry.'

He was the chief oncologist at the university hospital. He should know.

'You won't let her suffer.' It wasn't a request. My hand came up by itself and covered my mouth and I turned away from them both. My gaze came to rest on a silver-framed photo on a side table of Nonna and the children. Her bright blue eyes shone out at me and a mischievous grin seemed to share a joke with the camera. Gods.

'Marcella.'

'Lady?'

'Will you call the council for tomorrow morning, please? Eleven will give them all time to get here. Liaise with Junia about food and so on.'

'Of course, Countess.' She nodded and left.

I went for a swim to distract myself. After ten minutes or so of rhythmic up and down the pool, I felt calmer. The soft dappled light and the soothing motion of the water sliding over my skin acted like a balm. I became aware of another body gliding through the water. I shook my head to clear it and saw Allegra beside me. She swam up beside me, extended her arm across my shoulder and stroked me. We sat on the side, weeping together for a while.

She sneezed, breaking us out of it. Dried, dressed and clutching hot drinks in my study, we discussed what would come next.

'You know you have to come to the council tomorrow?' I hated pulling her into this; she was only a kid. She'd have to talk to a load of old people, all sad and pompous, some genuinely upset about Aurelia, some curious, some jockeying for position in the changeover.

'I know, Mama. It's fine. Really.' Her father's hazel eyes looked out of her strangely worldly-wise but soft, unformed face and she laid her hand on mine. 'I know what to do. Helena's been going over it all with me. I'm going to help you with everything. Don't worry.'

Juno! She was comforting me. She'd been raised as a Roma

Novan, of course. She knew this stuff far better than I did.

At lunch in the nursery, I let Allegra explain it all to the others. Gil and Tonia cried. She let them carry on for a few minutes, then told them to shut up and get a grip. Great Nonna would be embarrassed if she could see them.

'But, Legra, it's horrible. Why does she have to go?'

I wanted to intervene, but Helena shook her head at me. Allegra was doing just fine.

'C'mon, Gil, you know that's how it is,' she said. She looked at them sternly. 'If you want to go and see her this afternoon, you have to wash your faces and behave with dignity. The last thing Great Nonna wants to see is cry babies. We're supposed to cheer her up and make her proud of us.'

I had to look away. Where had I got this strong daughter from?

I woke with a start, a loud trill ringing in my right ear. It was the house intercom.

'DJ *custodes* for you, lady,' came Junia's voice. 'Do you want to take it, or shall I say you're unavailable?'

'No, no, I'll take it.' I sat up on my bed, the papers I'd fallen asleep over falling off my chest.

'Mitela. *Salve*.'

'What's the matter with you, Bruna? Slacking again?' Lurio's sarcastic tone woke me up instantly.

'Go screw yourself, Lurio. What do you want? It's the weekend, for Juno's sake.'

'Oh, sorry, I forgot you PGSF lot only work weekdays.'

'Don't be a smartass. I've done ten solid days. Conradus's on shift all weekend, until Tuesday, in fact.'

'That's why I'm calling you at home.'

'What do you mean?' I heard the suppressed excitement in his voice.

'I thought I'd tell you first.'

'What?'

'We've trapped your little bird.'

'She was on the Italian border in a hire car when some bright spark in the border guard spotted her.' He consulted the screen. 'Fake passport. Turns out to be a Brit called Sandbrook, ex-armed forces.'

He turned from his screen and fixed me with a stern eye. 'Now suppose you tell me what's going on here, Colonel?'

I glanced at the investigator, Pelonia, who was running the case. 'Would you excuse us for a few minutes, Inspector?'

Lurio nodded and she left, none too happy by the look on her face to be thrown out of her own office.

'Well?'

'Have you done all the prelims?'

'Yes. And?'

'Including DNA?'

'Well, she's a foreigner. She's hardly likely to match up, is she?'

'You may be surprised. Can you run it discreetly?'

'Why? Who is she?' He smirked. 'Not your long-lost sister?'

'No, but she may be Conradus's daughter.'

I was on my thousandth cup of tea when Lurio came back.

'You're right. We ran it against Tella DNA. It's a match with very little deviation in the markers.'

Hades.

He glanced down at me. 'How do you want to play this? Will you bail her?'

'No way. What did you detain her on?'

'Acting suspiciously on a public highway.'

'Well, draw up a formal charge of misdirection of minors and corruption of youth. I'll sign the papers now.' I could hear the hard tone in my voice. It was only a glimmer of what I was feeling inside. The seriousness of the charge would ensure she'd be held in custody for the whole twenty-eight days pre-trial – the same period Allegra had to serve as her punishment.

'Jupiter, that's hard, Bruna. Are you sure?'

'Oh yes. The formal complainant is Allegra, of course.'

'Very well.'

He called Pelonia in and she did the paperwork, her dark head bending over the print-outs. She fixed me with a steady gaze from her grey eyes as she passed the file over to me for signing.

'I must offer you my apologies for asking you to step out, Inspector. I didn't mean to undermine your authority. But I think you understand why.'

'Yes. I see now. We'll keep it confidential until it becomes critical to the investigation. Of course, it'll come out when it goes to court.'

'Thank you. Here's the direct number for Senior Centurion Flavius who led the surveillance operation. He'll clue you in and make the team available for you to interview. You'll get full cooperation, I assure you. My daughter will be available when convenient to you. Just call me.'

Pelonia thanked me and took herself off, presumably to begin questioning.

'Do you want to see her?' Lurio asked as we walked down the corridor.

'No, thanks. I want as little to do with her as possible.'

Lurio gave me one of his 'don't bullshit me' looks.

'Look, I don't want to, okay?'

'Chicken?'

'Don't be ridiculous.' I glanced up at him. Hades' teeth, he was right. I flicked my hand backwards to hide my embarrassment. 'Oh, very well, let's go stare at her if it'll make you happy,' I grumped, but now I was curious.

In the custody suite, I watched Nicola through the observation window as she answered the DJ interrogator's questions. Her hair was loose now, straggling, darker than I remembered but her eyes were exactly the colour of Conrad's. Why hadn't I spotted that in England? Because I hadn't been looking. She wore the standard bright yellow prison tunic; one wrist was cuffed to the plastic-topped table. I felt a fleeting wave of sympathy. It didn't last when I heard her tell the DJ interrogator sitting opposite her to go fuck a sheep. He gave a contemptuous laugh back.

Pelonia was relaxed, shoulders glued to the back wall, one leg bent at the knee so her foot was flat to the wall. She looked bored and was examining the nails on her left hand with intense interest. Lurio and I listened in for around ten minutes. Pelonia and the other DJ *custos* swapped and she turned into the bad cop now, quite frightening when she got going. But they weren't getting anywhere. It didn't help that they were forced to do it all in English.

'Do you want to go in?'

I was sorely tempted; I wanted to beat Nicola to a pulp for what she'd done to Allegra and what she was doing to Conrad.

'No, it'll contaminate the process. I'm only here as *parens per procurationem* for Allegra. Some smartass lawyer would use it to throw it out. I want this little bitch to go down.'

More importantly I wanted Conrad to see what she was.

Lurio walked me back to my car. I'd thrown it in the nearest space at an angle.

'Lurio, promise me you'll keep her in custody for the statutory twenty-eight. She's a crafty tough egg and'll try to find some way to slide her way out.'

'And suppose your husband turns up armed with a fancy lawyer?'

'You know what the law says. Tell him no.'

IX

I reached home only to find regular Praetorians on the gate and more in the courtyard. The guard saluted correctly, but didn't risk a single muscle on his face by smiling. A slightly anxious Galienus greeted me with news that the imperatrix was here.

'Yeah, I got that, Gally, from the toy soldiers outside.' But I smiled at him to take the sting out of my tone. I made my way through the vestibule into the atrium. Another one. Juno, how dangerous did they think our house was? I waved her aside and went upstairs, but she trailed up behind me. I arrived just as Silvia came out of Aurelia's bedroom. She looked pale, her eyes glistening, but she was keeping it together. Aurelia wasn't only her senior cousin, but her counsellor of many years, back to the time of the rebellion.

'Silvia.'

'Oh, gods, Carina. It's so wrong.' She held out both hands which I gripped and squeezed in sympathy.

'Hey, come and sit down for a minute.' I drew her down on to the day couch and, ignoring the damn guard, fixed her a fruit juice. She rarely drank alcohol during the day.

'Aurelia will have been so pleased to see you.'

Silvia looked strained, the white amongst her glorious red-brown hair was gaining more ground. She was only in her mid-fifties, but the loss of her husband all those years ago had been a savage blow. She'd married Andrea Luca, when she was barely twenty, only two years after returning to Roma Nova. Nonna had reckoned Silvia needed stability and kindness after forcible exile following the terror of Caius's rebellion. Andrea was an Italian academic who'd led the team clearing and restoring buildings damaged during the rebellion and the take-back. He'd loved Silvia deeply and supported her through the tough years when although still young, she had to rule a ruined country attempting to re-establish itself. On their sixth anniversary, he was diagnosed with cancer. He'd been in remission for a year when the cancer had come back suddenly like Nemesis herself. How bitter that her beloved cousin was being hunted down by the same killer.

'When Andrea was dying, he faded a little bit each day in front of me. I felt so helpless. It's the same now.' She shivered. 'What a colder place the world will be soon.'

'I know, darling, I know.'

When the imperial circus had left, I stripped off and showered, sloughing off the grubby smell of the *custodes* stationhouse as well as Silvia's despair. I played around making a big production about what to change into; in the end, I chose a simple tunic and laced leather belt and dried my hair in the most time-consuming way. But habit wouldn't let me drag it out for more than thirty minutes. I sighed. I had to get it over.

'Senior Legate's office. *Salve.*'

'Good evening, Prisca Rusonia. Is the legate available?'

'He's down in the watch office, ma'am. Shall I patch you through?'

Crap. Had he seen the joint watch report already?

'Mitelus.'

He'd seen it.

'Hi. Can we have a private talk?'

'I'm working. I don't have time for personal matters.' And, unbelievably, he cut the connection. I couldn't have been more stunned if Juno herself had materialised in front of me and slapped my face.

Well, screw him.

'Gather you had a visitation this afternoon.' Daniel smiled at me across the supper table. We'd chosen to eat together, Helena, children and Michael included. Was it some kind of tribal pulling together in a time of crisis?

'Yes. Silvia was so upset. It brought Andrea's death back.'

We ate on in silence, cowed by events. Once finished, I kissed the children good night, smiled at Helena and Michael and took Daniel into my study and updated him.

'Well, catching that little tart's one bit of good news, isn't it?'

'Yes, but Conrad's taken it badly.' I told him about our non-conversation.

'Maybe he's a bit pressured or was in the middle of something important.'

'Right. And catching the person responsible for nearly killing our daughter isn't important?'

'You know I didn't mean it like that.'

'No, sorry.' I gave him a tight smile. And tried to catch my mental breath. 'He just won't talk to me.'

'Do you think it's that bad between you two?' he said.

'Nonna thinks it's some kind of emotional crisis. Apparently, my grandfather went through something like it.'

'I haven't noticed anything different about him at work. A little pre-occupied, perhaps. But if you're right, now is not the time, not with everything else you've got to deal with. Daniel snorted. 'This bloody girl is just on the make. Why can't he see it?'

'I wonder if it goes back to his own bad childhood. Caius Tellus used to beat the crap out of him. That's why Conrad went for the low-life beating up on that kid just before his accident. That's why he's desperately protective of his own children. '

'Yeah, but that was forty years ago. He's a mature adult now, in a very responsible position. And you need all the support you can get.'

At eleven o' clock precisely the following day, I sat down in Nonna's place at the head of the long oak table that Junia's staff had set up in the atrium. Allegra at my right side and twenty-five of my senior blood relatives occupied the remaining seats. More cousins perched in a line of chairs along the side. They gazed at me expectantly. I felt numb; I couldn't think what to say. I'd completely forgotten how Nonna started these councils. Gods. I'd sat through enough at her right side. A movement at my left broke my trance; Dalina Mitela, Lucy's mother, handed me a sheet of paper. Of course, she was the family recorder. She'd have the protocol ready. I threw her a grateful look, read the sheet and got a grip.

'Thank you all for coming at short notice. I've called the council meeting to advise you of Aurelia Mitela's condition. My grandmother is very seriously ill; the doctors don't think she will live beyond the week.' I swallowed hard. 'I know some of you have visited her in the last week or two and this has given her a good deal of pleasure.'

Yeah, especially when afterwards she whispered clever ironic comments to me about the more pompous ones in the hoarse tones of what was left of her voice.

'The imperatrix was gracious enough to visit yesterday and sends us her support and love in such a difficult time. If you wish to say your farewells to Aurelia, please liaise with Marcella. But please keep your visits to a few minutes only. I will not have Aurelia's last breaths spent fending off crowds.'

Some looked shocked. Tough.

'I apologise if you are upset by my plain talking. She is really very frail.'

Allegra laid her hand on mine. Encouragement shone out of her eyes. I closed mine for a few seconds, before looking at them all again through a blur.

'I will advise you immediately of any further developments. In the meantime, I will continue to act as *de facto* head of the family. Does the council support my decision?'

For once it was unanimous. Nobody said anything further; they just sat there like parallel rows of stuffed movie extras. I brought the meeting to an end. Dalina handed me the record and I signed it off. I drew my hand across my mouth and brought it around to support my jaw. How in Hades was I going to carry on with this?

Dalina gathered up the folders and el-pad, zipping them up in a soft brown leather case. When she'd finished, she stood there, waiting. A little uncomfortable, but waiting.

'Dalina? What is it?'

Allegra saved me. 'Dalina Mitela will be staying with us now, Mama. Shall I ask Junia to sort out a room for her?'

'Yes. Yes, thank you, Allegra.' She jumped up and trotted off on her mission.

'Sorry, Dalina, I'm a bit lost in all this,' I said. I looked at Allegra's retreating figure. 'But luckily I have some expert help.'

'Please don't worry, Countess Carina. I should have realised you wouldn't know. I'm here to help you, not cause you any worry. My recording activities will keep me in the background anyway, so please try to forget I'm here.' That made me smile. Even her formal black suit and solemn expression didn't subdue her striking appearance and personal attraction. In a family with some reasonable lookers, her dazzling eyes and luxuriant waving chestnut hair made her outstanding.

'Thanks. Appreciated.'

I watched the fifty or so who'd fallen on the light lunch Junia's staff had set up. I gave Dalina a tight smile and we headed for the crowd. People darted out of our way as if afraid of catching an electric shock.

Galienus appeared out of nowhere with a tray of glasses full of Castra Lucillan white. Nonna's favourite, from our own vineyards. I grabbed one, and took a good swig. Fortified, I turned to go talk with the horde of cousins, with a smile on my face and a nagging ache in my heart.

I went into work as scheduled next morning. In one of her waking periods, Nonna had told me to stop moping around the house as it didn't do anybody any good. Once I'd got there, I agreed. But Sergius had everything under control. I'd really have to get him promoted; it was woefully overdue. If anything I said had any weight any more.

At the senior staff meeting first thing, Conrad had all but ignored me, calling for my report almost as an afterthought. He hadn't picked over it, but had given the impression it was pretty irrelevant. Daniel gave me a sympathetic look and even Sepunia, the Intelligence director, known for her cool detachment, looked puzzled.

'Everything okay, Carina? Anything I should know about?' she asked as we walked back afterwards.

'No, nothing for you, just a personal matter.'

'I heard your grandmother was very ill. How is she?'

'We've got about a week, the doctors think.'

'I'm very sorry.' She laid her hand on my arm and fixed her green eyes on me. 'Let me know if I can do anything. Please.'

Predictably, I couldn't get a slot in Conrad's schedule. I don't know why I tried; he was freezing me out and taking advantage of his position to do so. Rusonia said he was taking personal time again that afternoon. What in Hades was going on? I paced up and down my office, trying to think it through. Sure, it didn't take a genius to work out he was pissed at me about Nicola. Why wouldn't he see me and talk, okay, have an honest fight, about it? But why was he ignoring Allegra and giving even a second to thinking about Nicola?

And what was all this personal time in work hours? Then the worst thought struck me with the force of a marble wall. My head felt weightless, then the room started turning. I stopped, grabbed on to my desk.

No.

Impossible.

He'd never shown any interest in anybody else since the day we'd met. Incredible, considering how he'd screwed around before then. I was a hundred per cent sure he would have said something.

Roma Novans weren't squeamish about relationships; they wouldn't have survived the centuries without a pragmatic approach. Unlike that first break fifteen years ago when I'd thrown him out,

Conrad and I would try to have a civilised conversation and work out the practicalities. It sounded so cold-blooded to Westerners, but it cut out a lot of hysterics.

I was waiting, not directly opposite the PGSF barracks as CCTV scanned the whole area in front of the building. I'd been crouched down by my Ducati in a narrow pedestrian alley for nearly half an hour. Assaulted by the worst autumn storm this year, I huddled up against the wall. The damned rain dribbled down my leathers and over my boots in miniature drunken rivulets. The roof overhang three floors up gave no shelter.

In my foul mood, I nearly missed him.

Right on 14.00, he came out of the service gate. I glimpsed a silver pool car and the driver's dark blond head. I scrambled on to my bike, hit the gas pedal and curved out of the alley in pursuit. The driving rain smashed against my body but I didn't care; it would help hide me. I followed his vehicle's taillights at the furthest distance I dared, only once having to make an evasive manoeuvre.

Ten minutes later, he stopped outside our own front gate. For the gods' sake! I watched as he passed the entry scan and disappeared through the tall gateway.

What was he doing home at such a time of the day and why was it so secretive? I knew I hadn't triggered the house CCTV from where I was, but I couldn't risk getting any nearer if I wanted to stay unobserved. I waited.

Twenty-five minutes later, he drove out again, heading southwest. He parked on the street in the *macellum* quarter, once the central market, now expanded to include a large shopping centre and streets of individual outlets. He didn't get out of the vehicle immediately. I was too far away to see exactly what he was doing. I searched in my inside pocket and cursed when I found I didn't have my scope.

As he opened the door, I saw him thrust something in his pocket. Probably his cell. He opened the trunk and took out a messenger bag. While he was feeding the meter with coins, I stripped off my leathers and stuffed them with the helmet into the lockbox on the back of my bike. Only just in time, before he'd set off down the street. Pulling my sweater hood up over my head, I loped after him, keeping a good distance and occasionally fiddling with my fake music player headphones.

When he glanced up at the street name, I stopped and pretended to gaze into a display window full of new generation communicators. In the reflection, I saw him go through a door three metres up on the other side of the road. I picked up a brochure, wrinkled with damp, from the literature stand by the shop entrance. Why hadn't they taken it in when the storm started? It was raining less intensely now, still steady enough to soak through my jeans and sweatshirt.

After five minutes, I lurched across the road, running for the wall for shelter. When I reached the door Conrad had vanished through, I dropped down, re-tied my sneaker and, as I stood up, read the brass plate.

I jogged down the street some way, then doubled back to my bike, pulled my leathers on and headed back to the PGSF building. In the garages, I parked up and hung my leathers up to dry. Even after I was back into my uniform, I was still puzzling it out. A lawyer. I guessed he wanted to try spring Nicola. But neither Allegra nor I was backing off on that one. I really hoped he wasn't consulting her about divorce. But Claudia Vara, of all possible lawyers?

I got home to find Marcella waiting for me, grim-faced.

'She's not—'

'No, but she insists on seeing you as soon as you get in.'

'Why in Hades didn't you call me? I would have come immediately. You know that.' I glared at her.

'She wouldn't let me.'

'Gods! Next time, Marcella, you call me.'

Why the hell was I saying, 'next time'?

I took the stairs two at a time. The nurse was sitting at the bedside, reading a magazine. He started up, a slightly guilty expression. However dedicated, time must have dragged for him. My grandmother looked so peaceful. Even the oxygen mask she now wore didn't hide her wrecked face.

'She's had a good afternoon. Your husband visited for a while, then she slept,' he whispered. 'She woke a little while ago, wanting to see you, but said she would wait. She ordered me not to call you.'

Oh, Nonna. Impossible to the end.

I bent over and kissed her forehead. I sat on the chair next to her and held her hand against my cheek.

'Carina?'

'Here, Nonna,'

'Call Allegra. And the recorder.'

I looked at the nurse and he went out.

'Carina. You have to stop this girl,' she gasped. 'She's Caius. All over again.'

No. Not Caius Tellus the traitor who had wrecked Roma Nova. How could Nicola be like that monster?

'Don't agitate yourself, Nonna, please.'

'No, listen.' Her eyes glinted, hardened, surrounded by bloodshot and discoloured whites. 'Promise me. Or she'll destroy you all.'

'It's all right, Nonna. We've got her. She's in prison, awaiting trial for what she did to Allegra. Please don't worry.'

'You don't understand. Ask Quintus.' She sighed and shut her eyes. I froze. I thought she'd gone. But I saw her shoulders move and she took a few breaths.

I turned around at the noise of the door opening. Dalina and Allegra, followed by Marcella and the doctor, who came forward, took Nonna's pulse. He looked at me and shook his head. I signalled Allegra forward. She kissed Aurelia's cheek and her hand, then placed it in mine.

'Carina. My ring,' Aurelia whispered. 'Take it.'

I hesitated, glanced at Dalina, who nodded. I drew the heavy gold ring off Nonna's right hand, untying the ribbon that had kept it fastened to her shrinking finger. Not knowing what else to do with it, I slipped it on the middle finger of my right hand.

I sat down in my chair, scarcely believing what was happening, what I'd done. I leant forward, gently took Nonna's hand and held it until it went limp.

'Take her breath, Countess,' prompted Dalina. I stood up, bent over and kissed Aurelia's lips. I reached out and closed her eyes. Cold drenched through me. I shivered.

'Nonna,' I whispered. 'Nonna! Come back.' She couldn't hear me, of course.

'Aurelia Mitela,' piped up Allegra. '*Vale.*'

Gods! I'd forgotten what I was supposed to do.

'Aurelia Mitela, *vale*,' we repeated twice more. The shouts behind me nearly deafened me. The room was full of people I hadn't noticed arriving.

I sat frozen. I barely registered the rhythmic patter outside of rain falling steadily. Grey outside and grey in my heart.

X

I didn't have a clue how long I sat there. A touch on the shoulder; it was Allegra with a hot cup of tea. She stood there while I drank it.

I woke suddenly, a cold draught sliced across my feet. My neck ached and my back was stiff. My watch said four in the morning. I glanced at the bed. Aurelia was resting peacefully, but her hand in mine was like a block of ice. Then I remembered. Oh, gods.

A hard cramp in my stomach woke me up. I was in my own bed. How had I gotten here? My head thumped and my eyes were sore and desiccated. Half eleven! I struggled to the bathroom, showered and dressed quickly. As I reached for the bedroom door handle, my head swam and my stomach retched. I ran back to the bathroom and threw up. I leaned over the john, spitting out liquid, draining my core.

A gentle hand wiped my face, handed me a glass of water to rinse my mouth.

'Marcella?'

'Gently, take it gently.'

'I have to—'

'No, you have to do nothing. I've called the Senior Legate's office. You are on a month's leave.'

Had she spoken to Conrad or just Rusonia? I couldn't summon the effort to care one way or the other.

'I've called the council for this evening at six. The undertakers are preparing your grandmother's body. Countess Allegra and Helena are looking after the children.' Her face relaxed a little. Gods, she must be mourning herself; she'd been with Nonna for at least twenty years. Yet she'd done all this stuff. I hung my head with shame.

'Come and have a sandwich. Dalina Mitela is waiting for you. She'll take you through what has to happen next.'

I moved on automatic but felt as if I was watching somebody else being me. I shivered as I closed the door on my apartment.

Everything around me looked as clean and serene as usual; no noise, no bustling, no chaos except in my head. I felt like a victim ripped out from a war zone and set down in the middle of Pleasantville.

At first glance, everything looked normal in the atrium. Then I saw that the huge planters full of luxurious ferns and fronds had been moved from the centre over to the alcove opposite the large plate glass side doors. Beams of light fell from the bulls'-eye in centre of the roof of the great hall no longer onto the plants, but now onto a raised platform with a figure lying on it.

My grandmother was laid out, dressed in a white *palla* and purple *stola*. She rested surrounded by flowers and greenery on a deep-pile blue velvet cloth draped over the platform. I smelled myrtle and cypress. Myrtle for Mitela. From the walled garden. A single tear escaped and ran down my face. Was I going to fall down and weep? But I was numb, motionless. I had nothing to give.

The open flames on tall black stands at the four corners flickered, the only artificial light as the electrical lighting had been switched off. I felt Dalina press a metal disc into my hand, a gold *solidus* which I placed in Aurelia's mouth to pay Charon the ferryman to take her safely into the next world. I'd never laugh at one of her wicked jokes again, flinch from the bracing tone of her voice, watch her negotiating through the shark waters of corporate life or in the Senate. Nor would I find comfort in her arms when she consoled me.

I stepped back to join Dalina and we stood quietly. I couldn't watch Nonna enough. Illogical, but I thought she was sleeping and would wake up, asking what we all thought we were doing, standing around like dummies. Cousins, colleagues, friends and one enemy drifted in during the afternoon to pay their respects or perhaps to see if the supposedly indestructible Aurelia Mitela really was dead.

A good half hour had passed since the last visitor when I felt a tingle in my shoulder, caught an impression out of the corner of my eye of a beige-clothed figure entering the atrium from the opposite corner. My gut clenched. Was it Conrad? Had he come back? I swivelled around to get a better look in the gloom and took half a step forward. Not blond hair, not his cat-like walk. I shouldn't have been so disappointed, but it was Daniel. Another figure behind him, in dark pants and jacket. They walked in step, their solemn faces coming into focus as they approached the bier.

'Carina,' was all Daniel said. His eyes shone with emotion.

Ignoring all and any protocol, he seized my hands, bent over and kissed my forehead. I grasped his hands firmly in return.

'Daniel—'

'I know.'

I gave his companion a thin smile. 'Michael.' I waved my hand vaguely. 'This is not quite what you expected to see during your visit with us.'

'Carina, I'm so sorry. I hope you will accept my deepest condolences.'

'Thank you. You're very kind.'

'And if you need help with that other matter or anything else, you know I'll do anything I can.'

'You're going now?'

'Yes, I thought it best. You don't want any tourists at a time like this.'

'Have a good flight, then,' I said dully.

He dropped his bag, placed his hand on my shoulders, bent down and kissed my cheek.

I laid my hand on his forearm. 'Thank you,' I said and sniffed. I gathered my wits and smiled at him. 'Thank you for all the help with catching that girl. We'd never have gotten her without you.'

He shrugged. 'We have to stick together, you know. My pleasure. I hope it all works out.'

He and Daniel turned to go and we found Conrad behind us.

Juno! Where had he come from? And so quietly?

Contempt and anger fought it out on his face.

'Yes, thanks to the over-efficient captain,' he said, his tone stripped of all warmth, 'my daughter is now stuck in a foreign prison, friendless and helpless. Good work, Captain.'

Michael fought to contain himself; his common sense won out.

'Conrad,' snapped Daniel, 'leave it. Not the place or time.' He nodded towards Aurelia lying on the bier. 'Back off.'

'Or what, Daniel?'

Oh, gods. Luckily we spoke in English and no outsiders were present, only Dalina who tried desperately not to look curious.

'Don't be so childish, man,' Daniel said. 'You're upsetting Carina and making an arse of yourself. Go away and calm down.'

He turned to me. 'We have to go or Michael will miss his plane.' He gave me a fleeting smile, turned his back on Conrad, and left with Michael.

I grabbed Conrad's arm. 'Get over here,' I hissed at him, pulling him to the side, away from the bier, 'and shut up. I've had just about enough of you acting dumb.'

'Dumb? What a quaint expression,' he smirked.

I almost smacked it off his face.

'Just what in Hades do you think you're playing at? Or has that little tart so bewitched you?' I felt tears of rage and frustration pooling in my eyes. 'Yes, she's genetically your daughter, but what about the other daughter she tried to get killed? If I remember, you were going to break every bone in her body.'

'She's misguided, that's all.' His face was sullen.

'Misguided? She's a murderer. Can't you see that?'

'She's got nobody. I've been to see her. She's in a bad way, miserable and depressed.'

What was he talking about? Cocky and aggressive weren't strong enough words to describe her when I'd seen the DJ *custodes* questioning her two days ago.

'Look, Conrad, try taking a step back and thinking this through. She's trying to manipulate you right where you're most vulnerable. Don't fall for it. We've got to think of Allegra, our daughter.'

'Huh. My *fourth* daughter's got her powerful and tough mother to protect and coddle her. My first one is abandoned and alone.'

How could he be so illogical? I glowered at him.

He glared back.

I put my hand out and placed it on his forearm. 'Conrad, don't.'

He shook it off as if swatting an insect and stomped off.

What in Hades was happening to him?

Seven days later, as dusk was falling, we prepared to burn Nonna. As I slid the white stola over my black palla and tied the white cloth belt that morning, I still could not weep. Nor when they collected the bier and loaded it on to the carriage. As we drove past the forum, I knew I was lucky nobody expected a lengthy public oration, the *laudatio*, these days. Allegra, in identical dress, her hair loose like mine, smiled and squeezed my hand.

At the family mausoleum, several kilometres out of town, I watched the bearers lift the heavy bier. Nonna was light enough, Juno knew, but still the eight of them struggled. I recognised most; three senators, Aurelia's corporate henchman, Martius Bullo, Crispus Mitelus and his brother, one dark-haired younger man, a cousin whose name I couldn't recall but recognised, and Daniel.

Silvia joined Allegra and me while we were forming up for the procession and as we were about to set off, I saw Conrad, in funeral black, tap the young cousin on the shoulder and take his place at the back opposite Daniel. The look they exchanged was nuclear. After that they ignored each other. I didn't know whether to be happy or annoyed. The old Conrad had loved and respected Aurelia. Was he doing it for her or to support me?

Gil carried a palm and basket, Tonia the traditional slim spade. I'd protested they were too young, but Helena had intervened.

'They desperately want to be involved, Carina. Give them something to do, they'll feel part of the ceremony. It'll be more frightening for them if they think they've been left out. Better Mitelae than strangers, in any case.'

And Allegra had backed her.

I'd drawn the line at mask-carrying and noisy professionals – too much pantomime. I gathered it had pretty much died out anyway. The soothing music from the band at the front was much better. Hundreds turned out, not just Mitelae, but many of the other Twelve Families, two-thirds, I guessed, of the Senate plus the general ranks of the great and the good. I felt so disconnected; I couldn't register anybody beyond two metres. It was like being on some film set. At the walled burning ground, I stopped, my stomach in my throat. I could smell the pyres from the past, the wood, the perfumes, the aromatic branches and herbs. And the burning flesh. Allegra looked up at me, concerned, but Silvia grabbed my arm and murmured, 'Keep going.'

I turned to her, but she was facing forward, expressionless.

I got a grip, stood in front of the bier while people flowed in on each side and found a place. The music stopped, silence took over. I felt a thousand eyes on me, curious, tolerant, but expectant. I stepped up to the microphone and delivered the speech Dalina had helped me prepare for this private audience; gracious, celebratory and short.

I followed the rehearsal to the letter; torch in hand, lead in my heart, I walked around the pyre three times with Allegra and Silvia following, and came back to the start. I put the torch to the pyre and turned away as the kerosene-assisted flames erupted. I stepped back, not merely to avoid the rising heat, but in emotional retreat. My grandmother was gone; we wouldn't be burning her else.

People stepped forward when the flames began to rise, throwing on branches, oils, wine, scarves. I never felt more of a stranger, an alien, than at this ceremony.

Nonna's old friend Senator Pia Calavia kissed me on both cheeks and looked me direct in the eye.

'Never a truer or more passionate servant of Roma Nova,' she said, her voice breaking. She was accompanied by a tall man with grey curly hair and black brows. His Latin was good but accented. 'We were friends during the time of the rebellion. And afterwards.' He took time to scrutinise my face, ignoring the people queuing behind him. 'You are so very like her.'

Senator Calavia said, 'Come, Miklós,' and they went together to throw on their libations. His was a red rose, a colour Nonna had forbidden in her rose garden for a reason I didn't know until her will was opened.

I was thankful when the pile was burnt down. It was fully dark by now, only a thin sickle moon; the burning ground was lit by flame torches in sconces. We sprinkled wine over the embers, calling out our last farewells. By now, I was certain our faces were covered in dirty smuts; my lungs felt full of smoke, in a way full of the essence of Aurelia. Were my tears from the smoke or grief? It didn't matter. It was enough appropriate display for people shaking my hand, murmuring condolences as they left.

After the last mourner had gone, and Silvia, Helena and the twins were on their way home, I looked around for Conrad. No sign. I pulled Allegra to me; she gave me a teary little smile. As per tradition, we wouldn't leave until Galienus's crew had gathered up the ashes and bones. The cold water sprinkled over us by the old priest to purify us woke me up from my near trance. Galienus solemnly presented me with the urn to be interred with the other ancestors and I carried it to the sepulchre proper, bowed and turned away, not able to bear the finality. We left the priest to it.

At least we had eight more days' respite until the Novendiale when the cousins, close friends and colleagues of Aurelia and anybody who felt entitled would descend on us for the funeral feast. I was dreading it; the idea of people talking platitudes while stuffing their mouths with food and using it as a networking event.

We passed the intervening days confined to the house, no real hardship as the quiet time let us concentrate on mourning Nonna. Allegra had even been given a reprieve from her community sentence for the mourning period. Junia's team deep-cleaned the house from attic to basement, the priest blessing the mops, brooms and even the central vacuum system.

I told the children about Nonna's earlier life and service, the rebellion, and about how kind she'd been to me when I'd arrived sixteen years ago after fleeing the Eastern United States, how she'd supported me in my dark days. But I didn't know if I was comforting them or myself more.

By day eight, Tonia and Gil were bored stupid, no longer enjoying the novelty of being off school and even Allegra had slipped from her perfect daughter role, flouncing out of the atrium one afternoon after a lame remark by Gil.

The ninth day, we assembled in the vestibule, Allegra firmly holding one hand of each twin. I had hoped Conrad might turn up. I hadn't seen him since we'd burned Aurelia. Allegra and the twins had had text messages, but nothing for me. The car drew up and as Helena and I got the children in, a motorbike raced into the courtyard, parked, and the tall rider walked towards the car with a familiar cat-like grace. Oh gods! I swallowed hard. Not a scene. Not now. Please.

'Room for one more in the front?'

The smile he directed at the children faded as his gaze reached me. It was hard, but neutral. I guessed that was an improvement. Under his leathers, he wore mourning dress, so we all set off for Nonna's tomb like an average unhappy family on their last day of formal mourning. After a brief ceremony where a number of cousins joined us, wine and savouries were passed around. We toasted Aurelia and said final farewells.

Conrad rode back with me, somehow parcelling off the children to other relatives' cars. I wasn't going to start anything, so I stayed silent.

'You can't sulk forever, Carina.'

'I'm not the one sulking. You may have forgotten, but I'm mourning my grandmother. I'm entitled to be quiet.'

'Now she's gone, we have something more serious to deal with.'

'How can you be so callous?'

'She's gone. She'd be the first to tell you to get on with things.'

I remembered Nonna's words. All of them. I swallowed hard. We were just coming into the city limits.

'What do you want, Conrad? You've got ten minutes, unless you want to come in?'

'Don't you want me to sit by your side during the bun-fight?'

We were expecting nearly two hundred for the Novendiale funeral feast. Normally, I would have dreaded it without him there.

'Of course, I want you there.'

'Well, let's call a truce for today.'

I hadn't realised we were at war.

XI

Dalina packed up and went home to her own family, the last of the long-distance cousins departed and the house was quiet again. Allegra refused to do anything special for her fifteenth birthday; I asked if she wanted to go out with her friends someplace, but she preferred to read, swim and mooch around the house. She still had a week to run on her community service and said she wasn't in the mood for celebrating. She showed me a text she'd received from Conrad and later that morning signed for a gift delivered from him. We looked at the box, exchanged glances, then she picked it up, took it to her room and came downstairs after ten minutes without saying anything.

I went back to work a week later. I had to get grounded in my normal life. At least here it wasn't shifting under me all the time. Or so I thought. I dropped my side arm in at the guard office and got a strange look from the duty sergeant.

'Something wrong?'

'Nothing really, ma'am.' But her eyes said something different.

'Spill.'

'Well… it's just that your access code has been suspended until further notice.'

'Because?'

'No reason given.'

'I see.' I couldn't see anything. I was too furious. How dare he?

'Putting it back in now, Colonel.' And she tapped on her terminal.

'Thank you. I think it must be a system error.'

'I think so, too, ma'am.'

I stomped upstairs, into my office then flung myself in my chair. As the screen flashed up, I stared at my schedule with horror. I tapped frantically and within seconds Lurio's face looked crossly out of the screen at me.

'What?'

'Morning.'

'Humph.'

'You still have that little tart there. Nicola Sandbrook?'

'Ah!'

'"Ah" what?'

'You won't like this.'

I shut my eyes and waited for it.

'She's calling herself Nicola Tella. Says her father told her to.'

'I don't give a shit what she calls herself.' That was a huge lie, but I wasn't going to admit anything in front of Lurio. Had Uncle Quintus approved it then?

'Her hearing comes up in six days' time. Apart from the first three days, she's been a model prisoner. Mitelus has brought in Claudia Vara as her brief.' He snorted. 'She's as bloody annoying as ever.'

So it was for Nicola that Conrad had visited Vara the same afternoon he'd said goodbye to the dying Aurelia. Nice. Vara was hard-hitting and tricky with problems of her own. If I remembered correctly, she'd had two reprimands from the Legal Guild for borderline misconduct plus the complaint I'd made against her seven years ago through the Family Codes Court. That had cost Livilla Vara, her family head, a five thousand *solidi* fine. So we had history.

'How long will Nicola get?'

'Depends on who we get rostered as magistrate, but if proven, I reckon five. That's what we'll push for.'

'Sertorius will sort Vara out. See you in court.'

Sertorius reassured me and Allegra that it was a formality. He had the girls' statements, Michael's affidavit, and the reports from my ART's surveillance operation. Solid case.

Nicola was escorted to the defendants' bench by the court officer. She looked around, completely composed, paused at Allegra, half-closed her eyes then passed on to me where she stopped for a few instants. Her eyes were like tiger's eye stones. Unbelievably, she tipped her chin up at me in challenge.

She took her time walking up to the bar to hear the charges. The demure look on her face made me want to throw up. She looked at the magistrate as if she were a wounded pet, nodded briefly and put her hand to her eyes as if to wipe tears away. But from the side, I caught the tiny smirk. Allegra glanced at me, furious; she'd seen it, too. The magistrate shifted in his seat and coughed. His harsh features softened when he looked at Nicola. It was as if she was running the court – they all seemed in thrall to her. Conrad sat behind her, where he'd supported Allegra a few weeks ago. I nearly choked when he looked across at me; his eyes were so accusing. What right did he have to look at me like that? He was the one that had deserted us.

Vara picked at everything, but couldn't dent Sertorius's case. Allegra gave her evidence, hesitating, but not giving a centimetre under Vara's vicious cross-examination even when Vara tried to make her out to be an unnatural sister. Allegra, her face pale against her black mourning, retorted that no natural sister would try to get the other killed.

Some bad fate had allocated the same magistrate that had heard Allegra's case, but the evidence was solid. Even he couldn't dispute that. Allegra's hand had mine in a steel grip as we waited while he consulted with the two auxiliary judges. Hands flying, head bobbing in staccato movements, he was hammering some point home. They looked dubious, but from his mime he seemed to overrule them. A hard glint shone out of his eyes set deep in his wrinkled face.

'We find the defendant guilty as charged.'

Thank the gods!

'But several attenuating circumstances impact my sentence, leaving aside the fact that the chief witness is herself convicted recently of a misdemeanour. Not that that should sway us in this case, of course.'

Sertorius jumped up to protest, but the magistrate waved him down.

'The defendant is foreign-born, ignorant of what is an offence here, so some leeway must be allowed. Secondly, a guarantor has stepped forward to support and guide her future behaviour. Lastly, unwarranted in my opinion, and possibly illegal, heavy handedness has been used against her by law officers.'

Lurio sat impassively, but the muscles on his face tightened.

'One year's community service, level 2.'

A gasp ran through the audience. Then the courtroom exploded; talking and shouting, not least from the newsies, ramped the noise up. Allegra's face went white; she swayed on the bench. She looked as though all the air had been sucked out of her. I held her for a few moments while she caught her breath and steadied herself. Red hot anger rolled up through me and my head started thumping.

I watched as Conrad guided Nicola out of the courtroom, curtly nodding to Vara on the way. A loud rushing noise filled my ears and I fell back, crashing on to a bench. I covered my face with my hands and cried. I cried my heart out, I cried for Allegra, for Conrad, out of frustration, but most of all for Nonna.

I sat in the atrium for a long time after dinner that evening, nursing a glass of Nonna's favourite French brandy. She would have had plenty to say on the court case, especially about the way Conrad had leaned forward and whispered into Nicola's ear, put his hand on her shoulder and helped her through the crowd. I wondered for a moment if there was any insanity in his family. Sure, the Tellae had rotten olives like every family, but more the conspiratorial, power-seeking types. Like Caius Tellus who'd married Conrad's mother and three years after her death launched a coup, overthrowing and killing Imperatrix Severina, Silvia's mother. I shuddered. Quintus rarely talked about it, too raw, I guessed; Caius was his brother. Within eighteen months, Caius himself had been deposed and executed and Quintus set about repairing his own and Conrad's lives.

I had Marcella make some discreet inquiries at Domus Tellarum; she had contacts there, not surprising given our families had been connected for over fifteen years. She confirmed my suspicions; Conrad was living there now along with Nicola. Marcella looked at me gravely as I asked her to make a formal request for Quintus Tellus to call on me, one family head to another. I sure as hell didn't want to go there and run into Nicola. I might not have been able to control myself.

Quintus turned up the next evening, in a black business suit, flanked by two of his family officers, one of them the recorder. No problem, I'd taken the precaution of having Dalina and Crispus Mitelus with me. Quintus limped across the atrium leaning on a cane. I'd seen him at the funeral in a blur along with the other Twelve Families' representatives. Only two years younger than Nonna, he was the last of old Countess Tella's direct living descendants apart from Conrad. And she'd been old when Aurelia was a young woman. A strange family in a way, without direct female heirs for much of their history; old Tella had inherited from her father.

I kissed Quintus on the cheek, giving him both hands, then

invited him to sit in the one of easy chairs. The others I ignored.

'I'm sorry for dragging you out in the evening, Uncle Quintus, but it's very important we talk.'

'My dear Carina, I'm remiss in not calling on you before to pay my formal mourning visit. A touch of sciatica.'

Some kind of pain in the fundament, I was sure.

'Aurelia was one of my oldest and dearest friends as well as political colleague,' he continued. 'I feel a strong tree has been cut down, leaving less of a shelter in this cold world.'

His face betrayed his age, crumpled almost, cheeks sagging as if the muscles had given up.

I reached out and touched his hand. 'I know. I do know.'

He gave me a wry smile. 'It doesn't make it any better, does it?'

'Not a stitch.'

'So how can I help you, Carina?'

'I need to talk one-to-one. Let's have my people take yours for a coffee.'

He said nothing for a minute or two. I waited. The only movement was his recorder stepping forward and whispering in Quintus's ear. Quintus looked up at him, looked at me and shook his head. The recorder tried again and Quintus waved them away. Dalina and Crispus led them to sit at the other side of the atrium, where they could keep us in view and ensure I didn't beat up on Quintus.

I leaned forward. 'How is he?'

'Confused and upset.'

'I'm not surprised, with that little tart working on him.'

He raised his eyebrows. 'Do you really hate her that much?'

'Hades, Quintus, she tried to kill Allegra.'

'Are you sure? I mean, they were stupid and irresponsible, but—'

'For Juno's sake, even that malicious little bastard of a magistrate found her guilty.'

He sighed. 'Yes, unfortunately, I fear you're right.'

'You do?'

His fingers travelled up the back of his other hand and played with the silver link in the white shirt cuff.

'I've seen them all in my lifetime; the innocent, the crafty, the triers, the tough, the manipulators and the plain cruel. She's in a class of her own. If I didn't know better, I'd have thought she was Caius all over again.'

'Gods, that's exactly what Nonna said just before she died.' The tears welled in my eyes, but I refused them an exit. 'Tell me.'

'Caius used his clever manipulation skills in every part of his life. He oozed charm and confidence. His hard work guaranteed our mother's approval and she was delighted to open political doors for him.' His fingers curled. 'I was his victim since we were children. He was only three years older than me and like many brothers we shared a bedroom. When he started touching me, I tried to keep out of his way. During the day, our tutor was there most of the time. But I was terrified at night. Caius would slip into my bed and—'

Quintus looked away, his eyes seeming to focus on something a long way distant. 'You can imagine the rest. If I didn't lie there and take it, he'd thump me and then kiss the place better.' He flinched at the memory. 'I pleaded with him to leave me alone, but he laughed. My mother didn't have a clue. She thought it was boys' rough and tumble. My father tried to stop him hitting me, but got nowhere. Caius slithered out of every attempt to restrain him.'

He stared down at the coffee table for some moments. A sour taste filled my mouth and I rubbed my throat to try disperse it.

'I recovered when I ran away at twelve to live with my father,' Quintus continued, 'something my mother never understood. She thought me rather dull, a plodder, in comparison. She just shrugged the day the court gave Dad custody 'for family incompatibility'. He snorted. 'Dad and I kept out of his way. When Caius started on Conrad years later, I thrashed him, I nearly killed him. I wish I had. He'd married Constantia, charmed her away from Conrad's father, Richard, who was a good man. She died three years later, "of natural causes" they said.' He shook his head. 'She was thirty-two.'

I was riveted; fascinated and repelled at the same time.

'The public history is well known. I won't bore you. For some reason, after our fight, he left me alone, even during the rebellion. That was more frightening than being one of his victims; I never knew when, or if, he was going to pounce. But to the day of his execution he didn't see what he'd done wrong. He was completely amoral. He'd killed Imperatrix Severina Apulia, a nice woman if a weak ruler; he would have got Silvia if the PGSF hadn't got her away to New Austria. He wrecked the country, brought misery into so many lives. People were starving and terrified, the economy had plunged and the old *vigiles* police force had become brutalised and corrupted. It was hellish.'

He turned to me. 'You know yourself, what safeguards and systems were put in to guard the imperatrix and the state against a repeat.'

I'd used one of those same protocols seven years ago to prevent another bunch of would-be rebels.

'So where does this leave us, Quintus Tellus?'

He drew his gaze back and looked at me, startled at my formal tone.

'She is indubitably Conradus' daughter and I couldn't refuse to acknowledge her.' He studied his sleeve, his fingers flicked non-existent dust off. 'Much more serious, she is the only female Tella born within the past hundred years in the direct line who is still alive.' He glanced up at me, as if waiting for my reaction. I couldn't move or speak; I was frozen with horror. The four family aides stopped talking between themselves and stared in our direction. They couldn't hear us; it was as if they sensed something hovering in the air.

'You can't possibly mean what I think you're saying,' I managed eventually. The Tellae had no female heir within four degrees. Quintus had once suggested formally adopting Tonia, our second daughter – she had Conrad's genes and blood – but I'd said she was far too young for such a step. Maybe when she was older and could decide for herself. Quintus was now floating the idea that Nicola could claim to be his heir. Hades' teeth!

'I will watch her, Carina, and attempt to check any developing tendencies. If she starts acting like Caius, she'll use a mixture of relentless charm and attrition.' He looked up and smiled, but the rest of his face didn't mirror it. 'We may be being overly pessimistic. Perhaps she may settle now she has family around her.'

Don't kid yourself, Quintus.

'Can you give it a little while to see what unfolds?' he asked.

'All I want is my husband back. He looked so angry in court.' I waved my hand in a vague backward movement. 'She's sucking the life out of him. Why can't he see it? He's sharp enough.'

Quintus looked away, and spoke to the marble column. 'I think he's feeling guilty over what he thinks is neglect of this lost child.'

'And she's playing it for every *solidus*.'

'Perhaps.'

'Well, lock up your money, Quintus,' I urged him, 'as well as your virtue.'

Part II

The Furies

XII

The annual fitness–for-task exercise kept my department fully occupied for the next few weeks; training the visiting arms and preparing tasks, logistics and staffing for the whole thing. Almost the entire four hundred strength went out on this exercise. The worst thing was having the regulars move in as caretakers in our facilities. This year, I sprang a surprise and changed the location on the second day; we went up to the mountain tactical area. I'd found training in the pine woods with the British a rewarding challenge earlier in the year. It had sharpened up the skills of the whole detachment. Interesting to see how the rest of them took it.

At six thirty the first morning after the move, the teams had all gone out and I paused in the chilly air in front of the thick canvas staff tent, a hot bacon and egg roll in one hand and a mug of strong tea in the other, drinking in the diamond-sharp morning sunshine coming up over the pine forest. Gods, it was cool at this altitude, around zero degrees up on this mountain shoulder. But so pure and clear.

'Jupiter's balls, Carina, what possessed you to drag us all up here?'

Daniel, his dark brown eyes almost hidden by the fur round the hood on his parka.

'Ha! Can't take a bit of cool weather?'

He rubbed his gloved hands together. 'I'm a desert boy at heart.'

I grinned back at him 'I thought it got cold at night in the Negev?'

'Yeah, but that was over fifteen years ago. I'm old now.'

I chuckled.

He didn't say anything. I sensed him gazing at me.

'What?'

'Lovely to hear you laugh again. It's been a while.'

'Yeah. It hasn't gone away, Daniel, just buried a little further. And it's good to keep busy.' I turned to him. 'This is where I should be, in the middle of my people, working with them, caring for them, bollocking them if necessary, but with them.' I made a face.

'Gods, I sound like something out of a TV soap. Slap my face if I start again.'

'I wouldn't dare!'

I burst out laughing at his mock-horrified face, tapped him on the chest with the back of my hand. He laughed back.

'So pleasing to see my officers enjoying their work.'

A shutter fell abruptly on our happy mood. Senior Legate Conradus Mitelus had joined us. Disapproval on his face contradicted his words, combined with the now-familiar guarded expression he wore when he came near me. He hadn't stopped treating me like any other member of his team, but now his manner had an edge and no intimate smile ever burst through. It was like skimming over a large bowl of Jell-O. So far the surface tension hadn't broken.

'Cup of tea, sir?' Daniel said, seeking to break the mood.

'No thank you, Colonel. What time are you checking the sub-command posts?'

Daniel recognised his exit cue, saluted and went.

I snuck a sideways look at Conrad. His eyes were red and puffy and I saw from this close distance he'd gained a few more white hairs sprinkled over the whole of his head. That damned girl. According to Junia's contact, Nicola had settled into her new life like some Scarlett O'Hara, irritating the hell out of the whole household, provoking them into subtle retaliation against her imperious and unreasonable demands. And Conrad was caught in the middle.

'Every team get off without problem?'

'No problem at all, sir,' I said. 'All in good spirits, a few grumbles at the cold, but I'd be worried if there weren't.'

'Good, good.'

Juno, he wanted to talk and he didn't know how to start. He really was losing his confidence.

'Is there anything you wanted to discuss?' I tried.

'Why? Do you have a train to catch?'

I stared at him. 'Not at all. I just had the impression you wanted to say something. I—'

'I'll let you know if there is,' he said curtly and stomped off.

Misery washed over me. Would we ever be able to talk without snapping or bickering?

The week after we arrived back from the exercise, I found a meeting request from Pelonia, the DJ inspector who'd handled the case against Nicola Sandbrook. Nicola Tella. Damn. I hated calling her that.

'Colonel Mitela here. How can I help you, Inspector?'

'I wanted to run something past you, ma'am, given your unique experience and connections. Could we perhaps meet outside or here at my office, if you didn't mind?'

What in Hades did she mean by 'experience and connections'? She didn't want to come here, that was obvious. Her tone was tense, but diffident, so I'd be doing her a favour.

'Sure, no problem. Or we could meet informally for some lunch, maybe? What about tomorrow, at Dania's, off the Via Nova?'

'That would be perfect. I'll see you there.'

Dania was one of my protégées; I'd given her seed capital years ago and now she had a thriving business. When she'd started up, it had been a plain bar providing good food and personal services. Unknown to almost everybody, Dania had played a pivotal role fourteen years ago in my Operation Goldlights, to defeat organised drug criminals. After that had finished, she'd relentlessly driven her business further upmarket each year and now ran an exclusive restaurant which needed at least two months to get a reservation. I never had that problem.

I arrived early and stamped my feet on the entrance mat to shake off the icy slush. Snow had fallen steadily during the night and had turned into charmless sleet. Dania greeted me warmly, with a tight hug, but appraising eyes.

'How are you, Bruna? Is it any better yet?'

'Getting there.'

Since she'd stopped colouring her hair and gained a few pounds, she'd taken on a gravitas that could intimidate the shallow and callow. She had to be in her early fifties by now.

She smiled. 'Glad to see you out of black. I've put you and your friend in one of the private rooms. Go up, there's a bottle on ice.'

Pelonia arrived promptly, in designer jeans and leather coat which revealed a cashmere sweater and silk scarf looped around her neck. No way did she look like a cop. I poured her glass of Brancadorum champagne which she sipped carefully. Dania brought up our food herself and left discreetly.

'So how can I help you, Inspector?'

'I've received a piece of information which if true is explosive.

Unfortunately, it's more likely to be malicious gossip. But—'

She stopped, glanced at me almost furtively. I had the impression she was embarrassed.

'Pelonia, you don't know me very well. If you have something to say, however trivial, I'm all ears. I work a lot on instinct. I respect others who do the same. But I react badly to time-wasters, so go.'

'Since Operation Goldlights, we've been able to keep a tight control on most of the drug trade,' she said. 'We'll never stop them all, but—'

She shrugged, eloquently, and dug into her food.

'I wasn't aware you worked in narcotics.'

'I don't. My remit is special investigation.' Ah, one of Lurio's personal hunters. I hadn't known that when we'd first met at Nicola's arrest. Unkind colleagues and the ungodly called them ferrets, but they pulled in results.

I ate in silence waiting for her.

'A piece of trash we swept up a week ago claimed he'd seen a new dealer, a foreigner. She was accompanied by another girl, whom he thought he recognised. He was seriously fried, shouting his head off, so the uniforms sent him to the public detox unit to get stabilised. I followed it up a few days later, but he'd expired. We ID'd him, I ran him, but he only had minors. Nobody claimed the body, so it went to the public crem.'

'Why your interest?'

'The *custodes* who picked him up wrote up a full report and passed it to the Senior Commander's office.' She slipped a bunch of folded A4 sheets out of her bag and slid it across the table.

I flicked through the crime report, to the doctor's piece: death by narcotic overdose, subject verbal, but incoherent, until unconsciousness shortly before death. When I read the description of events and the junkie's description of the two women on the incident form I almost had a cardiac arrest.

Pelonia looked at me steadily. 'If it hadn't been for the previous case, I'd have put it down as pure gibberish. Now I wonder.'

I read the report again. I could hardly believe it. I had no doubt it was Nicola. She had wealth and position, and had Conrad tied up in emotional barbed wire, isolated, separated from me and our children. She was extracting revenge on a daily basis. So what in Hades was she doing dealing on the street? If it was her.

Yeah, right, Carina. Like you don't know it's her.

'Okay.' I cleared my throat. 'Stepping back a bit, there're a lot of tall blonde young women around, some with criminal records, drugs included.'

'Agreed, but this one's foreign, unknown on the street,' Pelonia pushed. 'And her companion – nobody could fail to recognise Stella Apulia.'

'That's quite a leap, Inspector. And all from the ranting of a stoned junkie who's now dead.'

'I see.' Pelonia said. She stood up, reached over for the report, and said, 'Sorry to have wasted your time, Colonel.' The look she shot me was contemptuous and angry, but she quickly stifled it.

'Sit down, Pelonia. I didn't say I didn't believe you.' I sighed. 'Unfortunately, I do. I just don't want to.'

Her face relaxed.

'I understand it may be difficult, but the Senior Commander thought you should be informed.' She looked down at the table, nearly smiled, as if remembering something else he'd said. 'He also thought you might have a unique insight on the problem.'

'Ha! He did, did he?' I paused for a few moments assembling my thoughts. Pelonia would have been cleared up to a very high security level; Lurio would never have sent her my way otherwise.

'Nicola Tella lives with her father at Domus Tellarum. I haven't seen her since the trial.' I looked over Pelonia's shoulder at the wall. 'Her father appears to have separated himself from my household, so I only have hearsay about her activities. I was under the impression she was enjoying the benefits of her new-found prosperity and position. I have no idea personally about her social circle.'

I brought my gaze back to look her straight in the face. 'But if that junkie was telling the truth and Nicola Tella has contaminated her half-sister, the imperial heir, and dragged her into criminality, there's very little I won't do to bring her down.'

We promised to liaise and Pelonia left, quietly closing the door behind her. I listened to the sound of her footsteps fade down the stairs. I bowed my head into my hands. Gods. Everything was coming apart. I was just about keeping the everyday in balance: the children, the wider family stuff, business meetings, the Senate. Oh, and sometimes I grabbed some sleep. Now this. I felt like running away from it all. With Nonna gone, I had no wise counsellor, with Conrad gone, no clever, sharp and witty companion. I loved

Daniel dearly, but he was no comparison. Tears trickled between my fingers down the back of my hands. This was so lame. I thought I'd stopped crying.

My phone pinged – a routine check – but it pulled me out of my self-pity. I had to get a grip. This was no ordinary danger. The source was inside and had not only split our family, but also now threatened the state. I was a Praetorian, for Jupiter's sake. I had to get off my butt and do something about it.

I left Dania's, took a taxi to the staff entrance of the palace. Flashing my ID at the guard detail on duty, I made my way through the admin area, upstairs into the private family quarters. Another guard stood there solemn-faced and checked me in. Silvia's private secretary materialised after a few minutes and looked a little disconcerted to see me, but he recovered quickly. He ushered me into an alcove with blue velvet easy chairs and a coffee table. After ten minutes I stood up to greet my cousin. And fellow mother. She was frowning.

'Carina? Is something wrong?'

She hovered by the double doors and didn't come forward immediately. I bowed and she eventually moved into the room. In response to her outstretched hand, I sat down again. She fidgeted; I guessed I'd interrupted something.

'Silvia, I apologise for butting in but I have just received some disturbing information.'

'Yes?'

'How much has Stella been around Nicola Sandbrook, I mean, Tella?'

She looked baffled. 'What do you mean?'

'Exactly that.'

'Would you care to elaborate?' Her tone was distinctly frosty.

'It may be nothing, but the DJ have reported a woman resembling Tella making what looked like a drugs deal down in the Septarium area.' Not a pleasant place. I doubted, and hoped, Silvia had ever been there.

'And how does that concern me?'

'She had a companion whom the informant recognised instantly. He couldn't fail to, I guess. Stella.'

'Impossible.'

I shrugged.

She stood up and disappeared though the door. After a few

minutes, she returned and focused on me like a scientist on an exciting new specimen.

'Details, please.'

I ran through the report. 'It's inconclusive, but enough to cause the head of the Urban Cohorts to send in a special investigator.'

'Very well. I'll have a word with Stella. Thank you for bringing this to my attention.'

I knew I was dismissed, but I couldn't leave it there.

'Would you mind not doing that?'

'Why ever not?'

'Because if Nicola Tella has had the face to drag the imperial heir into the dirt, I want the chance to nail her hide to the floor and stomp all over it.'

'Oh. I see. But I won't have Stella put in danger, in any way.' She sighed. 'I know she can be difficult. I was as disappointed as Conrad when she didn't pursue her career in the PGSF. She's been at a loose end ever since. Yes, she does some public appearances if she has to, but she's not really interested in any of my charities or foundations, nor in shadowing me.'

Silvia looked away. She was a hard-working decisive leader. Deprived of the luxuries of security and leisure of her early life, she'd had to grow up quickly in the aftermath of the wreckage left by Caius Tellus's dictatorship.

'I don't know what she wants, Carina. I thought she might like to go to the university – she's always got her head in a book – but she gave that up after a semester. She goes along with things, she's pliable despite the sullenness but she's got no staying power.'

She turned back to me, with a carefully bright smile. 'Well, that's my problem. How dangerous is this?'

'Have you met Nicola Tella?'

She shook her head.

'Look, Silvia, will you trust me on this?'

'You've only saved my life and my country twice, so I think I can cut you a little slack.'

I stared at her. How could she joke in this situation? I could never be so strong. No, it was gallows humour, a kind of protective irony.

I reminded her about Allegra's trial and gave her a summary of Michael's input. But when I repeated what Quintus had said, she shuddered.

'But what's Conradus doing about her? Surely he can see through her?'

'Have you seen him recently?'

'Not since after Allegra's trial. He came to eat with us one evening. Oh, Juno, Stella knows all about the trial. Conradus was very open about his anger at this "Zenia". Of course, he didn't know who Zenia was at the time. He wasn't too happy either that night at Stella giving up on the PGSF and he struggled to be understanding about it.'

'Before she died, Aurelia thought he might be going through some sort of emotional crisis. Something reaching back into his own childhood that was triggered by guilt over Nicola.' I threw my hands up in the air in exasperation. 'Nicola was not deprived as she likes to claim. Sure, she didn't have a wealthy background, but her mother had a good job teaching.'

'How do you know that?' Silvia asked.

'I'm an intelligence officer, right?' I grinned.

'Okay, silly question.' She smiled back.

I stretched and placed my hand on hers. 'I tried once to tackle Conradus openly about Nicola and he shut me out. Maybe I was a little clumsy. When Nicola was caught at the border and arrested, it caused a huge breach between us. I thought he'd understand why I pressed charges. She tried to kill our daughter, for Juno's sake! Any normal father would have been one hundred per cent behind Allegra and me.'

I stopped to swallow the bitter taste in my mouth.

'For some reason he's eaten up with guilt. Nicola's playing it for all it's worth. Now I'm sure she's targeting Stella. This time, I'm going to use her own tricks against her. But I need to take it very carefully.'

'We can put a stop to this easily. I'll have Conradus relieved of duty, pending investigation.'

Sometimes I wondered where Silvia got these autocratic ideas. Then I remembered she was descended from both the Julii and the Flavians, both ruthless clans.

'Um, you can't – it's a Senate-confirmed post and they re-confirmed after his accident. Unless he's convicted of a major felony or gross dereliction, you're stuck.'

She looked like she'd drunk a whole amphora of bitter *garum*. She shook my hand off, got up and went to savage a flower in the arrangement on the side table. The red petals fell in an untidy heap on the floor.

'Yes, I know. I was being self-indulgent. Much easier a couple of hundred years ago.' She shrugged. 'So what do you suggest?'

'I'm going to set up surveillance on her and get some solid proof we can use in the courtroom.'

'Can you do that without Conradus knowing?'

'I have to persuade him. It would be so much better if it was out in the open, but if I can't, I have, er, private resources, outside the PGSF.'

She waited for me to explain, but I didn't.

'Could you bear to invite Nicola here,' I continued, 'and let me know what you think?'

'You want me to be one of your operatives?'

Gods. I swallowed. That was exactly what I was asking. My face must have said it all as she laughed.

'Don't look so worried. Of course I will. Who doesn't want to be James Bond?'

'Yes, well, it's not like that really.'

'I know. I was only teasing.'

Her face became serious again. 'You'll watch over my Stella, won't you?'

'You know I will.'

XIII

I sat in the gloom that evening, nursing a small brandy. I'd taken to using Nonna's special glass, an exquisite red Hungarian crystal tumbler, a gift from an admirer, she'd said. Apart from my grandfather, Euralbius, she'd rarely mentioned anybody else in that way. It was only when Sertorius opened and read her will in front of the witnesses and handed me a large sealed envelope with a pompous flourish that I'd discovered she'd been held in the grip of a 'grand passion' for nearly forty years.

They'd met in Berlin, when she was in her twenties, then later in Vienna when she was in exile during the rebellion. He came back to Roma Nova with her but couldn't settle. He left, but they met from time to time and he always gave her a red rose to bring back. She'd kept and pressed every one. The colour photo tucked inside the letter showed a younger, black-haired version of the man with Calavia at the funeral – the man who had thrown the red rose on Aurelia's pyre.

I needed to fix a time with Calavia for a serious talk about this. Or maybe I should just let it go. My own 'grand passion' wasn't burning so bright at present.

I stared into the glass trying not to see her.

A cough interrupted me. Junia stood there, el-pad in hand.

'Sorry, Junia, I was in the clouds. Sit with me, please. What is it?'

'Saturnalia. I need to talk to you about it.'

Gods, no way could I think of partying. But I guessed I needed to – the household would expect it. We could avoid the public ritual on 17 December; that was mostly for the priests and enough family council members would go to represent us. But normally the house would be overrun with noise, people, stupid but fun dares, overeating, games, theatricals and stand-up of dubious taste, arguments, falling in lust, laughter and progressive drunkenness.

But gift-giving on Sigillaria, a few days, later usually balanced up any ruffled sensibilities. Conrad, Helena, Daniel and I usually took part in full. Last year, Daniel had climbed onto the roof and abseiled down through the bulls-eye, the *oculus*; wearing a garish tunic, conifer garland round his head, he'd sung his mind out to the booming music, jumped the last few metres to the ground and run up to Aurelia and presented her with a white rose. It sounded so stupid now, but the shouts, catcalls, laughter and applause had sealed the evening.

'Countess?'

I produced a bright smile. 'What's the programme this year?'

'Galienus and I called a staff meeting and we agreed it would be inappropriate to host the usual celebrations. Rather—'

'But—'

'Rather than the boisterous week here, we are proposing a shared meal on the 17th, family and household together in the atrium, everybody helping. We'd have the usual pork roast, and gifts afterwards. No *princeps*, no gambling, and no theatricals.'

'Good grief, Junia, they'll go on strike. At least let them have music and a card-playing book.'

'We'll allow something in the domestic hall, but I think you need peace more than anything.' She looked down at her el-pad, her face set. After a moment or two, she looked up, made a moue, stood up and went.

How she managed to excise ninety per cent of Saturnalia, I'll never know, but she did. It passed smoothly, pleasantly even, but it was dull. I know Daniel and Helena snuck downstairs one night for dancing and an evening show.

The next time I saw Silvia was at her private fifty-fifth birthday party. Grouped around her under the rose silk gazebo set up in the cavernous palace atrium, we looked on as sixteen-year-old Hallienia Apulia solemnly proposed the toast for her mother. Silvia leaned over to give Hallie a kiss of thanks on each cheek. A wide smile burst across Hallie's lips. She'd received her emancipation and officially left childhood behind only six months before, but she was still kid enough to grin at her mother.

The ceremony finished, servers were quick to circulate with glasses of champagne amongst the hundred or so family and friends. Silvia was caught up immediately by a couple of senator cousins.

I stood at the side, sipping from my glass while Hallie and Allegra pored over the table of gifts that people had brought for Silvia. In the noise of people talking and laughing, I felt rather than saw

Conrad approaching. He gave me a brief nod, not even attempting to give me a kiss, even on the cheek. He stood behind the girls gazing at them as if willing them into awareness of his presence, but they ignored us as only teenagers can. I coughed, Hallie looked up, a little guiltily. She stepped back, turned to Conrad, raised her brown eyes to his face and smiled.

'Hello, Dad. Brilliant you're here. Mama will be really pleased.'

'Of course I'd be here, silly.' He stroked her hair, pushing a stray brown lock back behind her ear, but he looked hurt that she'd doubted him.

'Yes, of course,' she replied, a little flustered. 'Only I thought you might be busy with—'

'Yes?'

'Other things.' She flushed red. 'Oh, there's Marcus Calavius. I must go and talk to him. Catch you later.' And she skipped off towards a dark-haired young man around twenty, grinning across the room and waving at her.

'Hmph. Calavius. Not sure about that,' he said almost as an aside.

'Good family, one of the Twelve, with a sound history,' I said.

'Not really good enough for her.'

'Keep it cool, Dad,' Allegra said in a bored voice, 'it's not as if she's sleeping with him yet.'

I somehow kept my lips clamped as his eyes bulged and he swung around to glare at Allegra.

'What in Hades is that supposed to mean?'

'Like I said, she's not slee—'

'Yes, I heard you, Allegra. How long has this been going on?'

She shrugged. 'A few months. Aunt Silvia's got it, so don't worry.' She took a deliberate breath. 'Well, Hallie said you haven't been around at the palace, so you won't have seen him.'

Allegra stole a glance up at her father and said nothing further. Good call – he looked murderous. She took off, looking for better company.

'I suppose you knew,' he accused.

'No, I didn't. I've been a little too occupied recently to keep up with teenage crushes. Like Allegra says, it's Silvia's affair.'

'Silvia might have discussed it with me.'

'Why? You weren't there, I understand, so she's dealing with it.'

He said nothing. I watched the other guests, laughing, drinking, eating canapés, greeting and gossiping, as if they were separated from us by an impenetrable wall of glass.

'And where's Stella?' I asked. 'She should have been here for her mother's birthday.'

His furtive expression rang alarm bells.

'Conrad, where is she?'

'She's... she's got another appointment, I understand.'

'You're kidding me. More important than this?'

'She has her own life now. I can't tell her what to do.'

I couldn't help myself. I really couldn't.

'No, you seem to be capable of only doing what you're told these days.'

'So what happened after he flounced off?'

Silvia and I were sitting by ourselves in her not very comfortable designer chairs on the glazed terrace overlooking the private garden. Subtle lights cast cream arcs over statues and the fountain jets threw living light into its circular pool. Only the distant sounds of teenage giggling and shouting invaded our private talk.

'That was it – I didn't see him after that.'

'Well,' she said, 'I think there's something going on under the surface but he just seems distracted, nothing more. Are you sure it's that serious?'

'I don't know, Silvia, maybe I've got it all wrong and we're just going through a bad patch. It started in London with that letter and has been getting worse ever since. But even if it's personal, it shouldn't be clouding his judgement on professional matters. Maybe he was more affected by his accident than we thought.'

She said nothing immediately, but her eyes narrowed slightly as if looking into the far distance. Outside, frost was starting to coat the rose bushes stretching away from us in two formal beds. Like Apollodorus, my old friend and enemy, Silvia loved her roses. Bobbing between individual plants, she could be found in the rose beds, secateurs in hand, followed by an anxious gardener too polite to say anything. Apollodorus had crossed in Charon's ferry six years ago after a traitor's death. I shut that door firmly.

Silvia pulled a quick tight smile, glanced up at the open door leading back to the atrium, stood up and closed it. Settled back in her chair, but still staring through the glass, she said, 'I met Nicola Tella at the end of last week. You're right. Completely right. She could be Caius's twin.'

She pulled her gaze back from the far distance to my face.

'You don't forget somebody like Caius Tellus. The Tellae were one of the Twelve, some illustrious, some not, mostly solid service to the state. That last time I saw him before the rebellion, he was talking to my mother. I was Hallie's age. It was some formal event. I remember my dress – it was new, green silk with gold shot through and a gold *stola*. He smiled down at me. I was frightened. He was overpowering in an uncomfortable way. He stroked my arm. I remember that vividly. I shivered and he smiled at me knowing exactly how revolted I was. He made my mother nervous – she was tongue-tied in talking to him. For Olympus' sake, she was no amateur rhetorician. He was proposing an alliance between our families. I didn't know whether it was her or me he had his sights on.'

She shuddered.

'I found my mother crying one evening later that week. It was as she waited for the councillors to arrive during the night of the fire. She stopped when she saw me. I think she knew what was coming. She hugged me close and told me to hold true. That evening, Aurelia ordered the Praetorian Guard commander to take me away, to escape. Julian stayed and helped hold them off. They killed him. I remember being made to run through the street, car doors opening and shutting, the grim silence of the guards. We crawled through farmyards, back into cars and hiked up the Geminae and through the northern passes to cross the border.'

'I never saw my mother again. I lived in Vienna for eighteen months, guarded twenty-four seven by PGSF who'd chosen exile over serving Caius.'

She gave a bitter little smile but there was no humour in her eyes.

'They thought he'd try and snatch me. They wanted me to go to America for safety, but I refused. I knew I had to stay near. Volusenia the Younger, the senior Praetorian, was tough and strict – I was terrified of her. But she was unbelievably kind when she told me my mother was dead. The official story was that she'd committed suicide, but nobody believed it. Later, the forensics proved she'd been murdered. Aurelia and Volusenia kept me from going insane as I was forced to grow up so fast. I was only sixteen.'

She paused and swallowed.

'I saw Caius on the television, parading round as First Consul. I felt so much hatred for him. It was like a tight lead lump in my heart. I vowed I'd get even. I wanted to kill him, but didn't know how.'

'When I came back to Roma Nova, everything was broken, people desperate and fearful. We had no food, the hospitals were empty, the power stations were off line, no fuel, looters were rampant. The old police service, the *vigiles*, was enforcing its own kind of law. But the Praetorians stayed loyal. They re-imposed order and the PGSF led by Aurelia hunted Caius Tellus down.'

She stood up and walked to the balustrade. She turned to face me, her figure outlined in the red and amber of the setting sun. Her voice was hard as she finished her story.

'They brought him in to me. He stood there arrogant and indifferent. He couldn't see that what he'd done was so wrong. Even at his trial, he managed to convince one of the judges he'd been treated unfairly. Cruel, manipulative bastard is a soft and tender description of Caius Tellus.' She turned away, her head bowed. Rare tears running down her face glistened in the dying light.

'He was a traitor, but more than that he killed my mother. He deserved his execution.'

XIV

The next morning, I marched along the second floor corridor, determined to see Conrad. In my heart and gut, I knew it wasn't going to be any good given the way things stood between us, but I had to try. Damn Nicola to Hades. Maybe I was too involved, but as a Praetorian I had to do my duty however uncomfortable. Silvia's story had confirmed that Nicola was no longer a private pain in the ass; she was a threat to the imperial family. I knew it instinctively, but had no proof. I had to try to persuade Conrad to authorise an investigation. He could step back and let Sepunia and her intelligence department run it. In fact, it might not be the world's worst idea for me to brief her.

Rusonia wasn't guarding the entrance for once. What had happened? World revolution? I knocked and hearing 'Come', pushed the door open, went in, saluted and waited.

'Oh, it's you,' he said. 'What do you want?'

He flicked his fingers towards the chair on the other side of his desk.

I sat and folded the fingers of my right hand around the left so my hands didn't fidget in my nervousness.

'Well?'

'A new threat has been identified and needs to be investigated,' I started.

'Really? I may be mistaken, but the last time I looked we had an intelligence department for that. What's the interest of Training?'

I ignored the sarcasm. 'It's the duty of all PGSF personnel to be constantly on the watch for potential problems and report them. One of your reform principles, if I remember. Sir.' I added.

'Oh, very well. Write it up and circulate it in the usual way,' he said and reached for a folder.

No way was I going to be dismissed like this. And why didn't he want to know what the threat was? Normally he'd be demanding details and listening with laser-like attention.

'I don't think that's advisable in this case,' I persisted.

'And why is that?'

I took a mental breath and let the words fire out.

'The DJ has reported a sighting of Nicola Tella dealing drugs and involving Stella Apulia.'

His eyes blazed. He struck his desk with both fists.

'Jupiter's balls! What in Hades are you trying to say?' he bellowed.

He thrust his head towards me, challenging me to continue. A stab of fear ran through me. I let it ground itself and sat back against the soft pad on the back of the chair.

'Exactly what I said.' I stared straight at him and he eventually dropped his eyes. After his face had lost the red flush, I gave him the details of Pelonia's report. 'It's inconclusive overall, but a definite ID of Stella. Given her status, it comes within our remit.'

'Who else knows about this charming little tale?'

'Stella's mother.'

'You went running to Silvia on the strength of some junkie's ravings? How bloody stupid are you?'

'How blind are you? Silvia agrees with me, your precious Nicola is unequivocally a threat. Don't you get it, Conrad? Silvia figures she's Caius all over again.'

He blenched, gripped the edges of his desk so tightly I thought it was going to cut off the blood supply to his fingers. Sweat broke out on his forehead, his lips took on a blue tinge. I leapt around the desk and gripped his arms. Gods! He was having a heart attack.

'Conrad.' No reaction. 'Conrad.' I eased him back down into his chair. I reached immediately for the desk commset to call the medics, but although speechless, he waved me away with an abrupt gesture. After a few breaths, he threw such a savage glare at me that I dropped my hands as if I'd been shocked by a thousand volts.

His colour was gradually coming back. I roused myself and poured him a glass of water which he grabbed and drank. Over the rim, he glared at me.

'You keep your damned nose out of it. Leave it to the scarabs. They can waste their time on it.'

'Conrad, I know you're upset but don't you think we should maybe have at least a preliminary look? Stella *is* the imperial heir, as well as your daughter.'

'I'm perfectly aware of that. I don't need lectures from my juniors.'

His eyes sunken in their sockets darted around the room. They glinted like he had a fever. He was unaware or he didn't care that he was letting his fingers drum on the desk. He was more than sore at me – he was coming unglued.

The muscles on his face drooped and he looked exhausted. I wanted nothing more than to protect him from all this horrifying business. Sure, Nicola was the trigger, but the demons chasing him since his brutalised childhood with Caius needed flushing out and defeating; he needed rest and safety more than anything in the world. I loved him. I would never stop, but he was making my working life a misery and, much worse, destroying our marriage.

He emerged from his stasis after a few minutes. His face settled back into neutral as if an exterior shell had re-formed over it. I could still see some inner tension from the hard lines sloping from his mouth to his nose.

He turned to me and said in a bone-cold voice, 'I've given you a direct order. This is a formal warning. If I find out you've been investigating, I'll have your hide.'

I was calm as I walked back to my office, numb even. His order was completely against logic and reason. Or was it me being unreasonable? Nobody else had mentioned anything to me about his behaviour. But would they have? For all the openness I practised and encouraged in my team, I doubted any of the more traditional members of the PGSF would have dreamed of reporting such a thing about a superior.

Disobeying a direct order carried a severe penalty though – several years in the central military prison. I broke out in a sweat when I thought about it. I took several deep breaths. I'd risk my chances in a court martial.

I hustled paper, schedules, asset packages. I typed, chewed my pen, approved, signed and stamped until my eyes blurred. I was scheduled to carry out performance and appraisal reviews on the senior staff, but I delegated most to newly promoted Major Petrus Sergius and switched Lucy in as his exec. By seven that evening, I'd freed up significant slices of time in my week, but I didn't mark it up on the internal calendar. Satisfied at my victory over time, but depressed about the subterfuge, I packed a few clothes into a small duffle, collected some equipment from the field room and set off into the city.

★

I munched some sour olives and nuts with the over-tart dry white I was nursing at the bar in Via Cloelia. Weak lights hung above the length of the black counter, making it appear more intimate and sophisticated than it really was. A crowd of noisy office workers in one corner were halfway to the stupid level. The more dubious patrons eyed them with a knowing and cynical air, half-resentful, but half working out how much they could rip them off for with offers of gambling or some other action. In amongst them was a mix of ages, more men than women.

I'd fended off one proposition, a total slimeball, a tourist who'd mistaken me for a working girl. Okay, the short black leather skirt revealed a lot of leg, but my dark top and black jacket weren't typical sex worker uniform. I was flirting with a much cuter guy, self-assured and keen to imply he knew where the action was. I was about to pursue this subject when his smile turned into a line of pain, his eyes bulged and he fell out of my sightline.

A tall, burly figure with a humourless smile on his round face had stretched his hand around my companion's neck, pulled him off his bar stool and thrust him back into the crowd. Another one slid in behind me. I was trapped.

'What took you so long?' I asked.

He laughed. 'Might have known it was you.' His eyes slid over me. 'I didn't think a new tart would have the temerity to wriggle her arse in here without asking. What do you want?'

'To talk to you, Philippus.'

He nodded, turned his back, and headed for a door at the rear. His companion grabbed my arm like I was a piece of meat to be bagged and weighed and pushed me in front of him. I nearly laughed when I saw the office I was herded into; it was a crude imitation of the one I'd run Goldlights from.

I shook the heavy's hand off and sat down in the chair on the opposite side of the table to Philippus, crossed one booted leg over the other and waited. Philippus dismissed his companion with a flick of his fingers.

'So what are you doing here?'

His round eyes narrowed and the permanent smile looked a little under duress. Both hands lay peacefully on the arms of his chair, but the pinkie on his left hand tapped the plastic, driven by a motor independent from the rest of the system. I could understand it; the last time we'd met, we'd both been on the point of having our heads blown off. In the end we'd only been spattered with the bad guy's warm blood and brains when a PGSF marksman had taken him out.

'Not running an operation against you,' I said.

The pinkie stopped.

'What then?'

'Information first and perhaps your help.'

'Go on.'

'I'm looking for a new dealer, a young woman, blonde, tall. A foreigner. She's been spotted once, but by chance. She's as wily as all Hades, so I don't think it'll be easy.'

'You never did easy, did you?' He grinned, a proper relaxed all-teeth, laughing-eyes Philippus grin.

'No point.' I chuckled back at him.

'Anything else?'

'She's ex-special forces, a surveillance and reconnaissance specialist.'

'Oh, good.'

He lifted his hand, inserted the nail of his thumb under the nail of his once over-active pinkie. His sleeve fell back and I saw he still wore the silver wrist torc with chased myrtle leaves I'd given him seven years ago. He followed my gaze and quickly dropped his hand.

'Philippus, can I ask you something personal?'

He didn't answer, but his expression tightened.

'I was surprised to discover you here. Why aren't you still working at the Foundation?'

He shrugged. 'It went so clean I was out of a job. Hermina's running it now, very corporate and respectable. She wears suits and talks goal-orientation, cost balancing and strategic planning.' He snorted. 'I didn't want to end up as her glorified security guard.'

I'd noticed my shares in the Foundation accumulating considerable value, especially in the last two years, but hadn't looked at the detail. When I'd set up the Pulcheria Foundation nearly fourteen years ago, it had been as part of a cover for what became Operation Goldlights, the biggest drugs sting ever. I'd managed to save it and throughout the years it had turned from a tightly private organisation with criminal origins into an efficient, and legitimate, services company. I didn't know Hermina, one of the other original associates, had the entrepreneur gene in her. Efficient, sure, but she'd been pretty deferential at the time.

'I hadn't spent much of my pay-off from you, so I used it to buy this place. It turns a good profit, especially with tourists who want to flirt with what they think is the dark side.'

I ignored the challenge in his eyes; no way did I want to know how his profit was turned.

'Glad to see Apollodorus's training wasn't entirely wasted.'

His fingers curled around the chair arms, then relaxed. He chuckled. 'Don't try and needle me, Pulcheria. I know your—'

He'd said it. The name hung between us.

'Why did you come back dressed in those clothes?'

My turn to shrug. A retreat into my second skin? A desperate search for the memory of my undercover criminal persona as Pulcheria? Who knew?

All we could hear for a few minutes were snatches of music, clinking of glass and muffled footsteps the other side of the door. He needed to get the soundproofing improved, I thought idly.

'Philippus.' I stretched out my arm across the table and flexed the fingertips of my open hand in invitation. 'I need your help.'

'You've got it, you know that. But why? You've got the whole PGSF at your beck and call.'

'It's a little complicated,' I said.

He smirked. 'They haven't thrown you out, have they?'

'Of course not! What a thing to say.'

'So what are you doing? Freelancing?'

I kept my gaze steady, but didn't say anything.

A few minutes went past. Philippus rolled his eyes.

'No wonder Apollodorus called you stubborn. I give up.'

'Thank you, Philippus.'

'Huh. Don't make me live to regret it.'

He delivered. Within three days, I had a good lead. Nevertheless, I took additional precautions and borrowed one of Philippus's people to help the stakeout. We'd set up two hours before the supposed meet in an empty apartment in the Septarium. Perfectly named; little runnels of indeterminate humanity oozed furtively around, filling up the fissures between the shabby buildings. Our apartment was a plain box, musty with damp patches at the top of the walls near the metal framed windows. Now it smelled of instant coffee and salami.

Right on schedule, a shadow figure shuffled along the side of the building in front of us and detached itself, coming into the early evening half-light. I reckoned male, between eighteen and mid twenties. He looked slowly up and down the street that crossed his. Satisfied, he retreated down the street to just behind the corner out of the freezing wind and started playing with a cell phone. We remained statue still. Even a tiny movement could betray a watcher's presence. And we were trying to catch an expert.

A second figure approached. Gods! My hand almost leapt up to my mouth by instinct. She walked exactly like Conrad – a big-cat lope. Surely she would have disguised it. Basic field craft. Was she that confident? I swallowed hard, my eyes busy working through the telescopic lenses. At least she was alone. She wore a hooded sweater, but I could see wisps of dark blonde hair. I could only see part of her face, but the hazel eyes were unmistakeable.

She made a quarter turn, a discreet hand gesture and a slim, brown-haired figure joined her.

Shit.

The shorter girl took an envelope out of her light duffle and handed it over to the first figure and received a square package in return which she stuffed into the bag. She cast an anxious look up to the older girl, who nodded curtly and gestured her back. The man took off back up the street he'd come from and vanished behind the next block. The taller woman grabbed the arm of the younger one and they hurried off down the opposite street, avoiding retracing their steps. Better, Nicola. Much better.

I remained immobile, not just from good practice, but from shock and anger. That bitch had made Stella effect the trade. Clever. If they were being watched by law officers, Nicola couldn't be charged. Damn her to Tartarus.

'Shall I stop recording?'

The voice broke into my consciousness.

'Yes...yes. Thanks.'

I stepped back into the room and took my telescopic eyeglasses off, blinking and pinching my nose.

Philippus' man tapped at the keyboard and downloaded the sequence to my cell phone. I shoved it into my jeans pocket.

'I've deleted it from the camera as instructed.' He shot me a speculative look as he held the tiny camcorder up for me to check the memory display showed empty. We waited another half hour, drinking lukewarm coffee and exchanging inanities before moving off, he ten minutes before me.

I had proof now. Not as solid as I'd liked but enough to start a formal investigation, whatever Conrad said. Then I'd nail her ass.

XV

'Where in Hades have you been?'

I was so wrapped up in planning my next step that I ran straight into Conrad. His hands caught me and held me firmly away from him. His eyes bored into mine. I shook my head to clear it.

'Sorry?'

'You should be. I thought I'd drop in on the appraisal interviews this afternoon and you were missing. Major Sergius was handling it well, but you should have been there.'

How dared he attack me like this? I was a senior autonomous rank, head of my department, a department that had turned in the highest results index three weeks running.

'Are you telling me how to do my job? How to delegate to my staff?'

I very nearly told him what dirty work his two oldest daughters had been up to, but I canned it. I'd learnt the bitter lesson. He could wait until I reported it through the proper channels he so loved.

'Where have you been? And what are you doing in civvies?'

'Strangely enough, I do have a few other things to do in my life. For which I have a dispensation, as you well know.'

'You need to make up your mind where your duty lies.'

I glanced up and down the empty cream corridor.

'If you think I need lessons in duty, you can go screw yourself,' I hissed at him. Before he could say anything else, I turned my back on him and stomped off to my office.

I knew my nerves were raw and I was sick about the whole Nicola business, but I should have kept my temper on its leash. Bad though things were between us personally, he was my commanding officer. I chewed my lip, bent a paperclip into impossible shapes and scribbled stupid patterns on my deskpad as I calmed myself down. As I glanced at my screen to check my mails, my commset buzzed: report to the senior legate, stat.

I reached Conrad's outer office just as the inner door opened and Sepunia, the head of intelligence, came out, chuckling at something. I heard Conrad's rich, full laugh from inside before the door closed. My heart lifted. I exchanged smiles with Sepunia before she hurried off.

Conrad's assistant, Rusonia, sat impassively at her desk. She gave me a long look and for a moment, I thought she was going to say something. She glanced away, opened her mouth, but closed it like she'd decided not to release any words. I waited but all she did was nod at me to go in. Conrad was pretending to look at his screen. The fingers on his left hand were tapping the leather surface of his desk, causing his gold signet ring to cast shiny dancing reflections against the side display cabinet. He didn't invite me to sit down.

'I wish to apologise for my rudeness earlier, sir,' I said stiffly.

He frowned at me.

'I know what you were doing this afternoon.'

Crap! How? No, he was on a fishing trip.

'You're wondering how, aren't you?'

No way was I going to give him the satisfaction. I said nothing.

'You were running a surveillance operation, specifically against my orders.'

It hovered there between us like an unmentionable disease.

'You're not an easy mark, so I used the only person possibly capable of following you undetected. He saw everything you did, but couldn't see who you were watching. You're not Operations anymore, so this will be treated as a full disciplinary. I want a complete report on my desk tomorrow morning, but you will turn over your recording to me now.'

He stretched his arm out, the fingers on his hand beckoned imperiously.

I was paralysed. I was going to throw up. The unfairness of it hit me like a wrecking ball demolishing a building.

'Don't pretend you didn't make a recording. Come along, hand it over. Unless you want the indignity of a full body search.'

His eyes were cold and hard in a face of tense muscles. He looked completely stressed out. What kind of strain was he under to switch from laughing a little too heartily with Sepunia one minute to freezing me out the next?

I battled through the numbness and misery to reach into my pocket and placed my phone on his desk, bypassing his hand. He played the sequence. Not the hint of a reaction.

'You're on suspension. Immediate.' He pointed at his desktop. 'Badge.'

I didn't move.

'Now.'

I unclipped the badge from my waistband and plunked it on the edge of the desktop. I could hardly drag my eyes from the crowned gold eagle raised away from the shield. I'd worn it for fifteen years. It symbolised my adult life's work.

I hovered there in front of his desk. I didn't know what to do next. He looked down at a folder on his desk like he was studying it. He even turned a page, completely ignoring me. I didn't move.

When he looked up with an eyebrow raised, rage boiled up in me. The paralysis that had gripped my mind dissolved.

'Keep it. I resign.'

I bent over the desk so my face was millimetres from his.

'And you can go to Hades with that junkie tart of a daughter. If I see either of you again, I'll kick both your butts back there.'

'You're drunk.'

'Yeah. And?'

Two Helenas swam in front of me and the atrium seemed unsteady. Did we have earthquakes? I couldn't remember. Everything was a little fuzzy, but fine now. Why had I been so mad? Oh, yeah, I'd told Conrad to screw himself and his job. I giggled. Now the Helenas were frowning at me.

'Come on, Carina.' They yanked me up, I thought rudely, and pulled me along the swaying passageways into my apartment. I fell on to the bed and they started pulling clothes off me. I giggled. Two Junias appeared. Why was that cup steaming? Was it on fire? I must have a strict word with her about the dangers of fire. More pulling into the bathroom. That's right. Must brush teeth before bed. Why was I sitting in the shower?

Gods! Aaah! I was drowning.

I woke up. I was in bed. The Junias were making me drink something warm. I pushed them away, but they must have dodged. Crafty!

Head buzzing. Going to sleep now.

The thirst woke me. My head was spinning as I searched for water. I leaned over to throw up, but I didn't. My head was falling off. A deep sadness washed over me and I wept.

'Here, drink this.' Junia's voice. The smell of ginger and malt.

I gulped the delicious drink down. Nectar. A sharp pinch in my upper arm as she gave me a shot. I fell asleep again.

The next time I woke it was daytime. The drapes were half drawn back. I reached over for the glass of water in front of the clock. Gods. Half one! I groaned. My back and legs were stiff and trembly. I hardly had the strength to press the housecom screen. Ten minutes later, Junia came through the door with a plate of sandwiches and, thank the gods, a workman's mug of strong tea.

She pulled up a chair, watched me eat and waited.

'Bad?' I said between mouthfuls.

'I've seen you worse.'

Yeah, fourteen years ago when I'd gone off the rails after I'd thrown Conrad out for deceiving me.

'I apologise, Junia. I didn't want to cause you such trouble.'

'Please, don't worry, lady. It's finished.'

'Yes, this time I really think it is.'

I turned my head away and sniffed.

I apologised to Helena. She shrugged it off.

'Hey, not a problem. Want to tell me about it?'

'Well, I don't have to go into work anymore.'

Her eyes widened, 'What?'

'I quit.'

'You are joking? Aren't you?

'No. I did.' I took her hand, but couldn't look her in the face. 'It became unbearable. He's become vindictive. No, that's the wrong word. It's as if he can't help himself.'

'Making excuses for him, now?'

'Not really. I think he's losing it. You know, an emotional breakdown.'

'What? Going off his head? Conradus?' She shook her head. 'Not possible.'

'Helena, he's changed so much. It's not natural. He's cut off, like withdrawn from everything.'

'Well, I haven't seen him for ages.' She fastened her eyes on me. 'So why did you quit? I mean what triggered it?'

'I can't tell you the details, but I want you to ensure that none of the children has any contact with Nicola Tella—'

'Juno, no!'

'Or Stella Apulia.'

★

Swimming had always been my retreat. As I glided up and down the pool in the basement, I attempted to settle my thoughts. Firstly, I had to see Silvia; there was a conversation I really didn't want to have, but it had to be done. As head of the senior of the Twelve Families, I reckoned I could throw my weight around enough to fix an appointment with her at short notice.

I couldn't march into the palace any longer unchallenged like any PGSF officer. That privilege had gone. I hadn't worked through that yet in my head. It wasn't as if I didn't have enough to do; the family, the businesses, let alone the children. At least I'd have more time to spend with them now. But my life would lose a whole dimension; the spark of the chase, stopping the bad guys, the privilege of serving, of making a difference. Worst of all, there was no doubt at all that I'd lost Conrad, literally the other half of my mind and body, my heart and soul.

I drove myself on for countless more lengths but gave up when my legs shook with exhaustion. In the hot shower afterwards I remembered the times we'd played, laughed, made love under the falling heat. I know I sobbed, but the salt tears mingled with the shower and washed down the drain in one flow.

Allegra and Helena were quiet at supper, Helena knowing and Allegra sensing my distress. I gave Allegra the short version. She stood up, wound her arms around my shoulders and hugged me. I laid my head against her and squeezed her hand.

'On a more positive note,' I said, 'I'll be able to get a bit more involved with your school activities and maybe we can have more girl-time together.'

She looked at me, love, tact and dread fighting it out. Her eyes betrayed her internal wince.

'Ah, no. Sorry,' I said. 'Fifteen out of ten for stupid.'

'Mama, don't. Of course, I'd like that. A lot.'

'No, don't you, Allegra. Sorry, I'm a little rusty—.'

'For Juno's sake, stop acting like two tarts in a soap opera,' Helena interrupted. She held her wineglass out in Allegra's direction 'Give me a top-up, Allegra, before I choke on all this emotion.'

After dinner, I passed a quiet half-hour alone in the atrium, thinking of nothing in particular, glancing through the paper without reading it. I folded it, laid it on the coffee table and was depressed to find I was considering an early night when Junia's son, Macro, interrupted me. Was I at home to a Senior Centurion Marcus Flavius from the Praetorian Guard? I considered refusing to see him, but that would have been truly petty.

'Show him into the small back study, please, Macro.'

Macro looked surprised, but bowed and went off.

I made Flavius wait a full ten minutes. I kept looking at my watch, not allowing myself to go before then. This was childish, but I was taking my small revenge.

I crossed the atrium and entered the narrow corridor. At the end, I took a deep breath, drew myself up and grasped the brass door handle. The back study had a desk and chairs, a bureau but not a lot else. Flavius jumped up as I entered. We stared at each other for several minutes. I made damn sure he broke first.

He cleared his throat. 'I brought a couple of boxes with your stuff.'

'I'm surprised internal security let you.'

He said nothing.

'Oh, I suppose they ransacked everything first. Nice.'

A painful silence hung there, refusing to relent.

'I see it was a mistake to come here,' he said. 'I'll go.'

'Why *did* you come?'

'To see if you were okay.'

'I'm okay. Satisfied?'

He looked away, staring at the plain wall. His fingers kept flipping his car key shaft open and shut.

'Why did you do it, Flav?'

'He made it a formal order. He even printed it out and signed it. I can't remember when I last had a hard copy order.' Flavius paused. 'He knew I was the only one who had any chance of tracking you without being spotted.'

He looked miserable, desperate, caught in an impossible choice.

'I'm sorry, Bruna, really sorry.'

I couldn't make it any worse for him. I put my hand out and touched his forearm.

'It's okay. Come on, come and have a drink and talk with me. I need all my friends right now.'

XVI

Flavius and I chatted for another half hour, but I didn't bring Stella and Nicola into the conversation. If, as Conrad said, Flavius hadn't seen the girls dealing, then I wasn't going to tell him. He'd feel bound to take it further and get himself enmeshed in the mess between Conrad and me. But we agreed to keep meeting, falling back on the old Pulcheria security protocols of changing times and places to a numerical pattern. It brought our old comradeship back. Strange, I'd been the catalyst fourteen years ago for him joining the PGSF and now he'd been the trigger for me leaving.

The next morning, I put on my black business suit, Nonna's heavy gold necklace and had Marcella dress my hair formally. Disguised as a big shot, I had the chauffeur drive me up to the palace in Nonna's cream Mercedes. We managed to pass through the two security checks, mostly by me doing what my old New York friend, Amanda, called 'the gracious stuff'. I'd hardly ever used my social rank; I'd been so embarrassed by it when I'd first arrived. My military status I'd earned. Now I was cut adrift from that.

Favonius Cotta, the head of protocol, came out himself to greet me. Nothing about him had changed since Washington apart from a little grey in the luxuriant black hair. His green eyes still challenged, but in a very careful way.

'Countess Mitela, we are honoured. A pleasure to see you, as always.'

Smartass.

'*Salve*, Favonius Cotta. I see you're well. How's Aelia?'

He smiled, but not warmly. 'She's working in the Paris Argentaria Prima office. I understand from her mother that she's doing well.'

Gods, he was a cold bastard. Didn't he follow his own daughter's progress?

'In a bank? Aelia?' I said. She'd been a rebellious teenager and a regular smartmouth when she'd helped me learn street Latin back in the Roma Nova legation in Washington. 'Well, good luck to her.

Please pass on my warmest regards when you speak next.'

'Of course, Countess,' he murmured.

'Now, I've come to see my cousin on an urgent family matter, so I'd appreciate it if you'd announce me.'

Anger at being treated like a servant flared in his eyes, but died quickly enough as he started on his payback.

'The imperatrix has a very busy schedule today, so I'm not sure that'll be possible.'

'Oh, I think I'm already in her schedule under private time, so let's get on with it.' I'd short-circuited the official channels and texted Silvia last night. She'd allocated me a twenty minute slot in which I would ruin the rest of her life.

In her private drawing room, Silvia and I did the safe thing and kissed cheeks. She smiled and gestured me to sit.

'You look very formal today, Carina. Something important?'

'Silvia, just remember the thing about not killing the messenger.'

Her jokey manner vanished; she'd seen the stricken look I knew was in my eyes.

'This isn't about your resignation, is it?'

'No, that's insignificant in comparison.'

'Of course, I was very sorry to hear about that. Are you sure? It's selfish of me, but I've always felt safer having my own cousin protecting me.'

Juno. I'd never thought of it like that.

'No, no, that's finished. I'm sorry if you feel I've let you down, but it was becoming impossible. In fact, it's connected to why I've had to come and see you.'

The studied professional look she kept pinned on her face for most of the time melted away as I recounted everything that had happened since we spoke at her birthday party. She brought her hand up and covered her mouth with it. She bowed her head and tears fell over the smooth surface of her made-up face. She got up swiftly and dabbed her face with a delicate lace handkerchief. She kept her back to me while she tried to recover, her shoulders bent with tension.

'And where is this recording now?'

'It should have been filed on the system, probably security passworded by Conradus. Only the minister can override it.'

She strode over to the phone, plunked herself down in front of the screen and tapped out a number. A nervous private secretary put her through to the defence minister.

'*Salve consiliaria,* I hope I am not interrupting you?'

Silvia gave the minister date and time and we waited. And waited. To break the tension, I went out and called for some coffee. Halfway through drinking it, the commset beeped. I just caught Silvia's abandoned cup as she rushed over to the screen. I kept out of camera range, but could see and hear everything. Silvia switched her calm face back on and smiled pleasantly like they were about to discuss the weather report.

From the minister's embarrassed face, I knew it wasn't good.

'I have to report, Imperatrix, that we can find no trace of this surveillance recording. The search has been carried out with thoroughness and utmost discretion as ordered.'

Silvia's neutral face didn't change as she thanked the minister and switched off.

Shit.

Now it looked like I'd made it all up. My fingers curled into my palms.

'Silvia, I—'

'Don't bother, Carina. I believe you.'

'I know you wouldn't say anything this serious unless it was true.' She looked away for a few seconds. 'I'm disappointed with Conradus, but that's nothing compared to how you must feel.'

I was too choked up to say anything.

'Now, you must be my advisor on this. Last time you asked me not to say anything to Stella. I think I must now.'

She poured me another cup of coffee and the hot liquid cleared my throat.

'Let me go talk to her, Silvia, if you wouldn't mind. If there's trouble, she can let me have it. You'll still be there to comfort her when evil Aunt Carina has finished with her.'

'Oh, gods, Carina, I can't let you take the flak like that.'

'I'll choose my moment, of course.' I got up and walked around. I glanced at my watch. 'Your schedule must be shot to Hades. Look, can you give me a pass to come and go here? I won't abuse it.'

She snorted. Inelegant from her but expressive. She jabbed her commset and her private secretary was in within ten seconds to receive instructions.

As she leaned towards me as we exchanged kisses, she said 'Come back later. After lunch?'

I nodded, bowed and left. After a few minutes, the secretary came out and escorted me back to Favonius and my clearance was arranged within the hour.

I found Stella in her room, lying on a couch, white wires running from her ears to the tiny square in her hand. Her head bounced side to side and her hand tapped her leg rhythmically. She didn't hear me shut the door, but her eyes bulged as I walked around in front of her.

'Aunt Carina! What are you doing here?' She pulled the earphones out, sat up and looked at me suspiciously.

'I need to talk to you, Stella.'

'Oh, yes?'

I sat down and said nothing. I just looked at her as neutrally as I could.

'Sorry, that was rude,' she muttered.

'Yes, it was, but I'm not here to talk about your manners. It's more about who you've been hanging with.'

'What do you mean?'

'I think you've been seeing Nicola Tella quite a lot recently.'

'So?'

'She's not exactly the best friend you could have.'

'I like her. She's fun and quirky. She doesn't tell me what to do. Anyway, Mama invited her up here the other day, so she's happy about it.' Her eyes narrowed. 'Is this because of Dad? Are you jealous? Losing it, are you?'

Gods, she was so contemptuous. I'd always found Stella difficult. Her personality was as slippery as her moods, but she was worse than usual.

'Don't go there, Stella. You don't have a clue what you're talking about. And this is about you, not me. You're getting into very dangerous territory with Nicola Tella. Don't forget, she nearly got Allegra killed. She's the type to use people and then throw them away without a second thought. Be very careful.'

She was trembling. Tears sprang from her brightened eyes, her face became red and flushed as her voice rose in pitch.

'You can't talk to me like that.'

'Stella, calm yourself.' I got up and fetched her a glass of water. As she grabbed it, I smelled her breath. She gulped the water down, looking down at her knees. She choked and I went over to tap her back to ease it. I was struck by how pale she looked. Mixed in with her defiance was anxiety. And fear.

I gave Silvia my report and recommendations when we met later. Her face shut down after I'd finished. At last she nodded and said 'Do it,' in a low voice. I don't think she liked me one little bit at that moment.

I met Pelonia and her team at the staff door and signed them through. She and her two assistants pulled on plastic suits and gloves, unpacked baggies and evidence boxes and took Stella's room apart. Silvia watched the whole thing with me and flinched when the taller man upturned Stella's laundry hamper and brandished a baggie with pale green plant remains and a part-opened pack of rolling papers. Her hand covered her mouth as Pelonia pulled the lid off a shallow plastic box she found inside a speaker and revealed around a dozen yellow pills with a stylised E impressed onto the surface. I pulled Silvia away, back into her sitting room and gave her a small brandy.

She looked like any other wounded parent, despairing about how she'd gone wrong.

I felt sorry for Stella when she came back from her tennis practice and was escorted straight to her mother's office. Silvia didn't give Stella the warm smile she normally greeted her daughter with; the ruler had replaced the mother. On the other side of Silvia's desk, Stella hesitated. Her eyes widened when she saw the evidence tray on Silvia's desk. She ignored Pelonia and glanced once at me. Her skin was mottled with red patches as if she'd been making a superhuman effort and had run out of breath.

'Sit down, Stella.' Silvia indicated the chair the other side of her desk.

'Mama, I—'

'Be quiet and listen to me.'

Stella narrowed her eyes; her mouth drooped.

Silvia waved her hand over the drugs. 'These items were found in your room. What is your explanation? The truth, please.'

'What's the use? You won't believe me.' Stella tipped her head in my direction. 'You always do what she says. I don't count.'

I heard a tiny gasp from Pelonia who glanced at me, then stared at Stella.

'Cut the "woe is me routine", Stella,' I said, 'and answer your mother. Politely.'

Silvia waited, a grim expression on her face, I stared down at Stella, Pelonia looked unhappy and awkward, but stood silently. Stella started coughing, the red blotches on her face getting worse, highlighting the pallor of her skin. Nobody moved. The hacking subsided. Stella swallowed, but said nothing.

I went to crouch down by her chair. 'Look, Stella, you're in a difficult place,' I said, 'but if you tell us everything, it'll go so much easier for you.'

She continued looking straight ahead, but not meeting her mother's eyes, instead looking over her shoulder at the display filled with ancient glass.

'Think of your mother, then,' I said. 'She has no choice but to uphold the law. Inside, she's weeping blood for you.'

She looked away. I suppose it was something, some kind of realisation that she had done something wrong.

After an eon, which was really just over five minutes, Silvia nodded at Pelonia who went over to Stella and pulled her to her feet. Stella stared unbelieving at Pelonia's hand gripping her arm. She tried to pull away, but the cop turned Stella and cuffed her hands behind her back.

'Stella Apulia, I am Inspector Pelonia of the Department of Justice special cases team. I'm arresting you for possession of Level I illicit substances and for suspected dealing. You will undergo medical examination and detoxification in a secure unit pending trial. Do you submit to the court?'

Stella stared back at Pelonia like she was an alien. She cast a pleading look at her mother.

Silvia looked at her daughter and said in a low voice, 'She submits to the court.'

Pelonia nodded to the two other *custodes* standing by the door and they all marched out, Stella stumbling between the two blue figures.

Silvia turned a shattered face to me and said, 'Go with them. Watch over her.' As I left, I heard her sobbing.

XVII

Stella was brought into *Custodes* XI Station through the back gate, taken to the medical room and given a thorough examination. She said nothing as the techs carried out the blood, urine and vitals tests. Normally robotic in their neutrality – testing druggies couldn't have been the pleasantest of jobs – they were more circumspect in their actions than I'd ever seen. One assistant dropped a tube that clattered on his metal instrument tray. Stella jumped at the noise and Lurio frowned at both techs.

I stayed with Stella throughout, but she more or less ignored me, only giving me a pleading look once when they gave her an intimate search. I took her hand and squeezed it in sympathy, but once they finished she shook it off. The medic gave her a drink and a shot – vitamins he told me later – and she was taken away to a locked room.

Lurio took me to his office and dosed me with coffee. He looked as grim as I felt.

'How the fuck did it get to this? She's had every chance. Jupiter, I'd strangle her myself if she was my daughter.'

'Don't, Lurio. Please.'

'What is it with you lot? First your fluffy bunny, now this one.'

'That's unfair and you know it, but if you want to have a temper fit, be my guest.'

He stopped pacing up and down and threw himself into his chair. He tapped his fingers on his desk, reached for his keyboard and attacked that.

'We can hold her in the medical unit and stretch out the detox, but she'll have to go to trial eventually. I'm sorry for your cousin, personally, but it'll send shock waves through the whole country. Bloody glad it's not me having to deal with that.' He looked at his watch. 'Pelonia will want to get started. I'd better wander down.'

In the detention suite, he nodded to the custody sergeant, and as I went to follow him down the corridor to the interview rooms, Lurio barred the way.

'Sorry, no further.'

'C'mon, Lurio, don't be such a hard-ass. She's only a kid, she needs somebody there for her.'

'She's a legal adult arrested on narcotics charges, suspected dealer and uncooperative. Nothing doing.' He relaxed a centimetre. 'Look, I'm sorry about your professional trouble coming on top of your family problems, but I can't bend the procedure for civilians. Even a prominent one like yourself, Countess.'

I stared at him, dumbstruck. I really was excluded now.

His eyes were full of understanding, but his mouth went into a tight line. He turned and disappeared through the scanlocked door.

I struggled back to the palace in my car, cursing the evening rush hour traffic as it sucked me in from the Dec Max and dropped me like a discard at the palace gates. Favonius met me in the staff car park and escorted me through to Silvia's office. His smooth shell seemed a little cracked.

'I wanted to have a quick word first, Countess,' he said as we strode along. He looked like he was swallowing a box of steel tacks. 'I confess I have not handled our relationship well in the past.'

An understatement of all time. When he'd been chief of staff years ago in the Washington legation, his political machinations had nearly gotten me killed.

'It's essential we work closely together on this crisis. I hope you will accept my apology.'

I stopped dead. Even more than his words, his eyes confirmed his genuine concern. Apart from his over-gracious smile having vanished, creases running down the side of his nose to the corners of his mouth had deepened markedly since I saw him twenty-four hours ago.

'Sure, Favonius, I accept it, but don't try anything fancy. I may not still be in uniform, but my priority is protecting the imperatrix and there's very little I won't do in pursuit of that.'

He half-bowed and we continued in silence.

I gave Silvia details about what had happened to Stella. She frowned when I reported how I'd been barred from the interviews. She glanced at Favonius. He shrugged. He must feel secure in his role and have Silvia's full trust to make such an informal gesture. Silvia signed a document on her desk and gave it to her secretary, who hurried off with it like it was on fire.

'I've issued an imperial order to Quintus Tellus demanding he produce Nicola Tella immediately.' She studied her watch. 'I'll give him an hour.'

'Juno, Silvia, can you do that for this kind of thing?' I blurted out.

'An attack on my heir, and this is undoubtedly what this is, is an attack on the state. Tellus will be here, with or without her. I very much hope for his sake it's with.'

The imperial courier reported that Quintus Tellus was indisposed. She'd insisted on seeing him to verify it. Quintus was in his bed, one arm in a sling, a bruised face and sleeping. The order was delivered to his nephew Conradus Tellus. I stared horrified at the messenger as she recited the facts.

Tellus?

He'd renounced my name? I choked.

I retreated to the far corner and called Conrad's cell. No reply. I called the Tella house landline, but all I heard was the steward's voice on the voicemail. If Conrad didn't answer Silvia's summons, I couldn't imagine the trouble he'd be in. I wanted to go over to Domus Tellarum right away, but Silvia forbade me. While we waited, she sat composed at her desk, seeming to push on with her normal paperwork. Perched on the sofa I pushed my caffeine levels through the ceiling, alternating with pacing up and down by the tall windows.

Time crawled, the only sound was Silvia opening and closing files, clacking on her keyboard or moving paper. I knew every stone in each archway after forty minutes. Favonius kept popping in like the cuckoo on a clock, but shook his head every time. Right on the hour, Silvia looked up at both of us hovering, jabbed her desk commset and summoned the guard commander. It was Flavius.

'Senior Centurion, I require you execute an imperial order with any means required. You are to bring me Count Tellus or his senior representative together with Nicola Tella. Without fail.' She studied his face. 'Do you understand?'

Flavius drew himself up and saluted. His eyes were impassive; he was too good a soldier to react.

'Imperatrix, if I may speak?' I said.

She raised an eyebrow and looked down her nose at me with the force of over a thousand and a half years of ancestors behind her.

Well, ditto.

'I know the house as well as any Tella, better than Flavius. Also, if Quintus Tellus is incapacitated, it's appropriate under the Codes that the senior of the Twelve is there to assist.' It sounded lame, but I had to go and find out.

'No, you are too close. Flavius will deal with it.' She looked up at him. 'On your way, Senior Centurion.'

He saluted again, turned, shot the briefest of glances at me and marched off.

'Would you excuse us, Favonius?' Silvia said, as soon as Flavius was out of earshot.

He bowed and shut the door softly behind him.

Silvia half-closed her eyes as if measuring her words and stroked her eyebrow with her middle finger. She rarely touched her face like that.

'I know you're tired and probably overwrought. And I am deeply grateful for your support for Stella. You are not only my cousin but my friend. But please don't ever speak across me like that again.'

The heat rose up my neck into my face. I felt like a kid being unfairly admonished for answering the teacher back. Something broke inside me.

'I apologise, Imperatrix. I did not mean to be discourteous,' I said at my most formal. Gritting my teeth, I bowed and left.

Back at home, I used my anger to fuel me. The hell with it. Silvia could be as autocratic as she liked but as head of the Twelve Families' Council I was perfectly within my rights to go to Quintus. More than that, I had to find out what had happened to Conrad. Capturing Nicola would be a bonus.

No way would they let me in the front door. I hurried into black t-shirt, fleece sweater and pants and fastened on black sneakers. I strapped on my carbon fibre knives and made for the service exit. The adrenaline was already coursing around my body.

At Domus Tellarum, a long wheelbase and a limousine, both with drivers, were parked up in front of the gate. Keeping close to the high wall, I ran the hundred and twenty metres to the back of the block. Frost was already forming on the sidewalk and I left ridged footprints. Too bad. No sign of any PGSF at the back. Sloppy. There was no entrance there, but still sloppy.

The soft pop of released air echoed off the wall as the carbon fibre hook flew up from the launcher. I glanced around, waited, but there was nobody, nothing. An intermittent buzz of traffic in the distance.

I'd targeted one of the tall oaks growing at the back of the long garden. Sure, their height and generous foliage guaranteed privacy, but appeared to be a housebreaker's dream. But I knew the system of beams and motion sensors made up for it. As long as I didn't touch the internal wall sensor which would detect my body warmth, I'd be fine. I scrambled up the outside wall and swung into the tree, right into a dead branch which cracked as I hit it.

Crap.

Clinging on to the main bough, I waited for figures to pour out of the back of the house and start shooting at me.

Nothing. I used up three precious minutes waiting.

I took a deep breath, fished out my beam reflector and progressed down the trunk. Landing softly on dead leaves which crunched with frost, I paused to scan the still silent garden.

I trotted up through the trees of the mini parkland, into the cultivated garden, made for the left side wall, sheltered by ornamental trees. I passed the pool and outdoor *triclinium*. I fished out the card to get through the electronic perimeter around the terrace, praying as I flashed it across the reader that it would work.

Green.

So far, so silent. The back door optical reader also let me through. Juno, that was a relief. I thought my access might have been cancelled.

I slid into the domestic hall to check the house system. Three biosignatures in the atrium, two on the stairs, two upstairs, but nobody else. The five would be the PGSF detail. Where were the servants? Normally at least four lived in at any time.

I ran up the service stairway and emerged in Uncle Quintus's suite, in the corridor outside his bedroom. I crept along, checked out his private study and sitting room, opening each door with a knife in my hand. I hesitated at the bedroom door, but grasped it and entered.

The bedside light was on and in the bed lay Uncle Quintus, bandaged head, a large red and purple bruise on one cheek and arm in a sling. His closed eyes were sunken, brown shadows surrounding them. Juno, he looked dreadful. On a chair by the side of the bed sat his steward, Ternia, her eyes terrified as she lifted them to see who had come in.

'Oh, thank the gods,' she cried out.

Quintus's eyes opened, apprehensive. Then he saw me.

'Carina,' he croaked and raised his chin a centimetre. I saw a vivid red weal on his neck. I took his hand.

'It's okay, Quintus, I'm here now.' The steward handed me a glass of water. I put my arm around Quintus's shoulders and raised it to his lips. Before I could ask him what had happened, there was a loud knock on the door and two PGSF guards burst in followed by Flavius. He stared at me, thunder on his face.

'What the hell are you doing here?' he spat at me. 'The imperatrix expressly forbade you to set foot in this house.'

'Well, too bad, Senior Centurion. I am here at the request of Quintus Tellus under the provisions of the Families Codes.' I squeezed his hand and felt a weak but definite response. 'And I would thank you to remember who you address.'

We glared each other out. In the end, he turned to Quintus. 'Count Tellus, I am commanded by the imperatrix to require you to produce Nicola Tella and to bring you both into the imperatrix's presence without delay. An imperial order was sent to you an hour ago.' Flavius stared down into Quintus' face. 'Where is Nicola Tella?'

Quintus closed his eyes and moved his head a few millimetres from one side to the other and back again.

I insisted on calling an ambulance, my back turned to Flavius as I spoke to them. The imperial order was still on Quintus's system and the hardcopy on the vestibule table. The courier said she'd handed it to Conrad. Where the hell was he?

I made Quintus drink a restorative which I laced with painkillers and between us the steward and I managed to wrap him warmly. The paramedics carried him downstairs with utmost care. I was relieved to see he'd dozed off.

Flavius turned to me. 'Do you know where the girl is?' His eyes were hard and his voice cold.

'No. If I did, I would have great pleasure in handing her over. You must know that.'

'Very well. You have two choices. You can help us search it or you can watch us take this house apart.'

'Why are you being so hard, Flav?' I laid my fingers on his forearm. He looked down at my hand. After a few moments, he slid his hand out from under my fingers.

'I'm trying to stay professional. Do you think this is in any way pleasant for me?' His eyes softened. 'We'll be as careful as we can, but no favours. Understood?'

I nodded.

'Anywhere special we should look?'

I gave him the guided tour and the guards with him broke out and searched individual rooms. I lingered in the rooms Conrad was obviously occupying. The silver frame I gave him last year of the children was on his desk. I opened the top drawer and gasped as I found the one of the two of us, smiling, happy, arms entwined, on the top of the drawer contents. A guard came in to search. I stood back but followed her every action. In a strange way, I felt I was defending his privacy. She looked at me, murmured, 'Excuse me, ma'am' and started opening the desk drawers. I stepped aside, hating every moment. In the end, I had to leave. I went downstairs and talked to the steward.

'Where's Conradus Tellus, Ternia?'

'I don't know, lady. I really don't. I came back this evening after visiting my sister and found the house deserted apart from Quintus Tellus lying in bed.' Her voice as she went on was bitter. 'That girl chased them all away in the end. Even old Marius who'd been here for twenty years. May the Furies find her and tear her into little pieces!'

I pressed her forearm and smiled at her. 'You and me both, Ternia.'

'Countess. With me, please.' Flavius beckoned me with an imperious gesture. We went upstairs again to a large room, formerly Conrad's mother's room. The closet doors were open, a single white shirt hung in one, a plastic bag on the floor. In the bathroom, grease marks and loose dark blond hair marked the basin, a shampoo bottle lay discarded in the shower enclosure. But these and the rumpled bedding were the only signs of recent occupation.

Almost by instinct, I dropped to my knees and searched under the bed. Two guards came forward and turned the bed on its side. Some loose stitching in the base revealed a now empty space – a classic hiding place. In fact, a little too classic. Even obvious. So she was capable of making a mistake? I saw a tiny light in our dark search.

The guards pulled the drawers out of the rest of the furniture, examining the undersides of each drawer and inside the carcass.

I climbed on to a chair and searched the top compartments of the closets.

'We've looked,' Flavius said, impatiently. 'Forensics are on their way. Leave it. Let's get back to the palace.' We trudged downstairs and he signalled the rest of his troops to follow. He turned to me and frowned again.

'You can ride with Count Tellus in the ambulance or with us in the back of the long wheelbase. Either way, consider yourself under arrest.'

I hadn't expected anything else. I was bracing for Silvia's reaction. Flavius would have messaged the uncomfortable fact of my presence through by now.

'I wouldn't dream of abandoning Uncle Quintus to your care, even if he weren't an injured eighty-year-old.'

I sat by Quintus in the ambulance, holding his hand. The movement of the road journey had roused him, but he didn't say anything, just kept his eyes glued on my face. I walked by his side into the atrium where Silvia was waiting with a small group. The wall lights between the columns cast distorted shadows but not much light.

She stood immobile, head pulling the rest of her spine upright. Her eyes flickered over me and settled on Quintus lying on the gurney. She waved one of the group forward who was clutching a medical bag. I hovered while the doctor examined Quintus, checking vitals and gently lifting his head to show the bruising on his neck.

'The arm's been set in a rudimentary but effective fashion, Imperatrix, almost an emergency battlefield procedure. But it'll do. I suggest immediate hospitalisation. We need to give him a whole body scan and monitor him closely for the next few days.'

'Very well, doctor, but first I need some answers.'

The doctor didn't look happy, but he had no choice.

Silvia bent over and asked, 'Where is she, Quintus?'

'I don't know,' he whispered.

She looked over at me, one eyebrow raised. I shook my head.

'Conradus?'

He shut his eyes. 'He went after her.'

'Has he realised yet?' I asked.

But Quintus had floated off into unconsciousness.

Silvia straightened up. She instructed the doctor to have

Quintus admitted to the Central Valetudinarium guarded twenty-four seven by regular Praetorians, no visitors allowed.

'You come with me, Carina.'

Her eyes were hard as agates, glinting above cheekbones pushing out against her skin. I shook inside. I had deliberately disobeyed her express wishes. She didn't look especially forgiving.

'I activated Conradus's tracker. It was the first thing I did when I went home,' I said in a pre-emptive strike. All senior members of the Twelve had trackers fitted. It replaced the personal guard of previous centuries. But only the family head could activate it for a purposeful search and only in the presence of the family recorder. 'Unfortunately, there's no signal.'

Silvia continued to look at me with hostility.

'The only explanation is that he's reverted to the Tella code.' To which of course I didn't have access.

'Was the girl fitted?'

'I don't know. Only Quintus Tellus or the Tella family recorder can answer that.' I lifted my cell. 'Shall I?'

Silvia waved impatiently, sat down on one of the blue couches and tapped her long, immaculate nails on the wood arm. At least we were conducting hostilities in her private sitting room. When I'd finished my call, she at last stopped the irritating staccato.

'The recorder says no tracker was fitted to her knowledge. And Conradus's is switched off.'

'Damn and blast them all to hell.' She called Favonius back in and her secretary. 'Tell the DJ to conduct a national search for both Tellae. Draw on the PGSF if they need, but with care. Too many owe loyalty to their legate.' She turned to me. 'Go home, Carina, and stay there this time.'

XVIII

I was catching up on emails later that morning, including presenting my excuses to the Senate for non-appearance yesterday, when Allegra and Hallie interrupted me. Serious didn't start to describe the expression on their faces.

'Mama, Hallie and I are going to visit Uncle Quintus.'

I had to hope my mouth didn't drop open. I admired their initiative but no way would I let my child, or her half-sister, get entangled in political, possibly treasonable, affairs.

'That's a kind idea, Allegra, but just not possible.'

'Why not?'

I waved my hand in a vague arc. 'It's too dangerous. I don't want you in the crossfire.'

She took my hand and held it to her cheek. 'Mama, I've already been in it.' Her tone was gentle, but her eyes fixed on me with that steady, stubborn Tella look.

'Don't worry, Aunt Carina, please,' Hallie piped up. 'We'll stay together and we'll be able to ask Uncle Quintus questions for you. We'll be your operatives.' Her eyes sparkled at the thought.

Oh, gods! Nancy Drew and sister.

'No.' I held my palm up.

'But—'

'No. Final word.'

Their angry faces reminded me so strongly of Conrad, I had to look away. They trooped off, not understanding I was trying to protect them.

'I thought I could rely on you to stop them,' Silvia said.

I didn't reply; I was too angry. Firstly at the girls, but secondly at the guards who hadn't stopped them. I could only guess that Hallie had exerted her charm and traded on her status and Allegra backed her up with her dignity and new rank as my heir. Damn useless Praetorian regulars. Mainly, I was stung by the easy way Silvia assumed I'd dragged the girls in when really I'd forbidden them to go. I hadn't relished being rousted out by her Praetorians this Saturday evening like some petty criminal. I stood there silently keeping my gaze focussed two millimetres above her right shoulder.

'Well?'

'I have nothing to add to my original answer, Imperatrix. They disobeyed me.'

She threw me an ironic look. 'Now you know how that feels.' She flicked her hand impatiently to dismiss the guard and sighed. 'For Juno's sake, let's stop acting like a couple of tarts arguing over a *stola* at a thrift sale. Sit down.'

I obeyed, but was wary. We were cousins and had been friends. She hadn't rescinded my appointment as one of her advisors. I hated being ranged against her, but I had to stand up for Quintus.

'This has to be resolved, and quickly. The Imperial Council meets in emergency session on Monday afternoon. I can't conceal this from them. Ideas?'

'You have the DJ scouring around with PGSF backing. To be honest, I think you were harsh in your comment about the PGSF. Given a conflict between bringing their senior legate in or obeying you, they wouldn't hesitate.'

'Really? They're intensely loyal to Conradus.'

'No contest. You saw how one of my oldest friends, Flavius, had no hesitation in arresting me.' I glanced at her. 'He didn't like it, but he did it.'

She rested her face in her hands. 'Yes, I know that really. I must be tired to even consider it.' She switched on a brittle smile. 'So what now?'

'The girls didn't get far with Quintus. He just smiled at them, thanked them for coming and said he'd only talk to me. So that's a priority, with your permission.'

She nodded and waved at me to continue.

'By now Senior Commander Lurio of the Urban Cohorts will have released his pack of ferrets. I suggest you establish some kind of direct liaison to control the operation.' Although I'd defended the PGSF in front of Silvia, I hoped they'd keep the line, knowing the DJ were hunting their chief. Tempers were sure to flare. And there was no love lost between Lurio and Conrad personally.

'However, you can't be seen to be micro-managing it directly, however tempting. You have to distance yourself from both Stella and Conradus.'

'You don't do easy, do you, Carina?'

'I've had to learn exactly that lesson over the past months.'

Neither of us said anything for a minute.

'Very well. I'll appoint you imperial agent.'

I opened my mouth but nothing came out. I was too surprised.

'You're the best placed,' she continued, 'you know the structures and the personalities. And you'll push over the limits if you need to.'

'But—'

'What?'

'Juno, Silvia, apart from Lurio exploding when he finds out, I doubt the PGSF will be happy to have their black sheep telling them what to do. And it would be a massive conflict of interest for me personally.'

'You exaggerate.' Her eyes gleamed with a calculating look. 'You want to find Conradus. You know how he thinks in the field, you know what techniques he'll use. And you want to nail this girl. So I think you're fairly motivated. And you're always saying how capable you are compared to others.'

That was a cheap shot. Anger rolled up through me.

Calm down, Carina. This is the imperatrix.

I pressed my lips together and swallowed my temper.

'It's decided,' she said, looked away and stabbed her deskcom to summon the chancellor. He nodded to me, but looked steadily at Silvia. He pursed his lips when she told him of her decision. He had no choice but to acquiesce when Silvia was in determined mode. But he insisted I should report at the Monday Council meeting on my progress.

I was reciting the oath within thirty minutes and received a rectangular gold embossed plasticard for my wallet bearing the imperial commission. I entered my tracker release code in their chip reader and the chancellor entered my upgraded status and his code. As he ran the scanner over my bare skin to check it was correctly entered I shivered. Not from the cold.

Back home, I yanked on my jeans and grabbed a leather jacket, my knives and emergency back pack. I calculated I had just under forty-eight hours to get a result.

At the Central Valetudinarium, I knocked on the door of Quintus's room and entered. He pulled his gaze away from the window when he heard the door open. He glanced at me, then resumed studying the window. The bruise on his cheek was turning yellow-black, a contrast to his washed-out face. I kissed his forehead, avoiding the broken and grazed skin.

'Hello, Quintus. You wanted to talk to me.'

He didn't reply. His free hand picked at the cotton sheet. There was no sign whatsoever of the crafty, confident politician of previous times.

'I have a tight schedule leading up to the emergency Imperial Council meeting on Monday, so if you have something, let's hear it now.'

'You know,' he rasped, 'I gave her an allowance and a card for any shopping she wanted.' He looked down and fidgeted with the mesh sling with his good hand. 'Conradus asked me to put no limit on it.' He sank back against his pillow. 'When I queried anything, she made me sound so unreasonable, like a mean old man. She has that soft commanding voice that verbal bullies use. The worst thing is that I knew she was doing it. I've come across Mars knows how many of those in my political life. Why I couldn't deal with her, I don't know.' He looked up at me. 'She wanted the access codes to the treasure account.'

Jupiter! That would have been at least half a million *solidi*, even though Quintus had started again from nearly nothing. But it was a trust to be handed down through the generations, not for personal spending.

'When I refused, she got up, came over to me smiling. I thought she'd accepted it.' He snorted. Well, more of a wheeze. 'How stupid was that! She put her hands on the arms of my chair, leant in and asked me again. I tried to push her away without hurting her, but she brought her foot up on to the seat, grabbed my wrist and elbow and broke my arm over her knee.'

I sat on the bed and took his good hand in both of mine and pressed it lightly. His eyes drooped along with his shoulders as he told me.

'It was so clinical. She's as strong as Hades. And that's where she belongs. She asked again in that soft voice of hers. When I refused again, she seized my wrist and jerked it. The pain exploded up my arm and shoulder. I passed out. When I came round I was choking. Her hands were round my throat and pressing down hard. She was kneeling on my chest. I didn't have the strength to push her off me. I was sinking into the Styx.'

His eyes closed for a few moments and he was so still I thought he'd fallen asleep. He had to be on strong painkillers seeping through the drip line attached to his good arm.

His eyes jerked open. 'It was going black, but suddenly, the pressure of her weight eased. For a few seconds I couldn't feel anything. Then I realised she was no longer sitting on me. The pain rolled back in and I couldn't stop coughing. Gods, it was worse than her throttling me.'

He was hoarse by now. I poured him a glass of water and helped him drink several mouthfuls before he could continue. Conrad had grabbed her and pulled her off. She'd fought him, kicking and punching. But he was stronger. He tried to restrain her, but she kept jabbing and punching. Eventually, he hit her so hard she fell to the ground.

'He looked shocked at what he'd done,' Quintus said, 'He shuddered and kept staring at his hands as if they weren't his. But I think at last he'd realised what she was. She lay there for a few moments, winded, and stared up at him with a death look, like a wolf assessing its prey. But after a few breaths she sprang up and ran.

'I begged him to go after her and stop her, but he wouldn't leave me. He hardly said a world but set my arm and helped Ternia put me to bed. She was the only one left. I kept telling him to go. I thought he had, but he came back ten minutes later, in his outdoor civvies, carrying a bag and pushing his service pistol into his shoulder holster as he approached. He looked deathly white and said he'd only come back when he'd caught her. I told him to go to you, but he bowed his head and wouldn't meet my eyes or answer me.'

'Did he give you any idea where he was focusing his search?'

'He thought she was running home, back to England.'

XIX

I abandoned my Moto Guzzi in the *Custodes* XI Station parking lot and trotted up the steps to the security barrier. Nobody was more surprised than I was when it lifted automatically. I glanced at the optireader, my palm on the panel, and I was in. More than a little disconcerted, the duty Senior Justiciar stared at me.

'Senior Commander Lurio?'

'Upstairs, 106, er, ma'am.'

'Don't call him.' I said as his hand stretched out towards the commset.

I ran up the stairs, and found Lurio's office. I knocked and went straight in. He was frowning, staring at his screen, tapping the index and second fingers of his left hand. His head swivelled round, an annoyed expression on his face which turned to incredulity. I plunked myself down in the chair in front of his desk.

'Who the hell let you in?'

'I let myself in.' I slid my imperial commission over the desk.

'Mars' balls! How did you barrack her into giving you this?'

'It may surprise you, but I didn't want it.'

He snorted and leaned back in his chair. 'I suppose you'll be all over us now.'

'No, and yes. I'm not going to interfere in your operation. You're perfectly capable of carrying out the search for Conradus. The problem is I doubt you'll even see him, let alone find him. No reflection on you.'

'Do you know how bloody patronising you can be?'

'It's a fact.' I shrugged.

'All right, superhero, tell me what you think.'

'He's gone after Nicola. His tracker is de-activated, so we can't use that. The key is Nicola. I want access to her file, all of it, and I want Pelonia to check Nicola's accounts and cards. But first, I need to see Stella.'

★

I stood over by the window, out of direct line of sight when Stella was brought into the governor's room at the detox unit. The DJ medical file recorded only level one addiction, but nudging level two. Her skin looked clearer since I'd seen her in the DJ cells three days ago. Her hair was neatly gathered in a single plait down her back. She said nothing except 'Yes, ma'am' when the governor informed her she had a visitor. Stella followed the older woman's open hand gesture toward the window but the girl flinched when she saw me. She flashed me an angry look, but dropped it and returned to a subdued attitude within a second. The governor left us to it, closing the door behind her almost without a sound.

'Sit down, Stella.'

Slumping on the plastic-covered couch she held her legs together and her arms crossed hard across her chest.

'How's it going?'

'All right.'

'Is there anything you need?'

She stared at me for a few moments, looked away and kept her eyes fixed on the other side of the room. Her shoulders were tensed up as high as shoulder-pads in an old fashioned jacket. A spasm racked through her. She gulped and sobbed silently. I dropped down beside her and put my arm around her shoulders. When she stopped, she glanced at me, stiffened and moved away. She shook her head when I offered her a wipe.

'What do you want?' she said. 'You've got me locked up. Isn't that enough?'

'You brought yourself here, Stella. You knew it was wrong to have those drugs. And you weren't very clever at hiding them. Darius or Hallie could have easily found them.'

She stuck her chin out.

'C'mon, the speakers? Your wash basket? Classic. The first places the *custodes* search.'

She reddened, looked down as if embarrassed.

'Did Nicola suggest those places?'

Her hands gripped the edge of the couch as she gave a tiny nod.

Poor kid. She'd really been taken for a ride.

'I'm going to try and find Nicola to bring her back to face the damage she's caused you and your father. And Uncle Quintus.'

'What do you mean?'

I told her about the brutal beating Nicola had dished out to the eighty-year-old. Her mouth opened, but nothing came out. Her eyes widened with the shock of my words. Unlike her awkwardness with many others, she'd always seemed relaxed and happy bantering with Quintus when I'd seen them together. In a way, I was gratified by her reaction now.

'Why did she want to hurt us?'

'I don't know for sure. That's one for the psychs, but I think jealousy and an imagined need for revenge. I guess she thought your father owed her something.'

I was too wired to sit still, so I got to my feet and helped myself to a glass of water from the governor's tray before resuming.

'I saw you with Nicola in the Septarium that evening when you handed over money for a packet of drugs.' She opened her mouth to speak. 'Please don't deny it. I watched the whole thing. What happened to the drugs?'

'I don't know.'

I didn't say anything. I stood within millimetres of her leg, gazing down at her, waiting. She wriggled, but I kept my eyes on her face, willing her to tell.

'I don't. I really don't. She snatched my bag as soon as we reached her car. She ignored me until she dropped me off at the service gate. She didn't even say goodnight.' She swallowed hard. 'I phoned her, but she wouldn't pick up. She didn't accept any of my messages. I thought I'd done something wrong, upset her.' Her voice puttered out.

'Okay. Here's the deal. You write out all the times you spent with Nicola and everything you did. Don't worry about getting it all down in one go. Write the dates, if you can, then fill in things as you remember them. If you make full disclosure, it'll go a long way to helping your case when you come to trial. And it could give us some leads to help catch Nicola.'

'Get anything useful?'

Lurio slouched in his chair, his eyes intense.

'Nothing immediate,' I said, 'but I think she's admitted to herself how stupid she's been. She's a little fragile and has lost all her self-belief. I told her to write out everything that's happened for Pelonia. The governor will send it via the DJ secure net.'

He grunted. 'Pelonia's got something for you.' He swung his screen around and spoke the display command. Reams of credit card statements scrolled down. Hades, Nicola knew how to spend. Quintus would be paying the Argentaria Prima back for years.

'Look at the last two transactions.'

A thousand *solidi* cash withdrawal and an airline ticket. London.

'Pelonia says she'll run through it all whenever you want.'

'Tell her I'll leave her to put it together for the court herself.'

'Why? Where are you going?'

'Hunting.'

I stabbed Lucius' number into my cell. As Conrad's closest comrade in arms for years, as well as PGSF adjutant, Lucius was a good first bet. It rang and rang. I was about to cut the call when he answered.

'Lucius? Carina. Have you heard from Conradus?'

He paused.

'So that's a yes. Stay there, I'm on my way.'

'Carina—'

'Just do as you're told.'

I cut it. Pelonia's ferrets were already at the front and back of Lucius's building and searching the underground garages. She nodded as I scanned and overrode the building access panel. I went up the stairs, she in the elevator. In the lobby outside Lucius's door, I gave her brief nod and knocked. The door flew open.

'Who in Hades do you think you are, ordering me around like that?' He shot an angry glance at Pelonia. 'Who's this?'

'May I present Inspector Pelonia from the DJ Special Investigations Unit?'

He looked up and down the lobby. 'You'd better come in.'

I strode straight through to the living room.

'Where's Paulina?'

'Gone to a charity meeting,' he said almost too easily.

'Oh, really? Venue? And her car registration, please. Now.'

'You can't march in here like a stroppy barbarian. You produce a warrant with our names on and I might listen to you. Until then, you can whistle.'

He folded his arms and glared at me.

'Lucius,' I said and laid my hand on his forearm. 'You won't help him like this. He's in so much shit, running won't help.' He opened his mouth to speak, but I held my hand up. 'He's in no fit state to deal with her once he finds her.'

He snorted. 'You don't have much faith in him.'

'On the contrary. That's why I need your help. Look, you can waste my time, but all you'll get is a long-term reservation in one of the DJ's best cells.'

'Are you threatening me? On what grounds?'

'Obstruction, harbouring and assisting a proscriptee for a start.'

He went pale and swallowed hard. It was a few moments before he spoke. 'He's been proscribed?' His voice was almost a whisper.

Although Silvia had stopped at stripping Conrad of his citizenship, he had lost all protection under the law. But it hadn't been published in the *Acta Diurna* yet and wouldn't be until after the emergency Imperial Council meeting on Monday.

I showed Lucius my warrant. He looked at it like it was radioactive. He flopped down on the small couch and recited the details we wanted in a monotonous voice. Pelonia relayed it over her commset.

'If they even so much as frighten her I'll have their hides.'

'They'll be discreet.'

'The scarabs couldn't know discreet if it smacked them in the face.'

Pelonia stiffened and threw Lucius a hostile look.

'Don't be childish. Where's she taking him? And please, please don't let's pretend any more.'

'The airport. They went hours ago.'

Paulina arrived half an hour later, accompanied by a *custos*. Her eyes flew to Lucius, who smiled at her and drew her to him, his arm around her to protect her.

'Paulina Carca, I require you to answer questions honestly and fully,' I said. 'If you do not do so or I think you are answering dishonestly, you will be arrested and detained until you do. Is this clear?'

She didn't say a word, just nodded.

'Lucius Punellus can stay, if you want him to, but I will not tolerate any interruption or attempt at interference. Please look at me while you are answering.'

I nodded at Pelonia who started recording.

'Please state your name, address and profession.'

She trembled as she recited them in a high-pitched nervous voice, but spoke clearly enough.

'What time did Conradus Tellus arrive at your apartment?'

'Eleven o'clock this morning.'

'Describe what happened after that.'

'He and Lucius went into the study. After a while, Lucius asked me to book an airline ticket for this afternoon and pay with my card. I made lunch and we left afterwards for Portus Airport. I left him at the departures and went back to the car park. I stayed there for three hours as he'd asked. I listened to some music and dozed for some of the time.' She paused and ran her palm over her face. 'As I was leaving the car park, the *custodes* stopped me and brought me back here.'

'Thank you.' I gave her a brief smile. 'Okay, Lucius, what did he look like?'

'Sorry?'

'You know perfectly well what I mean. Don't be a smartass.'

He shrugged. 'He dyed his hair dark brown and I gave him some old clothes, but you know yourself how good he is at changing his walk and persona. And no, I don't know what passport he was using.'

Lucius was right. Pelonia was already on her cell asking them to check the CCTV at the airport, but I knew we had little chance of identifying him on it. And the passport would get through every check. He'd have hitched up with somebody else and gone through security like friends, or a couple if it was a woman.

Lucius and Paulina stayed, hands locked together, on the couch; she anxious, he thunderous.

'Okay, so where was Conradus booked to go?'

Paulina glanced at Lucius.

'Paulina. Answer me.'

'Munich, then London.'

Pelonia called her colleagues in the Bavarian National Police to stop him in Munich, but I was sure it was too late. He'd be in London by now.

Part III

The Hunt

XX

As the Imperial Air Force transport touched down at London's military airbase the next evening, I gathered my thoughts together. The emergency meeting of the Imperial Council that afternoon had been like facing a firing squad. I'd felt so angry at the way some had made such easy judgements. Conrad's uncle Caius had been thrown in my face. Quintus's years of service and Conrad's own were conveniently forgotten. To my surprise, the chancellor stomped on the whiners after a while. When one of them had suggested suspending me as tainted by association, I just stared at him until he looked away. In the end they endorsed Silvia's decision. I had twelve days to get back with Conrad. Nicola would be a bonus.

I thanked the uniformed steward and stepped out of the warm cabin on to the first metal tread. A blast of sleet came out of the dark and slapped me in the face. I pulled my collar up which covered half my face. Juno, it was colder in the wet than the summit of the Geminae.

Michael Browning stood smiling at the foot of the steps like it was a summer's day and not early February. I shivered even more. He guided me to a waiting car.

'Good flight?'

'Sure. Thanks for meeting me.'

He pulled the car around. 'We'll stay in the mess here overnight, then head into town tomorrow morning.'

I was settling in my room, when somebody knocked on the door.

'Courier from your legation left this for you this afternoon, ma'am.' The young steward was solemn as he handed over a large plascard box in a transparent cover, sealed with a digital fastener. As soon as he'd closed the door, I stowed the shielded mailing box in the closet. Later, I'd unpack it, open the backpack I knew was inside and check out the equipment.

Over a drink and dinner in the officer's club, I updated Michael.

'So, can you help?'

'I'll do as much I can.'

Which didn't sound too enthusiastic.

Full of traditional breakfast and characterless coffee, we set off at seven the next morning along the freeway into central London. Even this early, the traffic was dense and crawled through a landscape of orange-lit grey gloom. Michael said little beyond polite things. We reached the elevated section as the sky was lightening.

'Where are we going?'

'To meet an old friend.'

'Yes?'

He just smiled.

We drew into a dingy street of 1970s office blocks; concrete panels, large dirty windows in metal frames. At a recessed doorway halfway along, Michael stopped the car and we got out. A younger man, who moved like military, emerged from the revolving door, opened Michael's door and slid into the driver's seat and drove the car off, disappearing around the corner. Michael led me through a pale yellow foyer smelling of stale paper to a desk where I collected a guest pass, signing in a register with a ball-point pen.

'Not as high tech as yours,' he said, 'but all the same, don't lose it.'

On the third floor, we stepped out of the elevator into a lobby with an armed guard – the first I'd seen. No doubt they had hidden CCTV and detection fields, but this place looked as open as a picnic ground on parents' day. Michael nodded to a female assistant tapping on her keyboard. She spared him a glance and a nod towards the door behind her counter and resumed processing her pile of papers.

I wasn't too surprised to see Andrew Brudgland getting to his feet, coming towards me, his hand stretched out, a standard issue smile on his face.

'Lovely to see you again, Carina. Coffee?'

'No. Thank you.'

'How can I help you?'

He sat back, entirely relaxed. I glanced over at Michael, but he sat on an upright chair at the left, quiet and expressionless; the perfect subordinate.

'You've been helping Conrad with his domestic problem from the start, so you know the background.' I tried not to sound resentful. His smile crystallised on his face, although it didn't falter. 'Since Captain Browning here ID'd Nicola Sandbrook four months ago, it's all gone in the crapper. She's systematically attacked my daughter, nearly killing her. Yesterday morning, I left her great-uncle, who took her into his household, lying in a hospital bed with a broken arm, strangulation bruising and destroyed faith. As well as blackmailing Conrad emotionally, she's resurrected and played on demons in his past and brought him to the edge of a breakdown as well as professional ruin. He's been proscribed.' I let that sink in. His file said he'd been to one of their preppy schools, Marlborough, so he must have studied Latin history.

'You still proscribe?'

'Rarely, but in crisis cases, yes. We don't stake the head on the town gate these days, but he's lost all protection under the law. Basically, it's open season on him.' I shrugged. 'Anybody informing on him could be paid a reward plus a portion of his assets; the state would take the rest. All the Tellae would be blighted. And Conrad wouldn't even come out of prison for his pension.'

'But why so harsh a measure?'

'Your precious Sandbook, Hargreve, whatever, targeted another of Conrad's daughters, made her an addict, and involved her in dealing. All this using the skills she learnt here. Don't you ever screen for personality? Don't you do thorough documentation and DNA checks?' I heard my voice rising and swallowed back my anger. 'But she made a serious mistake; when she did that, she attacked the imperial heir. Imperatrix Silvia Apulia was distraught at her daughter being so abused. And twisting her tail is not recommended.'

'I see.'

I fixed him with a hard stare. 'The Imperial Council have designated it as an attack on the state. I have twelve days to find Conrad, and Nicola, or we'll have to consider other measures.'

'What exactly do you mean by that?' Brudgland asked in his cool voice.

'Let's just say that helping me is your better option.'

Michael took me to his office and let me read the file on Nicola. It added a few details, but didn't tell me much more.

'Any guesses where she might go?'

'The local plods are checking the mother's house and we're booked to interview her last unit CO later this afternoon.' His voice was subdued, technical even. I had the impression he was dancing around the point.

'What's the problem?'

'What did you really mean by "other measures"?'

'C'mon, Michael. You've studied us more than most. You know we go in and do what's needed. Your boss looked upset enough to believe it. It's the last thing I want to happen, but I can't stop it. I had to fight the Imperial Council for this twelve day concession, so shall we get going?'

I dozed on the road west. The sleet had been replaced by driving rain that thudded ruthlessly on the windshield. The young driver seemed impervious to it. The line of his military haircut on his neck stayed in the same place the whole time. He didn't even flex his neck.

We'd briefly called in at the mess where I'd left my travel bag. I presumed the security services here had searched and scanned the contents. But I had my field service backpack in the box the legation had sent me. The digital seal showed no sign of breach. Brudgland's people had either been too polite or too sloppy to insist on searching it.

Three and a half hours after leaving London, we cruised along the peripheral circling around the market town leading out to the barracks. The pale green roofs, visible as we drove along the access road, glistened with recent rain. Crowning the hill behind, a kilometre or so away, the woods looked dark, closed and strangely malevolent. Crazy thought. Maybe I was tired. Inside the complex, we went straight to the colonel's office.

'Good to see you again, Major.' Colonel Stimpson was still the slim figure who'd hosted our visit all those months ago in Norfolk. His thick, almost brush-like hair was a little greyer, but the air of decisiveness and constrained energy bursting to escape hadn't changed.

'No longer major. I'm an imperial agent these days. I take my instructions direct from the imperatrix.'

'I see.' He obviously didn't. He exchanged glances with Michael who said nothing.

'Look at it like a roving inspector, if it helps.'

'Well, I have Sandbrook's service records here, which I understand you've been cleared to see. And RSM Johnson will be joining us shortly.' He paused. 'Michael's told us a little about the background to your, ah, mission. If you think we can help in any other way, you will let me know.'

'I'm not here to make trouble for you, Colonel. I just want to find Conrad Tellus and Nicola Sandbrook and take them back.'

Johnson was as I remembered from the exercise; a wall of muscle with an ironic sense of humour. After some formal stuff in the colonel's office, he and I sat over a beer in the senior non-coms club, he embracing the dark bitter, me wimping out with a lager.

'So, Sandbrook, she's been causing trouble, I gather. Not really surprising.'

'What do you mean? She seems to have excellent reports all the way through.'

'Precisely. Now what does that tell you?'

'Ah! Nobody that perfect exists?'

'Don't get me wrong, she carried out her duties well, but she didn't blend. She never went on a bender or got into a fight, like they all do here sometimes. It's mostly operational stress coming out.' He shrugged. 'She never went with anybody that I know of. The boys called her a dyke behind her back, and probably to her face, but I heard elsewhere that wasn't the case.' He placed his glass on the table, refusing my offer of a third one. 'She had an edge in her manner, a sort of snottiness, and was as stubborn as hell. You'd watch her smile, looking as if she was listening, but knowing she wasn't. She'd get people to do the thing she wanted them to do by eliminating all another possibilities. We put her in for leadership tests but it was the one thing she didn't shine at.'

'Did she have any friends, or even work buddies?'

'The reconnaissance work she did was individual, quite lonely, but she said she liked being on her own.' He gave me some printed sheets. 'These are her previous two years' schedules showing team rostering. I don't know if they might tell you anything. Let me have them back in the morning.'

'*Salve*. That you, Fausta?'

'Colonel?' The voice was thick and blurry. Damn. Rousting the head of digital security out of her bed probably wasn't a good start.

'Sorry about the time. I'm sending you some lists of people. I want you to run them. See if there's any kind of linking thread or common factor.'

'What's the background?'

'All UK military, the odd colonial, possibly. Send me anything you find as soon as you have it.'

I was too busy downloading Fausta's report to go for a run that morning. The sleet had also returned. Placing a crystal pyramid on the table in front of me to jam any surveillance, I called Fausta.

'Saw your bursts. They're the only two possibilities?'

'That's it, ma'am. I'll re-analyse and 3D cross-reference to narrow it down, but it may take an hour or two.'

'That's great, Fausta. Excellent job. We'll drive north and visit number one. Out.'

At breakfast, I advised Michael that our destination was a place called Birkenhead where one of Nicola's retired army buddies lived. First, I had to return the schedules. I found Johnson's office, but he wasn't there. I begged an envelope from his assistant, marked it 'Private and Personal – Urgent' and signed across the flap closure. She assured me he'd get it as soon as he was back. I didn't like leaving it like that, but we had to go.

Three hours later, we drove along 1930s urban sprawl as we entered Birkenhead. It looked as grey as the rest in the mizzle. We left the car in Hamilton Square, a grand Victorian plaza looking a little run-down at the edges now, and walked towards the street of dirty brick row houses. I left Michael to buy a paper. My East American accent would be remembered.

As we made our way toward the docks area, the day brightened and a light breeze brought the salty tang of the sea along with the smell of maritime fuel. I called Fausta to check for progress. Before I could ask her anything, she confirmed her earlier report that Christopher Newton as the most likely colleague, a 74% score on her 3D crossmatch; he'd been on three missions with Nicola.

We checked watches and Michael disappeared down the back alleyway behind the street I started walking along. I stopped at the ninth house. A white plastic door matched white plastic windows whose glass was slightly distorted. A satellite dish sprouted from the front wall along with an unlit Santa light decoration coated with a beige sheen of pollution. I checked my watch and knocked on the door.

'Christopher Newton?'

His eyes narrowed. 'Who?' He shook his head. 'No, sorry.'

He was good, but spoilt it by not looking puzzled enough.

'Don't mess with me, Christopher. Let's go inside and talk.'

He nearly shut the door, but I was a second too quick for him. I had my foot in the gap and body-slammed it back open. As I came through, my carbon fibre knife was in my left hand. I jabbed it in his face. He recoiled instinctively.

Within nanoseconds, he recovered and barrelled toward me. As he slammed into me, I kneed him hard in the groin. He gasped and curled up groaning in agony. Before he could catch his wind, I chopped the back of his neck with my right hand. He collapsed in a heap on the floor. I waited a couple of breaths then sheathed my knife, fished cable ties from my jacket pocket and secured his hands behind his back.

Michael burst through, Sig Sauer in hand. I jerked my head up and he rushed upstairs. I checked the rest of downstairs. There was only the lobby, living room and knocked-through kitchen. Nobody there. Michael clattered down the narrow stairway. He shook his head. I left him to heave Newton onto a chair.

I checked the answering machine. No light flashing for new messages. Juno! It was ancient and used plastic tape. I ran it back. One from a male asking him to go for a pint, then a marketing call for insurance. But the last one was in a female voice. No soft tones as Quintus described, but three abrupt words, 'No food. None.'

I stared at the machine and pressed the repeat last message button. No mistaking the words, or the speaker, but what did they mean? Was she holed up somewhere and had run out of supplies?

Michael shrugged and shook his head. 'It's not a code message we use. Not a clue.'

I continued checking; the unit drawers, papers heaped on the kitchen table, envelopes crushed together in a metal frame balancing on the mantel shelf.

Michael pulled the understair cupboard open and half disappeared into it. 'Look what I've found.' And waggled a black padded bag in the air. 'Now I wonder why it was hidden at the back behind the Christmas decorations. The router's in there as well.'

He fired up the laptop, but it refused to go past the login page without the password. He tried once more, but nothing.

'No, leave it,' I said and brushed his hand away. 'If it's a standard system, it'll lock up if the third attempt fails. Let me make a call.'

I picked it up off the table, walked into the kitchen, shut the door and called Fausta.

'We've found this laptop,' I said when she paused for breath. 'Can you hack into it?'

She broke into convulsive laughter. 'You have to be joking! Of course I can. I thought you wanted me to do something difficult.'

Sometimes Fausta sounded like too much of a smartass. She talked me through the set up and I called Michael in.

'Fausta thinks she can crack this, but you'll have to be her fingers.' I laid my phone down by the scanner and laptop and handed him the earpiece. 'Play with it while I have a little conversation with our friend out there.'

'Remember there are rules.' He gave me a long, steady look.

'Sure.'

XXI

Michael had blindfolded Newton and tied his legs to a dining chair.

'Now, Christopher, you and I are going to have a little talk. You know how it goes – hard way or easy way. Your choice.'

He opted for the silent routine.

I sighed and smacked one of his kneecaps hard with a steel ladle from the kitchen.

He grunted and flinched.

'Last chance. Ten seconds not to get me annoyed.'

I tapped his shoulder ten times as I counted the seconds. Nothing.

I was annoyed.

'What have you done to him?'

Michael's voice was sharp. Newton was unconscious, but he'd come round in about ten to fifteen minutes.

'He's having a little sleep.' I shrugged. 'I gave him a standard relaxant. Like we gave your Lieutenant Wilson on the exercise.'

'Well?'

'He admitted he's been in contact with Nicola, she's staying nearby, but she won't tell him where. He says that he has to wait for her to contact him. He went a little vague when I pressed him about an emergency contact number for her. He was trying very hard to conceal it. Or the relaxant was making him ditzy. What have you got?'

'We're in and I haven't found anything startling yet. Fausta's downloading the entire hard disk to work on. She wants a couple of hours to run analyses on it. She says she'll message you. A remarkable young woman.'

I grinned at him. 'You sound like something out of an old movie.'

He gave me a reluctant smile back.

Before we left, we laid Newton on the couch in the recovery position and found a blanket to cover him. I prised the back off his cell, inserted a miniature tracker bug. I seeded bugs throughout the house including his landline phone, and two in the coat hung on the back of another chair. Michael relocked the back door and after cutting the cable ties around Newton's wrists, we gave a last look around and left.

Back at the car, we drank coffee and ate sandwiches Michael bought at the subway station and waited as the rain folded over us again.

'Nic?'
  'Sorry, wrong number.'
  'It's Chris.'
  'Get off this line. Go to a public phone box.'
  'Round here? You're joking.'
  'Meet at 302.'
  The line went dead.

The tracker bugs in his coat were working perfectly until he dove into the subway at Hamilton Square. Gods, these tunnels had to be deep! Michael followed him. My screen showed Newton could take a train in any direction; this part of the network was underground, so untrackable. He could disappear and our lead would die. Hades.

It was a tense ten minutes until Michael called.

'In the open now. Just passed Birkenhead Park. Out.'

I hit the gas on the rental car. Luckily, the road was straight and wide. No right turns, thank Juno.

My cell rang again. 'Going north, Wallasey now. He's heading for the terminus at New Brighton.'

I met Michael at the entrance of the red-brick station at New Brighton with an umbrella to shield us from the freezing rain. As I kissed him like he was an old friend visiting, I watched Newton out of the corner of my eye as he walked down the street, head hunched down, hands in his pockets. He was easy to mark; he had that soldier's light rolling gait. He made for the promenade by the sea wall; it was completely open, no cover of any kind.

He dove into a decorated Victorian shelter, the kind with slatted wood seats to rest on, a sloping swayback roof, but sides open exposed to the sea air. Rain dripped off the pointy black ironwork edging the roof. Michael drove on and we parked up at the other end of the grey marine lake. I hooked my field glasses around my head and snapped off several shots of Newton and the figure he was talking to while we listened in on my receiver. It was Nicola Sandbrook.

'What happened?' Nicola.

'Some American woman. She burst in like a bloody tank. I didn't see her face, just heard her voice. And she was pissed, really pissed with me.'

'Mitela.'

'Who is she? CIA?'

Nicola didn't answer.

'C'mon, Nic, if she isn't Company, what is she?'

'Worse.'

A pause, ruffling cloth.

'What the hell have you got me into?'

'Don't sweat it. How long was she there?'

'About half an hour.'

'Tell me in detail.'

After he finished, she told him to sweep his house; there'd be bugs everywhere. Through the glasses, I saw her pat him down and search, her hands into every pocket, under the shirt and jacket collars, into his belt. She made him take his shoes off.

'Got it!'

Her foot stamped down, crushing the tiny metal disc, causing a spike in one of the lines on my screen and then its death.

Michael looked worried, but I smiled at him.

'Jesus, that's small,' came Newton's voice.

'Yeah, well,' Nicola replied. 'The people we're up against are clever bastards.'

In the car, Michael looked puzzled.

'Decoy,' I whispered to him, still watching the two figures through my field glasses.

'You've been out too long,' Nicola said, her voice sharp. 'You should have searched more thoroughly after being turned over like that.'

'Don't do the stroppy madam with me. I'm the one doing you a favour, remember.'

Newton stood up, walked over to the railing, crossed his arms and leant them on the top. He looked out over the grey waves, towards the old squat fort. Nicola followed him and wound her arm around his waist. He didn't move away from the intimate embrace, but continued staring out to sea, like he was trying to ignore her.

She bent her back, moving closer in and looked up into his face, ignoring the hair whipping around her head in the breeze.

'Don't be angry. I'm sorry, Chris. I need you so much.'

I snorted at her manipulative tactics, but my irritation was punctured by his next words.

'Look, Nic, I can't keep that bloke in my brother's warehouse forever.'

'Is he being trouble?'

'No, he just looks like some wounded animal.'

'That's what he is.'

'He's going to die on us if we don't feed him.'

'And the problem is?'

'Christ, you're hard.'

My head exploded. I went to wrench the car door open. I was going to throttle her.

Gods, I'd been so stupid. Asking Newton direct about Conrad hadn't occurred to me. I'd been so convinced Nicola was the key to finding Conrad, I'd concentrated on her. I struggled against the weight stopping me but it wouldn't budge. Michael had both hands on my upper arms, bearing down on my radials. The pain woke me up.

'No,' he said.

I swallowed hard.

'Focus.' He shook me.

'I'm good. You can let go,' I said, and took a long breath

The scanner pinged.

'Okay, Chris,' came Nicola's voice, 'I'll try and find somewhere else, but you know it's not easy. If I can't, we'll just have to dump him.'

'Dump him? No way, I'm not getting involved in topping him.'

'You said you were going to help me.'

'Not that.' Newton said.

She sighed, a little theatrically. 'Okay, Chris. Shame you're no longer up to it.'

'Just shut it.'

The lines on the scanner display dropped to the baseline. A beep, then silence.

'Oh, shit,' Michael whispered, 'she's walking this way.'

We dove into the wells in front of the seats, curling up as tightly as we could. Luckily, we'd left a few millimetres' gap at the top of each window, so they hadn't steamed up. I counted a full minute before peeping over the rim at the base of the window. Newton had stayed, looking out to sea. I could just see Nicola in the distance walking away at a smart pace.

Hades and all the Furies. I had around thirty seconds to decide whether to follow my instinct and go after her, or go for Newton who could lead us to Conrad.

XXII

Driving back to Hamilton Square, I concentrated through a red fog of worry and anger on the late afternoon traffic. My gut clenched hard. It didn't help any being on the wrong side of the road and the vehicle. I cruised around until I found a space. I fed the meter then went to lounge on a bench in the square, pretending to play with my cell. Only it wasn't a cell. The mini scanner showed Newton exiting the subway entrance. A minute later, he appeared around the corner.

I tugged on my green woollen hat and pulled the scarf tighter against the cold as anybody innocent would do. The rain had stopped, but the temperature was dropping fast. I held my breath as Newton walked past me, followed at a discreet distance by Michael who pretended he was looking for somebody. I waved at Michael and we greeted each other like a couple meeting up and set off arm in arm diagonally across the square to collect the parked car.

'Are you okay now?' he asked when we were inside, sheltered against the wind.

'Sure.'

'Humph.'

'Don't push it, Michael.'

'Fausta's sent me a report on the hard disk,' I said, 'email, porn, games, music – the usual. We have his brother's cell but nothing else. We go back in and sweat it out of him.'

'He was upset at Nicola leaving the man—'

'It's Conrad. I'm sure it is.'

I had to be sure after my decision on the seafront.

He coughed. 'Well, after Nicola's act this afternoon, Newton may feel guilty enough or sorry for him and go and check him.'

'You're such a romantic.' I snorted. 'We go in now.'

This time I had Michael take the front entrance. I parked up, glanced both ways, to check nobody was around and climbed over the gate leading to the back alley. At Newton's house, light shone through the kitchen window. I crept across the small yard. The shadow of a figure through the dimpled frosted glass stood up, then faded, presumably to answer the door to Michael.

I pulled the pick set out of my bag and unfolded it. As I went to insert the tool into the door lock, I had the sudden urge to stop. A tingle in my neck. I pulled back and retreated behind the garbage can seconds before the lock clicked and the door swung open, letting the light flood out into the half-dark.

Nicola.

She stood on the back step and scanned around. My heart thudded. Had she seen or heard me? Or was it a reaction to Michael knocking on the front door? And what in Hades was she doing here now?

I wanted to grab her. But if I did, would I lose the chance of finding Conrad alive? If she ran true to the Tella type, she'd never give up where he was. Even pouring industrial amounts of relaxant into her, by the time we'd extracted the information, Conrad could be dead. No, Newton was the key. She'd have to wait.

She cocked her head like she was listening. I couldn't hear any noise from inside except a faint sound from some soap on the television. No noise of anybody else, or shouting. No fight. After a minute, she went back in.

As I slid out through the gate at the end of the row, Michael was waiting for me. He pulled me around the corner and across the road.

'What the hell happened there?' I asked.

Around five meters from Newton's house, Michael had seen a taxi draw up in front of it. Nicola jumped out and ran up the steps. He didn't dare call or even text me, he said. The last thing you needed when you were covert was your cell phone sounding, even with a tiny message ping.

But what was she doing there?

We took up station further down the road shielded by a camping trailer wedged into a front garden. Holding the scanner clear of the metal box, I switched it on. Nothing. The lines bubbled along the bottom of the display. They couldn't have found every single bug and certainly not the thread bugs. I turned the volume up to max and heard cloth rustling, then a noise of wood against wood, a cupboard hinge creaking. They were searching in silence. I chewed my lip while we waited.

★

Five minutes later, the line on the display spiked as Newton's exasperated voice blasted out.

'Satisfied?'

I winced and hit the volume control.

'I suppose so.'

'Jesus, Nic, I know you're anal, but this is stupid.'

'I'm going now. I'll be back tomorrow to settle this permanently.'

'Why don't you stay here instead?'

'Security. Nothing personal, Chris. If you don't know where I am, you can't tell anybody else.'

'Please your bloody self. Don't expect me to sit in waiting. I'm going down the pub.'

As soon as she'd disappeared, Michael dawdled along the street past Newton's house. He paused a metre or so beyond the door, took out a packet of cigarettes, put one between his lips and patted his pockets as if searching for a lighter. Right on cue Newton came out of his house, slammed the door shut and stomped past Michael, his head bent forward and shoulders tense. Michael turned and followed him.

I drove down Newton's road and parked up between dull orange street lights thirty metres beyond him. I let myself out the driver's door, opened the trunk, bent in and rummaged around like I was looking for something. I tightened my grip around the hilt of my knife and stood up as he came level with me.

A flash of panic crossed Newton's face as he recognised me. He spun around, ready to run, but Michael grabbed his shoulders, jammed his knee into the back of Newton's and rolled him into the trunk. I slammed the lid down.

Observing the speed limit – the last thing we needed was to be picked up by the cops – we drove to the docks and found a deserted yard with no CCTV. Parked in the shadow under the shelter of a semi-derelict delivery hatch, we approached the trunk, prepared for attack by an angry hornet. Michael had his Sig Sauer ready, me my knife and cuffs.

'One, two, three, mark!'

Michael pulled the lid up and I swung in sideways to body block our captive. I deflected him enough for Michael to push him back in on his face so I could cuff him.

'Fuck you, you bastards!'

We let him rant for a few moments, his breath pluming in the cold. He stopped trembling after a minute or two, took a deep breath and coughed.

'Finished?' I said.

'Not by a long way, you bitch.'

I laughed at him, which made him angry again, but I said nothing. I stared into the back of his eyes until he broke his gaze.

'Now, Christopher, last time we had a little chat, I hadn't realised what a lot you knew. This time, we're going for full house. Same choice. But having two doses of this relaxant so close will make you feel sick for weeks.' It was a lie, of course. It wouldn't do a thing to him. 'Or you could cooperate.'

'Screw you. Nic was right.'

'Right. So it's right to kidnap, brutalise and starve a man who's done nothing to you? A man who's obviously ill? Her own father?'

He stared at me. 'Her father?' His voice rose several notes. 'You're lying.'

'Your Nicola is a very devious young woman. But you know that, don't you, Christopher?'

He looked down and said nothing.

'You know, don't you, in your heart, that she's been manipulating you all along?'

'Remember the training accident out on the Brecon Beacons when she made you take the rap? Or the failed reconnaissance in Mogadishu when you lost three comrades? Now she's trying to make you an accessory to murder.'

He looked away.

I nodded at Michael who brought me a plastic folder. The chill breeze ruffled the pages, but I held two stapled sheets up and turned my flashlight on it.

'The top one is a translation of the DNA test done a few months ago.' I held up Conrad's photograph. 'This is the man, isn't it?'

He glared at me, changed to sullen, but gave a quick nod.

Back at his house, accompanied by Michael, he fetched the keys. We'd taken his cell phone, money and ID.

'You'll get these back when we're finished, Christopher. If you try escape, or fuck with us, you'll be so finished, you won't need them back. Understood?'

He nodded.

'If you cooperate, you may even find something in your bank as our thanks. Oh, and I'd go on a little trip someplace a distance away for a few weeks. For your own good.'

We met nobody around the warehouse yard. It was approaching midnight and frost had already coated everything with a light sheen. Newton unlocked the padlock on the chain linking the corrugated metal doors together. The concrete floor was patched with oil stains. Workbenches strewn with tools, machine parts, half-cars, a ramp, gas canisters and welding equipment screamed illegal bodyshop. The acrid smell of paint came from a taped-up glistening shell in the far corner.

'Remember. Nothing stupid.'

He led us around a partition into a dark passageway with two doors off. He stopped in front of one and unlocked it. I signalled him to go in first. I nearly choked on the smells of oil, unwashed body and faeces filling the room. A rim of orange from the street lighting showed around a boarded window opposite. As my eyes adapted to the gloom, I saw the figure huddled on the concrete floor and dropped to my knees.

XXIII

Orange light reflected off the links of a chain ending around the figure's ankle. I swallowed hard.

'Take the key off our friend here.' I said, 'and lock us all in. I don't want him taking off if we're a little occupied.'

I fumbled in my pocket for my flashlight and shone it on the body. It hadn't moved since we'd arrived. My other hand trembled as I reached down to touch it. The face was hidden by the shirt collar but I didn't need to pull it back to see it was Conrad. I pressed my fingers on his throat hoping, praying, to find a pulse.

His head jerked back at my touch, eyes gleaming like a wounded animal fearful of the hunter's knife. His hand came up to shield his eyes.

He croaked, 'No.'

Alive. He was alive.

I sat back, releasing my breath and closing my eyes for a moment. Then my brain re-engaged. I cradled his head and put a bottle of water to his mouth and let the first drops dribble over his lips. When he drank, from it, he swallowed like he was never going to stop. I prised it away for a few seconds. He couldn't afford to lose more liquid by throwing up.

'It is really you?'

'Yes, I'm here. You're safe now.'

The imperial transport landed late next afternoon at the local air force base, disgorging Antonia Faenia, the PGSF's chief medical officer plus Livius, Paula and Atria from my ART. No, Hades, my *former* ART. I no longer had a team. They were all dressed in casuals, mostly jeans and fleeces. Not Faenia; designer suited, carrying a polished doctor's black satchel and striding across the tarmacadam, she looked like any medical prima donna. But a load fell off my shoulders when I saw she'd come in person.

At the hospital, she gave staccato nods at the British medic as he gave his report to her, nervous under the piercing stare and the frown of concentration on Faenia's strong face. She gestured impatiently as soon as he spoke his last word and followed him down the glaring white corridor to a door guarded by two armed cops. Inside, Michael, who was sitting opposite the doorway, rose to his feet, wary at the sudden invasion.

'Professor Faenia, Captain Browning.'

She nodded briefly and went straight to the patient. While she was scanning and checking, and exchanging terse comments with the British doctor, I told Michael we'd take over security.

He frowned at me.

'I'm grateful, Michael, very grateful, but he's our problem.'

'Commissioner Brudgland instructed me to stay until the transport was in the air.'

I smiled, almost to myself. 'Yeah, he's a real careful Harry, isn't he?'

'No comment. I have to stay, but I'll stand the police down.'

A knock and Atria and Paula entered, glanced at me and took up position on the back wall. Faenia came over to me after she'd given the patient a shot and bundled her stuff back in her bag.

'He'll sleep for about twelve hours. I've instructed this doctor to give a vitamin injection every four. I'm going to eat now and sleep. I'll be back at seven.' She scrutinised my face. 'I suggest you come with me, Countess. You look exhausted.'

Faenia woke me as promised; I thought she might ignore my instruction and do that 'we left you to rest as you looked as if you needed it' routine. She didn't say much as we drove from the air base mess back to the hospital.

A suit was arguing with Livius outside the door to Conrad's room.

'I cannot have a private security force in my hospital. It will intimidate and unsettle the other patients.'

'We have taken over from the uniformed police who were armed, so I think we are not so menacing.' Livius was smiling, releasing all his charm on the man in his accented English.

'It really won't do. I insist on speaking to your supervisor. Where is he?'

'She's right here,' I said, stepping up to face him. I left two centimetres between us.

He stumbled back.

'Countess Carina Mitela, representing Imperatrix Silvia Apulia of Roma Nova. How can I help you?'

'Oh.' His eyes darted between Livius, Faenia and me. Faenia shot a look of contempt at him and went in to see her patient. The administrator waved his hand in a vague circle. 'Your people are upsetting the other patients. You'll have to remove them.'

'I'm very sorry you think that. I'll ask for a squad of your armed police to replace them. That'll be so much more calming.'

'That's an extremely unhelpful attitude.' His face flushed with anger.

'Look, I apologise. I didn't mean to be rude. What have my people done? Have they caused a problem or been discourteous, or annoyed anybody?

'Not specifically, no.'

'Any complaints made by individual patients?'

'Well, no.'

I said nothing. I folded my arms across my chest, raised an eyebrow as my grandmother used to do and stared at him.

'Oh, very well. When are you leaving?'

'That will be the professor's decision, but I'll be sure to keep your team advised. Anything else?'

He shook his head.

I went into Conrad's room, leaving the little man puffing outside.

The ginger and malt aroma of the restorative hit me first. Conrad was sitting up in the hospital bed, drinking it out of the aluminium cup matching the flask Faenia held in her hand.

He smiled up at me hesitantly. I reflected it automatically. He looked exhausted; brown shadows surrounded his eyes and the skin over the bridge of his nose was tight, emphasising the scar from his broken nose. Dark blond and grey stubble covered his lower face making him look even more like a fugitive. But more than that it was the anxiety in his eyes as he searched my face.

He'd torn my personal life into shreds, destroyed the trust between us and blighted my professional career. I should hate him. I kept my gaze steady. After a few moments, he tipped his chin up like a defiant child, then blinked and looked away. His face crumpled like a piece of discarded paper. He was at rock bottom. Despite the hurt, I wanted to fold him into my arms and hold him there safe.

But I couldn't. Never more did 'servant of the state' sound as meaningless as it did now. I retreated into banalities.

'How do you feel?' I asked.

'Hungry. I haven't eaten for four days.' His voice was light, but his hand trembled.

'As soon as you've drunk that, Legate,' Faenia said a little too briskly, 'you can eat some cereal and one piece of fruit.'

I frowned at Faenia. She was wrong to call him legate, and she knew it. I beckoned her outside.

'How long before he can travel?' I asked.

'Tomorrow at the earliest.'

Atria and I worked the night shift. She took up station outside, but I spent most of the night watching Conrad and thinking. I must have dozed off as it was light when Livius shook my shoulder next morning.

From a plastic shopping bag, Livius handed Conrad a battery shaver and Conrad took himself into the shower. We kept the bathroom door open. As he towelled his hair, now free of the brown dye Lucius had given him, I was shocked to see how much white there was amongst the dark blond. His arms and torso were bruised, and a cut on his forehead had opened and was seeping. I handed him a gauze pad, but didn't say anything.

He tore open the clothes pack Livius handed him, glanced at the two of us, but we didn't move. No way was I going to have fewer than two people in the room with him at any time. He shrugged, slid off the towel around his waist and dressed in the casuals. He hovered, uncertain what to do. He rubbed his free hand along the hairline by his accident scar, but looked at the floor.

I chewed my lip and tried to find some way to break the awkward atmosphere.

'I presume you've come to take me back,' he said.

I nodded, swallowing the ache in my throat. Why the hell had Silvia forced me to do this?

'Did they revoke your resignation?'

'No, I work under a different authority.'

'Not a scarab?'

'No.'

He gave up.

'Did you find Nic...Nicola?'

'For a while.'

'What stopped you taking her?'

'You did.'

'What do you mean?'

'My orders are to prioritise finding and bringing you back over her capture.'

'Mars! That was hard for Silvia.' He spoke with the sympathy of a husband. I felt a bloom of anger. Although their eight-year partnership had finished before we met, I could never forget the emotional bond Conrad and Silvia shared because of their three children. I batted it away and pulled my shoulders back. Time to do my job, however shitty.

'By my authority as imperial agent, I am placing you under arrest. Do you submit to the court?' As I said the formal words, my heart was breaking.

'I submit to the court,' he replied after a few moments in a cold, despairing voice.

'I am not going to cuff you in front of foreigners, but you must give me your personal word of honour that you will not try to escape.'

He nodded.

'Aloud.'

His face tightened, producing a peevish look.

'You have my word. Aren't you going to read me my rights?' he asked with an ironic tone.

'You don't have any rights. You've been proscribed.'

Ever efficient, Michael provided an SUV to transport us from the hospital to the airbase.

Conrad had collapsed into the hospital chair like his bones had dissolved into powder when I told him about the proscription. He stayed there, frozen, not believing it and staring at the floor. In the end, Livius had taken Conrad's arm in a firm grip and hauled him to his feet. Conrad hardly reacted, but followed automatically. Atria and Paula fell in close behind as I led the group down the hospital corridor to the glass door. I gave the hospital administrator an ironic bow before making our way out to where Michael was waiting. Wedged between Livius and Atria with Paula watching him from the opposite seat, Conrad slumped and still said nothing.

As we rode along, Michael made light conversation in that

polite way the British do in tense situations. At the plane, the others took Conrad up the steps, Faenia following. On the tarmacadam, Michael and I waited until they were out of earshot.

'I'm truly grateful for all the support you've given us, Michael. I don't know any other way except to say thank you. Please convey my thanks to Andrew Brudgland for putting you at our disposal.'

'No trouble at all. I mean it. We'll keep an eye out for Nicola Sandbrook. If she resurfaces, we'll have her before she can move.' I knew he was saying that to comfort me. She was an expert at living below the wire and they just didn't have the resources. I gave him an understanding smile.

He looked at me steadily. 'I think you're in for a rough time on all fronts in the next few weeks. Give me a call if you think I can help or you want a sounding board.' He bent down and kissed me lightly on my cheek. 'Take care.'

Conrad flinched as I touched him on the knee. We'd been in the air for an hour. I glanced around in the half-gloom of the transport deck. A crate and our bags were secured by heavy nets to bolts in the centre of the floor. A row of tubular-framed canvas fixed seats lined each side. Paula, Atria and Livius sat along the opposite side towards the back, Faenia eight along from us.

'Are you okay?' I raised my voice against the aircraft noise. Unlike a cosy civilian aircraft this military transport had no plush cabin with insulation. 'Do you want something to eat or drink?'

He shook his head and stared at the opposite wall of the fuselage.

'You have to talk to me sooner or later. I prefer not to do it in Interview 2 with half of the Interrogation Service listening.'

'She beat Quintus, she broke his arm.' He shivered. He seemed so fragile. 'Her hands were locked round his throat and she was shaking him. He was making choking sounds like an animal. She would have killed him if I hadn't dragged her off. Gods, she's vicious. I knew then I had to go after her. But I was so unprepared. She took me as if I was a one-day cadet.' He looked at the floor.

'That's the least of your troubles. Silvia is furious, boiling. When you disobeyed her summons, I thought she was going to implode. Quintus tried to take the rap, but she wouldn't accept it. She's devastated, Conrad. She knows Stella has been difficult and is impressionable, but she expected you to rein Nicola in.' I stopped before I went too far.

'She's Caius, all over again,' he whispered.

I remembered Conrad's haggard face the day he'd talked about Caius Tellus. We'd been at Castra Lucilla, our summer home in the country, lying on a rug drying in the sun after a vigorous swim. Conrad wouldn't detail the personal abuse Caius had imposed on him; he stayed silent for a few minutes at that part, his breath light and eyes unfocused.

After the city had been re-taken by Imperial forces and Caius' brutal rebellion defeated, Quintus had discovered the nine-year-old Conrad cowering, filthy and terrified, in a locked cellar in Caius's suburban villa. During the journey to the derelict farm in the east that the ruined and disgraced Tella family had been allowed to keep, Conrad remembered pulling the blanket over the back of his head and huddling on the seat of an old utility truck, refusing to let go of Quintus as they drove through the night.

When Conrad had stopped talking that day by the lake, I'd held him in my arms while he wept at the memory of his ruined childhood. That was nearly fifteen years ago. I'd thought it was all behind him; he'd never mentioned it since. Now he looked haggard, lost somehow. He took some short breaths and gazed out of the aircraft window.

'It was that kid being beaten, the day of the accident. That man was Caius and the kid me.' He closed his eyes for a few moments. 'It was a nightmare when Caius came to live with us. One day my dad wasn't there. I ran all round the house, looking for him, crying for him. I kept asking for him. Instead, my mother said Caius was going to be my new dad. Even at three, I didn't like him. He'd pull me on to his lap and stroke me. I felt hot and uncomfortable. I wanted to run. Mama was cross with me and said I had to stop being silly, but in the end I saw she was frightened of him.

'When we came back from her funeral – I was six – I clung on to Uncle Quintus's hand praying that he would take me home with him. But Caius pulled me away. I didn't understand why I had to go with him, but later I learnt it was because he'd been named by my mother as legal guardian. That night he gave me my first beating. To settle me in, he said. Then the nightmare started.

'He made me sleep in his bed each night. I dreaded his weight on me, the pain, the soreness as he—' Conrad swallowed hard. 'I sobbed myself to sleep most nights. Then he'd beat me again. I ran away once. He laughed and joked with the *vigiles* when they brought me back, then he beat me unconscious. I was only a kid but I swore I would kill him when I was strong enough. He said I was nothing and would never be anything but his pet animal. He made me live outside in the day in a dog hutch. None of the servants would speak to me – they were too frightened of him.

'Later, I found out my dad had died, in an 'accident' they said, but nobody had told me.

'I didn't see Uncle Quintus except once. He came and fetched me from the hutch. I ran into his arms, begging him to take me away, but he gently set me down and told me Caius wasn't going to hurt me any more, but I would have to stay there. I watched with Quintus as the servants unloaded an unconscious Caius from the back of Quintus's car and carried him into the house. Quintus's eyes were hard and he looked as nasty as Caius as he watched his brother disappear into the house.

'I wept as I watched Quintus's car disappear down the drive, but he was right; Caius didn't touch me after that. He ignored me apart from giving me an occasional kicking. And later, he went away to the town and only came back occasionally. I would sneak into the kitchen by the back door and pilfer food from the servants' hall. Sometimes they let me stay inside.

'One day when I was nine, he suddenly appeared, beat me again and locked me in the cellar in the dark. He never came back again. Uncle Quintus rescued me.'

I seized both of Conrad's hands and pressed them. Tears trickled down my face, but I ignored them.

'Quintus says the farm we went to live on was almost derelict. I thought it was Elysium. Nobody bothered me. Quintus was so kind when he found me sobbing over a dead chicken or just nothing. He'd hold me until the sadness passed. The other kids at school showed me how children should be cared for. I vowed my children would be treated like gods and protected from everything. No child of mine would ever be deprived or suffer, even if I died in making sure that happened.'

His eyes flamed in his grey, exhausted face. He dropped my hands and clenched his fists. His whole body shuddered. I said nothing but pulled him into my arms.

Hours later, I woke at the sound of the plane descending. My left arm and shoulder were numb with Conrad's weight full on it.

I nudged him awake. He looked around, disorientated.

'It's okay, we're nearly home.' I said. 'Here, drink this,' and I handed him a water flask. He shook his head, sat up and glanced at the guards sitting with impassive faces.

'It'd be easier if I just threw myself off the plane,' he said and sighed.

'No way.' I tried to smile. 'Too late, anyway, we're nearly down. Look, I'll find you the best psychoanalyst, therapist, whatever. And Sertorius will do the legal stuff. But you are undoubtedly going down for years. Or if the judge is really pissed, they'll make you stateless and deport you.'

His Adams apple bounced as he swallowed hard. Exile was the worst punishment any Roman could be given; a living death cut off from every connection and family and friends forbidden to communicate with or see them.

'But you,' he said, 'and the children? Gods, the children!' He reached out and grabbed my hand. 'Divorce me. Now. That'll stop the worst.'

XXIV

'You need to come with us, Conradus Mitelus.'

He stood and Paula drew his hands behind him and cuffed him. He stared down at me as she grasped his arm. I couldn't stop myself following him with my eyes as she led him down the back ramp at the open end of the transport. Nor watching him climb in the back of the short wheelbase, hardly needing Paula's assistance. I swallowed and wiped an imaginary speck of dust off my cheek as my heart left and went with him.

Faenia gave me a measured look. 'Go home, Countess, and rest.'

'Thanks for your concern, but I have an appointment.' I cleared my throat. 'Can I drop you anywhere?'

I had to wait for Silvia; she was in a meeting with the chancellor. Her assistant gave me a life-saving coffee, the first good one for five days.

I closed my eyes and wondered how Conrad was doing. He'd be processed much as any other detainee and housed in the PGSF cells for the pre-trial period. If he was convicted, I'd have the lawyer try to have him hospitalised for treatment, not sent to the central military prison or, Jupiter save us, the silver mines at Truscium. In his fragile state, he wouldn't survive a week.

My eyes snapped open as I shuddered awake. Silvia's assistant was touching my shoulder and looking worried. I smiled at her, stood up, patted down my creased clothes and followed her into Silvia's office.

'Welcome back, Carina.' She searched my face. 'You look shattered. I won't hold you up. Just give me the basics.'

She indicated an easy chair and took the one opposite. She listened, her concentration on full. She didn't move until I'd finished.

'It was a choice, bring Conradus back here ASAP or go after Nicola. I had to come back with him. You do understand that?'

'I admit those were my instructions,' Silvia said. 'I don't often proscribe somebody – it must therefore be the priority. But I'm a little disappointed you couldn't neutralise the threat itself – the girl.'

Juno's tears! I was mentally and physically exhausted, my life was falling apart around me and she wanted a fricking miracle. I jammed my lips together. No way could I give her a polite answer until I controlled my resentment. And a little guilt.

'I'll do a proper report for you and the Council, of course,' I said after a few moments. 'Maybe you could remind me of the date? I've been a little busy lately.'

'In four days' time,' she replied as tersely.

She folded her hand and rubbed the tips of her fingers and thumb against each other. 'How is he?'

'Outwardly fine, inside, a total fuck-up.' I looked at her twitching hand. 'Sorry, that was a little strong. But he's a mess. I'm going to try persuade whoever to let him be assessed and start psychotherapy now.'

Whatever you might say, I thought.

I waited to be dismissed. I wanted a measure of Nonna's French brandy and my bed.

The awkward pause grew.

'Look, I'm sorry, Carina. I didn't mean to be ungrateful. You've done everything I asked and with your usual dedication. I shouldn't have thrown Nicola in your face. I just hoped you might have been your usual superhero self.'

Gods, she had unrealistic expectations sometimes. Still, I had to keep trying.

'Don't worry. She's next on my agenda.'

Allegra wound her arms around my neck and laid her head on my chest like I did with Aurelia when she was alive. Except Allegra tucked her feet under her legs as we sat on the big couch in the atrium. Tonia and Gil were behind us in the alcove absorbed in competing up the levels in some computer game.

'Can I see him?'

'I'm sure I can arrange something.' Older children could visit parents in a regular prison, but I'd never seen one in the PGSF barracks. But then we didn't get many parents held on treason charges.

'You look so tired, Mama.' She stroked my cheek. 'Why don't you go up? I'll chase these two out in a minute.'

I was bone-weary but annoyed everybody wanted to be my mother. But her eyes were large with concern.

'Okay, you win.'

I stumbled my way into bed, missing Conrad tonight more than I had in all the previous months.

Sertorius dropped his pompous act when I explained the seriousness of Conrad's case. He fiddled with his immaculate hand-woven silk tie and scratched the side of his open mouth before replying.

'Diminished responsibility is the only way out I can see. I say that, of course, without having consulted my histories.' He tapped on his el-pad. 'I'm free at 13.00 today for an hour. We'll go and register my representation with whoever is in charge,' He glanced at me. 'If, of course, you are available to accompany me then, Countess,' he added as an afterthought.

With me in my formal black suit and Sertorius in his lawyer's Italian tailoring, we looked like a pair of management consultants as we crossed the courtyard to the PGSF entrance.

Although I had full access privileges as imperial agent, I thought it more polite to wait in the entrance hallway. I studied the photos of ceremonial occasions without really seeing them. Sertorius fidgeted with his papers; he'd never been inside this building and looked disconcerted at the fully-kitted guard porting a bullpup assault rifle and helmet with black visor.

'Carina.' Daniel appeared from the side corridor. His face wore a solemn, but not unfriendly expression.

'You should distance yourself,' I said. 'Tainted by association and so on,' I added at his puzzled look.

He snorted. 'Don't be ridiculous.'

I held his eyes for a few moments, trying to convey my gratitude and a warning at the same time.

Sertorius coughed.

'Well, come on, then. You know the way.' Daniel spoke into his commset, telling them to bring the prisoner to Interview 2 where he had visitors. Sertorius registered with the custody sergeant for all-times access. The sergeant had to look up some regulation; they hadn't had a suspected traitor under their guard for a while.

'Usual rules; audio off, video on. And don't push it,' Daniel warned me as the guard unlocked the door.

Inside were a plastic-topped metal table bolted to the floor and three plastic chairs, two empty, side by side, the third on the other side of the table occupied by a yellow-clad figure curled over, away from the chair's back support, head drooping down with his hands in his lap. He looked up as we entered.

It was his eyes. The despair I read in those hazel eyes. I went up to him, pulled him up off his chair and bear-hugged him. He leaned into me. Something like a gulp echoed through my shoulder as he buried his face in my neck. I had the weird feeling of being a mother comforting a hurt child. I grasped his upper arms, pulled him gently away. The skin had shrunk into his face. I stroked the edge of his cheekbone. He closed his eyes for a moment.

Sertorius coughed. Again. I'd get him a bottle of syrup for next time. I moved my chair next to Conrad's and took his hand as Sertorius began to throw questions at him.

'Has anybody interviewed you yet?'

'Only preliminary facts. And advising me of the charges.'

Sertorius shot a look over his glasses. 'Did you accept the charges?'

'Of course not.' The old fire blazed in Conrad's eyes. 'I may be stressed, mental, or what you want to call it, but I'm not stupid.'

'Very well.' Sertorius's voice went down a few degrees in temperature. 'You will not agree to any interview or interrogation of any sort without me present. As you are a seasoned practitioner of techniques to get people to talk, I am confident you won't fall for any of them. Whatever the provocation.

'Next, I am arranging a full psychiatric examination for you as soon as possible. Please be completely honest. I also need you to write or record a full account of everything since you first learnt of Nicola Tella's existence. Everything. I don't want any surprises in open court from the imperial accusatrix when she starts outlining the case for the prosecution. It doesn't matter if it's not in time order. Note the day or date or peg it on to something else. My assistant will pull it all together.'

He held up a digital recorder, a pad of paper and a sealable folder to the camera in the corner of the room, turning them 360 degrees for the security staff watching us.

'Seal it in the plastic folder. My assistant will collect what you have produced every day and give you a new set. Clear?'

Conrad nodded. The simple recorder was passwordable, but somebody several degrees less good than Fausta could crack it within minutes. But it was something that all sides respected. Mostly. Sertorius dredged through some formalities. Conrad sat impassive as he listened, seemed to take it all in. At last, the lawyer pushed the representation order towards Conrad.

'I apologise for my rudeness earlier, Gaius Sertorius,' Conrad said as he signed and gave the document back. 'I'm feeling a little unsteady at present.'

Sertorius thawed and smiled. 'Understandable,' he replied, looking around the plain beige room with its concrete floor, plastic furniture and lack of windows. 'I'll call in tomorrow morning first thing to check when the interviews are scheduled.' He stood, shook my hand, pressed Conrad's shoulder briefly and knocked on the door to be let out.

I waited. Conrad's hand gripped mine. His eyes chased around the room. Eventually they stopped.

'I only wanted to make it up to her. Quintus rescued me, I wanted to rescue her from struggling. She was on her own, having to fight her way through. Everybody was against her, she told me. She said your attitude was typical.' He covered his face. 'Jupiter, I've been so bloody stupid.'

'Yes, but for the noblest of reasons and with all the pig-headedness of a true Tella.'

To be honest, I'd been frightened by his account of his three year terror at Caius's hands. Anything he'd had to endure in his later life was peanuts in comparison. No wonder he'd become so intent on doing the right thing, making sure that even the tough military structure he lived in was fair and just. At that moment, I respected him more than ever before.

'You've carried around the trauma of when you were a kid buried inside you,' I said, 'and it's come out at the same time as Nicola's attack. Did you never talk to anybody seriously about what Caius did to you?'

'No, we were too busy trying to keep alive. We slaved in the fields on that farm, every hour there was. I was nine. Until the vegetables came through we had nothing to eat except occasional eggs the scruffy hens laid and what the charity people gave us. Quintus got a school voucher for me and I ate midday at the school and they'd give me milk and bread before I walked back to the farm each evening. No, we had no "time to talk" as you Americans call it.'

As I checked out, the custody sergeant said the legate had asked if I would drop by his office. I stared at him for a moment. Then

I collected my brains; of course, he meant Daniel.

No assistant in the front office, so I walked past their desk and knocked.

'Come!'

He was concentrating on his screen, glanced up to see who it was.

'Give me a couple of minutes.'

I looked around the room. Conrad's books were still there, but not the personal stuff. Daniel had a photo of his mother and late brother on his desk but that was all.

He finished, grabbed a folder and opened it. His shoulders were hunched, rigid, just as his mouth was set in a straight line. Any sign of jokiness, of the overgrown schoolboy had vanished.

'This is the most awkward situation I've been in. No doubt it's the same for you. The only way to get through it is to do it all by the book. As Conrad's accused of threatening the state, the PGSF is the only body legally enabled to hold him. But the politicos are watching us like hawks to make sure we don't do him any special favours.'

'I'm sure you'll carry out your duty meticulously, Legate.'

'Don't get huffy with me – that's exactly what I mean.' He fixed me with his eyes. 'You have to promise me not to get up to any of your heroics. If I suspect anything, I'll close him down into isolation.'

Only Sertorius would be able to visit on nominated days; none of the rest of us.

'I'm too tired, Daniel, I just want to get him out of the dark hole he's living in. And I'm going to give him my hundred per cent support.'

'Well, you'll probably have to surrender your imperial warrant. You can't be part of the state machine and fight it at the same time.'

I emailed my report late the next morning to the Imperial Council secretariat for the meeting on Wednesday and copied it to Silvia. After lunch, I took Allegra to see her father. We signed in at the front desk and she received her bio-pass. As she looped it over her neck, her eyes widened at the armed guard at the back of the lobby where it split into the two-way corridor. At the entrance to the guard zone, at the walk-through scanner arch, she was checked again.

'They're very strict, aren't they? Nobody could get in. Or out.'

'No, darling, nobody.'

Only from the inside like that traitor Petronax had done years ago.

She held her arms out, perfectly calm, when the custody team scanned her, and took her coat off and turned out her pockets like she did it every day. I was so proud of how she read the declaration sheet with a firm clear voice, more at ease than most adults.

After giving Conrad a smile and a peck on the cheek, I left them alone. As the door shut, I saw his arm came around her waist, hers around his neck.

I leaned on the wall outside Interview 2, my eyes closed. I shook my head when the guard asked if I wanted a chair. Twenty minutes later, Allegra came out. Although outwardly calm, the skin was tight across her face and her cheeks glistened.

Nicola Sandbrook's account had just gone into double deficit.

XXV

After the Imperial Council meeting, I went straight back to the PGSF barracks, walked into the bar and swallowed a brandy in one. The mess steward said nothing, glanced at me and poured me another. I had nearly stopped trembling with anger when I sensed somebody next to me.

'Hey, Bruna, it's a bit early to hit the hard stuff?'

Livius. And Paula, approaching fast.

I hunched over on the bar stool. 'This is the only place where I can be among rational human beings.'

'Come and have some lunch or you'll fall over.' Paula guided me to one of the long tables in the mess room. I saw so many familiar faces, talking, laughing, hands waving in discussion. The noise filled the room, but who cared? I desperately wanted to be back here, in my beige, talking training, strategy, promotions and foul-ups, joshing with my comrades. I ate on the familiar government stamped plate, used plain steel cutlery and drank from the moulded glass beaker. And nearly wept.

How Silvia dealt with the Council every second week, I didn't know. I thanked the gods I'd been too busy to even think of standing for election to it. Being an independent advisor might have drawbacks like twenty-four seven on-call, but I'd take it any day.

The rational, wiser members seemed to get talked down by the malicious windbags. A high percentage of them were on an ego trip of some kind. They should be grateful I wasn't the imperatrix; I'd have shot half of them. But they accepted my report; two made facetious comments, which were squashed by the chancellor and a senior senator. They agreed with Silvia's proposal to lift the proscription but insisted the charges against Conrad stood. Without Nicola Tella, they said, they had no option. They passed on to something else and I left the room after a curt bow to Silvia.

★

I dropped in on Fausta to thank her, but she just said, 'Sure, anytime,' and waved it away. Even though a captain heading the digital security section, she wore just her black tee and the worst ironed uniform pants ever with scruffy sneakers as she sat in her electronic bat-cave. She still looked like the teenage black hat hacker she'd once been.

I checked in with Sepunia to see if she'd found anything new on Nicola.

'We've added a considerable amount to her personality profile after interviewing Quintus Tellus and his household and collating reports from your daughter and Maia Quirinia. The scarabs picked up some circumstantial detail from the drug dealing, but it doesn't conform to the usual pattern.'

'How so?'

'Apart from the deal you reported, she only made a few other contacts. If you're going to make any money from it, you need to establish a wide network quickly. But she didn't. And reading through the whole file, it's obvious she doesn't lack the drive and intelligence to do it.' She fixed her green eyes on my face. 'It's another indicator she was only using it as a method to compromise Stella Apulia.

'Of course,' she continued, 'we hope to gain a great deal more when the Interrogation Service start questioning Mitelus.' Confused, she stopped and looked over my shoulder at the far wall of her office. 'I mean, Conradus Mitelus.'

'Don't be polite on my account. That's nothing to what the Council called him.'

Sepunia touched my arm. 'Be very careful if you go after her, Carina. She has an abnormally low score on the personal morality scale.'

'So surprise me.'

That evening at home, crouching over my desk, I hesitated. My finger rested on the Send button. Exposing my life, my family and my personal opinions to be picked over by the Interrogation Service made acid flow up my gullet. I'd poked around enough in other people's lives, but it was entirely different when it was happening to me. But if I didn't volunteer my digital diaries, the IS would subpoena them, so I was saving myself a lot of unnecessary hassle.

I hit the key and copies of both work and personal flew off into

Interrogation Service chief's inbox. At least she was handling the interrogations herself, but her number two and Inspector Pelonia would pick through Conrad's and my life like a pair of assistant vultures.

'I've consulted every case going back to the recodification of the Tables in 1718.' Sertorius jabbed the screen of his el-pad at our meeting the following morning. 'Quite simply, there is no way out of this without Nicola Tella.'

I glared at him.

'Er, Sandbrook, rather.' He didn't apologise, just a flicker of his eyes in reaction. Quintus had filed the declaration disowning her days ago. Sertorius would do well to remember it.

Junia interrupted us, breaking the awkwardness.

'An urgent call from the legate, *domina*.'

I glanced up at her. A straight, sewn-up mouth. Now what?

She handed me the miniscreen with a frowning Daniel looking out of it.

'What—' I started.

'No, listen,' Daniel said. 'It's bad news.'

'Yes?'

'The imperial accusatrix is so confident of conviction,' Daniel said, 'she's moved the trial opening day up to start in ten days.'

I prepared with a few practice rounds in the small PGSF training arena with Livius. Covered in sweat and tired after twenty minutes intensive close quarter combat, I was stupid enough to ask for his opinion.

'You're good, Bruna, good enough to still give me the run around.' He clasped the back of his neck for a few moments with his free hand and looked down in the sand. 'Why don't you take those two who came to England on the exercise, Pelo and Allia, along as insurance?'

It only took five minutes to surrender the power I'd had as Silvia's direct representative. She understood. She always did, except when she lost her temper.

'Are you sure you don't want any official back up?' she said.

I'd stomped off the training area after refusing Livius, but with Silvia I merely shook my head. This was my call. I didn't want anybody else becoming entangled in what I couldn't decide was personal or official.

She fixed me with her eyes. 'I am going to have the PGSF commander at the London legation informed of your presence and tell her to keep a small detachment on twenty-four hour call. If you get stuck and I find out you didn't call on them, I'll throw you in the Transulium myself.'

'No. Don't. Not for me.' Conrad grabbed my hand and pressed it. His eyes narrowed and tilted up.

'Too bad. I've handed my warrant back and booked my flight. Allegra will come and visit you each day while I'm away and I'll catch up with her each evening.'

I reached out and he closed his eyes and breathed hard as my fingers ran over his cheek. The temptation to stay here bit me hard, but I batted it away before it had a second try.

'I might not get back before the start,' I said, 'but I'll bust my ass to drag hers into court.'

Conrad stuck his chin out and his face set like hardstone. 'Even if you bring her back she won't talk to help me.'

'There are ways.'

'Don't be bloody stupid. They'll discard that sort of evidence.'

His eyes were shining, anger flashing through them. A mixture of joy and relief rolled through me as he swore at me. He was starting to climb out of the black pit.

Eating an early supper with the children, doubts flared in my head. Was I overreaching? Tonia and Gil grinned at some joke Allegra made, then collapsed in giggles when she added another twist. They'd only just celebrated their eleventh birthday. Suppose they lost their mother as well as their father being in prison for years? I nearly called Livius to roster Allia and Pelo. I nearly reached for the keyboard to cancel my ticket.

But Allegra had more backbone than I did at that moment.

'You have to go, Mama. We'll be fine. Helena is here, and Dalina. Junia will look after us all.' She smiled at me. 'Don't worry about Dad. I've got his visiting schedule covered. I'll make sure I go every day. Uncle Daniel has promised these two can go as well. If they behave.'

She gave them an 'Aurelia' look and their boisterousness fled.

They were used to me being away, but this time, I had a really bad feeling I might not be back to see them grow up.

XXVI

The suburban shuttle from Paris-Leclerc airport stopped at each and every station on the way, but eventually we reached the Gare du Nord. I dodged the rain as I trudged across the street, pulling my case behind me like a kid's stuffed dog on wheels into the bright, brass-decorated lobby. The receptionist's eyes ran over me and my dusty chain-store appearance. He dipped his respect and upped his condescension as only Parisian men can.

The next morning, hair dyed mouse-brown, dressed in jeans and fleece, I fought my way upstairs in the rush hour to collect my tunnel tickets. It had been a while since I'd had to stand in line to travel – a salutary experience. The clerk hardly looked at me as I handed over my print-out and a fake US passport as Carly Jackson. She stuffed a UK immigration card in my passport, thrust it back at me with the chequered tickets and looked through me at the next passenger. I bought a throw-away cell phone; '*jetable*' the sales assistant called it. I couldn't help having a vision of cell phones with super-thruster back-packs zooming in and out between people walking along the street.

As I neared the barrier, I saw the police checking every passport thoroughly. I knew mine was good, but it didn't stop a nervous ripple passing through me. My hands were a little sweaty, but I forced myself not to wipe them. I swapped my purse and case from one hand to another to get rid of it on the handles. I gave an all-teeth American smile and a cheery 'Hi' which the gendarme ignored. He scrutinised my face, feature by feature, flicked back to the photo and back to my face really, really slowly.

Eventually, he handed my passport back with a brief upward nod. I waited until I was at least two metres away before I let my breath out. Why was I so jumpy? I hadn't even reached England.

As we emerged from the railroad tunnel on the English side, rain battered the window. The rich green countryside was spoilt by unremitting dullness under the grey sky. After an hour, the train stopped at a sleek modern station in the middle of nowhere, but my GPS screen showed it was near the peripheral freeway around London. I threw the jetable into the trashcan at the station. I had made the calls I needed to.

I had to decide where to try first: back to Birkenhead to find Newton; or Nicola's old army base in the west; or her mother's home in the north. I reckoned Newton's house was a busted flush. After losing Conrad for her, he would be long gone. I'd visited her former unit once; I'd do that afterward. So it was north for four hundred kilometres in a rental.

The motel south of Darlington was bleach white, charmless and smelled of second-hand cigarette smoke despite the notice in the lobby. I was washed-out by driving on the stupid side of the road, harassed by rigs and tanker trucks blocking the freeway as they struggled past each other, frustrating other vehicles including mine. I wanted a soak in the tub, but contented myself with a quick shower.

The rain had been replaced by a cold wind that sliced at my ears as I set off for Nicola's mother's place. No lights were on at the house, one of a pair of twin homes in an old development. I sat in the rental car which I'd parked between two street lights. I finished my take-out coffee and pretended to look at a street map book when anybody passed by. But it was too dark for the casual person hurrying home to see, let alone suspect, me.

Just after six, a silver hatchback drew into the driveway. A medium height dumpy woman with long dark hair tied back at the neck opened the driver's door. At the back hatch, she lifted two bulging shopping bags out. She opened the house entrance door and stepped inside, but came back out within five seconds to fetch a briefcase and book-bag. She pointed her key at the car and it replied with a mechanical squelch and a flash of trafficator lights.

I initialised my new audio scanner, moving it in a fan pattern to find the best signal. The lines wavered across my screen as she unpacked. The noise of tins plunked on a solid surface echoing through my earpieces.

I heard every small sound: kettle boiling, spoon as it hit the cup sides with vigorous strokes, the click of two buttons. I had to congratulate the quartermaster on this latest piece of kit – it was outstanding.

Disembodied voices chattered with beeps in between. Answering machine. Two blanks, a whiney voice about a charity collection and a man's voice about some school meeting. As I heard the television start, I settled in for a long, boring evening.

What had I expected? Nicola ringing in with her location?

After another twenty-four hours tailing her mother as she did her Saturday chores, made a gossipy call and hummed along to the radio as she flicked pages over, I accepted Nicola wasn't there. It had been a possible, even though the cops' report to Michael from my last visit stated the mother hadn't seen her for around a year. Although it was a routine function of a surveillance operation, it felt intrusive listening in to this stranger who had shared intimate time with Conrad, a slice of his life I would never know. Maybe curiosity was mixed in with duty when I knocked on her door the next morning.

'Yes?'

Janice Hargreve was a tired woman, face sour at the interruption on her day off.

'Hi.'

Her face clouded over and she flexed her arm to shut the door.

'No, I'm not selling religion,' I said, 'nor anything else. I want to talk to you about Conrad Tellus.'

She paused for a second or two. 'I don't know who you mean.'

I pulled out my gold warrant card and held it up. Janice wouldn't know it was only a piece of meaningless plastic. 'I'm an investigating officer from Roma Nova. He's in a load of trouble and I hope you can help me.'

'That was years ago. What's it got to do with me?'

'It's not so much you. It's your daughter.'

Her mouth drooped, the shadow lines at each end of her mouth deepening.

'You'd better come in.'

'She walked out when she was seventeen.' Janice's eyes darted over at me.

'She started stealing from my purse at five. Kids do that sometimes when they feel neglected. I've seen it myself with parents at school.' She lifted her cup to her mouth but it was already empty. 'But she wasn't. Neglected, I mean. My sister Marian came to live with us. She was like a second mother. Well, as Nic grew up, more like an older sister. They were real friends, doing girly things together. Marian thought the world of Nic and said it was a shame her dad didn't know her.'

She looked away and stopped talking.

I waited.

'He was the most attractive man I'd ever met. When he took me out, he always made sure we had a good table. He was never late or stood me up.' She looked straight at me. 'I fancied myself in love with him, but he was only here for another few weeks. And I knew deep down he didn't love me enough to take me back with him.

'Maybe I was stupid, but I wanted to keep a little bit of him for always.' She shrugged. 'Cheap condoms don't always work. I made sure they were cheap. Marian said I should have written and told him I was pregnant.'

The whumph of a central heating boiler broke the silence. As the water trickled through the radiators, Janice brought her eyes back into focus. She looked at me, her lower lip caught by the top one, blanched by the pressure.

'Where's Marian now, Janice?'

She bowed her head and cupped her cheeks in her hands. 'She's dead.'

'What happened?'

She dropped her hands into her lap and raised her head. Not looking at me, she spoke to the picture of dreary landscape above the fireplace mantel.

'Marian wouldn't believe Nic had been in trouble at school. She'd been caught bullying the other kids for their lunch money and making them steal things for her. She got the bright ones to do her homework for her. One day, she'd gone too far and they excluded her. It was the worst day of my life, sitting in that headteacher's study and hearing the whole story. Marian and I had a massive row about it. She said I was always down on Nic and ready to take other people's side against her. But Nic always turned the charm on for Marian, never the tantrums or the spite.

'Marian stormed up to Nic's school and was told some home truths. She was devastated, tried to talk to Nic about it but got the door shut in her face. Nic ran off with both our purses. I held Marian while she rocked in my arms, crying herself out.

'The police found Nic and brought her back. She was barely fourteen. We went through psychologists, probation advisors, we changed schools, tried to get her involved in helping other kids, doing outward bound, you name it, but all she did was get more crafty, learning from the gangs she hung out with.

'One evening, a week after Nic's seventeenth birthday, Marian was taking the short cut back through the flats from her keep-fit class. I told her I'd always come out and fetch her if the weather was bad. It was bucketing down that night and half the streetlights didn't work, but she didn't call me. Marian spotted Nic with some other kids who were joy-riding. Nic was shouting with a gang of them, tins of drink in their hands, egging the drivers on.

'Marian tried to stop her. She ran towards Nic, waving her hands. The boy driving one of the cars turned it towards Marian full speed and crushed her. The other kids were so shocked, they ran off.'

Tears ran down her face now.

'I stayed with Marian until she died four days later in hospital. Nic had vanished, but the afternoon before Marian passed away, Nic appeared at the room door. Her clothes and hair were filthy and her eyes all red. She stared at Marian for ages, then whispered, "I didn't know it was her."

'The police came and questioned her, but she said nothing. After Marian's funeral, she picked up her coat and bag from the hall, pushed past me and walked out of the house without a word. I haven't seen her since then, well, not until a year ago.'

Janice's shoulders slumped. 'She was hard, efficient, somehow more frightening. She said she'd been in the army, but was out now and going to get her due. I'd told her when she was younger that her father was a foreigner, from Roma Nova, but I had no contact with him since. She laughed, asked me for her birth certificate, her real one, she said. I only had the real one. The police said she'd used her friend's one, another Nicola, but Sandbrook, when she joined up.'

She fell silent for a minute or two.

'He was such a lovely man. I don't know how we had such a difficult child between us.'

'You still love her, don't you?'

'Of course.' Her voice was barely a whisper.

'She's a very clever girl,' I said, 'but she's done some seriously bad things. She nearly killed her great uncle, and has ruined her father. She's made one half-sister a drug addict and nearly got another killed. My daughter.'

Her eyes flew up to my face, then she flinched.

'God, are you his wife, then?'

'Yes, but my job is to find Nicola and take her back.' I stretched forward and touched the back of her hand. 'I don't mean you any trouble, Janice, but she must face up to what she's done, to stand her trial.'

'What—, what will they do to her?'

'She's likely to go to jail for some time, but they'll run a rehab program for her, counselling and so on, during her term to try make her see what she's done.'

'God forgive me, but I don't think you ever will.'

Janice didn't have any clue where Nicola might be. She was almost apologetic, like she thought she was responsible. I stood in her hallway, awkward about how to say something comforting, but finding nothing. She stretched out her hands, a pleading look in her face. I took them, pressed them, gave her a smile but couldn't say anything.

I gave her my personal number and explained it would be re-routed to me wherever I was. Well, not to the little pre-paid cell phone I bought from a vending machine in the services area on my drive here. But I'd make sure I checked my voicemail every two hours from now on.

I handed the rental car in at the railroad station next day and took the train south and west to the town near Nicola's former base. I had over two thousand euros in cash left in my money pouch, but didn't want to spend any more on car rental. No way was I going to leave an electronic trail by using a card, even to replenish my cash, unless I really needed to.

The budget hotel was modern, big and smelled of fresh paint. All the clerk could manage was 'Name? How many nights?' and 'Sign here,' followed by a grunt. She hardly looked at me, which was good.

The next morning, I walked to the town centre, my parka protecting me against the chill February wind. After buying a large scale walker's map, a sandwich which I transferred into a plastic baggie and some bottles of water, I stowed them in my black field bag and took the bus that travelled up past Nicola's former army base. I rubbed the dirty window but didn't see any better what my next step should be. I was eighty, no, ninety per cent sure Nicola's mother would call me if she showed up there. Not out of spite or resentment, but so her daughter would be stopped and contained.

Nicola must have known I'd be on her trail. If I were her, I'd stay out of population centres. Her unit had been pretty pissed with her, causing them the trouble I'd brought them on my previous visit. Sure, they cooperated, but their senior non-com Johnson's narrowed eyes and his expression like he was eating raw chilli was enough to show me just how much. If they found her, she'd get a rough ride. So it made perfect sense for her to hide here right under their radar, so close they wouldn't see her. But if I didn't find her here, I'd have to start over.

One problem – I didn't have enough time to start over before Conrad came to trial.

XXVII

Crawling around in a wood in an elite special forces' backyard was not the safest thing I could think to do. But it was somewhere to start. I'd stepped off the bus at the entrance to a garden centre, two stops before the base gate. I wandered past the special offers, through the shrubs out to the trees section at the back where the delivery gate would be. Nobody hauled two-metre high trees in heavy containers further than they needed to.

I slipped behind the last row of conifers, picked the gate lock and exited on to a country road. After an intersection where the delivery trucks had to come, it narrowed and started climbing. A little over a kilometre further on, a wood came into view over the rise. Green stuff started to appear in the raised centre of the road which finished up at a farm gate. I hiked along field boundaries keeping a northwest direction, sometimes crouching, sometimes lucky to find some sheltering hedgerow, but always below the sight line.

A hundred metres from the edge of the wood, I hunkered down behind a hedgerow. If Nicola was there, she'd be watching. No way was I attempting anything until it was dark. I ate my sandwich, pulled my microfibre bag over me, covered it with dead leaves and recently-live green twigs and grabbed a few hours' sleep, knife in my hand.

Exactly four hours later, I woke. Completely. I couldn't hear any wildlife except a few birds. Moving my hand at an excruciatingly slow pace, I fished out my pocketscope and swept around for body heat. Two adult signatures and a small animal blazed out in red.

They kept many of their training areas open-access here, except during exercises. Michael had told me some walkers even tried to continue in the face of live fire. Asserting their rights, they said. How dumb was that?

I stayed where I was until I saw an older couple emerge from under the tree canopy. A pointy-eared, long-haired dog trotted near the ground in front of them. It stopped, sniffed and cocked an ear; far better detector than the best Brown Industries scanner. The man bent and attached a leash to the dog's collar and they walked away, following a trail down the opposite hill. The dog tried to pull back but was dragged away by the impatient owner anxious to get home before dusk turned to night.

I folded my microfibre bag and stuffed it back in my field bag, swapping it for a bottle of water. While I swallowed, I scanned for electronic or thermal detection fields. The fibreglass and aluminium linings to my clothes and face scarf would blur my signature on good equipment, I doubted Nicola had anything that efficient – it was too expensive. No, it would be the old-fashioned way.

Thankful for a sickle moon, I crawled forward into the chilly night. My coat was covered with tiny water beads from ground dew as I brushed over it. At the edge of the wood, I crouched and paused for a few minutes, searching away from the trail. Nothing. Just standard nocturnal fluttering of birds and scurrying of small mammals. I headed for the rise and stopped for frequent sampling with my pocketscope. Nothing, just an even blue-green image. I made my way up towards the highpoint – an Iron Age hill fort, the map said. Ten metres from the top, I lay in the shelter of undergrowth. I waited twenty long minutes. I stowed my field bag inside a group of hawthorn bushes and crept forward, my carbon fibre knife in hand.

In a dense thicket, I found a camp; two DPM groundsheets, one slung over a rope and each side stretched taut at an angle to deflect rain and the other on the ground, edges tied up to form a bundle. Inside were a sleeping bag, cutlery, mess tins, bottles of water and a khaki backpack with basic field supplies. And a gold *solidus* with Silvia's portrait, a thin ribbon tied through a hole in the top of the coin.

Batting away satisfaction, I started looking around for a good ambush point. Once I had her, I could hold her in this isolated spot and get an evacuation team here in hours. I didn't think this was one time Daniel would go stiff-rumped on me. The Brits wouldn't even know I'd been here.

I did a regular scan every fifteen minutes, but it was getting a little boring. I'd been here five hours and she hadn't shown up. Had she found any trace of me? Maybe she was out getting supplies. She couldn't forage during the day – the risk of running across somebody who knew her would be too great. I stretched my arms and legs where I lay. The last thing I needed was slow reaction from stiff muscles.

Leaves swishing apart and rebounding. Too much movement for a small animal. Human. I tensed. The adrenaline sparked and started flowing. I moved quickly into a crouch, knife in my right hand, scope held to my eye in my left. More movement to my left. Hades! There were more of them. Six, seven. Maybe eight. Too late to run. I shrank back, flattening myself against a tree trunk and froze. It had to be a night exercise. It could be why Nicola wasn't here. But how had she known?

Before I could work out any answer, something hit my head, pain exploded. I dropped to the ground and went out.

The jolting woke me. I was lying on a ridged metallic floor, my hands tied behind me. I was bouncing along in a vehicle without any suspension. A shortbase jeep. It smelled of gasoline and human sweat. My head hurt like the Furies having a bad day. When I tried moving, everything swam in front of me. I closed my eyes and made the effort to breathe deeply and slowly. I forced myself to visualise blood flowing around my veins and arteries healing my wounds, open flesh closing, endorphins being released.

Ten minutes later, the vehicle stopped. The driver's door swung open. The whole vehicle shuddered as it was slammed shut. Boots on concrete, then the tailgate was released, the side chain clanking. The beam from a flashlight blinded me. Hands grabbed my ankles and yanked me out into a heap on the ground. Catching my breath, I struggled up on to my knees. A figure with a balaclava mask over his face thrust his arm out, hauled me to my feet. A second, shorter figure jabbed a barrel into the back of my neck. The first one dragged me towards one of the buildings on the edge of the parking lot and shoved me through the door.

A twin neon light hung in the roof space from a crosswork grid. Benches ran around three sides of the room with tools scattered over them. Some kind of workshop. I flexed the balls of my feet, looking for a pathway out of here. I made to pull away, but the figure squeezed his grip on my radial. It was excruciating.

'A mistake. Please, let me explain,' I didn't have to fake the shaking in my voice.

He swung his arm back in a full arc. I tried to duck, but he still managed to punch me in the mouth. I staggered back. As the blood rushed back in, pain throbbed through my cheek. Liquid from my nose on my upper lip. Salty, iron. Blood.

The shorter one stood a metre away training his Glock on my head. The taller one thrust me down on a chair, looped a second cable tie between my wrists to the back of the chair. He secured my ankles to the chair legs with more cable ties and stood back like he was satisfied with his day's work.

'Water,' I croaked. 'Please.'

A bucket of water hit me full in the face, but at least it cleared my head. Did they think I was part of the 'enemy' for the exercise? These guys played hard, but this was beyond that. And why only two of them?

The shorter one advanced on me. Through the balaclava eye holes, I saw quarter moons of light reflected by the copper tones in the hazel eyes.

Shit.

'Hello, Nicola,' I said, who's the boyfriend this time?'

Maybe it was stupid to annoy her but it was satisfying.

She seized her balaclava in a claw-like movement, dragged it off her head and threw it on the ground. Her face was red from temper. She kicked me several times in the same place on my shin. My leg starred with pain and I felt something give. She'd broken the bone. I struggled to heave air back into my lungs, water welling in my eyes. I refused to scream, but bit my damaged lip.

'Later. You can have your fun later, Nic.'

I knew that voice. Where from? Native English, military from his walk. As he pulled his own balaclava off, I recognised Lieutenant Wilson from that joint exercise an eon ago.

Crap.

'Well, Major, my turn.'

I didn't update him on my career development.

He brandished a syringe, upended a bottle of transparent liquid, punctured the rubber seal with the syringe needle and slowly drew the liquid into the reservoir.

I coughed and swallowed more of my blood.

'What's that?' I whispered.

'Something, as you told me several months ago, "that'll have you chirruping like a mongoose on holiday".'

He yanked my sleeve up, stabbed the syringe into the crook of my elbow and rammed the plunger deep into my flesh. I gasped at the pain. Vindictive son of a bitch.

Faenia's chemical bombs would protect me for a while from whatever it was, only up to a max of forty-eight hours. And I'd forgotten to take a booster this morning.

'Where are the rest of your team?' Nicola shouted in my face.

I didn't answer.

I collapsed as she jabbed her elbow in my stomach. Sour fumes throbbed their way up my gullet. The rest of my sandwich followed.

I woke up choking on a mix of blood and saliva and the smell of machine oil.

Light was creeping in at the strip windows running along the top of the walls. How long had I been here? I was woozy from the drug they'd pumped into me. Juno, I was stiff. And sore. My face throbbed and my leg pulsed with pain.

I craned my head around as far as I could. Nobody. No sound except a machine hum like a refrigerator from the far wall. I risked closing my eyes for a few moments and took some deep breaths. Even that tiny movement made my face ache.

Only years of training had made me keep my tongue behind the shelter of my teeth. I ran it around the inside of my mouth and found a loose tooth and a pool of blood. I bent my head over and let it dribble out, taking the tooth with it. Swallowing blood just made you throw up more. The hurt from my stomach was painful enough; if I threw up again my middle would implode from agony.

I scanned around. The workbench was three, max four metres away; it could have been four kilometres. But if I did nothing, I'd be killed like a stuck pig.

I twisted my good foot left and right. The cable ties were tight on my ankles, but I could place my feet on the ground. But one leg was going to have to do the work of two. I leaned forward, causing the back chair feet to move millimetres off the ground. Swinging to my right to gain momentum, I forced the right chair leg another millimetre up and pivoted on my left foot nearly 180 degrees to my left. I gasped at the pain that shot through my abs. I reckoned ten more to get to the bench. And next time I'd have to swing on the other leg.

The sweat running into my eyes was nearly blinding me and I was sucking in lung-wrenching breaths as I prepared for the last turn. I had just sixty centimetres to navigate to reach the bench. Maybe I would make it out of here.

Then I heard voices outside the door, one higher than the other. The inside handle travelled down a couple of centimetres. I was overcome by a wave of bitterness at the wasted effort of the past fifteen minutes. I had so nearly got there. And they'd start breaking more of me until there was nothing left.

Holding my breath, I stared at the handle. I could hardly believe it as it travelled back to horizontal. The voices disappeared abruptly. I released my breath and burst into silent tears of relief.

I spotted a hand file and manoeuvred it with my bruised mouth into a vertical bench clamp and pushed the lever round with my shoulder, tightening it with painful slowness. Ignoring the ache of stretching I moved my wrists up and down against the file edge. After a few minutes my arms ached with the agony, but when the ties snapped, the release of tension in my shoulders was blissful. I eased the file out of the clamp and freed my legs. I rubbed my good ankle and wrists to get blood flowing again. The adrenaline was pulsing already.

With shaking hands, I took off my jacket, pulled off my tee and ripped it along the underarm seams to make a bandage to strap my leg up. I tied it so tight my leg went numb temporarily. I only hoped I hadn't damaged it further. I stood and tried putting some body weight on it. Not one of my best ideas. But I had no choice.

At the door, I huddled against the wall. Grasping the handle I opened the door half a centimetre. A short wheelbase outside but no people, no boots on gravel. Nothing.

I hobbled out and dragged myself along the edge of the metal-clad building. At the corner I stopped and waited for the pain in my damned leg to subside. I eased my face around the edge and jerked back as I saw a soldier cross to the brick building opposite. I was on the base but I didn't have a clue where. The silver and white comms dishes and antennas on the headquarter building stood out against the night sky, so I staggered from shadow to shadow in that direction. I didn't know how long I had before they discovered I'd escaped. But I knew I had to get medical help soon or I was going to pass out again.

All I had to do was cross an open grass area about twenty metres deep. I leaned against the cold brick, resting for a few breaths. No way could I let myself slither down the wall and sit. I would never get up again.

Like some hunted animal, I didn't want to leave the protection of the shadows. But I had no option. When I fell to my knees after a few metres, I didn't have enough strength to push through the pain and stand up, so I crawled, dragging myself along the ground with my elbows. I was halfway across when somebody slammed into me, crushing me into a heap of agony.

Wilson. In the moonlight, his face was livid, monstrous even.

'No!' I shrieked. I was pinioned like a beetle on its back, too weak to do anything except protect my face. I balled one fist and tried to swing my arm, but I was losing the struggle as he pinned me down.

I screamed, half-choking on the blood that had started to flow again in my mouth. I spat it out into his eyes. He jerked back, then brought his arm up to smash his hand into my face again.

'What the hell is going on here?'

A bulky figure blocked the light from the entrance. It was RSM Johnson.

I endured the medics cutting the damaged clothes off, the swabbing down, the dressing of cuts and bruises. I knew from the doc's expression that I wasn't about to enter any beauty contest. The analgesic anti-inflammatory took the jagged edge off, but tomorrow would be worse. They were fixing a drip up as Colonel Stimpson arrived, looking thunderous.

'I spoke to your legate. He said a civilian recovery team will be arriving as soon as he can muster one.'

He waved his hand towards the medics. 'They're taking you to the theatre to set your leg, but first, I want you to tell me exactly how you turned up at the front door of my camp looking like a victim of a gangland beating. And what the hell you're doing here anyway.'

XXVIII

I gave him an outline, but my mouth became too swollen to say much. The medics interrupted and wheeled me away on a gurney and I knew nothing else until the recovery room.

Apart from the broken shinbone and a fractured rib, my face throbbed and my stomach was purple and sore. Despite the pressure-relieving foam under the sheet, I couldn't find a comfortable way to lie in the bed. They changed the ice-pack round my head twice in the night. I passed the next day in a haze of drugs and exhaustion, but on day three, I woke up to see a face with freckles topped with wavy dark blond hair.

'Michael,' I croaked and mustered a half-smile through cracked lips.

He didn't smile back.

'When you said you'd take 'other measures' to hunt Nicola Sandbrook, I thought you were sabre-rattling. Now it turns out you're not even official. Give us a good reason not to hand you over to the police as a terrorist.'

'S'great to see you, too, Michael.'

I should have expected Andrew Brudgland's ball carrier, but he could have lightened up.

'What?' I said, 'I go hiking in a public open space and your government's security forces beat up on me.' I took a painful breath. 'My lawyers will be in touch.'

'You knew we were keeping a watching brief. Why didn't you contact me?'

'I have a tight deadline.' I struggled up to half-sitting. Pain stabbed through my middle up into my skull. I nearly blacked out. 'Date. What's the date?'

I'd been away for a week. Conrad's trial started in two days. And I didn't have Nicola to take back.

After he'd stopped me trying to get out of bed and we'd both calmed down, Michael took a full statement from me. At first, he refused to tell me about anything, but I coaxed it out of him. Wilson was in custody being questioned about Nicola by military police detectives. Michael said his career was over. A forensic team was going over Nicola's camp and would take the case from here on.

'But they'll send you their report?' I said.

'No, you can't have a copy,' he replied. 'It's confidential.'

I stared at him through swollen eyes.

'Oh, very well, I'll see what I can do. No promises.'

An air ambulance flew me home, and I was helicoptered straight to the Central Valetudinarium where Faenia tutted at me as I lay on the scanner bed.

'You're getting too old for this sort of beating, Carina Mitela. Get a team of twenty-year-olds in next time. Your tooth we can fix. The broken bones and bruising will self-heal. And we'll use electric therapy to accelerate it. The plastic surgery on your face will leave a few faint scars, but your internal organs are not as immortal as you seem to think they are.'

'Just patch me up so I can attend the trial,' I grumped.

'Out of the question,' and she pulled the switch to insert me past the blinking lights into the gaping maw.

Only when I promised to have a medic with me at all times and return immediately to the hospital after my part in the proceedings was finished did Faenia release me two days later, on Monday morning. My pride was dented by having to use a wheelchair, but no way could I walk with a leg strapped from knee to toe and hurting like a minor Hades.

Allegra collected me. She'd burst into tears the evening I arrived when she'd pushed into the hospital and insisted on seeing me. I'd held her hand and waited until she stopped trembling. This morning she wore a neutral, serious face along with a neutral, serious suit. She bent and kissed my forehead.

'Are you ready, Mama?'

I ached from head to foot, my ribs were strapped tight, my stomach stiff and sore, my broken shinbone aching with pain and my face a mess of cuts, bruising and dressings.

'Sure, I'm fine. Let's do it.'

★

As Allegra guided my chair between the seating, people stopped talking. The silence expanded throughout the courtroom and every face seemed to be angled towards us. Some looked as if their eyes were going to fall out with the strain. We reached our ringside seat right behind the bench where the defendants and their lawyers sat. Sertorius turned, rose to his feet and bent over us, his hand extended.

'My dear Countess, how are you?' he said in an overloud voice. 'Are you sure you're well enough to attend today?'

'Don't worry, Sertorius. I have a sick-note.'

He leaned closer and whispered, 'Speaking tactically, you couldn't have made a better entrance. I'll call you early.'

He was a cynical bastard, but the best there was. I just smiled back, trying to look heroic. He hurried back to his front bench as the judges and the examining magistrate filed on to the dark oak-carved podium which hovered above the rest of the mortals.

When Conrad came in, he looked pale but composed. Until he saw me. He stared, eyes wide, travelling from my wrecked face down to my lower legs showing below my tunic hemline. He stopped and put his hand out to steady himself. When he didn't move, Sertorius took his arm and guided him to the defendant's bench. Conrad bowed his head, shoulders hunched forward for a few moments, then twisted around. The skin bunched around his eyes which shone with anger, or was it anguish? Despite the jagging pain when I moved, I attempted a smile. He just stared back.

A treason trial involving two prominent families was rare; with the added spice of a lost and renegade daughter, I thought we'd be in for a circus, but after some shuffling about the audience settled down to quiet. Hungry to hear every one of the details, I guessed.

Sertorius had filed all the statements including my abortive trips to Britain. He called me early as promised, and Allegra wheeled me over to a spot in front of the dark wood carved witness stand. As Sertorius declaimed about duty and sacrifice and blah, blah, I studied the audience. Amongst the sensation-seekers, smug politicos and the plain curious, I found familiar faces: my former Active Response Team, Paula sending me a smile; Lucius, frowning through new eyeglasses, Lurio, leaning back, his arms folded across his chest, Pelonia by his side, plus half my household, Dalina Mitela and her Tellus family opposite number. There had to be around a hundred PGSF. I wondered who was left minding the store.

My written deposition and IS reports had been filed before I'd left to hunt Nicola. Sertorius praised the generosity of the British government for their cooperation and asked me to describe Nicola's attack in detail. He read out Faenia's report which shocked even me. I didn't know I had half of what she listed.

'And this, magister and learned colleagues, is what this daughter of Hades did to a special forces officer at the height of her powers and experience.'

The imperial accusatrix stood up, cleared her throat, raised her papers, looked over her spectacles and was about to open her thin little mouth to aim a question at me, when the main court doors were thrust open.

Two Praetorians in formal dress marched in and took up position one each side of the entrance. From between them stepped a tall young woman, red-brown hair and light brown eyes. She walked slowly, but with great self-assuredness, to the front of the court and bowed to the magistrate.

'I apologise for interrupting the proceedings, magister, but I have come to court to support my father.'

A collective gasp went up from the audience and everybody started talking at once. Thank Juno, there were no photographers allowed in.

Hallienia Apulia might only have been a bit over sixteen, but she stood there with the full dignity of sixty generations of rulers behind her. She seemed to ignore the babble and excitement around her. When the magistrate had recovered herself, she called for silence and gestured to a court officer to bring a chair.

'If you do not object, I will sit with my sister.' And made her way to Allegra's side. And Sertorius thought *I'd* made an entrance.

The imperial accusatrix gathered herself again, emphasising I was no longer a member of the PGSF and that my illicit operation had endangered the good relations with the British. Sertorius objected quoting Michael's report which the magistrate upheld and the fact I'd honourably surrendered my imperial warrant. The accusatrix tried her best, but Sertorius was on firm ground. The morning ended with him in the lead.

In the prisoner room, we sat round eating a takeout lunch, surrounded by Hallie's bodyguards, Conrad's escorts and court officers, all watching for some false step. Hallie and Allegra looked like two teenagers again, shucking off the dignified act, reverting to normal girls. Except they weren't.

Conrad had hugged Hallie as soon as we'd reached the shelter of the room and turned to pull Allegra in. His face was tight with emotion and I saw his hand wipe across his eyes.

As we finished our surreal picnic, Sertorius went off to prepare for the afternoon session, mainly technical stuff with shrinks and profilers, leaving us to work out what to say next to each other as a family.

'I'll stay this afternoon, Dad,' Hallie said, 'and I'll ask Mama if I can come back tomorrow.'

'Darling, just this morning was wonderful.' Conrad ran his finger down the side of her face. 'I'm sorry I've let you down, you, Allegra, all of you.' He glanced at me.

She took his hand. 'Don't worry, we know you were off your head – it wasn't really you.'

He looked at her, astounded at the teenage brutality, then broke into laughter. 'Thanks.'

I glanced at my watch. 'Five minutes to go. You two girls go back up. I need to say something in private to Dad.'

They shot a worried look at him, but he smiled back, I thought, to reassure them.

'Before you say anything, Faenia's said I'm fine, just a bit bruised, so don't worry. Okay?'

He gave me a measured look. 'Don't bullshit me, Carina. I was tri-aging wounds when you were still designing adverts in New York. And I wasn't afflicted with sudden deafness when Sertorius read that injuries list out.'

Despite Sertorius's attempts to have me excused, the imperial accusatrix was allowed another thirty minutes to grill me. I guessed it was her job to try discredit my testimony. I was disconcerted by being opposite her after years of working with her team, but I was damned if I was going to let her even glimpse that. But I was almost passing out with fatigue by the time I flopped against the back of my wheelchair.

I woke later, feeling like a lump of Aquae Caesaris granite was lying on my chest. I was hot, burning. I felt a tiny rectangular alarm sensor in my palm and pressed it.

'How are you feeling?'

The young doctor in a white coat too big for her had such a wide and friendly smile, I didn't have the heart to tell her. I tracked her movements as she ran her scanner over me, felt my middle and studied the digital panel behind me.

'What time is it?'

She carried on as if she hadn't heard me and played with a switch on the drip.

'Professor Faenia instructed you were to be kept quiet and calm. I think you have visitors shortly, but they can only stay for ten minutes.'

'What time is it?'

'You don't need to worry about the time at the moment.' She tapped on her el-pad, not looking at me. She came back to the bed, standing close.

I grabbed her wrist. 'What's the time?' She looked down. 'Wait a minute, what day is it?'

The door swung open. Allegra.

She nodded at the doctor, who easily freed her wrist from my feeble grip and retreated.

'Relax, Mama. Calm down.'

'Don't you tell me what to do!' I tried to turn away, but I was too stiff.

'Mama, please don't.'

Around her eyes the flesh was puffed, her cheeks sagged. She was trying too hard to smile. She pulled up a chair, sat down and looked at me gravely. I could see she was struggling to find some years to add on so she could deal with all the shit being thrown at her.

'It's Wednesday. Yes, you've missed a day, but you needed the rest. It's almost finished. They've recessed for two days to consider the evidence.'

'Juno, that's unusual. So final defence and prosecution speeches the day after tomorrow. And the verdict. Nobody else to be questioned?'

'Sertorius said he wasn't calling anybody else after the psychs as everything was in the depositions. The magistrate just nodded at him. Perhaps she doesn't like long trials. I don't know how these things go.' She shrugged and looked a little lost. 'Uncle Quintus gave his testimony this morning. But he came across like Dad.'

She studied the stiff white sheets I was enclosed in. 'I—'

'Say it, Allegra.'

'They looked – weak.' She lifted her head. 'The former imperial chancellor and the PGSF senior legate. How could that be?'

XXIX

Imperatrix Silvia's circus was next. I was obviously so dangerous, her Praetorians stayed in the room with her. She didn't order them out. While she was perfectly friendly, asking how I was, her eyes didn't meet mine. She kept behind her neutral persona.

'How's Stella?' I asked.

'Progressing well, the governor says. She's been on field trips under supervision to a rehab centre and a social aid hub. Apparently, she took a real interest and wanted to know more.' She shrugged. 'Perhaps she's not as hopeless as we all think.'

Juno, that was a change. Silvia always defended her daughter, even to herself. She looked tired, almost brittle. Ignoring the pins and needles, I stretched out and touched her forearm.

She looked me full in the face at last. She waved her hand backwards and the two guards left.

'Tell me,' I said.

As she left, trailing the hospital director and a load of fussing in her wake, I thought about the difficult place she was in. Her eldest child aimless and in rehabilitation, her former partner, father of her three children, on trial for treason, her cousin and friend incapacitated. All brought about by a new version of the man who had murdered her mother and destroyed her early world. And no wise Aurelia around to guide any of us. But over the fear and the heartache, she had to bolt on a detached, even-handed persona.

No way was I going to miss the verdict in less than thirty-six hours. I dragged my legs across so I could sit on the edge of the bed. Ten minutes later, after falling over only once, I reached the bathroom, and a mirror.

My body was a mass of black and yellow blooms, some still red and violet, the skin on my abdomen red and blotched in patches. But my face. Black eyes above parallel deep weals where she'd drawn a metal comb, heated in a blow torch flame, across my right cheek.

My swollen lips healing into crooked taut lines revealed the gap in my teeth. Faenia said it could all be repaired once the bruising had receded. Right now I looked like some Gorgon.

I steadied myself by grabbing onto the basin and glanced at the shower. Another thing where I needed to accept help. I passed my hand over the emergency sensor panel and waited.

Sertorius was outperforming himself summing up the defence case; he wove together the IS reports, our depositions and testimonies, Nicola's brutality, her attempts to destroy her sisters, the attack on Quintus. His voice carried without booming, his vowels were oil-smooth as they wrapped themselves around his tongue, his pauses for effect not quite tipping over into pathos. But there was one big fat thing missing – Nicola's testimony – and the imperial accusatrix leapt on it. She trashed Sertorius' hard work in two minutes and sat down on her bench with a smug smile.

When the judges went into a huddle, I stretched my hand out and met Conrad's halfway as he twisted around.

'You shouldn't have come,' he whispered, 'you need the rest.' But he smiled at me.

'I have to know where to come and visit you,' I said and smiled back.

'That bad, you think?'

'I'm so sorry I couldn't bring her back. You have no idea how sorry.'

'Don't.' He glanced at the judges still conferring. 'Whatever happens, I will owe you for the rest of my life.'

I pressed his hand. It was scary to see just how diminished he was. More white had appeared in his hair. Not passing through grey, just straight to white. I wanted to pull him in and hold him.

The judges separated and the buzz melted. Conrad was called forward, flanked by Sertorius.

'Conradus Mitelus, you are accused of *crimen lasae majestatis*. Treason is a grave charge with an appropriately severe punishment. We have taken time to consider all the circumstances. It is regrettable that Nicola Sandbrook, previously known as Tella, is not here to be questioned.' She glanced over at me. 'The court absolves you of *crimen lasae majestatis*—'

Yes.

Sertorius' hand patted Conrad's back. My mouth hurt as I tried to grin. I seized Allegra's hand and she fell into my hug. Tears rolled down both our faces; mine mostly from pain from the ferocity of Allegra's hug, but it didn't matter. Shouts from the audience, a buzz blooming into a deafening roar.

'Silence!'

The magistrate's gaze panned around, fierce and commanding, willing the audience to quiet down. What more had she to say? Allegra looked at me, her face frowning. I shook my head at her.

The magistrate brought her gaze back to Conrad.

'However, we find a probable case of *indiligentia majestatis* against you. You will be held in custody for a later hearing. This session is closed.' She stood, nodded at the other judges and disappeared with them through the door at the back.

'What the hell was that about? What does it mean?' I demanded.

Conrad had flopped back on to the bench. We clustered around Sertorius, blocking the guards.

'It means,' Sertorius said, 'we're not clear yet. I'll file an application to transfer to house arrest immediately. Fortuna only knows when they'll schedule the hearing.' He laid a hand on Conrad's shoulder. 'We've cleared the worst. At least you won't end up in Truscium.'

After the guards took Conrad away to PGSF headquarters, I grilled Sertorius.

'Explain, please, exactly what this *indiligentia majestatis* is.'

'Basically it covers minor acts of treason. They brought it in two centuries ago as a warning measure and to deal with rabble-rousers. It didn't carry the death penalty, mostly punishment by short-term imprisonment and/or fines. I'm afraid I'll have to look into my histories to find the details.'

Sertorious brought his hand up to push back some strands escaping from his normally immaculate hair. He gestured his assistant to gather up the files, slipped the cover onto his el-pad and pocketed it. 'Right, let's get to the magistrate's clerk. Then it's the night shift.'

Faenia grudgingly let me home after three more days, but insisted on sending a nurse with me with a load of instructions. He would continue the electric therapy on my leg for the next week. She had booked me back in in two weeks to start repairing my face. Something to look forward to.

After a week, I ventured into the swimming pool. Four lengths up and down and I lay on the side like a struggling turbot. Plasseal kept the water off my leg, but the leg brace didn't help. Five days later I managed ten, although my legs shook as I climbed out. I picked up my robe and trudged over to the stairs, wishing the elevator extended down to the basement. Head bowed and my hand groping for the stair rail, I contacted another human hand. I looked up, expecting one of the hovering servants, but found a copper-brown and green gaze fixed on me, a smile below it. My heart squeezed. He drew me in and I fell into his embrace.

We said nothing. He half-carried me upstairs, helped me dry off and put me into the bed. We lay there, warm and content, and slept.

The next morning, we sat behind the three-metre high wall that enclosed a private garden full of lavender, sage and rosemary, edged with mulberry and fig trees between walkways covered with the skeleton of bare vines. It was March so the honeysuckle that ran all over the summer house in the corner was just breaking bud; a tentative start to the year. The rich scents of the summer were months away. We talked about the trial, the lesser hearing to come, my next medical treatment, a possible holiday and then we ran out of polite conversation.

'Carina,' he said, 'I'm sorry, truly sorry for everything.'

The ache in his voice made me want to put my arms around him, but this wasn't the moment. I leaned back on the teak bench circling the large myrtle tree at the centre of the garden.

'I thought I would hate you for the rest of my life when I walked out of your office in the PGSF building,' I said, my gaze fixed on the flagstones. 'You destroyed my work, our marriage and my trust. So nothing too major.'

He said nothing, just hunched over, holding his hands palms together, elbows resting on his knees and looked at the ground. He scrubbed his foot in a circle on the rough stone.

'You put me through eight months of hell.' He went to speak, but I held my hand up. 'No, let me finish. I know now you were going through a terrible time, but you were so cold and discarded me from your life.'

A tiny breeze passed over my arms and I shivered.

'I thought once I'd brought you back to Roma Nova, that

would be it – divorce for me, prison for you. I never wanted to be involved with you again.'

He didn't move. Two finches chased each other around the trees, eventually settled and chirruped melodies at each other.

'Do you want me to go?' he said to the ground.

'No, it was in the transport, on the way back here, that I realised I couldn't walk away. You were in such a state.'

'Oh, so you just felt sorry for me.' He sat up, anger and hurt in his eyes.

'Don't be ridiculous,' I retorted, but maybe there was a little truth there.

'So what now?'

'We get through this *indiligentia majestatis* hearing, then try to get back to some sort of life together.'

He looked up at me. 'I don't deserve you.'

'No, you don't,' I said, 'but I'm not going to give myself the heartache of throwing you out.' I took his hands in mine. 'I am bound to you by something I can't explain. You know the ancients' marriage vow "*Ubi tu Gaius, ego Gaia*"? Well, it seems to apply even in the 21st century.'

On Monday, Sertorius came back with the goods; *indiligentia majestatis* was like neglect or failing to stop a crime against the imperium, which probably fit what Conrad had done better. After wriggling around, protecting his rear with 'all things being equal', the lawyer was confident the worst sentence would be a large fine and some community service.

Sertorius had also applied to the imperial accusatrix for an arrest warrant to be issued against Nicola Sandbrook, formerly Tella. If it was granted, although *in absentia*, she could be detained immediately if she ever set foot again in Roma Nova. Being realistic, Pelonia and the DJ couldn't do much more than issue border alerts, but the application didn't hurt Conrad's case any.

Hallie came to see him that afternoon and I left them to walk in the park, brown and white heads leaning together. Stella, confined to the rehabilitation centre, was still out of his reach.

I came upstairs, wiping my face from a remedial session in the gym with the therapist and found Junia talking to a tall, brown-haired man in casuals and trainers. Flavius. His face burst out in a smile. He hurried over and kissed the less ruined part of my face.

'How are you, Bruna?'

'I don't know if I can still use Bruna as a *nom de guerre*.'

He scanned me, 'Oh, I don't know. I think you qualify on the *guerre* part.'

He'd been on an exchange mission; Daniel had sent him to Bavaria and he had missed the trial.

'Well, you've got the most expensive legal team going,' he paused to grin. 'So I expect they'll get the legate off.'

'He's not the legate any more, Flav.'

'I know, but... Well, you know.'

I cleared my throat to break the silence.

'It's lovely to see you, Flav. Please give my regards to the others.'

'You'll be seeing them soon yourself. We're going to help you get fit again.'

Stella's trial came up and, apart from Conrad who was still under house arrest, we all went along to support her. Silvia didn't make anything like the sensational entrance Hallie had at Conrad's, but slipped in with me. Not completely unnoticed.

Stella stood quietly as the charges were read out and Silvia's advocate listed the attenuating circumstances. I was questioned on my deposition, but there were no surprises. Stella was sentenced to two years' full-time residential community service, level four, and was directed to work in the addict support centre where she'd been helping out. She held her head up as she took the sentence, looking the judge in the eye. Before leaving with the *custodes*, she turned and smiled to her mother. Silvia nodded back, her eyes moist. I remembered how I'd felt when Allegra had been in court. Ignoring the frowns of her Praetorian security detail, I put my arm around Silvia's waist to support her as we walked out.

Faenia had performed the last operation on my face, thank Juno, and a new tooth had been implanted two weeks ago. Flavius and the others had been soft training with me in between times and I figured I was rested and pretty much recovered. Until I ran a cross-country trail. After that I kept to our park until I had rebuilt my stamina. The plus was that Conrad could come with me.

Our low-key life settled into a routine; I was kept busy with the spring Senate hearings and budget wrangling. The gods knew we had a sound economy. Why did they need to pick over every *solidus*?

It struck me that verbal debate had become the most dangerous thing in my life. I regretted my and Conrad's PGSF careers ending the way they had, and although we hadn't eliminated the menace of Nicola, we were healing from her attacks and reckoned we had thrown her out of our lives for good.

Part IV

Nemesis

XXX

'Mama!'

I jumped. Sheets of paper fell on the floor. I'd been absorbed in a stack of Senate papers. Why they had to issue commission minutes in hard copy, I didn't know. I could have easily signed them digitally.

Allegra bounced into my study, fine brown hair flying. Hallie followed less energetically, with a serious expression, no sign of her usual sunny smile. She bent down and picked up my papers and set them back on the pile.

'We had to come and tell you immediately,' Allegra said.

Her eyes shone copper brown, the green drowned out. Pink flooded her usually pale face.

'What's his name?' I winced internally. She wasn't going to be sixteen until November and I wasn't ready to play the hardliner mother.

She batted that away with an impatient hand and frowned. 'No, nothing like that. It's Nicola. We think we've seen her.'

Pelonia kept her manner professional and calm, but her eyes gleamed as she heard the girls' story. They'd been in the Macellum shopping mall, along with Hallie's Praetorian who didn't look much older than eighteen herself. Allegra said she was trying to stop Hallie buying a sweater that would make her look like a fat duck. Hallie tapped Allegra's upper arm at that point and grinned. I coughed and they subsided back into decorous.

'What made you convinced it was Nicola?' Pelonia fixed on Allegra.

'Her walk.' Allegra looked at me, her fingers fiddling with the pass around her neck. She dragged her eyes back to the inspector's face. 'You know I spent some time with her, when Maia Quirinia and I were taken in.' She coughed. 'It's really embarrassing now, but we used to watch her walk away from us at the school gate until she disappeared. We had it really bad.' She darted a glance at me, but it was Hallie's hand she grasped in comfort.

'Well, a skilled operator *can* simulate a walk,' Pelonia said, 'so that's not conclusive, but we can run some comparisons with vids of other women of her age and see what comes up.'

'I know it was her, Inspector. I'll never forget.'

Hallie and I sat behind Allegra as one of Pelonia's team ran a series of short films showing female figures walking, their faces blanked out, only white file numbers flickering in a black box at the top right of the screen. The *custodes* always videoed people they detained; a few steps were all they needed for their files. A person's natural gait *was* the most difficult thing to change. 'I want you to tell me as soon as you think you recognise her,' Pelonia instructed.

Some were from the public feed, most filmed in a custody suite or interview room. I jammed my lips together as I saw one walk into the courtroom, just seconds before Allegra shouted out.

'That's her!'

Not a muscle moved on Pelonia's face. She nodded to the tech to continue. More, this time all inside. When Allegra identified two more, Pelonia signed the tech to finish.

'Very well. We'll run these against the public feed from the Macellum. It may take an hour or so, so perhaps your mother can take you for a coffee. I'll call you when we're ready.'

An hour later, a tall figure loomed over our mess room table.

'Bruna.'

'Hello, Lurio.'

He slouched into a chair opposite me next to Allegra and gave her a smile. 'Well done, young lady, for observation. You got full marks on the vids.' He paused, glanced at me before going back to Allegra. 'But we couldn't find anything in the public feed. Perhaps it was somebody who looked like her. You may subconsciously be associating that image with Nicola's walk from before, when she was playing you.' He took her hand. 'Don't feel badly about it, Allegra. It happens all the time. And to people a lot more observant than you.'

Allegra stuck her jaw out. 'It was her, Uncle Lurio, it was.' Allegra's voice was shrill. She looked fierce, almost like Nonna.

'I know it's disappointing, but you have to accept it.' Lurio's voice was final. He stood up, nodded to me and left.

★

She was silent in the car on the way home and went straight to her room. She reminded me of those 'virtuous' men of old Rome and the early settlers of Roma Nova I'd read about who'd rather die than tell a lie or do something off the honourable path. I sighed for her; it couldn't be comfortable being such a serious soul.

Conrad went and fetched her down for supper.

'It's hard, darling,' he said, attempting to comfort her, 'but it happens. Very few people get it right all the time.' He glanced at me. 'Even your mother, who's got excellent instincts, has been known to fail.'

I opened my mouth to protest, but he gave me such a look, I said nothing.

'But it *was* her,' Allegra muttered into her soup.

School routine and public exams took her life over for the next few weeks and she thawed out of her frozen certainty. But a doubt nagged at me. Allegra was pretty smart and noticed things others didn't. I'd finished a boring meeting with my accountant, and needed some light relief so I headed over to the *Custodes* XI Station.

Sertorius' application for a warrant to detain Nicola had been granted within two weeks, but as nothing had happened, Pelonia had put the case on hold.

'We've been monitoring it from time to time, but I'm afraid we've got more active cases.'

'Sure, I understand, 'I said, 'but Allegra is pretty sharp for her age. I know you're pressured on resources, but do you have any objection to me sounding out a few of my former contacts?'

She paused for a few moments, her face serious and studying the papers on her desk. I guessed she was working out how to politely say, 'Butt out, you're a civilian now'.

She brought her eyes up and suddenly smiled as if she'd made a decision. 'Why not?'

I should have known better. I was out of the game. I had no legal warrant. But a frisson of excitement ran up me as I volumised my hair and changed into clubwear; short black skirt, silver strap top, what Conrad called my 'minxy' short boots, feather short jacket. He came in as I was applying the tenth layer of mascara.

'Jupiter, where are you going? You look like some tart.' His eyes ran over me, slowly. They drooped halfway shut and I saw an appreciative gleam in them as his lips parted.

'Going to see an old friend,' I said.

He raised an eyebrow. 'I'm not even going to ask, but you will be careful?' His hand came up and he stroked my cheek with the backs of his fingers. I know he would have come with me if he could. He must be so frustrated. Thank Juno, his hearing was due the week after next. Hopefully, he'd lose the damned tag.

I breezed past the bouncers by waving Philippus's token in their face and a heavy took me straight to him.

He sank his head in his hand in true Greek drama mode then looked up. 'I knew it was a shit day today, but what have I done to deserve another visit?'

'Don't be such a grouch.' I looked around. 'Much better, Phil. Good soundproofing and I like the bigger bank of monitors. So you used my voucher?'

'Yeah. I picked the most expensive they had.'

I just laughed. He gave a little smile.

'Did you get what you wanted from the lead I gave you?' he asked.

'Yes, and a whole load of grief. I lost my job.'

'So a good result.'

'You bastard.'

'Sorry. Their loss.' He glanced away, then brought back a serious expression. 'So what now? If you were stuck, I'd offer you a pitch here, on favourable terms, obviously. There's always a demand for well-preserved maturity,' he smirked. He paused when I didn't reply to his off-colour suggestion. 'But I don't think you're looking for a job.'

'No, more for a limb of Hades.'

I gave him the background, without mentioning Allegra by name or her relationship to me.

'You must trust your informant's judgement to be so sure.'

'She's been a victim of this bitch. It's scarred all over the back of her mind. I feel instinctively she's right, but none of the formal proof stacks up. But if I find this woman, she'd better kneel in the sand and say her last prayers.'

★

Philippus promised to put out feelers for me. He'd found her once, but Nicola had moved on, learning Latin, the way things worked in Roma Nova and she had contacts in our criminal world. She'd lost none of her internal violence nor her external brutality, as I well knew. Maybe it was the time it was taking me to recover my full fitness or maybe frustration at not finding her, but I felt helpless and despite Philippus' willingness to help, more than a little depressed.

I'd graduated to longer runs now and Flavius took me out to the PGSF open country training ground. As we wound in and out of trees and dips and ran up long hills, I gave him the whole story in between grabbing air for my struggling lungs. We got to the top of Muscle-Death Hill and stopped to recover.

'Lurio has a good point, but from talking to her previously, I'd say Allegra's likely to be right,' Flavius said, 'but the scarabs can't do a thing.'

'I guess. But how in Hades can Nicola hide like that from the public feed? I know she's skilled, but surely not that good?'

'Oh, please! You used to do it all the time. C'mon, remember that bet we ran years ago to see who got picked up first by the scarabs?'

I'd forgotten. We'd run book on trying to outdo the public CCTV. I'd slated it as a legitimate training exercise, but the local scarab commander almost had a fit. She wanted to throw us all in the pit for wasting their time and resources. But it had been fun as well as useful. I'd lasted over the two week deadline before they'd detected me. I remembered now they weren't too gentle when they'd brought me in. But I'd won the book.

'That was five years ago, Flav. The system's updated several times over since.'

'But you said yourself she was good.'

I shrugged, took a swallow from my water bottle, and stood up, my eyes ranging over the far mountains and forest and the green fields and city below.

'I love this country. My ancestors struggled for it. I'm not going to let some throwback poison it. End of.'

Sertorius was at his most pompous at Conrad's hearing as he delivered an eloquent pleading on his behalf, but the accusatrix's representative hardly bleated. The magistrate declared that in light of Conrad's previous service to the state, the character witnesses' testimonies and the malign influence he'd been subject to, his punishment would be light. But the judgement stood; he would never be able to hold any public office again. He swallowed hard as he heard these harsh words, but he said later he didn't expect anything else. A lousy end to a great career, I thought.

He was placed under probation for three years, a novel idea for Romans, but better than rotting in the pen. He'd wear a midnight to six curfew tag for the first six months and report to the *custodes* every month as well as undergo supervised counselling. Juno, it was humiliating, but the judge said as a member of the Twelve Families he should have behaved better.

I felt a hot, red wave rise in me at this public humiliation of a man who had given so much and done one stupid thing, but Helena pulled me back down to my seat. The magistrate fixed me with her fierce eyes for several seconds. I had to give way and she went back to her condemnation. If Conrad incurred anything more than a parking offence, the conditional release would be revoked and he'd be in the central military jail for the rest of the period.

'At least I can get out of the house now, thank Mars,' he said. 'And thank you, love, for not rejecting me, for helping me fight my way back.' He took my hand kissed the back, kissed my cheek and my forehead. He was well again, back with us in the family and free. I had to be content.

Conrad went to visit Stella that same afternoon. Nothing was said at supper, but he hardly spoke a word. After the children and Helena had gone, we sat together on a couch in the atrium, his arm along the back and his other hand cradling mine.

'She didn't rush into my arms or sit beside me, but she didn't pull her hand away when I took it. I apologised for letting her down, but she started mumbling one back to me. I've never felt so awkward with her. I thought that was it and we'd sit the rest of the visit out in guilty silence. But when I asked her about her work at the centre, it was as if a cold corpse had sprung into life.' He pressed my hand. 'You know something? I think we're all a bit irrelevant to her now. She is so centred on her work. Anything or anybody outside it doesn't count.'

XXXI

The festival of Floralia hit us in May and now her exams were over, I let Allegra out to go to the less wild parties her school friends were putting on over the next three days. She was fifteen. She wouldn't want to hang around a crowd of boring adults. I drew the line at being out after midnight, though; it got rowdy after that in the public squares. After the circus, open air theatres, processions and dancing, the all-night street parties meant drunk crowds and less inhibitions.

On the last night of the festival, around twenty-five of us were at home, sprawled around on couches and easy chairs in the atrium, a full dinner and several bottles of Brancadorum champagne inside us. Helena had brought her latest squeeze. We were in full flight solving the world's problems and dissecting the characters of our favourite pointless celebrities. Conrad smiled lazily at me, his fingers playing with my hair. I smiled back, the most relaxed with him I had been since the trials. He still had black moments that made me anxious. When my sympathy was thrown back in my face, I'd become annoyed and shout at him, then feel so guilty. He always apologised abjectly which I found embarrassing for him. But these incidents were becoming rarer, thank Juno.

I was speculating on what might happen later on tonight then there was a loud thump, followed by boots clattering on the marble floor of the vestibule hallway. The noise grew louder and two blue-uniformed figures marched across the atrium, one holding the waist of a slighter one between them.

Conrad jumped up and stared at the two *custodes*.

'What in Hades is this?'

It was Allegra, weeping and with a bandage across a bloodied nose.

Conrad pulled the distraught child into his arms, stroking her head as he half-carried her to a couch. I signed the release and we all listened while the *custodes* Senior Justiciar recited the details.

Allegra had been found in a street off the Cardo Max, lying in a heap on the ground between two dumpsters. They thought she was just another teenage drunk until they saw the blood on her face and the bruising on her arms. A paramedic had checked her out and said she could go home if there was a responsible adult there. If not, she would be hospitalised. Allegra was awake enough to insist on being taken home.

'We think somebody tried to rob her but beat her up when they found she didn't have anything on her.' The SJ looked at me, her eyes neutral but mouth straight. She didn't quite sneer. 'Such a young girl shouldn't be out by herself on the last night of Floralia.'

'She was driven to her friend's house earlier this evening and was due to be collected at midnight. She shouldn't have been anywhere near the street,' I said, stung by her tone. I called the chauffeur. He was still parked outside the friend's house, waiting to bring Allegra back.

'Very well, Countess,' she said and looked at her el-pad, 'but this is the second time she's been found inappropriately on the street.'

'Now wait a damned minute—'

'Leave it, Carina.' Conrad stepped in front of me, centimetres away from the SJ. 'Your business here is finished. Our thanks for bringing our daughter back, but I suggest you take yourself off and find some genuine law-breakers. There's enough of a choice out there tonight.'

He was as biting as if admonishing some recruit who'd fouled-up on the simplest task a ten year-old could have done. The Senior Justiciar's cheeks turned a dull red. She took a step back.

'We'll be copying our report to juvenile services.'

'You'd be better occupied in finding out who did this to Countess Allegra, than writing specious reports,' Helena piped up and came to stand by me and stare at the cop.

'Specious? Why do you teachers have to use weird words?' But I smiled at Helena. If her gaze had been any hotter and crosser, the SJ would have been a pile of ash. She'd followed the two *custodes* to the door, not quite stepping on their heels and stood, arms crossed, while the porter sealed the pad activating the electronic bolt behind them.

We put Allegra to bed; the doctor was on his way but it looked like bruising only. Allegra's poor face, now cleaned, would ache in the morning. Our guests slid out tactfully to their beds.

'Before you ask,' Helena said, 'it was Maia Quirinia's party—'

I groaned. Not again.

'—and Countess Octavia assured me she and her husband were going to be there the whole time, but in the back. They wouldn't let them outside tonight, they said, even for half an hour. They were going to watch the street show from the house balcony.'

My cell phone rang, interrupting us. Helena's eyebrow went up in question. I shook my head.

'Yes, yes, she's fine, Octavia, apart from the black eye, the swollen nose and bruises all over her arms. Do you have any idea how she got outside?'

I looked at Conrad's face as I listened. His frown deepened when he realised who I was talking to.

'Okay. I'll be over first thing. I'd appreciate it if you didn't tell Maia I'm coming. I want to get her impression fresh. And I'll need a list of who was invited.'

'Well?' Conrad asked.

'It was Octavia who alerted the *custodes*. Her husband and two of the male staff went outside to look when Maia said she couldn't find Allegra. Maia thought Allegra was playing some hiding game, but realised after a while she'd disappeared. There were around fifty kids there in the house.'

Helena's hand on my arm woke me next morning around seven. I glanced over from my pull-out bed at Allegra; her eyes were still closed. The doctor had given her a sedative once he was satisfied nothing was broken or torn. There was no sign of sexual attack, thank Diana. As I sat up, Helena tilted her head, signalling me to retreat with her into Allegra's sitting room.

'How is she?' she asked.

'Woke once in the night and I gave her some more panalgesic.'

'Poor chick, she's had a shitty year, what with that Nicola business, Aurelia dying, her father and you. She's been so worried about you, Carina.'

I looked at Helena and found I had nothing to say. I would have torn my heart out for Allegra not to have worried about me. Conrad came and sat with Allegra while I went to Domus Quiriniarum. He said I'd do better on my own with Maia.

Octavia Quirinia jumped up from her easy chair in the far corner of the atrium. She swallowed as I approached her. Her brown eyes, full of worry, searched my face. I bent to give her a formal kiss.

'Don't worry, Octavia, I'm not going to eat you. I'm thankful for your intervention in calling the *custodes*.'

'Gaius and the men couldn't find her anywhere; the *custodes* found her four streets away.' She turned her face away. 'Juno knows what would have happened to her if they hadn't.'

'Presumably the doors were secured?'

'Gods, yes! Only Gaius and I, the porter and the steward knew the code for the evening. You know how silly and headstrong these girls can be. I wouldn't put it past any of them to try and sneak out for a dare on the last night of the Floralia.'

Not in my house they wouldn't, but I didn't say so.

She handed me an el-pad. 'This is a list of those invited and the acceptances. You'll know most of them.'

I scanned it quickly, but mailed it over to Helena to double-check; she might recognise any names I should be worried about.

Octavia led me upstairs to Maia's room. It was more like a luxury apartment. A living room was complete with every kind of electronic device and screen, expensive laminated panels instead of traditional curled edged posters of rock stars and film actors, a huge pile of pastel, mostly pink, plush toys. The fine birchwood furniture was marred by coffee rings and scratches. Magazines, hair ornaments and empty glasses and even a bottle lay on the carpet. And I smelled stale smoke. Through an alcove, I spotted a workstation, a shelf of books above, paper and pens on the desk. A schoolbag leaned at perfect right angles against the desk leg. A little used and undisturbed area.

Maia sprawled in her bed, quilt thrown back covering only her lower legs. One arm curled around her head, the other was folded against her chest, hand under her face. One leg was bent at the knee, her left buttock exposed. And she snored.

I strode over to the window and pulled back the drapes, letting the harsh sunlight fall on to her face. Octavia handed me a glass of water.

'Maia.' I stroked her face and gently shook her shoulder. 'Wake up.' I shook harder and she opened her eyes, shut them and a second later opened them wide. She sucked her breath in.

'Here, drink this,' I said.

She struggled to hold the glass, but drank the lot in urgent gulps. She held it out to her mother who re-filled it. She stared at me like a terrified rabbit.

'I didn't see anything. When I saw Allegra wasn't there, I thought she was hiding or had gone off somewhere,' she gabbled before I could ask anything. 'She's got so serious these days. She's not much of a laugh.' She clamped her hand over her mouth. Her eyes bulged with fright. 'I didn't mean—'

'Relax, Maia. Tell me about the whole evening from when you greeted your first guest to when you fell into bed.'

Allegra had refused to stay in bed, Helena said, but she submitted to resting on the couch waiting for me to return. Conrad had brought her downstairs and now sat with her, the two of them reading books.

Both faces jerked up as I entered the atrium, one frowning, the other with bruises set against an abnormally pale skin. I kissed both, sat opposite in an easy chair and sipped the coffee Junia slid on to the table for me.

'Is it very sore?'

She waved her hand, exposed the black bruising on the top of her forearm. I looked down at the table and jammed my lips together.

'How was it at Quirinia's?' Conrad asked.

'I'll come to that later. First, I want to hear from Allegra.'

She'd been fine for the first two hours, happy to laugh and hang with the others and watch the street show together from the balcony. As she turned to go inside, she'd caught a face in the crowd.

'I looked again. It was true. I stopped hearing the others calling me in. Maia pulled my arm, but I couldn't move. It was Nicola.'

Conrad and I exchanged glances. He nodded at Allegra.

'Nobody had believed me before, so this time I wanted to make sure before I called. I knew Aunt Octavia would have locked the doors, so I looked for a window. The only open one was one floor up, but it had a downpipe just by it.' She gave me a little smile. 'Just like in the movies.'

I closed my eyes. *Please, no.*

'It was really easy. When I got to the ground, I crept along the side of the building.' She glanced at me then quickly away. 'I kept in the shadows. At the corner, I stayed behind that huge column base they have at the front. And the street was so full of noise, nobody would have heard me. She was still there in a red costume and stupid head-dress. But I knew her. It's the eyes, they're so like Dad's—'

Conrad hugged her to him.

'She was laughing and flirting with some guy in an old legionary costume, then somehow, she stopped and stared right in my direction as if she knew somebody was watching her. I pulled back, but I knew she'd seen me and knew who I was. I ran back to the drainpipe and was part-way back up it, when she pulled me off. She grabbed my arm and hit me on the nose. Then she started slapping and punching me. She said some really bad things about Dad, but she said she hated you, Mama, and would finish you off next time.' Tears poured down Allegra's face now.

'I don't remember much more,' she said and sniffed. 'I know she dragged me away from Aunt Octavia's but I couldn't see much. And my nose hurt. She threw me on the ground in a dark place and kicked me. Then it all went black.'

XXXII

I didn't get any sympathy from Lurio about the snotty Senior Justiciar; she'd been doing her job, he said. But he promised to have her copy report to juvenile services scrapped as unnecessary.

'You or your resident criminal must have pissed her off. And what in Hades was Allegra doing pulling a stunt like that? Jupiter, I hope she's not going to turn into a gung-ho idiot like her parents.'

I could hear the combined anxiety and irritation blasting down the line. Too bad. 'If you've finished bad-mouthing my family, I'll get on to the point of this call.'

He listened and grumped some more. Somebody would come round and take a statement, he said, when they had a gap in their schedule. I wasn't surprised when Pelonia knocked on the door that afternoon.

Conrad looked around, fidgeting in the unfamiliar and unappetising place. Well, he'd wanted to come. We sat in a corner booth in a shabby country inn. Yellow-orange subdued lighting from dirty ceiling fixtures attempted to bounce off unpolished brass and old dark-wood furniture. A folksy smell of beer, oak and uninspired cooking permeated the place.

I raised my hand as a figure paused in the doorway. His eyes narrowed as he looked us both over. He went to the bar, and a minute or two later stood by our table. Still standing, he took a swallow of his beer.

'For Juno's sake, sit down, Philippus. You're blocking my view,' I said.

'Didn't know you were bringing the family.'

The last time he'd seen Conrad was eight years ago when he cut manacles off Conrad's beaten and emaciated body.

I opened my mouth to reply, but Flavius walked in. He paused for a second, nodded to Philippus and sat down on the side bench without a word. Conrad tapped on the table with the fingertips of his right hand for a few seconds, but stopped when I glanced at him. He shrugged, looked away and studied the dime-store pictures hung around the walls. Nobody said anything until the server had finished bringing the rest of us drinks.

I outlined the attack on Allegra.

'Job for the scarabs, surely?'

'Have you listened to anything I've said, Philippus?' I glared at him. 'Do you have anything sensible to contribute?'

'Didn't realise we were at a fund-raiser.' He smirked.

'Don't be an arse-ache, Phil,' Flavius said. He must have kicked his former colleague under the table, as Philippus winced. 'This is too serious.' They stared each other out, steady brown eyes boring into the round, face, gleaming ones sending cynicism back.

'No, I haven't got anything.' He shrugged. 'Which is strange. I took on most of the Pulcheria Foundation's informers when Justus was killed and, excusing the delicate feelings of all those present,' he smirked again, this time at Conrad, 'they're bloody good.'

'Comforting to know that criminals have the same problems,' Conrad shot back.

'At least we have the balls to sort our own out.'

Conrad smashed his fist down on the table, jumped to his feet and leaned over, his face in Philippus's.

Flavius and I rose a second later, hands out, to stop it getting physical.

'Enough!' I said. 'We don't have time for playground bickering.' I turned to Philippus. 'You've obviously got a leak or someone's taking bribes. I suggest you deal with it.'

'You don't need to tell me how to keep control in my own organisation.'

'No, I don't,' I said. 'So do it.'

Flavius signalled to the barkeep who brought another round of beers while we sat in unhappy silence.

Conrad recovered first. Ignoring Philippus, he turned to Flavius. 'Anything from your side?'

'Sorry, nothing, sir. Now all the trials connected with the case have finished, it's gone into the cold store for us. According to the joint watch report, the *custodes* have marked it "on-going".'

'Very well,' said Conrad. 'We have a complete zero between us all. No sign on the public feed, nothing from the *custodes*. I think Lurio only sent the inspector around yesterday out of courtesy.

The attack on Allegra will be filed as one more Floralia incident. Anybody else think this is just too much of a black hole?'

'You *are* sure of your daughter? Allegra, I mean, not that Nicola.' Philippus corrected himself hastily after Conrad's fierce look.

'I thought at first she'd mistaken or muddled the face,' Conrad answered, 'but would you forget anything about somebody who'd tried to get you killed? Or beaten you up and abandoned you in a side street?'

'Suppose not.'

'She's not inclined to be hysterical.' Conrad said. 'If anything, she's a little too thoughtful for a young girl. I'm backing her judgement.'

'Okay,' I said. 'Anybody got ideas for trying to get out of this hole?'

'The public feed is a priority,' Conrad said. 'Somebody must have been tampering with it.' He shrugged. 'The CCTV *custodes* cameras cover the whole city. It's near impossible not to find anybody on there.'

'Um, problem, Conrad. Neither you nor I can access the public feed system any more. Even Flavius doesn't have clearance for that kind of search.'

'Can't you get your pet geek, Fausta, to break into the public feed by some back door?'

I looked at him, shocked. Philippus bellowed a laugh. Of course, he knew Fausta from when she worked years ago with Apollodorus.

'Are you suggesting she hack into an ultra level national security system?'

'Well, she's done it for you in the past.'

'And what exactly did you mean by that crack about Fausta?' I shouted in Conrad's ear as I clung to his leather-clad back as we tore along the Aquae Caesaris road back to the city.

He didn't answer, but I felt rumbling in his back; he must have been laughing.

We glided to a stop by the tall gates, passed through the security system and coasted into the courtyard where the night team were coming on shift. I swung off the back of the Moto Guzzi and went to talk to the house security chief.

'Paulus, we had a problem overnight. Not here, but I want you to halve the time between patrols and ensure at least one person is watching the screens at all times. Not playing cards or watching the TV.'

He frowned. '*Domina*, none of my people would do that.'

His face was neutral, but I saw a flash of anger pass through his eyes.

'I'm not doubting you. But would you personally re-check anybody taken on in the past six months, especially female personnel? If it's at all possible, you might see if anybody's acquired a new girlfriend, cousin or even 'sister' in the same period.'

'Are we under attack?'

'I hope not, but let's be extra careful.'

I met Fausta the next afternoon at my gym. Now Flavius and the others had got me past the basic fitness level, I was taking on the punishing regime of Mossia's training programme again. I sat at the bar on a stool drinking soda and had a direct sightline to the front lobby. Fausta lolled in, presented her guest voucher and collected the welcome patter and a load of hand-pointing from the receptionist. She passed through the swing door to the women's changing room. After a few seconds, I abandoned my drink and followed her. I caught up with her in the Japanese massage pool where the noise of the forced jet over-rode anything we might say.

'You want me to what?' Her eyes almost fell out of her head. She said nothing for a few moments, letting the water pound into her back.

'That's a ten to fifteen stretch.' Her face muscles contracted to resemble a cross cat.

'Oh, you think you might get caught? I didn't know you'd slipped that much.'

'Why do you always do that? You're such a cheat.'

'Fausta!'

'What?'

'Never mind. Will you or won't you?'

'Of course I will. You knew that.'

'Why did you insist we meet here then?'

She grinned at me. 'I've never been in here. I wanted to see it for myself.'

Hallie collected Allegra a week later to take her to stay at the palace for a few days. Allegra was so much better physically, but she'd moped around the house, wanting to be with other people and nervous of her own shadow. Too bad her brave little adventure had ended with a beating.

'Honestly, Hallie,' I said when I called her, 'she'll be so much better with some young company.'

'Brilliant idea, Aunt Carina, it'll be great to have her. At least you won't have to worry about security.'

As she stood in the courtyard ready to get into the black SUV with Hallie and the guard, Allegra clung to me for a few seconds, then drew back and gave me a little smile.

'I have to get over this, Mama. I hate being so pathetic.'

She turned, smiled at the driver holding the door open, pulled herself up into the back seat. Through the tinted bullet-proof window, her waving hand looked so small.

'I don't know how some of these people can breathe as well as stand,' I said, waving my Senate committee folder in the air. 'Who in Hades elected them? The first rulers had it right – experienced and clever only, and one hundred per cent appointed.'

'That bad?' Conrad had been waiting for me outside the members' room. His smile rose at one end of his mouth and he put his arm around my shoulders and gave me a quick sideways hug. He released me and watched the others as they filed out. Some scurried past, pretending not to see him, but one approached us and shook Conrad's hand.

'How are you, Mitelus?' she said.

'Volusenia,' he nodded.

'Glad your trial went well. Just need to get that other thing quashed. Any sign of that girl?'

'Unfortunately not, but the *custodes* are working on it,' he replied smoothly.

'Ha! Well, we've just locked their budget to last year's levels, so they'll no doubt put that forward as an excuse.' She turned to me. 'Whatever the others say, I think diverting budget to the addiction programme is entirely justified. We need more education and prevention as well as clinics. It affects us at all levels.' She glanced at Conrad, then back at me. 'You have my group's support all the way through.'

'Well,' Conrad said after the stout figure had hurried off out of earshot, 'that's a coup. What on earth did you promise her?'

'Nothing. I was as amazed as you when she stood up to

annihilate the opposition. Maybe it's not entirely unconnected with Stella. I caught a few rumours speculating about her position, now she's a convicted criminal.'

XXXIII

'So when Senator Volusenia gave my proposal support in the plenary, it flew through.'

'I'd like to have seen that,' Silvia said the following day at our weekly consultation. She laid my report on her desk. 'Volusenia's pretty formidable, not exactly famous for her work on social issues. So you think this is an expression of worries about the succession?'

'Nobody's said anything to my face. Yet. But it has to be there.' I smiled at her. 'It's not like Marcia and Maelia Apulia.' Three hundred years ago, two imperial sisters – the elder a waster, the younger a tireless servant of the state – had slugged it out the traditional way in the arena, swords in hand, in front of the Twelve Families. 'Hallie loves her sister even though Stella drives her crazy sometimes. Anyhow, you're not falling over yet.'

She gave me a sardonic look. 'Thanks. But it's something I have to think about. And soon.'

We passed on to other stuff for the next hour. I left her working on her reading and went to find Allegra. I heard the loud television in the hallway before I knocked on Hallie's door. Nobody answered, so I slipped in. She and Allegra were sitting on the couch laughing at some inane teenage film.

'Noooo! You dumbass tart!' I heard my studious daughter shout at the screen.

'Oh, for fuck's sake. This is total crap!' agreed Hallie.

I coughed loudly and both faces whirled around.

'Nice, girls. Really nice.'

Both went crimson.

'We didn't know you were there,' accused Allegra. Her face was open, eyes sparkling and chin out in defiance. I was thrilled.

'No, well, let's move on.' I hugged her to me and put my other arm around Hallie.

'Have you come to fetch me home?'

'Not unless you want me to. I had a meeting with Aunt Silvia.'

'We're going shopping tomorrow.'

I must have frowned or something.

Allegra drew back a millimetre. 'Don't worry, we've got Hallie's guard.'

'I know, darling. And I'm not going to say anything lame like "be careful". Okay?'

She docked her chin into the normal position and grinned.

After agreeing dates with Junia for our summer holiday at the farm at Castra Lucilla, which would include the inevitable estate meetings, I was trying to get my head around the allocations in the state budget. Problem was that I found it difficult to challenge the minister on funding requests for the security services. I had asked the senate president to reassign me, but she just smiled and said I was perfectly fitted for the job, so I would stay in the post until another more suitable opening occurred. Like never. I sighed and attacked the keyboard, drafting a few ideas for the hearing. Conrad and I were going out to our favourite restaurant, the Onyx, tonight so I gave myself an hour to write something half-reasonable.

I felt rather than saw somebody intrude on my concentration. Allegra stood there looking at me almost like a stranger. Her fine hair hung straight, framing an oval face dominated by eyes abnormally wide and round, shining like moss green agates. But her hands were trembling.

'Whatever is it, darling?' I got to my feet carefully, so I didn't startle her and took her hands.

I drew her down to the leather couch and waited.

'We went to see Stella this afternoon.' She turned her face away. 'Those poor, struggling people. She's so good with them. Some she coaxes, some she jokes with, others she pushes hard, but she knows exactly how to talk to each one to make them feel they're valued. One girl, about my age, was sobbing, sitting in the corner of the room, her face to the wall. Stella went and sat with her, hugged her and rocked her in her arms. She was still there when we left. She just turned, gave us a vague smile then went back to comforting the girl.'

'I'm glad you went to see her. She must have enjoyed having her sisters visit with her.'

'But that's it. We were just visitors. The centre is her home, her life.'

'Why does that worry you so much?'

'She can't do that all her life – she's the heir! But she'll be so upset when she has to leave.'

'Aunt Silvia knows, but for the moment, Stella has something purposeful to do and is obviously finding it fulfilling. She's settled there for two years. Working with people who've had few or no life-chances or who've become lost will make her a better ruler when her time comes.'

Allegra said nothing, but she rubbed the seat leather with the fingertips of her splayed hand.

'Is there something else?'

'One of the boys I talked to there, he was around eighteen, told me he'd only been injecting for five months. He couldn't believe what he'd done to himself. It was so sad. He'd been struck off the apprentice list and lost all hope of getting back on it. I asked him about his family and they sounded so normal, not a broken home or anything. He'd started when one of his friend's girlfriends gave them some stuff and needles. He said he must have been a bit drunk at the time.'

I laid my hand on her forearm. 'It's devastating, I know, darling, I saw so much of it in America when I lived in New York.'

'No, but listen, Mama. This girlfriend, he said, had eyes just like mine and blond hair and a foreign accent.' Her eyes fixed on me.

When I didn't say anything, she touched my hand.

'You know what I'm saying, don't you?'

'Unfortunately, yes. Well, I'm not surprised. I don't suppose he gave you her address and phone number?' I heard the bitter tone in my own voice. Fat chance.

'No, but he's only been at the centre for three weeks. He's in the detox stage. He heard she was squatting up near the old castle, in the caves.'

Conrad and I left the Onyx around ten, our voices a little overheated, and caught a taxi to the railroad station. Once on the train to Aquae Caesaris, we took turns in the restroom, changing into pants and sweats Conrad had brought in his casual bag. I'd cleared my face of make-up and stuffed the diamond earrings into my safety pocket. We walked through to the front of the train and sat in second class.

We jumped off as soon as the train drew in and at the ticket office, dialled in the code to release the keys for the rental vehicle I'd reserved that afternoon. Maybe it was a little risky RV-ing at the same old inn, but I'd never seen the same barkeep twice, nor the same customers. This time, Philippus was waiting for us. And there were two male customers in a corner who glanced across at us a little longer than was necessary. I smiled to myself.

'Friends of yours, Phil?'

'Well, you never know.'

'Chicken.'

He frowned for a few seconds, then laughed. 'One day you'll twist my tail once too often. You may regret it.'

Conrad went very still.

'I'll be ready when that day comes,' I replied in a quiet voice. 'Remember that.'

He grunted. He waved and one of his toughs went to the bar and fetched some beers over to us and withdrew to their corner.

Flavius arrived a few minutes later, swept his gaze around the bar area, taking in the toughs. He sat down and rolled his eyes at Phil.

'Even numbers,' Phil replied.

'Okay, enough of the playground,' I said. 'Where are we now?'

'Fausta gave me this for you,' said Flavius and handed over an envelope with a coded tab. 'Did you tell her we were meeting?'

'No, but she's not stupid.'

I entered the code we'd agreed on and read the contents. From the corner of my eye, I saw all three men pretending not to look, but I felt the pressure.

'She detected a tamper signature from a hacker, but more importantly she's found Nicola. She's given me a list of sightings and some screenshots.' I leafed through the photos. 'Oh, she's added a much earlier one. Well, damn.'

'What?' Conrad said.

'Remember those two tourists in the palace, one slinked off while the other, the journo, was locked up and Favonius Cotta called you in?'

'Well?'

'The one that snuck off, leaving the journo to shout blue murder, was Nicola. Presumably stirring things up.'

Conrad stayed silent, just looked down and made patterns on the table with a drop of spilled beer.

'Anyway, Fausta's had the hacker detained in private solitary, pending my instructions.'

'Jupiter, if the legate catches her on a non-sanctioned op, she'll be in the shit,' said Flavius.

'Not at all, Flavius,' Conrad said. 'She's ID'd somebody attacking an ultra level government network. Knowing her, she'll probably get a commendation.' He smiled at me. 'Reminds me of another insubordinate captain who pulled similar tricks.'

Philippus sat looking into his beer saying nothing. His brows were drawn together and lines at the side of his nose were pronounced.

'Did you sort out your leaks, Phil?' I asked.

'Nearly. One of them pulled a knife on me and damned near stuck it through my throat, hence those two.' He waved towards the two in the corner. 'A crack head who won't be needing his fix any longer. Another loser will be seeking alternative employment when she comes out of hospital. There's one I haven't caught yet. But I will.'

I coughed. 'Moving on. We've heard a rumour that Nicola's been squatting up by the old castle in the caves.'

'That's where the crack head lived.'

'Okay. I don't want the scarabs tramping all over it, so we'll keep it low-key. Flav, do you think any of the others would be willing to help?

'I know Livius would, and Paula. Not so sure of Atria. Nov's abroad in a legation somewhere and Treb's on maternity.'

'OK, set them up. We'll go for a little walk around the old castle and see what we can find. RV at 21.00 tomorrow in the turnout before the road splits off to the ruins.'

XXXIV

Calling it a turnout wasn't really accurate; further in from a large car lot was a grass area with picnic tables, overlooking the city. The view was open, but to each side, woods were threatening to reclaim the cleared area. But cars could park in between the trees at the edges; a perfect place for a romantic rendezvous. But nobody was here this evening except one small hatchback at the far left edge. Maybe it was too early for teenagers making out.

We parked the bike near a table and sat arms around each other, staring down at the city, enjoying the warm May evening. Immediately below us, soft floodlighting played on the Golden Palace, perched halfway up the castle hill. It had been built in the 1700s when the Apulians felt safe enough to abandon the medieval stronghold whose ruins were a short distance from us up the road.

Down in the valley, the square of the forum was more harshly lit, the Senate and temples stark in the contrast with the almost moonless night. The grid layout of the city fascinated me, like a Sudoku blank, but based on four instead of three. Lights blazing out from shop windows and restaurants added colour to the squares at the centre.

'Reinforcements,' Conrad whispered. Turning as if into his embrace, I looked over his shoulder. A black SUV had drawn up and driven into the trees. Three men got out.

'Phil has brought his monkeys,' I said. 'I'll try and get rid of them.'

But only Philippus came forward. He was dressed entirely in black, including a waisted leather jacket and soft boots.

'I expect you'd prefer them to stay here.' He perched on the next table, crossed his arms and jerked his head back to his vehicle.

'Well, yes.'

'I know you. You only trust the ones you know.' He laughed. 'I only want one little scumbag, then I'll let you get on with it.'

'We're just looking, Phil.'

'Yeah? So why's your soldier-boy packing, a Glock?' He smirked at Conrad who kept a neutral face.

Several seconds passed while I stared him out.

'Bruna.' Livius materialised behind Philippus. Close behind. 'Everything good?'

'Fine.'

Under the shelter of the trees, Livius handed out urbancam jackets, trousers and caps. I shucked off my leathers and pulled them on. Philippus hesitated.

'What?'

'Did I really need these?' He held the camouflage clothing out in front of him as if they were week-old laundry.

'Unless you want to stick out like a fairground target on the rock face, then yes.'

'Good thing Livius brought some double X,' Conrad murmured, not quite to himself.

Philippus took a step towards Conrad, face burning.

I stepped between them, my back to Philippus and mouthed 'shut up' at Conrad.

Conrad just shrugged and reached for some fatigues. I beckoned him away from the others.

'You'll have to stay here,' I said and pointed at his leg.

He grinned, bent down and pulled his pants leg away from his ankle. There was no tag bracelet.

'You dumbass! Get the hell back home and strap it back on.' He had a two-hour window before the *custodes* would be everywhere, hunting him.

'Settle down, I've by-passed it.'

'What? How? It's DNA-matched. And how did you get it off?'

'Easy. You bridge the security wire running the length of the band, then cut it. The circuit stays unbroken. They don't have internal light sensors since DNA-matching came in last year.'

'Yes but if it doesn't detect your DNA, it'll alarm.'

'I'm not the only one with male Tella DNA in our household.'

I was so horrified, I couldn't speak for a moment.

'Do not tell me you made an innocent eleven-year-old wear your tag?'

'Gil was fine about it. Quite proud to help his dad out.' He looked at me almost pityingly. 'Sometimes your moral sense is a bit asymmetric, love.'

Too furious to speak to him any more, I turned away and checked watches and comms with Livius.

'Paula and Flav are in place,' he said. 'Not a lot happening up there at last report.'

'So let's go.'

We kept to the line of the cliff edge, hidden by the trees. Old paintings showed the whole area cleared of any growth higher than half a metre, but tonight I thanked nature for taking it back over the two hundred years since then.

In front of the ruins ran a grassed area, bordered by wood stakes and an ornamental chain to keep visitors at a proper distance. One wing of the castle could be visited with a guide, but the part nearest the cliff was blocked off. Nobody wanted to fill out the paperwork associated with a foreigner falling out of a second floor window straight down the vertical cliff into the valley below. The granite walls showed orange in the floodlights, black empty rectangles where windows had been high in the walls and below them thin, tall arrow slits looked like they'd been drawn on with a felt pen.

Behind the castle, around fifty metres away, rose a sheer rock face dotted with cave entrances. Some had been built across, even with doors and the odd window. Once used by homeless people and those who lived on the margin, these days they were most likely to house runaways and petty criminals. The *custodes* raided them from time to time, when the media complained about 'lawless elements' or when the arrest statistics were low for the month and they needed to up their figures for an inspection.

I signalled Livius forward, timing him on my watch. He stayed close to the treeline, dodging behind the ticket kiosk for cover halfway when he ran across the open vehicle entrance. Nothing from the gaping holes. All I could hear was an occasional fox bark, and the buzz of insects around the floodlight lenses. Nothing else.

I left it a few minutes then signalled Philippus with my fingers that he had six seconds to get across. Philippus was surprisingly light on his feet for his sturdy build and nearly as fast as Livius. We waited another ten minutes. I nodded to Conrad and launched myself. He was barely a second behind me.

A ping in my ear.

'Bruna, Paula.'

'Report.'

'Last visitors left at 19.00. Staff locked up and went by 19.20.

We've seen nobody since then. Unable to verify if anybody was there before we took position, but no torch or other light observed.'

'Okay, out.'

Paula had the aluminium collapsible ladders ready at the base of the cliff. They were used by building surveyors in normal life but, sprayed with flat finish grey and black pattern, they were perfect for us tonight. I sent Philippus and Flavius up the right side of the cluster of caves, Livius and I up the left. Conrad took up station at the base of the cliff to guard our backs.

I reached up and edged my fingers around the lower corner of the nearest cave and very slowly eased the top edge of my periscope up. I scanned slowly and through the green haze saw no heat signatures.

'Flav, Bruna. Report'

'Nothing.'

'Okay, let's get in.'

Watching for any warning mechanisms, devices or wires, we hoisted ourselves up into the caves. Flavius and Philippus's cave met ours about ten metres in. We swept the area millimetre by millimetre with our green beam flashlights, but found nothing but a few cartons, some torn tarps, abandoned cooking and eating debris. The whole place stank of mustiness and stale urine.

'Bruna, here,' hissed Livius.

A sickly sweet smell, a buzz of flies. Livius shone his beam down. A face in agony grimaced back, all life gone.

'Oh, shit.' I covered my mouth with my hand. 'Paula, Bruna. We need a body bag up here. And some gloves.'

Philippus looked at the face made more sickly by the steady green light, bent down for a second or two and studied it. He stood up as if satisfied.

While Flavius and Philippus bagged up the corpse, Livius and I scouted around the back of the caves. In the corner, almost hidden, we discovered a passageway with some crude steps leading up to the next level, the ones where the entrances were built across outside. The air was fresher and behind a curtain hung to conceal rough wood shelves were blankets, three sleeping bags, two large water carriers – full, tins of food, and plastic boxes of rations and utensils. Everything was arranged tidily, the blankets packed in plastic ziplock bags.

'Military, no doubt,' Livius said quietly, 'No dust. Somebody was here very recently. High chance it's our target,' Across the other side, in a recess, was a cupboard under a homemade shelving unit. Livius bent down and picked the crude lock. Inside, we found a plastic storage box with a clip-down lid and containing bags of white powder.

I glanced at him. 'We'll leave this. I don't want to share with our, um, associate on this one. We can pick it up later.'

We closed the box and Livius relocked the cupboard. We checked everything was in its original place and he flicked over the cave floor with a telescopic fan brush to obliterate our footprints.

Back at the cliff base, Philippus was grunting after the strenuous effort of helping Flavius bring the body down. He slid his cell out of his pocket and spoke quietly into it. We gathered our equipment together and made a stretcher for the body out of the ladders. When we reached the castle, Philippus put his arm out.

'We'll take care of this,' he said and nodded to the SUV crawling along the road to the castle entrance, its lights unlit. The vehicle stopped and his two toughs strode up to us, quietly but purposefully, one toting a compact bullpup assault rifle.

Hades. Where did they get that from?

Conrad took a half-step forward. I shook my head.

'You can't just take a body, Phil. It has to be reported,' I said.

'Oh, please! This is what I came for. I didn't say it had to be warm and alive. Looked as if he fried himself anyway.' He smirked. 'An example to show others and one less thing for you to worry about.'

While his monkey covered us, he stripped off the urbancam fatigues and thrust them back at Livius. He bowed to me and said ironically, 'It was an honour to serve with you tonight.'

We tabbed back to the parking lot in silence. In a way, I couldn't help agreeing with Philippus. The *custodes* would have made the whole place a crime scene, Paula, Livius and Flavius could have caught a disciplinary, and Conrad and I would have had a heap of explaining to do. Even so…

I thanked the three others for coming along tonight. Paula smiled and walked towards the hatchback, Livius gave me a light thump on the back and Flavius? He just nodded and disappeared.

Back home, I laid my motorcycle helmet down on the side table without paying attention and it rolled off and crashed to the marble floor. Damn, something else to be thrown out with the garbage. I rubbed my forehead with my fingers.

'Something to tell me?' Conrad asked.

'Yes and no.'

He poured us a brandy each. I took mine over to the atrium glass wall and stared out at the budding roses – Nonna's favourites, which she wouldn't ever see again. My shinbone was aching after the clambering around in the caves so I flopped down on to one of the couches.

'Livius and I found a stash of white powder in little plastic baggies in the other cave. We couldn't test it, but I'm pretty sure it wasn't icing sugar.'

Conrad tapped his lower lip with the outer edge of his glass and said nothing. After a few minutes, he glanced up at me.

'Okay, so apart from concealing a death in suspicious circumstances,' he said, 'we're failing to report proscribed substances.' He half-smiled at me, but his eyes didn't reflect it. 'I thought you'd given up being a cowboy.'

Conrad and I watched the caves for the next five days and evenings, but nothing happened. On the sixth evening, we climbed up using the equipment Livius had left with us, but no sign of anybody or of anything being used or moved. I was torn whether to report the drugs, but it would have alerted whoever it was that we were on to them. And as Livius suggested, I was sure it was Nicola.

I woke late Saturday morning, alone, groggy from catching up on sleep and irritated at our lack of progress. I guessed I'd have to call Pelonia or Lurio and tell them what we'd found. Depressed at that thought, I headed for the shower.

I was still figuring out what to do when I entered the breakfast room and almost bumped into Daniel.

'Hey, watch out,' he said, protecting his mug of coffee.

'Sorry.'

'Are you okay? I haven't seen you for ages.'

I flicked my hand back. 'Doing this and that.'

'Really? Is that why Junia had to take in two messages from the Senate office and I had to sign for some hi-pri package last night? Where've you been?' He fixed me with an intense brown eye stare.

'Nowhere.'

He'd moved full-time into the PGSF HQ building when we'd

brought Conrad back from England. I'd insisted. Daniel was edging into the political sphere now as legate and I didn't want him tainted by association with us, especially if Conrad was convicted.

But only hours after Conrad's major treason trial had collapsed, Daniel's official car pulled up in the courtyard of Domus Mitelarum. He'd jumped out, hardly waiting for his driver to unload his cases from the trunk.

Now he held me with his stare, his brows raised, shallow lines crossing his forehead. I'd forgotten how astute he was under the boisterous manner.

'No, really. Meetings, committees, you know.'

'Conrad had to go as well?'

'I don't run his appointment book, Daniel. And he's curfewed as you know well.'

He set his coffee cup down on the table.

'No, sorry, won't wash. Tell me the truth.'

Daniel didn't comment except to promise not to discipline Flavius and the others. He shrugged. 'Just remember you have no warrant or authority. If you and they get into trouble, you're all on your own and Conrad ends up in prison.'

XXXV

I sat in the atrium late afternoon debating what treat Gil deserved for wearing Conrad's tag for him all this week. Somewhere along the gene pool, Gil had inherited the one that took him straight to dismantling and building things. He'd been in Elysium the week he'd spent with Conrad's mad inventor cousin, Sextilius Gavro, who I'd first met sixteen years ago in New York.

But Gil loved risks as well. Maybe a day go-karting, or some kind of challenge trail. I'd ask him; it was his treat. I closed my eyes and relaxed for a few moments. I was lucky to have children who were self-driving and ready to step up so willingly. And, like Allegra, to take responsibility well beyond her age. A little too much, to be honest.

'Um?'

An urgent hand shaking my shoulder broke me out of my doze. Junia, half behind me, frowning.

I turned and saw one of the palace Praetorians with a grim look on her face.

'Countess Mitela, the imperatrix requires your immediate attendance.'

Crap.

Now what had happened?

The instant I walked in I knew it was bad. Three awkward figures wearing grim faces stood in a semi-circle: Lurio in a quickly tidied up version of his everyday uniform, Pelonia in her svelte casual tailoring, but one hand twitching at her pants leg, some man I didn't know in jeans and sweat top. Silvia, arms crossed was standing away from them, studying some heroic battle scene painting on the opposite wall.

I bowed in the imperatrix's direction, nodded to the cops and raised an eyebrow to the man. He was around thirty, dark, stubble chin and petrified.

Silvia turned at the sound of my arrival. She flicked her hand towards the man. 'Fabius Pico, Countess Mitela, my security counsellor. Pico is/was Stella's supervisor.'

Is or was? I waited. Silvia's face was flushed. The skin over her nose and cheekbones was tight as if the underlying tissue had disappeared. She looked furious, but somehow chagrined at the same time.

Lurio coughed and fidgeted from one foot to another.

'Would somebody care to tell me what's happened?' I asked.

'Stella's absconded.' Silvia's voice sounded as drained as her face.

I had them all sit around the cherry wood table. Silvia's fingers ran along the grain markings slowly but persistently. Lurio relaxed, but not quite into his usual slouch.

'When did we know she was missing?' I asked.

Silvia nodded at Pico who sat a little away up the table, one hand grasped in the other, the shoulders of his skinny frame rounded.

I smiled at him in an attempt to reassure him. 'Just as it comes, don't try to put it in any order. If you suddenly think of anything you want to add to anything you said previously, just interrupt.'

Once he got over his nervousness, he was reasonably logical. I scribbled some notes down as well as recording everything on my cell.

'She was there at breakfast, then had a couple of counselling appointments. She's very good at those. She has that knack of getting them to open up, but not invading their dignity. She came in and grabbed a sandwich on a plate and went to talk to a new arrival, a young woman who'd walked in off the street.'

He pulled his cell out and handed it to me. 'I downloaded the footage from the CCTV at the front door, if it helps.'

I jammed my lips together as I watched the short clip. I passed it over to Lurio who grunted, then pushed it at Pelonia. Her eyes widened for a fraction of a second. She said nothing, but gave it back to me. I showed Silvia who stared at the screen, running the five second sequence over and over.

'Stella had nothing booked for the afternoon,' Pico continued, avoiding looking at Silvia. 'She usually used time like that for reading or talking to the others. Last time I saw her, she was in the garden. That was just after two. I had a group counselling session, a double, so I finished at half three.'

His eyes darted nervously towards Silvia. 'She's so happy there. You wouldn't think she's serving a sentence. I can't understand why she's gone.'

'Why don't you activate her electronic tag?' I asked.

'We found it stuffed in the back of her cupboard. It had been bridged and cut.'

Jupiter! Another one. Better go back to the light sensitive ones if these new DNA ones were so easy to shuck off. I batted that aside.

Pico gave me his mail address and I advised him I'd send him a statement to check and e-sign then send to Pelonia. He stood and waited, hovering like some summer fly. His eyes darted to the cell in Silvia's hands.

'Imperatrix,' I said, gently.

She looked up, her eyes blurred with tears which she didn't let escape.

'Fabius Pico needs his phone.'

I thought she was going to throw it across the room, but she let it drop from her fingers on to the table. Pelonia grabbed it, transferred the footage to her own and laid it back on the table. Pico darted forward like a nervous bird and scooped it up. He nodded to us, bobbed his head in a quick bow to Silvia and escaped.

I caught my breath and held it for a few seconds.

'That bitch has got my daughter again,' Silvia almost choked. She brought her hands up to her face and the tears leaked out between her fingers. 'I can't understand why you haven't caught her. Get out there and do something!'

I held my cell out to her. 'Give me Stella's tracker code, and your consent, and we'll find her.'

'All right, Bruna, I apologise. I was wrong,' Lurio said.

'Say it to Allegra, and the imperatrix, and I'll believe you.'

We were about to leave the imperial office area, when Favonius Cotta appeared. He didn't say a thing, just held out the scanner with my old warrant card sticking out, waited for me to tap my access code in, confirmed it and handed me the card which I stuffed in my pocket.

Lurio, Pelonia and I found a quiet corner in the palace atrium. When I'd seen Nicola captured on Pico's phone, I thought I was going to throw up. But somehow I knew it would be her.

I told Lurio about Fausta's discovery that the public feed had been doctored and promised to email them her list of sightings and screenshots.

'I'll instruct her to release the hacker into your custody.'

'Very gracious of you,' he grumped. 'Anything else you'd like to share?'

'I have an idea about where Nicola's hiding out.' I told him about our reconnaissance and observation over the past week. I didn't mention Conrad's part.

'I should book you for—'

'Yes, I'm sure you should but I was trying to figure out how to set a trap.' I laid my hand on his arm. 'She's good, Lurio, she's very good. You won't round her up in the usual way. She'll run, go to ground and we'll have to start over.'

He grunted, but seemed to accept it.

I hesitated as I held the scanner to activate Stella's personal tracker code. The tiny tracking device had been inserted into her shoulder tissue when she was a small child. It had never been triggered. Only the head of family could authorise it and in emergencies only. Unlike an external tag that convicted criminals wore, it was designed for protection not control. And she'd always had Praetorians around her.

I entered the code and tapped. The map grid disappeared as the signal zoomed in on a ten metre square at the ruined castle.

Pelonia hurried off to send a deep cover team into the woods and step up the overhead electronic surveillance on the caves. I called Daniel to ask him to release Flavius, Livius and Paula to RV at the far end of the palace gardens in twenty minutes.

'Very well,' he said. 'As it's official this time, you'll have proper back up, like it or not. Two squads will be covert in the garden.'

I didn't argue. Then I called on Conrad for the most dangerous task.

In the back of the private palace garden I gave the signal to disable the back sector of the electronic perimeter alarm. I watched as the inspection hatch of the overhead protective canopy opened with a soft hum as the hydraulic support arms were exposed.

The canopy arched away from the cliff over the back five metres of the garden, long struts parallel to the back cliff and shorter ones forming the curved structure. A beautiful piece of modern engineering and style, but lethal; all the edges were razor sharp to discourage interlopers.

I was already kitted up by the time the others arrived. I studied the climb up to the old castle rock. Although it was virtually sheer, it was sandstone and had enough possible handholds. The only risk was falling on to the barrier and getting cut up like salami. But it was the only way up that Nicola couldn't see. With the *custodes* in the woods, we couldn't risk inserting any more people up that road; it was too late for infiltration as tourists. Daniel and Lurio would sit in the PGSF control room and do the hardest part – waiting.

Livius and Paula would climb as a roped pair followed by me and Flavius. I nodded and we approached the base. As Livius set his foot on the rock, my cell vibrated in my pocket.

'Mama? It's Allegra.' Her voice was only just higher than a whisper.

'Can I call you back, darling, I'm a little busy right now.'

Livius rolled his eyes.

'No. This is important. I've found Nicola.'

I gripped the cell so hard, my fingers ached.

'Where are you?'

'Up behind the old castle. I saw Nicola with Stella in the town. I was on my way to visit her again. Nicola was dragging her along by the arm. So I followed them on my scooter.'

Shit.

'Where exactly are you?'

'Hiding. Down behind the last buttress on the west curtain wall, near the cliff.'

She sounded super calm. Unnaturally calm. Was Nicola holding a gun to her head? I closed my eyes. No, her voice would be more stilted. Was she in the grip of some trauma after her attack?

'Mama? Are you there?

'Yes. Yes, I'm here.' I swallowed hard. I wanted to shake her hard for plunging into this, but now was not the time to let my temper out. 'Now listen, Allegra, and don't mess with me. I want you to stay there. Do not move. If you get cramp, too bad. Do not sneeze – grab your nose and bury your head in your clothes. Do not fidget. Don't peek around the buttress even if you hear a scream. Set your cell to low vibrate only and put it next to your skin, but within easy reach. I won't call you unless it's crucial. Do you understand?'

'Yes.'

'Good. I'm on my way. Don't react if you see me, or Flavius or the two other soldiers. Nicola may have spotted you and be leaving you there as bait. I don't want to frighten you, but you have to understand why you must not react.'

'I understand.'

'Can you manage that, do you think?'

'Yes.' Determination sounded through her thin voice.

'One last thing... Where did you leave your scooter?'

'Oh! Behind the kiosk.'

'Okay. That's fine.'

'No, it's not, is it?' Her voice trembled at last.

'It's fine, Allegra. If she comes up the road, she won't see it. Promise,' I lied and cut the call.

'Fucking Pluto in Tartarus.' I leaned back against the cliff and closed my eyes for a few moments. All three soldiers looked at me with concern on their faces. I shook my head to clear it.

'Let's get up there stat.'

It only took twenty minutes. It was hard work but not fatiguing. Livius and Paula climbed five metres to our right. The temperature was dropping, but wasn't cold enough to plume our breath. Half a metre below the crest, I eased my night periscope up, a centimetre at a time. Sure, we were out of sight line of the caves, but this was Nicola we were dealing with, a trained and experienced reconnaissance expert.

'Bruna, Livius. Anything?'

'Zero. Wait five.'

After five minutes of seeing nothing, I eased myself up over the edge and crawled forward on my stomach, using my elbows to propel my body forwards. The curtain wall loomed and I saw the first buttress and the dark shadow of a figure slumped against it.

Unless Nicola had learned to see around corners, Allegra was safe. I let a breath out slowly and relaxed my shoulders. I unclipped my climbing harness and crept along the crest very slowly. I knew the fabric of my fatigues dimmed my heat signature, but I assumed nothing. It was only ten metres to the protection of the wall, but they seemed like a hundred.

Halfway there, the figure stirred and cast around with anxious eyes. It was my Allegra. She didn't make a sound, but gave me a little smile. Then her face crumpled and I saw tears, reflecting like drops of moonlight. But she kept still.

I covered the last metre and pulled her into my arms.

She sniffed. 'Don't suppose you've brought anything to eat with you?' she whispered.

XXXVI

A tiny movement behind me.

'Bruna,' Livius whispered, crouching down. The barrel of his sniper rifle stuck out above his shoulder like he was some bandit in a Balkan movie. He winked at Allegra. She stared back, wide-eyed.

'Livius, you and Paula go to the kiosk,' I whispered. 'Flav and I will go for the side of the entrance steps. When the diversion appears, move to the base of the rising cliff, left of the first cave as before.' I glanced at my watch. 'You have seven minutes.'

He turned and murmured into his mic and Paula appeared seconds later. He studied the far cliff with his binoculars for about half a minute, nodded at Paula and the two of them loped off. My arms triangulated in support, I zoomed my own scope to max and watched the caves while they deployed but saw nothing through the green light world.

'Bruna, Livius. In position.'

'Livius, Bruna. Noted. Cover us. Out.'

I smiled at Allegra. 'We have to go and do stuff. I need you to stay here and wait. You can move a little, but don't stand up. You may hear gunshots or other noises, but stay here. I or one of the others will come back and fetch you when it's over.' I searched her face, but she seemed calm enough. 'Can you do this?'

She nodded. I wrapped a cam survival blanket from my backpack around her and left her munching on a super-cal chocolate fruit bar.

My heart left by the buttress, I turned and crept after Flav.

Four and one half minutes later, the noise of a car engine broke the silence. As it grew louder, we readied ourselves. A compact, but sporty convertible, silver in the moonlight, came into view and parked up on the other side of the entrance steps where Flav and I were hunkered down.

A tall man pulled himself out of the driver's side, stood in the shelter of the open door and looked around casually, his hand and forearm resting on the soft roof. Seeming satisfied with what he saw, he stepped back and slammed the door. His shoes crunched on the gravel as he walked around the vehicle, leaned back against the other side and crossed his arms.

Beside me, Flavius took a sharp intake of breath. He'd recognised Conrad's features in the orange light from the floodlights. Before I could say anything, my earpiece pinged.

'Bruna, Livius. In position at the base of the caves. Nothing yet.'

'Maintain position and observe.'

Conrad looked at his watch in a very deliberate manner then started to walk around in a random pattern as if to relieve the boredom of waiting for the person he was meeting to turn up. We didn't know if Nicola was there or if she'd take the bait of Conrad. But she had to know we'd come for her when she'd abducted Stella.

I was getting a crick in my neck looking through the binoculars pointing up at the caves when I saw a tiny disturbance in the entrance to the middle cave. A thin line was let down the right edge. Spaced about a foot apart along the length were large loops for hand and footholds.

Conrad jerked upright when he saw two figures descending the rope. With my binocs, I saw Stella, clinging on to the line as it swung around, struggling to find loops for her feet. She missed one and slipped down the cliff face.

Juno.

I covered my mouth with my hand to stop myself crying out. Then she grabbed on to the next one with her flailing arm. I thought she was going to plunge all the way down. Nicola followed, her hands and feet finding the loops without any problem like it was a stroll through the park.

I swallowed hard then whispered into my mic, 'Livius, Bruna. Track target at twenty metres.'

At the base of the cliff, I saw Stella, hands stretched out towards Nicola, as if begging for something. Nicola's hand came up and struck Stella's face. Stella fell and disappeared from sight. Conrad ran forward but froze when a short volley of shots rang out. Nicola had a micro-bullpup rifle in her hand and had fired over his head.

'Bruna, TAC-1. We heard live fire. Report status.'

Pelonia.

'TAC-1, Bruna. All well. Stand by until further notice. Out.' I didn't want Pelonia's scarabs rushing in with their flat feet all over the site.

Nicola reached down and hauled Stella to her feet. She gave her a strong shove in the direction of the castle. Stella's figure wavered as she stumbled through the wild shrubs and brambles eventually reaching the grass area in front of the castle ruins. Her arms and legs were covered in scratches; unlike Nicola's sturdy jeans and blouson, Stella's thin dress and sandals might as well not have existed. She was trembling violently.

Around ten metres from Conrad, Nicola grabbed Stella's arm and jerked it hard. 'That's far enough.'

Through my binocs I saw her eyes dart around, pause for a second at the steps Flav and I were concealed behind, and then fix on Conrad.

'Well, isn't this nice,' she said. 'Quite the family reunion.'

'Let her go, Nicola,' said Conrad. 'Your quarrel is with me, not any of the children.'

'She's not a child. Mind you, she's as dopey as a child, a bit thick. Must get it from her mother's side.'

Conrad's figure became very still but he didn't say anything. I'd seen this reaction hundreds of times – he was concentrating his strength ready to launch himself.

'Come on, then, *Father*,' she said, beckoning him with the bullpup. 'You'd like that, wouldn't you? Sacrifice yourself nobly and all that. You lot make me sick, with all that service and honour crap. This is the twenty-first century. Get real.'

'Then why did you come back if you hate us so much?'

'Your dear wife was starting to really piss me off. After you, she's up the top of my list. You are such a bunch of losers, pussy-whipped every one of you.'

'Yet you took advantage of the system when you came to live with us. In every way. You destroyed me, personally and professionally, and nearly killed two of my other daughters. Why, Nicola?'

'You deserved it, deserting my mother without a penny after screwing her like some town tart for a few weeks. You deserted her when you found I was on the way.'

He moved his lips, but nothing came out. I could only see the side of his face, but the shock on it was obvious. Stella stared at him like he was Cerberus from Hades.

That was it. I was done with listening. I stood up, took two long strides away from Flav who looked at me like I was crazy, and stepped forward.

'You have that so wrong, Nicola.'

I kept to the right extreme of her vision, trying to divert her attention away from Stella on her left. She couldn't watch all of us at once. She swung her weapon towards me.

'Your mother tells it differently,' I said. 'She refused to write and let your father know about you. She didn't think it was fair to burden him, she told me. Sounds pretty noble and honourable and a sacrifice on her part.'

Nicola stared at me. The mirror of Conrad's face. I realised she didn't know about Janice's decision.

'And she didn't exist on benefits,' I continued. 'She's a trained teacher and doing well in her profession. No thanks to you, though.'

Crap, I shouldn't have said that.

'Shut your mouth,' she shrieked, grabbed Stella and jammed her weapon against Stella's head. Stella screamed.

Conrad threw me a death look.

'Okay, Nicola, try and calm down', he said. 'We don't want anybody getting hurt. Let Stella go and we'll talk about it.'

'Is that the best you can do?' She made a pantomime of thinking, putting her head to one side for a few moments. 'No, I don't think so.' Nicola's eyes flowed with antagonism. She shook Stella, causing her to whimper and dragged her over to the far side of the ruins, towards the cliff edge in the shadow of the curtain wall. Stella tripped over a large block fallen from the crumbling wall and fell, her shoulders and head landing over the edge. She stared down the hundred metres to the palace garden where she'd played as a kid. And screamed.

'What are you doing?' Conrad shouted at her. He started towards the two girls.

Keeping her eyes and weapon on us, Nicola bent and yanked Stella to her feet in one fluid movement. She swung the bullpup up to Stella's temple. 'Stay exactly where you are unless you want me to blow her head off.'

I'd managed to get a little nearer, but didn't want to get in Livius's sight line. I had to leave him a clear shot. If it came to it. Neither Conrad nor I could get to Nicola before she could kill Stella – we were just too far away. Stella was too terrified to do anything. She hung in Nicola's grip like some rag doll. And she was coming unstitched. Her eyes were all over the place, she sobbed and her whole body trembled.

'Livius, Bruna.' I mumbled into my mouth mic. 'Can you make the shot? To take her out?'

A pause.

'Affirmative.'

'Standby.'

Thank Juno, Conrad was too far away to hear me. But when it came to it, Stella was the one to save.

'Bruna, Paula,' the voice in my earpiece whispered. 'I'm circling round cliff base to vegetation perimeter. ETA three minutes.'

If Paula could get to the edge of the brushwood, she'd be only three metres from Stella. Snatchable distance. But Nicola was getting more agitated. She had to wonder what we were doing.

'Okay, Nicola. You have us where you want us,' I said and sighed. 'What now?'

She said nothing as if she'd run out of ideas.

'You've given your life to your revenge over these past months. Now you've got it, what are you going to do?'

Conrad sent me a warning look, but I signalled him that I had it under control.

'Oh no, I'm not there yet,' she said and gave me a tight smile that pushed a chill through my veins. 'I'm going to start with my dear father. His daughter can watch me execute him.' She gave Stella a shake. 'Ever seen a head explode, little sister? Pink bits and blood spraying everywhere.'

Stella stared back at her, hiccupped, fell to her knees and threw up.

'He'll do as I say because he thinks there might be some slight chance I might think his death is enough and stop there.' She stared straight at Conrad. 'Your gamble.'

He took a step forward, like a robot. Nicola placed her weapon on Stella's neck and her finger extended to curl around the trigger.

He froze.

'Not yet.' She looked at me. 'I can't see a red dot, but you've no doubt got a marksman somewhere with his sight on me. Believe me, my reactions are good. She'd be dead within the same second.' She tilted her head up at me. 'Stand your sniper down and let's all listen while you do it.'

XXXVII

A second after I'd stood Livius down, a fist-sized chunk of Brancadorum granite flew down from the curtain wall in a fast, strong trajectory. It landed square in Nicola's chest. She grunted and stumbled backwards. She swung her arm up and loosed off a series of rounds. Stella, left unguarded for a few seconds, dragged herself away from her tormentor. She placed one foot flat on the ground to lever herself upright, but Nicola recovered quickly and kicked her in the ribs. Stella collapsed in a heap.

'Five seconds to show yourself,' Nicola shouted at the wall and took a step forward.

Allegra stepped out from the broken curtain wall. My heart shrivelled. No.

'You can't kill us all,' she called. 'Even if you take one, the others will get you.'

'Oh, it's the little princess, the apple of her mother's eye. You'd be a good one to start with.' She raised the bullpup, settled her fingers on the pistol grip and tensed her index finger. Conrad launched himself at her. I barrelled forward. But the distance was too great. Nicola rolled away, escaping the tackle, and as she scrambled up, she fired a single shot at Conrad.

He grunted, clasped his arm and staggered back at the force, and fell.

'Back! Get back.' She waved the weapon in my face.

Nicola had nearly a full clip. We had no option but to obey her. I pulled Conrad back to the curtain wall and propped him up against it. I checked his arm out. It looked like a flesh wound, thank Mars, but messy. I tied it up tight with a field bandage which I took out very slowly and very obviously from my sleeve pocket.

Nicola raised her chin up at Allegra. 'You get down here. Now.'

Allegra stood where she was.

Move, Allegra, for pity's sake, do what she says, I prayed silently.

'Too scared, little girl?' Nicola said. 'Well, I'll have to use you as a shooting gallery target.' And raised her weapon, pointing straight at Allegra's heart.

If I moved, Allegra might die or be permanently disabled. If I didn't, Allegra would definitely die.

In the end, it wasn't my call.

Hunkered down by Conrad, my eye was caught by a movement behind Nicola. Stella was scrambling toward her.

'Make some noise,' I hissed at Conrad, 'to cover Stella.' His eyes flickered over to her, he blinked and started groaning loudly.

Nicola looked over at Conrad. 'Oh, for God's sake, shut the fuck up.'

Stella was there and bringing her hands up from her sides. With an almost feral look on her face, she grasped Nicola's ankle with both hands and tugged. The bullpup let off a volley into the air and dropped from Nicola's hand as she crashed to the ground. Allegra disappeared.

I launched myself at Nicola, but she leaped up and grabbed Stella. She was dragging her to the cliff edge. Stella was hanging on to Nicola for grim death, making no effort to escape.

Nicola heaved Stella over the edge, but Stella pulled Nicola over with her. My hand touched Stella's as I tried to grab her as they went over, but I lost her.

Paula kneeled over the edge, peering down and searched with her binoculars as I got into my harness.

'There's some kind of heat signature down there, but I can't say what. It could be either or both of them.'

'Okay, go for white light.'

Flav was by my side, letting out webbing and rope that he'd run and anchored to an oak tree. I checked the rope was well attached to the anchor straps, looped it through the belayer, twisted the lock on the carabiner. Checking through his scope, Flav threw the rope to the side of where the girls had fallen. My hand by my hip, I nodded to him, and walked backwards over the cliff edge.

Searchlights came from either side, but I didn't need them to see Stella's frightened eyes staring up at me. She was clinging to a spur of rock, but her hands were slipping. She was kicking her feet in her panic.

'Keep still, Stella, I'm coming to get you.' But I saw she was beyond it. I let the line out as fast as I could, pushing with my feet to bounce off the rock face. I reached Stella and grabbed her wrist just as her other hand lost its grip on the rock. She grasped at another rock but there was nothing to hold on to. The sweat on her hand and wrist was oozing between my fingers, loosening my hold every second that passed.

'It's okay, Stella, I'm here. You're going to be fine. Now, concentrate and stretch up with your other hand and grab hold of my sleeve.' She couldn't do it, but it gave her mind something to do. I reckoned I had only a few more seconds before she became too exhausted to hold on and fell into the dark below. If I tried to manoeuvre down, I could lose her instantly.

But then I heard the rasp and clinking of another set of ropes. Paula. She jumped to below Stella and put her shoulder under Stella's rear. Within seconds, Paula had fastened a leather belt around Stella's waist, then strapped two more around her thighs. Holding her between us, we got her back up to the top. Conrad pulled Stella into the safety of his good arm where she sobbed all over him.

Still roped, I stood on the cliff edge and looked down. The strong white beams highlighted a splayed four-limbed shape impaled on the barrier roof.

'Stern, Bruna,' I spoke into my mic, my voice as dead as my feelings. 'Turn out the troops to check for what's left of Nicola Sandbrook. They'll need a body bag. And gloves.'

'Bruna!' Livius shouted.

I whirled around. At his side, back straight and arms relaxed like she was on a geography field trip and listening intently to what the teacher was saying, walked Allegra. She looked up, waved and grinned at me. I fumbled at the steel loops, fighting to detach myself from the anchor as fast as I could.

I grabbed her to me, but after a moment, she patted me on the back and pulled away.

'Is it finished? How's Stella? You did save her, didn't you?'

Her voice was even, she scanned the area with calm eyes, assessing where everybody was and what they were doing. She waved in Stella's direction but her sister was too far gone to notice. I stared at Allegra. She was showing no sign of reaction – no trembling, no darting eyes, no stumbling – just calm. Maybe it would come later. I glanced at Livius. He merely raised his eyebrows and shrugged.

Allegra went over to her sister, hunkered down and took her

hand. She stayed there talking to her until the transport arrived.

Livius stood by me, but kept his eyes on Allegra.

'If I didn't know you'd be pissed at me, I'd say she'd inherited the right genes on both sides. I'd cry with pride if I had a daughter like her.'

'I already do, Livius.'

XXXVIII

Nicola was buried in the foreigners' cemetery outside the city two weeks later. I'd called her mother and met her at the airport. At the ceremony, Janice Hargreve looked tired, but in a strange way peaceful, content even. She hesitated as she held her hand out to Conrad and dragged her eyes up to his.

'I'm so sorry,' she whispered.

Still holding her hand, he drew her to him and held her for a few seconds.

'It's over now, Janice,' he said and took her arm. Quintus and I stood in the shade of a cypress and watched them walk along the broad gravel pathway back towards the entrance.

'How are you, Carina? Really?' Quintus asked. He looked better, still wearing a neck brace, but not really leaning on his cane. He held my arm as we followed Conrad and Janice slowly back to the cars. His family recorder and his assistant followed at a discreet distance.

'I don't know. I know that sounds lame, but I don't. I think the anger won't go for a while. I've forgiven Conradus, I can't do anything else, but I know Nicola's changed us, maybe more than we think.'

Stella spent a few days in hospital before she was released by the court on compassionate grounds to convalesce in the country. She returned to the rehabilitation centre after a week to continue her sentence. I went to visit her after she had settled back in.

As she came into the director's room, I saw she still had traces of scratches and grazes over her face and arms. She didn't smile, but her face was solemn rather than sullen like before.

'Sit down, Stella,' I said as she hovered there, one hand grasped in the other, fingertips worrying the skin on the back of the other.

'I want to say something first.' She pulled her shoulders back, looked over at the window, then dragged her eyes back to my face. 'Aunt Carina, I want to thank you for saving my life. I know you don't like me, you think I'm useless.'

'Stella, I—'

'No, don't deny it. Please.' She gulped. 'I don't think I've been a very likeable person, to be honest.' She put her hand out to grab the back of a nearby chair. 'I didn't know what I was supposed to do half the time. Everything seemed to be happening in a different world and I couldn't grasp any of it. I felt so pathetic – exposed – when Nicola had me.' She gave a smile that was not a smile, one corner of her mouth drooping. 'I should have taken more notice of what people wanted to teach me those few weeks I spent in the PGSF.'

She sat down on the chair and folded her hands in her lap and looked thoroughly miserable.

'What do you want to do, Stella?'

'I want to stay here, but they won't let me after my two years are up. I mean, Mama and the Council and all the rest of them.'

I reached out and touched her hand.

She brought her face up. Her eyes were shining as if somebody had injected some life force in an inanimate object.

'I love it here. This is my real world.'

And she burst into tears.

I gave her a few minutes to get herself together. I walked over to the director's desk and logged on to check something.

'There is a way,' I said after a few minutes. I laid my hand on her shoulder and looked down into her eyes, still full of tears. 'It's happened in other countries but I don't know if any Roma Novan has ever done it.'

Two months later, I accompanied her into the Senate house where a special meeting had been convened. I'd been more than surprised and a little touched that she selected me as her formal supporter for today.

I watched Silvia across the floor sitting upright in her carved chair. She was pale and her eyes moist, but she listened gravely as if she hadn't heard Stella practise it fifty times before.

In a low, but dignified voice, Stella Apulia stood in front of members of the Senate and the House of Representatives and made a formal renunciation of her inheritance in favour of Hallie. Some of the more conservative politicians looked shocked and one muttered her disapproval, including the word 'coward'. She was rewarded by a look from the imperatrix like the falling iron fist of Vulcan.

Poor Stella had geared herself up to this ordeal and didn't need a load of hassle. But she ignored it, the only sign of having heard it a double blink. She thanked the dual assembly, bowed to her mother and somehow managed to exit without running. I gave her a straight A+ for courage.

Conrad continued with the counselling and was eventually discharged from the court. The following week, he took himself off on a walking tour up in the mountains north of Aquae Caesaris and spent two months afterward at the boot camp I'd trained at years ago.

When he returned, I was sitting in the atrium reading through a company report when I heard his footfall. I looked up and watched the cat-like walk as he approached. He practically bounced. He was tanned, the lines around his eyes had faded and except for the white hair, he looked younger. But it was the smile that showed me he'd healed inside.

We settled down to living at a slower pace and Conrad took on some of my business affairs. But he surprised me, and himself, when he rammed decisions through sometimes with a ruthlessness acquired from his military life and made me laugh when he told me how he'd made some of the bean counters jump.

The biggest shock was Allegra. I'd settled her down on our favourite couch in the atrium to talk with her about the scene at the old castle. I figured that now a few weeks had passed, she would have gained some perspective. But I worried that it had been another toxic experience for her.

'It's fine, Mama. Really. I don't need "time to talk" or any of that.' She glanced over at me. 'In fact, I enjoyed it. It was exciting. When I threw that rock at Nicola, it wasn't just revenge or anything babyish. I was doing something powerful to help.' She looked out of the atrium glass door over at Nonna's roses, now on their second run of blooms. 'In fact, I wanted to talk to you about something. I know I'm not sixteen until November so you'll have to give your consent, but I want to join the auxiliaries and go through the legionary *cursus*.'

My face must have stayed fixed for several seconds. I ran through my head what she'd said. My daughter wanted to join the military reserve and then follow the tough training preceding a full-blown armed services career.

'Allegra, this is a big, big decision. What about your plans to travel, to go to university? You could join the auxiliary cadets there and see if you like it enough to make such a choice.'

'You and Dad travelled enough when you were in the PGSF, not just postings, but exercises abroad and holidays. It's really not a problem.'

She took my hand. 'I looked at death straight in the face up on that wall. I knew in a second that if I survived I wasn't going to waste time trying other things out when I knew what I wanted. You knew that the instant you met Dad all those years ago in New York. Now it's my turn.'

Also by Alison Morton

INCEPTIO
Book I in the Roma Nova series

New York, present day. Karen Brown, angry and frightened after surviving a kidnap attempt, has a harsh choice – being eliminated by government enforcer Jeffery Renschman or fleeing to the mysterious Roma Nova, her dead mother's homeland in Europe.

Founded sixteen centuries ago by Roman exiles and ruled by women, Roma Nova gives Karen safety and a ready-made family. But a shocking discovery about her new lover, the fascinating but arrogant special forces officer Conrad Tellus, who rescued her in America, isolates her.

Renschman reaches into her new home and nearly kills her. Recovering, she is desperate to find out why he is hunting her so viciously. Unable to rely on anybody else, she undergoes intensive training, develops fighting skills and becomes an undercover cop. But crazy with bitterness at his past failures, Renschman sets a trap for her, knowing she has no choice but to spring it…

PERFIDITAS
Book II in the Roma Nova series

Captain Carina Mitela of the Praetorian Guard Special Forcesis in trouble – one colleague has tried to kill her and another has set a trap to incriminate her in a conspiracy to topple the government of Roma Nova. Founded sixteen hundred years ago by Roman dissidents and ruled by women, Roma Nova barely survived a devastating coup d'etat thirty years ago. Carina swears to prevent a repeat and not merely for love of country.

Seeking help from a not quite legal old friend could wreck her marriage to the enigmatic Conrad. Once proscribed and operating illegally, she risks being terminated by both security services and conspirators. As she struggles to overcome the desperate odds and save her beloved Roma Nova, and her own life, she faces the ultimate betrayal…

AURELIA
Book IV in the Roma Nova series

1960s Roma Nova, the last Roman colony which has survived into the 21st century. Aurelia Mitela is alone – her partner gone, her child sickly and her mother dead. Forced in her mid-twenties to give up her beloved career as a special forces Praetorian officer and struggling to manage an extended family tribe, businesses and senatorial political life, she slides into depression.

But her country needs her unique skills. Somebody is smuggling silver – Roma Nova's lifeblood – on an industrial scale. Sent to Berlin to investigate, she encounters the mysterious and attractive Miklós, a known smuggler, and Caius Tellus, a Roma Novan she has despised, and feared, since childhood.

Aurelia discovers that the silver smuggling hides a deeper conspiracy and follows a lead into the Berlin criminal underworld. Barely escaping a trap set by a gang boss intent on terminating her, she realises that her old enemy is at the heart of all her troubles and pursues him back home to Roma Nova...

Lightning Source UK Ltd.
Milton Keynes UK
UKOW04f1805080115

244216UK00001B/49/P